# ANNIE'S WILD RIDE

She made his head spin. There. Finally. After four years, Paul could finally put words to how Anne made him feel. Single-engined planes, jets fast enough to break the sound barrier, Paul climbed in and out of those without so much as a flicker of motion sickness. But Anne—*Anne!*—made his head spin.

Standing in line for the roller coaster, she closed her eyes and spun in place. Her hair and the hem of her dress twirled in unison, like twin propellers revving to go. For the briefest of instants, Paul actually believed that Anne might take off, powered by nothing more than enthusiasm, joy and conviction.

What was worse, for that same brief instant, he, more than anything, wanted to go with her . . .

# ALINA ADAMS

# Annie's Wild Ride

AVON BOOKS ◆ NEW YORK

AVON BOOKS, INC.
1350 Avenue of the Americas
New York, New York 10019

Copyright © 1998 by Alina Sivorinovsky
Inside cover author photo by Mark Liberman
Published by arrangement with the author
Visit our website at http://www.AvonBooks.com
Library of Congress Catalog Card Number: 97-94936
ISBN: 0-380-79472-1

First Avon Books Printing: August 1998

AVON TRADEMARK REG. U.S. PAT. OFF. AND IN OTHER COUNTRIES, MARCA REGISTRADA, HECHO EN U.S.A.

Printed in the U.S.A.

WCD   10  9  8  7  6  5  4  3  2  1

# ===PROLOGUE===

The primary items of contention in Paul and Anne Gaasbeck's divorce proved to be custody of their five-year-old daughter, and of their twin-engine Cessna T303 Crusader—both of which were named Amelia.

For over a month, Judge Thomas Saul listened to arguments from both sides on why the other parent was an unfit guardian for their child. Or maybe it was why the other parent was an unfit guardian for their *airplane*. Mostly Judge Saul cursed the fact that his jurisdiction extended into Utah's Hill Air Force Base. Family court for civilians was bad enough; military personnel, though, inevitably turned every proceeding into an all-out war.

Captains Anne and Paul Gaasbeck, USAF, approached his bench as if intending to plant their flag atop his gavel. Both stated their cases eloquently; neither used a single, excess word to convey their point. Then they stepped back, confidently expecting their orders to be carried out without question, as always.

So it came as quite a shock to the plaintiffs when Judge Saul introduced the word "compromise" into this couple's vocabulary.

Trying to be fair, he granted Paul and Anne joint custody of the Amelias, decreeing that whoever had the child for the week would also receive access to the airplane.

Judge Saul, even if he did say so himself, thought his ruling uncommonly equitable. Not to mention easy to follow.

Anne and Paul did not agree.

In the six years since he'd dissolved their marriage, the pair returned to court nine times, battling for advantage over the other by hammering repeatedly at the agreement's finer points.

They argued whether custodial weeks accumulated or were lost when a parent flew out of the country on assignment, whether the parent taking care of Amelia and not flying the plane could deny the other its use, whether holiday weekends constituted a new week or part of the old, whether days lost crossing the international dateline could be made up, and whether Amelia's time at camp meant they still had to keep rotating custody of the airplane.

Such refusal to accept surrender probably contributed to both Anne and Paul's eventual ascension in rank from Air Force captains to Air Force majors. But it gave Judge Saul a headache.

The tenth time they showed up in his court, he was in no mood to be amicable.

According to the custody agreement, Anne had the Amelias for Christmas Eve; Paul was scheduled for Christmas Day. But Anne wanted to fly Amelia to Colorado for a ski trip. Paul said it was fine with him, as long as they returned by Christmas Day.

Anne accused Paul of caring more about enforcing their accord than about their daughter enjoying her vacation. Paul accused Anne of using the skiing as an excuse to cut short his week with Amelia. Anne accused Paul of being jealous that Amelia would rather be with her. Paul wanted to know when it was, exactly, that Anne had begun giving a damn about anybody's feelings but her own. Anne told Paul the day he finally got any, feelings, that is, she'd be the first one in line to care about them.

That they managed to complete such a spiteful exchange without raising their voices, Judge Saul attributed to military discipline—or to a pair who just really liked hearing themselves talk.

In no mood to dicker a truce between two who had clearly proven that their only interest lay in the other's complete capitulation, Judge Saul slammed his gavel and ordered the Majors Gaasbeck to obey his initial ruling—and next time, maybe, just maybe, could they give a shot at talking *to* rather than *at* each other, preferably without beleaguering the United States judiciary system.

Afterward, Judge Saul told his clerk, "Anne and Paul Gaasbeck must have really been something together. It takes an awful lot of love to turn into that much hate."

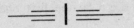

"Dad is not going to like this." Amelia Gaasbeck, age eleven, reclined in her copilot's seat, careful not to kick the rudders or the fuel-tank selector as she swung her feet. Halfway through sixth grade, she'd already logged eighty flying hours of her own inside a single-engine Cessna 152. When it came to her namesake, though, the twin-engine Crusader, the throttle and control wheel were so heavy, Dad didn't even like Mom going up in it alone.

"Dad," Anne said, "can lump it."

Anne sat on the left side of the *Amelia*'s cockpit, dressed in a blue sweatshirt featuring the U.S. Air Force logo and a leather bomber jacket; her dark blond hair, cut per regulations to clear her collar, tucked behind both ears. She was quietly seething.

Thanks to Judge Saul's stubbornness, Paul could insist that Anne return Amelia to his house by nine A.M. Christmas Day—"or you'll face contempt of court charges." She had no doubt he meant it, too. Her ex-husband nurtured an almost mystic faith in the written word. If it was on paper, it had to be obeyed, come hell, high water, or, God forbid, a spontaneous change of plans. Their custody agreement promised him Amelia on

Christmas morning, and so Anne had no choice but to go along—up to a point.

Instead of canceling their vacation, Anne simply shortened it. She and Amelia flew up to Colorado before dawn and spent Christmas Eve afternoon racing each other down the snow-covered Rockies.

Anne had invited her boyfriend, Lyle, to come along, but he begged off, proclaiming himself incapable of keeping up once she and Amelia got going. Anne made a show of attempting to change his mind, but her heart wasn't in it—primarily because Lyle and her daughter in the same room invariably made Anne uneasy.

Not that they didn't get along. Amelia was always impeccably polite toward Lyle. She was too much of her father's daughter to behave with anything less than perfect etiquette.

And that, precisely, was the problem. Amelia was her father's daughter. When Anne looked at her, she saw Paul. It wasn't their physical resemblance, though. Feature for feature, Amelia actually favored Anne: they had the same fine hair, blond in the sun, brown when wet; the same round eyes, fixing their expressions in perpetual wonder; and the same twin dimples on their right cheeks.

But Amelia was Paul's child in spirit. There was a . . . steadiness to her. Anne could think of no other word to describe it. Like Paul, Amelia was solid. When friends asked Anne if she felt afraid taking to the skies with only a child for her copilot, she replied, "I'm not with a child, I'm with Amelia."

And Amelia in a plane was fine. But Amelia in the same room with Lyle inevitably prompted Anne to compare him to Paul—an activity she tried to avoid whenever possible. And when avoidance didn't work, Anne used her own special reasoning so the right man could come out the winner. Whenever she recalled how she didn't laugh nearly as much with Lyle as she had with Paul, Anne rushed to remind herself that she also didn't cry as much, either.

Anne and Amelia exchanged early Christmas gifts over dinner at their Colorado hotel, then retired to their room for a quick nap. At two A.M. Anne woke Amelia and they hustled to the airport. With luck, and advantageous tail winds, they'd touch down in Utah forty minutes before Paul called out the military police.

Amelia reminded, "Dad doesn't like you flying at night."

"Dad doesn't like me flying, period."

She'd commanded a twenty-nine-ship fighter cover formation over Bosnia, ferried supplies to Panama and troops to Saudi Arabia, and piloted a Black Hawk helicopter over enemy lines in Iraq. But Paul still treated Anne like an aviation imbecile; asking, for instance, if she had remembered to check that the *Amelia*'s oil pressure and revolutions-per-minute were within their prescribed limits before takeoff.

Naturally, Paul's pre-flight routine included inspecting the aircraft's tires, searching its wings for frost, the propeller for nicks, and examining the fuel supply to make certain no water had collected in the tank overnight. He called the flight station for their weather report, then also checked DUAT, another government service, on his personal computer every hour before takeoff.

While they were married, when Anne could still view his caution as sweet and protective rather than macho and controlling, she used to kid Paul about being too dependent on gadgets and indicators and instruments. Whatever happened, she'd wondered, to pure, instinctual flying? The kind that poets wrote about?

"Ah, yes," Paul replied, "flying on instinct. The battle cry of the thoroughly unprepared."

No matter how much Anne reasoned, he refused to see things her way, to admit that, like parents with a child, a born pilot could sense something off-kilter before her gauges registered a tremble.

Like right now, for instance.

A barely perceptible vibration in her controls prompted Anne to look out the cabin window. Only seconds later did she hear the crack of hail against their cabin, indicating that enough rime had collected along her wings to break loose from the propeller.

"What was that?" Amelia sat up, more curious than alarmed.

"Ice." Anne replied, as if it were a natural encounter midflight. But under her breath, she muttered, "Damn."

Amelia checked her copy of the flight plan, reporting, "We're not supposed to be getting ice at this altitude, Mom."

The flight plan Anne filed before takeoff specified the *Amelia* cruising altitude as 9,000 feet. Air Traffic Control cleared her plan without reservation. As an afterthought, they mentioned that some snow seemed to be heading into the area, although, according to their calculations, the *Amelia* could easily beat it.

But now a message came over the radio from Colorado Springs Center. "Attention, all aircraft. SIGMET in effect."

SIGMET, Significant Meteorological information, was a severe weather warning for pilots. "Pilot weather and flight conditions report moderate icing at 8,000 to 10,000 feet."

Oh, great. Now they tell her.

Anne snatched up her nav/com microphone. "Colorado approach, T303 Crusader *Amelia,* overflying Colorado Springs Airport at 9,000 feet en route to Hill Air

Force Base. I'm starting to pick up some ice. Requesting weather condition clarification.''

The controller told her, ''Had a Moony land with a quarter inch rime on its wings about five minutes ago. That storm sure moved in faster than we anticipated.''

Anne's instincts told her to clear the ice area. But dipping below 8,000 feet meant skimming her belly against the Rockies.

Anne radioed the tower, ''*Amelia* requesting clearance above set flight plan, to 11,000 feet.''

''Negative, *Amelia*. Altitude occupied, risk of collision. Do you need coordinates to circle around the snow?''

Unable to lower or raise her aircraft, rerouting was her third option. And although it sounded like the most practical, it was also the one she liked least. Circling to avoid the snow wouldn't leave them enough fuel to return to base. She'd have to land and refuel—and risk missing Paul's nine-A.M.-or-else deadline.

Anne flicked on the microphone again, telling the Colorado control tower, ''*Amelia* is known ice-equipped.'' Unlike most smaller planes, she was outfitted to handle precipitation. If the storm wasn't too severe, they could follow their flight plan and deal with any icing problems as they arose. ''Requesting weather information up ahead.''

''Roger, *Amelia*. We've got a PIREP of moderate to severe icing for all sectors. Visibility, one mile. A United 737 came through five minutes ago with minimum problems. Same with American 747.''

That was all Anne needed to hear. She sighed with relief. If other planes had successfully cleared the difficult area, there was no reason why she couldn't. Even in these weather conditions, she felt confident they'd make it home before Paul blew a gasket.

She turned to Amelia. "What do you say, Ace? Up to a little low-visibility flying?"

Amelia tightened her seat belt, sitting up straight. "Cool."

"I'll take that as a yes."

Anne told the tower they would be sticking to their original flight plan, and received authorization to proceed. She winked at her daughter. "You're becoming quite the daredevil, Ace."

"Gee, I wonder how that happened? My mom's a pilot, my dad's a pilot. My *grandma* was a pilot, for Pete's sake."

Anne smiled, remembering that her daughter was also conceived on a plane, but she decided against sharing this with her eleven-year-old daughter.

So, anticipating the moderate icing forecast by PIREP, Anne pushed her deicer switch to full forward, inflating the boots around both wings and inspecting the ammeter needle to insure her equipment was working properly. For maybe fifteen minutes, the procedure proved adequate. Then, without warning, the temperatures outside dipped drastically. In less than thirty seconds, *Amelia* collected an inch of concrete ice on both her wings.

Anne felt the extra weight in her control wheel and attempted to cycle the deicing boots again. But they had frozen solid.

"Shit."

Her expletive prompted the first speck of fear to dot Amelia's face. Usually Amelia wasn't scared. From the time she could walk, she'd toddle on board an airplane fully confident that her mommy and daddy would never let anything bad happen to her.

Anne bit her lip to keep from frightening Amelia further. But there was nothing she could do about the ice chunks pounding along their cabin windows like a rock slide.

"What's going on, Mom?"

The terror in her child's voice frightened Anne much more than any threat to her own well-being. In fact, up to that point, being scared hadn't even crossed her mind. Her reluctance to ever believe the worst, no matter how dire the circumstances, used to baffle Paul. He thought she was just whistling past a graveyard.

*"If you can keep your head, while all about you are losing theirs . . ."* Anne regularly quoted Rudyard Kipling to him.

*"Chances are you're in serious denial about the whole thing."* Paul put a spin on the poem. *"What kind of tactic is that?"*

*"It's called positive thinking."*

*"Great. Wing and a prayer. Clap your hands, and Tinkerbell comes back to life."*

*"Worked every time I saw the play."*

She'd tried to instill the same self-confidence in Amelia, the conviction that you are well-trained, smart, and, most important, competent enough to conquer any crisis. Anne wished she could take a moment now to reassure her daughter that there was no reason to be scared, that everything was going to be okay. But there was no time. The added inches of rime were swiftly dragging their aircraft down toward the mountains.

And still Anne wasn't afraid. In fact, if truth be told, she was in her element. This was what drew her to flying. The speed, the excitement, and, more than anything, the exhilaration of knowing that she could conquer the elements.

Anne accelerated to full power, struggling to stabilize the plane. But it wasn't enough to keep them from losing altitude.

Fleetingly, she thought of Paul and his prepping for missions by trying to predict everything that might go awry. His contingency plan. He swore it was the only way to avert disaster. But all the contingencies on earth couldn't help him here. If their situation weren't real, it would almost be funny. Murphy's Law on an airplane. Everything that could go wrong was now going wrong. With a vengeance.

Her engine surged, airspeed declining rapidly. The controls went limp in her hands. At 9,000 feet, *Amelia* flat-lined into a full-power-on stall, lurching downward at a speed of 170 knots.

Amelia gasped, guiltily covering her mouth, embarrassed by the breech of etiquette; then gasped again, this time too terrified for guilt as their right wing dropped, turning the aircraft sideways.

With all of her strength, Anne yanked the controls, managing to straighten out her right wing moments before the *Amelia*'s nose dipped as well. Even if she could have steered, there was nowhere for them to go. Mountains encased in snow mocked them from every side. The *Amelia* would strike one in seconds. Unless . . .

Having attempted every defensive technique taught by the Air Force, Anne abandoned popularly accepted strategies and acted on reflex. She released her pressure on the yoke, briefly regaining just enough control to swerve her plane away from the mountains and toward a rocky plateau some 500 feet below them.

She hurled down her wheels, gambling that 800 feet of slippery terrain would cooperate by acting the part of the world's shortest, most makeshift, landing strip, and slammed on her brakes, employing the only contingency plan she still trusted. Prayer.

\*   \*   \*

When Paul Gaasbeck's phone rang at five A.M., he lifted the receiver already hearing Anne's voice conjuring up some fanciful excuse for why she was going to be late. In anticipation of such a stunt, he'd checked Colorado Springs weather before going to bed. The forecast indicated some moderate snow but nothing so severe as to impede *Amelia*'s takeoff.

"Nice try, Annie." Paul rubbed his eyes with the back of one hand, flicking on his overhead light with the other.

"What? Hello? Paul? It's . . . this is Lyle. Lyle Jellison."

Lyle Jellison? There was a new one. It wasn't like Anne to palm her dirty work off on someone else. Especially not on a sap like Jellison. Paul wondered what exactly it was Annie saw in that worm. Not only was he a civilian—an engineer, granted, but a civilian just the same—he didn't even fly.

Paul yawned, covering his mouth with one hand. "Listen, Lyle, I know Anne put you up to this. So, tell you what, you go back and you tell her that I don't care how—"

"Anne didn't put me up to anything. Paul, I . . . there's been an accident."

Despite all the pertinent details Lyle gave him by phone, Paul broke the sound barrier speeding to his base tower and forcing them to connect him with the Colorado Air Traffic Control office.

In turn, Colorado Air Traffic Control repeated word for word what Lyle had already told him. Unforeseen icing, loss of radio communication, presumed crash.

Paul made them play him their recording of the *Amelia*'s radio logs, flinching when he first heard Anne's voice across hundreds of miles. God, but she sounded so confident. So sure of herself. So thoroughly convinced that everything would be all right.

But Paul had expected nothing less. For better or worse, his ex-wife did not know the meaning of the word fear. At the start of their marriage, that feature had excited him like no other. At the end, it nearly drove him out of his mind.

Paul demanded of Colorado, "How the hell could you have given her clearance to fly into a snowstorm?"

"Mrs. Gaasbeck was—"

"*Major* Gaasbeck, damn it. She's a major in the United States Air Force. If Annie lost control of her aircraft, you guys must've screwed up royally."

"*Major* Gaasbeck was given access to both SIGMET and PIREP. It was her choice to continue with the designated flight plan."

"You told her the SIGMET, you told her the PIREP, and then you told her there were airlines flying through with no problems. Talk about sending out mixed signals. What was she supposed to do, read your mind about the actual weather conditions?"

Paul had been flying into Hill Air Force Base for eight years. Every air traffic controller employed by the tower had guided him in at least once. Even the time his instruments malfunctioned and he was forced to land blind, none of them had ever heard Paul raise his voice until now.

He grilled Colorado. "How many helicopters have you allocated for the search?"

"Actually, Major, the fact of the matter is—"

"Listen, I went to school at the Air Force Academy. I have contacts there. If we consolidate our rescue efforts, we can—"

"That's impossible."

Paul shook his head in disgust. "This is getting us

nowhere. Patch me through to whoever's in charge of your search-and-rescue. I'll take it from there.''

A pause. Then, ''I'm afraid that inclement weather conditions make any sort of search-and-rescue unadvisable at this time.''

Paul couldn't believe what he was hearing. ''Are you out of your mind? What do you expect them to do? Walk down the mountain? Hitch a ride, maybe?''

''Sir, you don't understand. Based on our data, combined with weather reports and Major Gaasbeck's last known coordinates, we feel that . . .''—the controller lowered his voice, choosing words with painful precision—''we feel that there remains little probability of the *Amelia*'s passengers still being alive.''

The night crew froze in their tracks, heads swiveling in near-comical unison toward Paul. Every air traffic controller at Hill knew Anne. Some were members of their Academy class. A few had been guests at their wedding, and at Amelia's baptism. As Paul glimpsed their alternately sympathetic and horrified faces out the corner of his eye, he sternly ordered himself not to look. Their reactions weren't relevant. They would only distract him. And he couldn't afford that right now. He had to focus.

''You don't know Anne. You've never seen her fly,'' Paul insisted for both the benefit of Colorado, and the premature mourners in Utah. ''She can pull hats out of rabbits when she has to.''

''That's all very well and good.'' The controller cleared his throat. ''But I can't risk the lives of my crew on a mission with no chance of success. We're experiencing blizzard conditions here. Even if our helicopters did manage to take off in this wind, their visibility would be non-existent. I'm sorry, sir. But the fact is we cannot mount a rescue effort at this time.''

Paul struggled to remain calm, swallowing all his anger in a single, disciplined gulp and managing to sound entirely reasonable as he explained, "If no one goes up to get them, my wife and child are dead. They could be injured. Not to mention the cold . . ."

"W-With all due respect, sir," the controller stammered, "it is our belief that Major Gaasbeck and her passenger are already dead."

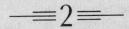

=2=

*1983*

"You're dead." Paul Gaasbeck, age twenty-two, and four months short of graduating the Air Force Academy, raised his voice to be heard over his paratrooper plane's howling engine. He stood by the cabin door, ready to fling it open and guide fifteen cadets through their virgin parachute jump. Enunciating each word, and referring to the Academy's top award for excellence in flying, academics, and leadership, Paul informed Anne, "The Commander's Trophy is coming home with me at the end of the year."

Anne warned, "I wouldn't rehearse my victory dance just yet, Gaasbeck. Last time I checked, you and I were still tied."

For even at the Academy, which billed itself scholastically equal to Stanford and Harvard, and reviewed thousands of applicants for 1,500 appointments, Paul and Anne were the best of the best.

Because of her family's constant traveling, Anne didn't attend a real school until fourth grade. When she finally made it inside a classroom, she was surprised to learn that, due to her parents' tutoring, she was now far ahead of everyone else. While other nine year olds recited all the planets in the solar system, Anne amused herself by sketching a periodic table, complete with each element's atomic weight. While they struggled with long division, she solved geometry proofs.

And when Mrs. Vega insisted that American Neil Armstrong, in 1969, was the first man to walk in space, Anne raised her hand to correct her: Armstrong was the first person to walk on the *moon*. Soviet Alexei Leonov, of Voskhod 6, was actually the first, in 1965, to take a spacewalk. An hour later, when Mrs. Vega used the terms mass and weight interchangeably, Anne spoke up again. "Mass is how much matter something has. Weight is gravity pulling it to the ground. They're not the same thing, you know."

She spent the remainder of the day out in the hallway, amusing herself by trying to see how many smaller words she could form out of the letters making up "impertinence."

In total, Anne attended thirty schools in twenty-two states. She headlined the honor roll, captained the forensics, tennis, and track teams—and was bored to death. When she got her Academy admission, Anne jumped in the air and laughed out loud. Finally she would attend a school capable of offering her a challenge! A school where the other students might prove smarter than herself.

She'd already heard about one specific wunderkind through the grapevine. Perfect S.A.T. scores, perfect A.C.T. scores. All-city quarterback. Class president. Eagle Scout. During his admission interview, when asked the secret to his achievement, Paul Gaasbeck allegedly replied, "I never make mistakes."

So naturally, on their first day of class, Anne made a point of seeking him out. But Paul didn't return her smile.

He barely acknowledged her presence. His facial expression didn't flicker. He appeared to be looking straight through her.

Puzzled at the unprovoked slight, Anne turned away, focusing her attention on the lecture taking place at the front of the room. Still, she couldn't get Paul out of her mind. He sat behind her, and twice Anne could have sworn she felt that peculiar tickle at the back of her neck, indicating someone staring, rather intently, in her direction. Yet every time she turned around to check, Paul was sitting with his eyes riveted on the blackboard.

When their instructor proposed a dire aeronautic scenario and asked the cadets for a possible solution to the imminent disaster, Anne immediately raised her hand and proceeded to expound that, since the crux of the problem seemed to be their hypothetical aircraft's excess weight, the best solution, in her opinion, was to jettison a portion of the fuel supply.

From the back, a voice pronounced, "That is, without a doubt, the stupidest suggestion I've ever heard. Jettison that much fuel, and what do you expect to land on? A wing and a prayer?"

Anne swiveled in her chair, resting her left arm on its back, and facing Paul head-on. Even as she formulated her reply, a part of her brain gloated that Paul could not avoid acknowledging her presence anymore.

Paul chided, "If I were your copilot, I would never let you pursue such a foolish option." Then he proceeded, for a good ten minutes, to reveal exactly how *he* would have handled the situation.

"You're right," Anne said. "You are absolutely right. If I'm ever in such a crisis, I most certainly will not relieve myself of excess weight by jettisoning my fuel supply. Instead, I'll just rid the cabin of its excess hot air, by jettisoning the copilot."

Anne heard a sharp intake of breath all around her.

A few cadets giggled. Those sitting beside them instinctively scraped their chairs out of radius, lest blood started spurting. Paul's features, however, remained stubbornly blank.

They spent the rest of the period arguing, and as she stood to leave, Anne overheard one cadet whispering to another, "I don't get it. Who won?"

From that day on, neither Anne nor Paul could make a statement in the classroom without the other swooping down to contradict it.

Knowing that he would always be there, delighted to pounce on any error she might make, kept Anne up studying long after *Taps* had sounded, while dreams of outsmarting him regularly woke her before six-thirty reveille. Thanks to Paul, Anne found herself producing much finer work than she ever would have without his spurring her.

In class, the fervor of their argument over odds and ends, ranging from the correct interpretation of NASA research to obscure military aerial precedents, dissuaded anyone else from joining in the daily debates. Their instructors abdicated trying to referee. After four years, Anne and Paul had established such a rhythm, that each could finish the other's sentences. It was almost as if they were reading each other's minds. There was nothing Paul could say that Anne didn't catch instantly. Conversely, Paul never failed to grasp any idea she expressed—if only so that he could expound on how ridiculous it was. She couldn't remember the last time she'd had this much fun in school—or with another person. Except for flying, nothing got Anne's blood pumping in quite the same way.

Not even parachuting. Although she did love it, and

had shown enough aptitude to be selected, along with Paul, to instruct cadets in the field.

Their fifteen charges sat on narrow benches along both sides of the plane, dressed in foam-cushioned paraboots, helmets, gloves, and floppy blue jumpsuits that made them resemble flying squirrels.

Their instructor, Captain Binnebose, sat in the rear, keeping his eye on the cadets, and also on Paul and Anne as they stood by the door, awaiting the pilot's word that they'd reached 3,000 feet.

Anne watched her students staring out their windows, some with anticipation, some with dread. One sat with his hands clenched in prayer, bent from the waist until his head touched his knuckles.

At 3,000 feet, the pilot cut his engine to idle speed. Paul signaled for the cadets to rise and check their equipment while Anne grit her teeth and shoved open the cabin door with all of her might. Paul stood beside her, jaw set in utmost seriousness, his blue eyes scanning the cabin, searching to solve potential crises before they mushroomed. He was a good deal taller than Anne, with shoulders so broad they made the parachute seem a perfect fit. He moved with brisk authority, expecting obedience without question.

Anne and Paul took their positions on either side of the door. He gestured for the first novice to approach. "Stand by!"

A trembling jumpsuit with tufts of red hair sticking out from underneath the helmet moved into the doorway. He sat on the edge, feet perched on the jump step that protruded just below the exit.

"On the step!"

Redhead gulped, rising unsteadily and leaving his left leg on the step while his right leg dangled over 3,000 feet. He clutched the wind strut with all of his might.

"Go!" Paul ordered.

Redhead's eyes twitched nervously toward Anne. She nodded reassuringly, miming a quick push with her hands. He took a deep breath, and stepped off the platform.

Anne snuck a peek at Paul, noting that his usual expression of barely disguised condescension had been replaced by a look that one might even interpret as concern. He watched the descent, and, even though Redhead obviously could not hear them, Anne and Paul counted out loud in unison, "Arch, one thousand. Look, two thousand."

Redhead checked his grip on the rip cord with the right hand, then threw out his left hand for balance. Anne and Paul exchanged glances, nodding their approval.

"Pull, three thousand." They held their breaths, knowing that a mistake here would prove the deadliest.

Redhead wavered, glancing not up at his chute but down at the ground, hand halting by the rip cord. The first jump was always so different from a cadet's expectations, it was difficult not to feel dazed. Despite lessons drummed in during ground school, they still expected a sensation of rapid, possibly painful, falling. But, in reality, at 3,000 feet, it was more like sailing on an air cushion. Anne described it as being cradled in someone's arms. Paul smirked at her hyperbole and suggested she should switch to writing purple prose for the Air Force recruiting manuals.

The problem with expecting to plummet, then finding yourself floating, was that such perception camouflaged the actual rate of descent. It became easy to get lost in the sensation. Everything moved in slow motion. Hard to believe that the process would ever reverse itself, that the ground could zoom up and crush you.

"Pull, three thousand," Anne repeated, stamping her

foot for emphasis. Beside her, Paul blanched, the color seemingly whipped from his face by the same wind that was violently flogging Anne's hair against her cheeks.

Redhead pulled the rip cord.

"Look, four thousand."

The canopy released over his head.

Laughter bubbled from Anne's chest, half in triumph, half in relief. She beamed at Paul. "I feel like a proud parent!"

He held up one hand, shaking it. "Don't start passing out the cigars just yet. He still has to land."

"Well, yes, but the hard part—"

"Something could go wrong. Something could always go wrong." Paul stepped out on the jump step for a better view of the landing site. Only after Redhead hit the ground feet first, rolling knees, hip, shoulder, then onto his back, did Paul allow himself a smile of triumph. He punched the strut with a gloved hand, whispering, "Yes! Yes!" before crawling back into the plane.

He spied Anne looking at him, eyebrow raised in amusement, and awkwardly dropped his hand.

Paul cleared his throat. "I . . . fine. It was a fine landing."

He rose to his feet, brushing his jumpsuit of imaginary lint, and turned away, beckoning a second cadet forward. "Next!"

For the subsequent jumps, despite needing synchronization to open the door and call out commands, Paul refused to look in her direction.

Jumper number twelve approached takeoff position with unusual trepidation. His knees trembled, and he stumbled walking from his seat to the door. Under the helmet, his skin went from kelp green to flour-white. Cadet Wakeman, Anne suspected, would be a problem.

She held out her hand reassuringly, gripping his wrist and half-leading, half-dragging him toward the exit.

"Stand by!" Paul ordered, a bit louder than Anne thought was necessary under the circumstances. The boy was obviously scared.

Wakeman inched toward the door, feet dragging like a prisoner in ankle chains. Then he just stood there, looking down, counting each of the 3,000 empty feet between him and solid ground.

Hoping to make things easier, Anne sat, legs dangling out the plane, and patted the empty spot beside her, imploring him to join her. Paul frowned, but Anne had no interest in worrying about his approval. Tentatively, Wakeman sat beside Anne. Still, it took a kick from Anne before his feet settled on the platform.

"On the step!" Paul's gaze met Anne's and he shook his head in disgust at her breech of protocol.

She urged Wakeman to stand, then mimed his gripping the strut with his hands. His features twisted into an agonized grimace, but with Anne's help, he leaned out of the craft, arms stretched like a sleepwalker's. She gripped his wrist and guided him toward the wind strut. But Wakeman only brushed it with his glove before falling back into the plane, knees to his chest in fetal position.

Paul grabbed him under the elbow, yanking the boy to his feet.

Voice perfectly level, and thus perfectly out of sync with the frustration visible in his actions, Paul asked, "Problem, Cadet?"

Wakeman squirmed, stammering, "I—I can't."

"You can," Paul said.

"I . . . what if my . . . what if my parachute doesn't open, sir?"

"That's why you have a reserve shoot."

"My landing position—"

"Your body will do it automatically."

"What if—"

"Everything will be all right, Cadet. I promise you that."

Wakeman's lips trembled. He gulped to keep his nostrils from quivering in advance of tears. Anne's heart broke for him.

She pushed Paul aside, seizing Wakeman's hand and suggesting, "How about we do the jump together?"

She couldn't ascertain who looked more stunned by her offer, Cadet Wakeman or Paul?

"Are you out of your mind?" Unlike most people, Paul managed to make the inquiry sound not like a rhetorical insult but like a valid, practically medical, question.

"No. Why?" Anne indicated the equipment. "I can pin myself to the parachute straps, like a harness. It's strong enough."

"It's too big of a risk. I forbid you."

"I beg your pardon?"

He insisted, "I am the senior cadet on this assignment."

"How do you figure that? We're equally ranked."

For the first time that afternoon, someone stumped Paul with a question he didn't have the answer to. He wasn't overjoyed. In fact, he looked like he wanted to strangle Anne, on the spot, and with his bare hands. He said, "I will not let you ruin my command record by breaking your neck."

Wakeman, who, for a moment, had seemed to be pulling himself together, once again turned green, thanks to Paul's "breaking your neck" comment. Realizing that their window of opportunity was even narrower than she'd assumed, Anne abandoned trying to change Paul's mind and, instead, moved to slip one arm in Wakeman's parachute.

Paul grabbed her elbow. "Since you won't listen to me, will you at least recognize Captain Binnebose's authority?"

The captain sat at the back, watching their unfolding drama with massive interest and an unreadable facial expression.

"Fine." Anne folded both arms across her chest. "We'll let Captain Binnebose decide."

"Fine."

"Good."

"Fine."

He turned, marching to consult with the Captain. And granting Anne enough time to maneuver herself into Wakeman's parachute, her shoulders buckled securely against his chest.

"Ready?" she asked him.

"Uhm. Yeah. I guess so."

"Nothing to it." They staggered like Siamese twins toward the door. Anne called her own commands.

"Stand by! On the step! Go!"

Her last sight before free-falling was Paul standing in the doorway, eyes blazing—an expression she'd never seen before and, for the life of her, couldn't identify.

Anne suspected that her summons to appear at the disciplinary hearing was drafted and officially stamped before she and Wakeman ever hit the ground. They'd completed an excellent jump, though.

"What do you think?" she asked the cadet after landing.

He glowed. "When can I do it again?"

As far as Anne was concerned, that should have been the end of it. She'd done her job. She'd introduced Wakeman to the thrill of parachuting. So what if her methods were unconventional? The ends certainly justified the means.

For everyone, that is, except Paul Gaasbeck.

They stood in the hall, waiting for the disciplinary hearing to begin, both wearing their formal-dress uniforms: navy pressed slacks in his case, a skirt in hers; matching blazers without bars, indicating their still unofficial status in the Air Force; and caps with a silver American eagle crest pinned over the brim.

Paul glanced down the length of his sleeves, checking if both cuffs were in alignment. Then, eyes focused on the opposing wall, he inquired politely, "May I ask you a question?"

She shrugged. "Take your best shot."

"Why do you think it was that Cadet Wakeman believed you, and not me, when you said everything was going to be all right?"

"That's easy," Anne said, "It was because *I* believed me."

He startled, as if an electric spark along his spinal cord had jolted every vertebra an inch to the left. Paul's jaw tightened.

Seeing that she had his attention, Anne pressed her advantage. "You shouldn't have tried to bully Wakeman into jumping."

"I disagree."

"Why? Because you think you know everything?"

"I don't know everything." She detected a strain of amusement running the length of his words. "Just everything I need to know."

Anne rolled her eyes and shook her head. "You know what your problem is, Gaasbeck?"

"Please. Enlighten me."

"You're a bully."

"Is that a fact?" He leaned backward, pressing his

shoulders along the wall and slowly turning his head to face her. His gaze bore into hers, refusing to let go.

Not that Anne ever gave the subject much reflection, but, for the record, she had always believed Paul Gaasbeck's eyes were blue. Not azure, not indigo, not sapphire. Blue. Paul's eyes were blue.

So why then did she find herself suddenly cataloguing the hues swirling within his pupils? It was rather distracting.

Yet not so distracting that Anne lost her place in the debate. "You tell people what to do, and God help them if they don't do it. That's a bully."

"That's a leader." As always, his tone remained level, albeit sprinkled with condescension. "The military depends on discipline within a chain of command. My superiors give me orders, which I obey. I, in turn, give my subordinates orders, which they obey. Does that make us all bullies?"

"Yes."

On Anne's confirmation, the door behind them opened. Major Sharon Danahay stepped into the hall. Looking from Paul to Anne, she inquired, "Starting the hearing without us?"

Both snapped to attention. "No, Major."

They followed her inside, waiting for "at ease," before taking seats across a conference table, behind which Captain Binnebose sat on the major's right, and Captain Zimmermann, their military ethics instructor, sat on her left.

Major Danahay looked down at her notes, then up at Paul and Anne. "I understand there was a disciplinary problem during the first-year cadets' parachuting excersise."

"Yes, Major," Paul said.

"No, Major," Anne said.

"I've spoken to Captain Binnebose. He's given me his opinion. Now I'd like to hear your statements about this problem that Paul had, that Anne didn't have. By the way, I do know who I'm dealing with. I've heard about your marathon debate sessions. As a favor to me, let's keep things concise, shall we? I have dinner plans."

"Yes, Major."

In as few words as possible, Paul and Anne summarized their respective positions, noting how they were absolutely right, while their fellow cadet was absolutely wrong.

Paul concluded, "She disobeyed a direct order not to jump."

Anne raised her hand, indicating she'd be adding an addendum to her statement. "Gaasbeck had no authority to issue me orders."

"Your jumping was not in the approved plan," Paul reminded.

"Well, then the plan needed to be changed."

"Oh? I see. And is this how you mean to conduct yourself in combat situations, too? Halfway through a mission, you decide you don't like how it's being handled, so you strike out on your own?"

"If halfway through a mission it becomes obvious that the plan of attack isn't working, then, yes, it would be time to revaluate."

"You just don't get it, do you? A plan is necessary so that all act as one, instead of each taking off to do their own thing."

"So, according to you, it's better for 'all' to do the wrong thing—rather than for 'one' to do the right thing?" Forgetting that they were supposed to address their remarks to the committee, Anne pivoted in her chair, contending, "Face it. It's impossible to predict everything. Unforseen problems come up. At that point, sticking to a set plan becomes stupid, not to mention dangerous.''

Paul shook his head, speaking as if to a dim child. ''Strategy agreed upon logically and reasonably beforehand inevitably defeats half-assed plans scavenged in the panic of battle. Decisions based on anything save sound judgment are invitations for calamity.''

''Enough!'' Sharon Danahay glanced from one cadet to the other. She noted the flush of Anne's cheeks, the way Paul tightly clenched his teeth to keep his breathing steady, and the animated glimmer in both their eyes.

''Would you two like to light up a cigarette?'' she asked.

Their twin blank expressions told Major Danahay that neither understood her reference. Yet.

Instead of following her instincts and immediately lashing out at Paul the next morning in class, Anne bided her time. She waited for the perfect opportunity to humiliate him as badly as he had her the previous day, when he'd convinced the disciplinary committee to issue Anne an official reprimand for her behavior with Cadet Wakeman. But as soon as they stepped on the athletic field—where Paul, as he did every day, proceeded to needle Anne on the obstacle course, easily scaling the fifty-five-gallon drums pyramid, then waiting at the bottom, arms crossed against his chest, for Anne to complete her own descent—she knew it was time to strike.

The ''confidence'' course had been her nemesis since enrolling at the Academy. Anne's national high-school records meant nothing compared to the upper-body strength required to excel along the Air Force obstacle course. Daily, she pushed herself to the very edge, coaxing out just one more pull-up long after all the muscles

in her shoulders retired in trembling protest. But as she
plunged to the ground, shaking her arms out to regain
feeling, Paul kept on going, even picking up his pace.
He refused to quit until he was the last cadet left clutching the chin-up bar.

Anne knew it would take a miracle for her to rack up
as many physical education points as Paul, much less
exceed his tally. But she kept trying. Academy rules dic-
tated that cadets participate in intercollegiate and inter-
mural sports. Anne played tennis. So did Paul. Anne ran
track. So did Paul. And even though they didn't compete
head to head, if Anne ended a meet with less victories
in her division than Paul had in his, she still felt like
she'd lost.

She watched him now, warming up beside the high-
jump bar, setting it at six feet ten inches from the
ground—one quarter inch higher than his previous jump.
He took four accelerating strides toward the bar. On the
fourth step, on his right foot, he curved to the left, so
that as he swung back his arms and rose off the ground
on his ninth step, he was slightly turned. Paul cleared
the bar, head and shoulders first, heels together, knees
apart, landing on his back in the twenty-two-inch foam
pit and celebrated his proficiency by triumphantly
punching one fist toward the sky.

Anne made up her mind.

Although unsure of just what she intended to do once
she got there, she impulsively crossed the athletic field,
heading toward the jump-bar. She trusted herself enough
to posit that, when she arrived where she was going,
she'd know why.

Anne stepped into the jump line behind Paul, observing the way every muscle at the back of his neck tightened into a solid-V as he squeezed his fists in
preparation. He squared his shoulders, knees bending

slightly. His shirt clung damply to his back, and, in the instant before he took off, Anne could read the ligaments and veins just beneath his skin like an aerial relief map. His body radiated discipline, not just in the lean lines and chiseled tones but in the way that every tendon snapped to attention on command, blessing his jump, from run to leap to landing, with a seamless fluidity, a natural grace that emphasized the strength necessary to achieve it.

Well, if he could do it, Anne figured she might as well give it a shot. She took a deep breath and leaned forward, preparing to spring up and duplicate his achievement.

"Hey." Paul slid in front of her, blocking Anne's path to the bar and forcing her to skid to a stop only seconds after starting her preparation run.

He asked, "What are you doing?"

"What does it look like I'm doing?"

He indicated the bar over his head. "It's set at six ten."

"I know."

"You want me to adjust it for you?"

"No. I want you to get out of my way so I can jump."

Paul shook his head. "No way can you jump six ten."

Anne's personal best stood at five feet eleven inches. She'd been struggling to break the six feet mark for over a year.

"Please, move," she repeated.

He shrugged. "It's your funeral."

"You're a prince."

Paul stepped aside with a sigh. "That's what they tell me."

Anne ran. She approached takeoff, turned left, and leapt into the air, swinging her left foot to shoulder height, arms to chin level, then stopping them abruptly.

The upward drive, combined with an arched run, turned her shoulder blades toward the bar.

For a moment she floated, sailing up higher than ever before. She forgot Paul. She forgot why she was doing this, what she was trying to prove, and to whom. She forgot where she was. Because, just for a split second, Anne was flying.

It ended much too quickly. Out the corner of one eye, she saw Paul step toward her, and Anne turned her head, ready to bark. The twisting affected her position in the air. Instead of soaring over the bar, Anne felt it slam her squarely against the cheek.

She flailed her arms, bouncing off the bar and plummeting to the ground. She braced herself for impact, attempting to turn over and avoid landing on her back.

Paul caught her. The shock of landing in his arms, instead of crashing down on gravel, jolted Anne more than any hard fall would have. At least she'd been expecting the gravel.

Her head spun, the vision in both eyes spiraling in and out of focus. She saw yellow, then purple, then both in a checkerboard pattern. Her cheek throbbed, swelling until she could barely hold up her head. Funny how it didn't hurt all that much. In fact, it felt kind of numb. Like Novocaine. But so heavy . . . Anne let her chin drop, resting it against Paul's shoulder. Just for a minute, though. Just until she could pull herself together.

"Are you okay?" She heard his voice through a distant filter. The words had to wrestle and defeat a ringing in her ears before she could make them out. "Anne? Come on. Are you all right?"

She tried to nod, but that only increased the dizziness. She tried to speak, but her tongue didn't feel like taking orders from her brain. The only physiology still working properly, seemed to be her eyes. Anne forced them open through sheer will, trying to stabilize the fireworks by focusing on the object nearest to her: Paul Gaasbeck. God, Anne decided, had a hell of a sense of humor.

Paul shifted his grip so that he held Anne with only one arm. He raised his other one to lightly probe along the swelling beneath her eye. "You're going to have one beauty of a bruise tomorrow."

"So are you," Anne snapped, "if you don't put me down."

He ignored her less-than-implied threat. Instead, Paul set Anne down gently. But rather than removing his hand entirely from her face, he slid it ever so slightly to the left, wrapping loose strands of her hair around two fingers and absently stroking the lock with his thumb, seemingly lost in thought.

Her own arm sprung up automatically, but instead of making contact with her hair, Anne's fingertips brushed the back of Paul's palm, skimming down his knuckles and settling, somehow, at the base of his wrist. His pulse leapt out at her like an electric current. Loath to be out-done, Anne's heart jump-started into double-time to keep up, and for the first time outside an airplane, her stomach bounced off the roof of her mouth and plunged to her knees before bouncing back and splattering around her rib cage.

She inhaled sharply, wondering how she could be feeling so suddenly cold while a bead of sweat trickled down her neck and disappeared into her shirt collar. Her fingers still grazed Paul's wrist, the steady beat of his pulse her only indication that time was indeed continuing. Otherwise, even the wind felt unnaturally motionless. The warmth of Paul's hand hovering inches from her cheek was exhibiting a most peculiar effect. Anne's every breath seemed to have grown heavier.

She slipped her hand in beside Paul's, easing the

strands from around his fingers and guiltily admitting, "I know. My hair's too long for regulations. But don't tell anyone, okay?"

It was her one vanity, and Anne figured she was entitled. Bad enough women pilots trained wearing men's flight boots, suits, and helmets, and makeup was forbidden because of interference with the oxygen mask. Such conditions didn't exactly boost her self-image. The only thrill she got, under the circumstances, was that moment when she stepped out of her airplane, whipped off her helmet, and watched the transient maintenance guys' eyes bug at the sight of a woman flying.

After seven hours of school, followed by physical conditioning, target practice, and parachute training, Anne needed that daily boost to keep going. So even though Air Force canon specified her hair had to clear the collar, she deliberately kept it down to her shoulders—for effect. She pinned it up, so no one could tell exactly how long it was. Unfortunately, her hair was too fine to stay put for long.

She waited for Paul to respond to her plea. The way he kept staring at her made Anne think he wanted her to say something else. But she couldn't guess what.

"I . . ." Paul started, then his voice trailed off. He took a step backward, withdrawing his hand and snapping it firmly to his side. He cleared his throat.

She'd never caught Paul strapped for a quick comeback before.

Finally, Paul offered, "Don't cut your hair. I like it long."

Then he walked away without another word.

Still stunned—from the blow to her face or from Paul's behavior, Anne couldn't be certain—she hobbled toward the dormitories, limping up the stairs to her room and clutching the rail to stay balanced. The throbbing in her ankle pounded in sync with her throbbing cheek. From the bottom of the steps, Anne heard her name called. She turned, wincing, just in time to see Major Danahay hurrying up the stairs, asking, "Are you all right?"

Anne stifled a groan. Wonderful. Twenty-four hours ago she'd received a condemnation for acting too reckless. Now this.

Major Danahay glanced from the bruise on Anne's face to her swelling ankle. "I saw what happened out there."

Anne shrugged. There wasn't much to say in her defense.

Major Danahay looked around, debating whether they'd be overheard. When she felt sure they were out of eavesdrop range, she motioned for Anne to take a seat next to her on the stairs.

Certain that she was about to be reprimanded, Anne braced for the worst. She lowered herself gingerly onto the step, and waited.

After a beat, during which she cleared her throat and lowered her voice, Major Danahay said, "You're a bright girl, Anne. Very, very bright. Too bright to be wasting your life here."

Anne's eyes widened. "Excuse me?"

Major Danahay sighed, resting her elbows on top of her knees and propping her head up with both palms. "Did you know that I was the first woman admitted to the Academy? Diana Paul was one of my instructors. Know who she was?"

"Of course I do."

During World War II, aviatrix Nancy Love convinced the Army Air Force to create the Woman's Auxiliary Ferry Service, so female pilots could deliver newly built fighters and bombers to overseas air bases, freeing up male pilots for combat. The WAFS's youngest recruit was Diana Paul, a fifteen-year-old crop duster from Iowa who'd lied about her age. After the war, she accepted an offer to teach at the Academy, where it took twenty years of training men before she saw her first female cadet pass through the door.

Major Danahay continued, "I was a big story in 1976. All the newspapers covered it. Television, too. One week, I was both an answer in *The New York Times* crossword puzzle and a punchline on the Carson show. Hell of a lot of pressure. I couldn't just get through the program. I had to excel. So . . . I did. I graduated number one. But when it came time to be commissioned, I got the same assignment as some man who'd graduated near the bottom of the heap. Only, he's flying. And I'm pushing papers for a career."

Anne didn't know what she was supposed to say. She met Major Danahay's eyes, then guiltily looked away. "I—I'm sorry."

"No. *I'm* sorry. I'm sorry that I didn't pick up the phone and call every girl who sent in an Academy application to tell her exactly what things are like around here."

"But, I . . . The Academy's the best school I've ever been to."

"Please. Are you trying to tell me you've always felt welcome inside this fortress that testosterone built?"

Anne seriously considered the question.

Sure, over the past four years there'd been moments. Moments when her male colleagues' jokes stopped being funny and bordered on the insulting. Moments when hostile TIs drilled their women cadets to exhaustion, then ridiculed them for failing to complete a man's job. Moments when a visiting alumni berated them for taking away an Academy spot that rightfully belonged to a man.

But Anne refused to let any of that bother her. She saw every offense as a challenge, a chance to prove all her detractors wrong.

"You're killing yourself for no reason, Anne. You are every bit the athlete Paul Gaasbeck is. You are more than his match in the classroom, and, hands down, you're the better pilot. Problem is, you are never going to be honored for those talents. Not in the Air Force. For four years, I've watched you killing yourself to be the best. That kind of ambition is commendable—but only if you're going to be rewarded for your efforts. Otherwise, what's the point of suffering the bruises, the insults, the lost sleep?"

"The Commander's Trophy—"

"The Commander's Trophy means nothing. Not unless you have a Y-chromosome to go with it. I'm telling you the truth for your own good. I wish someone had told me years ago. Save your strength. Finish school, get through whatever lousy tour of duty they stick you with, serve your five years, then get out. Go to the private sector. Airlines, corporate, whatever. A woman like you, there's no telling how high you could go. But save your strength. Don't waste it fighting battles you can't win." Major Danahay gripped Anne's chin with her palm, forcing her to listen closely. "This boys' club is never going to give you the attention and respect you deserve. Believing otherwise will only break your heart."

By midnight, Anne's eye had swollen shut. Her taped ankle pulsated with each heartbeat. She lay on top of her bed, arms by her sides, eyes closed, mind whirling at the speed of light. As a rule, Anne didn't believe in bad days. However, for a person who didn't believe in them, Anne felt pretty sure she'd just had one.

She played the afternoon over and over in her mind, until it was no longer linear. Paul's voice overlapped the major's, their words slapping her like sharp pebbles as she ran toward the high-bar. Anne leapt in the air, and she was parachuting with Wakeman, then crashing to the ground and landing in Paul's arms.

*This boys' club is never going to give you the attention and respect you deserve. Believing otherwise will only break your heart.*

She felt so tired. Every breath was a Herculean effort. And yet, no matter how much she wanted to, Anne couldn't fall asleep.

She'd never been faced with failure before. Growing up, Anne had simply assumed that, if she worked hard enough, she would get anything she wanted, no matter how impossible her goals might seem to other people. If she believed in it, then it would happen.

It never occurred to Anne that she might be denied a slot based on her gender. She'd expected to be judged solely on merit. That's why she worked so hard—well, that, and because she liked sticking it to Paul Gaasbeck. But mostly it was because she expected to be rewarded for her efforts. And now Major Danahay claimed it would never happen? How could that be?

For four years, the Commander's Trophy had been Anne's light at the end of the tunnel. As she winced while applying bandages to her shredded palms after attempting fifty pull-ups too many, as she clocked her seventieth consecutive hour without sleep studying for a final, as she accepted every task that came her way, from rinsing jets with freezing water in the middle of winter to reassembling an engine just to prove her toughness, Anne concentrated on her silver objective. And now, to find out it meant nothing?

Anne rolled over, searching for a spot on her body

that didn't hurt. She wondered how she ever judged herself bright. Killing yourself for a competition you might not win was one thing. But killing yourself for no reason whatsoever was just plain stupid.

For the first time in her life, Anne seriously considered the possibility that it might be time to give up. On everything.

And everyone.

In class the next morning, the first time Paul Gaasbeck raised his hand to answer a question and wasn't immediately contradicted by Anne, fellow cadets thought she was merely saving her energy for a later assault. The second time it happened, students snuck peeks at Anne out the corners of their eyes, brows wrinkled in confusion.

Anne, for her part, sat slouched in her chair, gaze locked on the paper in front of her as she covered first one side, then another, with a series of three-dimensional squares. The third time, when Paul tossed her a softball so easy no one had any doubts Anne could blast it out of the park, and still she said nothing, even their instructor stopped class to ask, "Are you all right?"

She looked up, as if waking from a dream. "Fine, sir."

On the confidence course, she made a halfhearted attempt at scaling the pyramid. When she slipped, cutting the inside of her wrist, Anne looked for a moment at the injury, then shrugged and walked away, ignoring the rest of the course altogether.

On the shooting range, Anne arrived late, ignored orders to wear protective ear cover, and fired a round while barely looking at the target. She missed the bull's-eye entirely.

"What the hell is the matter with you?" Paul grabbed

Anne's arm as she attempted to enter the cafeteria. "Been lobotomized?"

She didn't even fight to escape his grip. "What do you care?"

"Look,"—Paul softened his tone, sounding for the world as if he might really give a damn—"is something wrong? Are you sick?"

"No. I'm perfectly fine. I've just wizened up, that's all. Major Danahay, she explained how some things work around here."

"What things?"

Anne sighed. A week ago, she would have died rather than make a fool of herself in front of Paul. But considering her behavior at the high jump, Anne figured she didn't have a face left to save.

And so she told Paul the whole story, her voice devoid of any self-pity, or any other expression whatsoever. Why bother?

It was over.

By fourth year, Academy cadets were allowed to embark on solo flights, going up in sets of two and taking turns maneuvering the controls. Pairs were grouped by aptitude, so naturally, Paul and Anne ended up together. Their expeditions typically began with a debate over who would navigate first, and ended with a fight about who'd done the better job.

Since she had no intention of challenging Paul that afternoon, Anne didn't even bother checking his flight plan before they took off. Instead, she strapped herself into the copilot seat, mouthed through the pre-flight checklist, and then proceeded to stare out the window, while Paul meticulously executed each of their assigned drills. He didn't say a word to her. Anne preferred it that way.

It was only when she spied the sun setting outside her window that Anne emerged from her lethargy, realizing not only were they out much later than they were scheduled to be but that Paul had long ago swerved off their course.

"Paul?" Anne popped upright. "Where are we?"

He glanced out the window, "Somewhere over New Mexico."

"Is there a reason for that?"

"There is." He peered closely at the altimeter, then leaned back, satisfied by what he'd seen.

"Do you have any idea how much trouble you'll get into, taking an Academy plane off its designated flight plan?"

"I do."

This was starting to get on Anne's nerves. The look in Paul's eyes reminded her of kamikaze photos she'd seen. Total composure, mixed with an ample dash of madness.

Her stomach stirred uneasily.

"Paul? Where the hell are we going?"

He only smiled in reply.

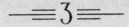

## 3

*The Present*

The minute the *Amelia*'s landing gear hit that icy stretch of snow- encrusted mountain, Anne lost control of her steering, and, in the instant before impact, she gave up on being an Air Force pilot and simply became a mother. She thrust out her right arm, blocking her daughter's head from smashing against the instrument panel, absorbing the brunt of the collision as her own head slammed against the steering wheel instead.

The splintering glass, the screech of wheels, the howl of the wind, and the groan of a tree ripped out by its roots and splitting a portion of wing off along with it, made it impossible for Anne to hear the bone in her arm shatter. She certainly felt it, though. She felt its severed edges slice her flesh, felt her elbow twist in the socket, muscles and tendons unspooling like thread.

Anne figured that passing out right about now would not be a bad thing. But Amelia shrieking her name quickly reminded Anne why she hadn't succumbed to that practical option in the first place.

"I'm all right, Ace," Anne managed to croak out. She tasted blood. A prod-and-nudge survey of her mouth revealed tongue and teeth still in place, albeit wobbly for the wear.

She grit her teeth and attempted to straighten up. The tip of her rib cage scraped painfully against her hip bone. Anne inhaled sharply, but continued gradually raising her shoulders. She felt her arm pulsate twice its size, and she couldn't so much as inhale without jolting her arm and firing nails of pain along her body.

Nevertheless, she twisted her head toward Amelia, ravenously scrutinizing the child for signs of injury. Anne's daughter sat in the copilot's seat, her sweater and jeans covered with the silvery sheen of broken glass. A slash across Amelia's forehead dripped plump ruby beads in two parallel lines down to her eyebrow, where they matted into a single, sticky clot.

"Mom?" Amelia's voice trembled. The glass dust quivered as she spoke, enveloping Amelia in a cascading, silver cloud.

"It'll be okay. Everything's going to be fine."

"You're hurt."

"I'll live." Anne raised her good arm and brushed its fingers across Amelia's forehead, relieved to record that her bleeding had already stopped. "Does your head hurt?"

"Just a little." Amelia's eyes filled with tears. "Mom, your arm. I broke your arm."

Following Amelia's guilty gaze, Anne found herself forced to look down and confront the sight of her right appendage dangling uselessly by her thigh. She tried to make a fist, but couldn't.

"I'm fine," Anne insisted. "How about you?" She squeezed her daughter's shoulder, her arm, both of her knees, feeling for broken bones. "If you start to feel dizzy, tell me right away. Promise, Amelia. Promise you'll tell me if something starts to hurt."

"I promise."

"Good girl," Anne said. Then, softer, "You're a good girl, Ace. And I promise you, we're going to be fine."

Now that the shock of the crash had passed, Anne's perceptions barreled through her immediate pain and fixed on another sensation. She realized it was freezing.

Peering outside her demolished cockpit via a shattered window, Anne spotted rocks, trees, mountains, and snow. Two kinds of snow. Snow laying on the ground in icy piles, and snow that continued to fall from the sky. Sideways.

That, Anne decided, couldn't possibly be good. When snow fell sideways, it suggested a rather stiff wind navigating its journey.

"We've got to cover these windows with something," she said.

Amelia unsnapped her seat belt and leapt to her·feet. She'd been waiting for a command to do something, anything, as long as it meant concentrating her thoughts outside of what had just happened.

Anne looked around for a makeshift shutter, rising from the remains of her seat and just as quickly crumpling back down as the pain in her arm effectively paralyzed any major movements.

"Okay," she said. "Won't be trying that again." Spotting the terror in Amelia's eyes, Anne lightened her tone, explaining, "What I meant was, we need to make me a splint. That's all. A splint is easy. Elementary first-aid stuff. You'll see."

Amelia wrinkled her nose. "What do we make it out of?"

Anne surveyed the cockpit, recognizing that their options were limited. She dismissed the throttle as too short to be effective, and the transistor radio antenna as too light. Her eyes settled on their passenger seat lying on its side amidst the scattered debris at the back of the plane. She asked, "Is that too big, 'Melia, or can you drag it over here?"

"I can bring it." Amelia dug her fingers into the plastic armrest and tugged. She needed to bore her heels in, leaning back so far that Anne feared if she lost her grip, she'd go sprawling. But eventually Amelia managed to drag the seat within her reach.

"I wish we had a screwdriver," Anne said. She picked up the shattered transistor radio and yanked out its antenna. "I guess this will have to do."

She wedged the antenna's cap into the first screw connecting the foam-filled top to the metal of the armrest. Working with her left hand, it took a couple of tries before Anne figured out how to keep the antenna from slipping out of her grip, and twice as many failures before she got the hang of turning it properly. She was so focused on her task, that Anne didn't notice Amelia disappearing for a bit, only to pop up minutes later with a flashlight.

"Where'd you get that, Ace?"

"Dad always keeps a flashlight on board. For emergencies."

Anne couldn't help it. She laughed. No matter how it hurt her arm, no matter how inappropriate it was, Anne laughed. "Oh, Ace. Of course he does."

Amelia aimed her beam of light onto the armrest, holding out her hand so Anne could, one by one, drop the loosened screws into her palm. That's when she noticed that Amelia was shivering. Her teeth chattered. Her hands trembled. She clutched the high-powered flashlight, fingers straining toward the negligible heat offered by its bulb.

"You're cold," Anne accused.

"No, I'm not. I'm fine."

"Amelia!" Anne dropped their antenna, awkwardly struggling to writhe out of her jacket without jarring her injured arm. "Do you think you could quit being Paul Gaasbeck's daughter for one second? If you're cold, just say that you're cold. Don't keep me guessing till your fingers fall off from frostbite. It'll be a little late to do anything then."

Anne supposed that another child might have started to sniffle at such a sharp reprimand. But Amelia simply raised her chin, eyes steeling in determination. Voice even, and in a tone so reasonable it was virtually a dare to contradict her, she justified, "You were busy. I didn't want to distract you. I'm cold. But it can wait."

No, Anne realized. Not even for one second could Amelia quit being Paul Gaasbeck's daughter.

"Your discipline is admirable, Ace. But it's misplaced. See, thanks to this," Anne indicated her worthless arm, "I'm counting on you to be my right hand—literally. So your priority has to be keeping in tip-top shape. Or else, we're both out of the envelope."

It was a test-pilot term. If a plane stayed within the limits of its flight envelope, it remained stable and flyable. If it went beyond it, the aircraft swept out of control, most likely crashing.

Amelia nodded. "Yes, ma'am. I understand."

"Good girl. Now, help me off with this jacket." Anne grit her teeth to keep from moaning when Amelia gingerly tugged on the right sleeve. "There you go. Tie it around your shoulders, good and tight. Perfect. You look like Superman."

Amelia giggled, dwarfed by the World War II bombardier jacket Anne once bought Paul to celebrate his reaching number one in the test-pilot percentile rating. After their divorce, Paul left the jacket at Anne's. Probably to make some sort of an obscure point. She'd considered throwing it out but then decided it was too nice, practically an antique, and proceeded to wear it herself. Just to see what Paul might say about it. True to form, whenever he ran in to Anne wearing his jacket, Paul said absolutely nothing about it.

But the jacket did look adorable on Amelia. More importantly, it diffused the blue tinge puckering her lips. She reached down to retrieve the antenna and stood silently cradling the flashlight until Anne had finished exorcising every screw. Anne wrenched the arm rest loose, turning it upside down. The hollow interior made a perfect splint.

She held her breath and crammed her arm inside the cavity, grimacing. Anne directed Amelia to fasten the rubber band loosely holding up her ponytail around the wound to stop the bleeding, then tighten another band around her wrist to anchor the splint.

Anne's head spun. Her eyes closed, fighting back the churning vertigo.

"Here," Amelia said, "you'd better take your jacket back. Or you'll get cold, too."

"No," Anne's eyes snapped open, and she waved away the offer. "No, honey, I'm fine. Honestly." She indicated the genuine sweat dripping down her forehead. Thank God pain was such an effective heat inducer. "Besides, we've still got a lot of work to do."

For the next hour, Anne and Amelia tore all of the fabric from the remaining seats, pinning the strips up to cover their shattered windows and cramming the surplus synthetic cotton used to stuff the seats into their clothes for insulation. They filled the empty seat frame with snow so it could melt and create drinking water. Eating snow directly, Anne knew, would force their bodies to waste precious heat, while drinking it already melted would conserve it.

They swept the piles of glass off into one corner, clearing an area to sit, and huddled together for warmth. Anne told Amelia to pull up the neck of her sweater until it covered her lips and nose, then cross her arms and tuck each hand under an armpit, cautioning that exposed extremities were the most vulnerable to frostbite.

Her daughter did everything she was told. When it looked like Anne had run out of things to say, Amelia prompted, "What do we do now, Mom?"

"Now?" Anne flexed and unflexed her one able fist, propelling circulation through pure force of will. "We sit. And we wait for your father to come get us."

Which was precisely what Paul intended to do—if every ring-knocker at Hill Air Force Base would quit trying to stop him.

Bad enough those bastards in Colorado Springs were sitting on their asses, refusing to lift a finger. Now, he was getting that same kind of crap from his own men.

It was not like Paul was asking for something unreasonable. All he wanted was for them to let him borrow a plane, pop up to Colorado, and straighten out this entire mess. If a plane was out of the question, Paul would settle for a helicopter. Considering his years in the service, Paul figured the least they owed him was this one favor. You couldn't even call it a wholly personal favor. Anne was an Air Force officer, after all. Paul was perfectly within his rights to launch a rescue effort.

"But not," his superior officer upheld, "in a snowstorm. You heard Colorado Springs Traffic Control. Even if I did allow you to take a plane or helicopter, you would still be unable to land."

"Let that be my problem, sir. I've landed in adverse

weather before. Sand in Iraq, hail in Bosnia, rain in Grenada.''

''You're an excellent pilot, Major, no one is questioning that. But what kind of commander would I be if I let one of my men take off in weather I knew, in advance, to be life-threatening?''

Paul wished he'd had more time to prepare an argument. Leave it to Annie to have an accident without any advance notice.

He looked at his watch, realizing that each second Paul wasted trying to convince a colonel who obviously harbored no intention of budging was a second during which he wasn't on his way to Anne and Amelia. Finally, he turned on his heel and marched out of the building and into the parking lot toward his car. Paul gunned the engine, not caring whether it was warmed up. He peeled out, tires squealing so loudly, he left black tracks on the asphalt. He didn't even care if anyone turned to look.

Assuming nothing went wrong, Paul expected to reach Colorado Springs by nightfall. He didn't know what he would do if something did go wrong. He had no contingency plan. Of course, arriving in the middle of a blizzard, after sunset, with no promise of a search helicopter available, wasn't exactly Paul's idea of a great primary plan, either. But he couldn't sit by and do nothing.

When Paul left the house that morning, he'd automatically put on his uniform. Now he unbuttoned the collar, resting one elbow on the window frame and propping his head up on his palm.

Damn her.

Damn Anne.

If she'd only listened to him in the first place, forgotten that asinine ski trip, none of this would have happened.

No matter how long he lived, Paul felt certain he would never meet another person quite like Annie. On the one hand, she was undeniably intelligent. Paul would even go so far as admitting her brilliance—although, of course, never in her presence.

How, then, could a girl that smart be so . . . so . . . reckless?

Anne threw herself, one hundred percent, into everything she did, mindless of the consequences. Leap-before-you-look wasn't an aphorism for her, it was a lifestyle. In battle, unpredictability made for a very dangerous opponent. But it made for an even more dangerous partner.

He tried explaining as much to Anne while they were still cadets. But each time Paul brought up a perfectly valid point in class, she shot it down with some whimsical argument. Her debates were all over the territory. Paul never had a firm grasp on where they were headed, and it only took a few moments in Anne's presence for him to feel the ground beneath his feet dropping away. Talking to her was like attempting to balance during an earthquake. An Air Force staffed by officers like Anne would crumble from the chaos. It went against everything Paul believed in.

That's why, by the end of his first semester, Paul had become convinced it was imperative that he win the Commander's Trophy over Anne. The decision was by no means personal. On the contrary, it was for the greater good of everyone. Anne's winning the trophy might inspire others to emulate her. Then where would they all be?

Paul knew he'd have no problems beating Anne in the classroom or on the athletic field. He never had trouble coming out ahead in any sort of objective testing. But he worried about his scoring in the subjective areas: flying and leadership. Paul hated subjective trials. They were always so gray, so nebulous. Point him toward a target, outline the parameters, and Paul would get it done faster and better than anyone else. But everyone had a different opinion of what constituted good flying or strong leadership. It was too intangible, not to mention wide open for interpretation. Arbitrary judging was the reason Paul quit wrestling. If Paul felt he'd won, he didn't take too kindly to a referee overruling his conviction.

So, determined to beat Anne at any cost, Paul took chances he otherwise would never have considered. If Anne free-fell for five hundred feet while parachuting, then Paul had to free-fall for six hundred. If Anne proposed a strategy where they accomplished their objective in twelve days, Paul cut the time to one week. When Anne touched down her aircraft under the 3,000-feet-landing limit, Paul ignored his better judgment, and aimed for the 2,000-feet marker. He ended up working the rudders too hard, and triggering a fire in the port wheel's brake gear. Paul didn't like what he felt himself becoming. But, he also couldn't seem to stop it.

The idea that he could be so easily controlled by the actions of another person was not a pleasant one. Paul prided himself on his self-discipline. He counted it among his strongest attributes. Yet Anne proved capable of shattering it with a minimum of effort.

Paul hated that.

She must have known the power she exerted over him back then. How could she not? She was on Paul's mind practically every minute of every day, no matter how hard he tried to fight it.

But Paul refused to give Anne the satisfaction of seeing how deeply she affected him. Except for his one minor slip, that day when she asked him to keep quiet about her hair being too long, he applauded himself on the distance he'd managed to keep.

But there was another problem. One Paul hated admitting, even to himself. Still, he couldn't lie—not even to himself. The military had an honor code. "We will not lie, steal, or cheat, nor tolerate among us anyone who does."

If Paul ignored that Anne's recklessness was dangerous, that it undermined the entire structure of the military, that it bespoke irresponsibility, capriciousness, and plain, old laziness, then, in the name of honesty, he felt honor-bound to admit that there was a part of him—a small part, but a part of him nevertheless—that also found her total fearlessness rather, well, alluring.

He wondered what it might be like to approach any circumstance so thoroughly devoid of worry. To believe in yourself so totally that the thought of failure was never even a possibility.

Paul believed in himself. Rather, he believed in his ability to prepare, to anticipate problems, and to conceive of the perfect plan for countermanding them. But it was different for Anne. Anne embraced a freedom that bordered on abandonment. The rest of them flew airplanes. Anne simply flew.

Paul envied that quality, even as he resented it.

But he never foresaw that her abrupt withdrawal, thanks to Major Danahay's idea of a pep talk, would so thoroughly shatter *him*.

Paul hadn't realized how much he'd come to depend on the light in Anne's eyes to bolster him, to hearten him, to liven him, until that light unexpectedly disappeared. When she told him the reason for her melancholy, Paul expected to feel pleased that someone had finally put Anne in her place. Instead, he was left with a sense of overwhelming sadness. As if he had lost something infinitely precious and irreplaceable. He tried rationalizing the emotion, and finally dredged up an adequate explanation. Despite Anne's undeniable rough edges, she would have made a commendable officer. Paul hated to see the Air Force lose such a talent. It was a waste of all the time and money they'd already invested in her.

Clearly, it was up to Paul to rectify the situation. He knew of only one way to do it. Unfortunately, it wasn't exactly by the book. Not that he'd specifically seen a rule against it. Still, he had a hunch that hijacking an Academy plane to New Mexico fell somewhat outside the code of acceptable behavior.

But that was the problem with Anne. From the beginning and to this day. She liquified his common sense.

She made him break the rules, take foolish chances, cast aside logic in favor of some hazy gut feeling.

And, worst of all, she made him like it.

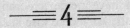

## 4

*1983*

Anne said, "The minute we get back to school, Major Danahay is going to be on-your-six so fast, you'll be blown out of the sky."

On-your-six was a combat pilot's depiction of his jet sitting directly behind another plane, ready to shoot it down.

"Probably."

Despite Anne's bravado, Paul could hear the uncertainty in her voice. She had no idea what he was up to, and it was driving her nuts. He figured it was about time she got a bit of her own back.

As a fringe benefit, Paul's stunt had succeeded in returning the color to Anne's cheeks. She sat up in her seat, eyes blazing, chin thrust out in defiance. When she soared in full battle-stance like this, Anne seemed to glow, to hum with energy. Paul imagined he could feel the air around her shimmering, scattering its zest onto everything in its path. He'd missed it these past few days.

"You mean you don't care that you're going to get into trouble for this? You? Paul Gaasbeck? Mr. I-Don't-Just-Go-By-The-Book-I-Wrote-The-Damn-Book?" Anne plopped back down in her seat, studying his profile. "Okay. It's official, now. You're scaring me."

"Good."

Her eyes narrowed. For a beat, Anne wasn't sure how to react, then she burst out laughing. "Gaasbeck, I'm starting to like you."

"I can die a happy man."

"Give me a hint, are you planning to do it on this flight?"

Now it was Paul's turn to crack a smile. He tried to hide it by turning his head and glancing over his shoulder, out the window.

"So where are we going?" Anne craned her neck for a peek at his scribbled flight plan.

Paul shifted the paper out of her view.

She pouted, "Come on, Gaasbeck. One itty, bitty hint? What's the big secret? You've got me helpless and defenseless up here. For all I know, your evil plan is to ravage me, then toss me into the Grand Canyon."

Paul snorted. "I can't imagine you ever being helpless, or defenseless. And, for the record, the Grand Canyon is in Arizona."

"I know that. Haven't you ever heard of poetic license? By the way, you haven't said anything about the ravaging part."

"No comment." Anne's words triggered a myriad of images in Paul's head, none of which were appropriate while flying, or, for that matter, anytime. He concentrated on the vista below, until the sensation passed.

Noting that Paul was preparing to land, Anne glanced out her window, searching the dusky landscape for a clue as to where he was taking her. All she could make out was a split-level ranch house, a barn wide enough to serve as a hangar, and an illuminated runway.

Paul coasted the Academy's Cessna in for a landing

as if he'd been doing it his whole life. He stopcocked the throttles, flicked off the engine, and turned to Anne, smiling.

"Follow me," he said.

Paul offered Anne his hand as she climbed out of the cockpit. He continued holding it while he led her toward the house. Paul told himself it was because she didn't know her way around. And it was dark. He couldn't risk her being hurt. Then Paul would really be in trouble back at the Academy.

Anne followed Paul's lead up the porch steps and to the front door. She gasped when she saw the name on the mailbox.

He knocked. A woman in her sixties, dressed in blue jeans, a gray work-shirt, and cowboy boots, her graying auburn hair brushed back into a bun, opened the door.

Paul said, "Anne, this is my mother, Diana Paul Gaasbeck."

"Your . . . mother?" Anne looked from him, to the face she was used to seeing only in portrait on an Academy wall. To clarify, in case she'd misheard, she repeated, "Diana Paul is your mother?"

"So I've been told."

"Oh. Well. That explains a lot."

"Doesn't it, though?"

World War II's youngest female pilot invited them inside. She said, "I'm so glad Paul finally brought you here. I've been dying to meet the young woman my son claims is almost as smart as he is."

"Almost?" Anne turned to Paul, hands on hips. "Almost?"

"You wouldn't want me to lie to my mother, now, would you?"

Anne stuck her tongue out at him. Paul smiled innocently.

Mrs. Gaasbeck laughed. "It's nice to know some things haven't changed since I was an instructor at the Academy. The competitive spirit is alive and well. Although," she turned to face Anne, "not lately, I hear . . ."

Anne ducked her head, shooting Paul a look of pure evil. He'd told his mother about her behavior? Wonderful. Now even her role model would know she was an idiot. "I—"

"You gave up." Diana Gaasbeck's voice was compassionate but firm. "The world stopped turning your way, so you took your ball and went home. That's one of the hazards to being an overachiever all of your life. No one teaches you how to deal with setbacks. Damn it, I could wring Sharon's neck for what she said to you."

"You mean it isn't true?" Anne experienced her first spark of hope in days.

"Of course, it's true." Diana Gaasbeck flicked her arm at the wrist, indicating a concern of no consequence. She wore gold pilot wings on a chain around her neck. They clicked as she spoke. "The Air Force Academy, the entire Air Force, is a boys' club. But, it is changing. Seven years ago, women weren't allowed to fly. Now, look at you. You have a chance at the Commander's Trophy. That's something. That's huge! Forty years ago, they said women couldn't fly fighters and bombers. Well, I did. Jacqueline Cochran broke the sound barrier in an F-86 in 1953. And mark my words, by next year, women will be flying the KC-10 tanker. I've heard it through the grapevine. I know it's going to happen."

"Really?" The KC-10 Extender was a heavy tanker and transport with a takeoff weight of 590,000 pounds.

Previously, women pilots had been deemed too weak to handle such a cumbersome craft.

"Yes." Diana Gaasbeck carefully weighed her subsequent words. "Progress takes time. That's something Sharon never got. When she was in my class at the Academy, Sharon wanted everything at that moment. She was in a hurry. Couldn't wait. Well, I'm sorry, but you don't get everything first time up. How does she think she made it into pilot training? Does Sharon think it just happened? Nothing just happens. Especially not when the majority are against it. For there to be a Sharon Danahay, there first had to be a Nancy Love. A Lillian Gatlin. An Amelia Earhart. A Jacqueline Cochran."

"A Diana Paul," her son offered.

"Yes," his mother's eyes danced mischievously. "Her, too."

Anne glanced at Paul. He was practically beaming with pride. Earlier, she'd suspected his hostility toward her stemmed from a typical macho airman's contempt for women pilots. In retrospect, she realized that theory begged for some serious rethinking.

Diana Gaasbeck said, "I apologize, Anne. But I taught at the Academy for so long, the minute I see a cadet, I start lecturing. I don't mean to go on and on. But I do think it's important that you hear what I have to say. You've chosen a very difficult road for yourself. Not only physically difficult. Although, I do know something about that." She displayed her hands so Anne could see the mounds of callouses across both her palms. "The hardest thing about military life, at least for me, was the unrelenting sense of responsibility. Civilians are responsible for themselves, solely. *We* are responsible for everyone. Each airman, from basic on up, is responsible for every other airman. Otherwise, the infrastructure falls apart. Any act taken by one, affects the whole. Any mistake made—and I've told Paul this since he was a boy—is a mistake that impacts not just on you but on everyone around you.''

"That's kind of scary," Anne admitted.

"It's supposed to be," Paul said. "It's supposed to keep us from flying off half-cocked."

Ah. There it was. Anne knew he'd get around to insulting her sooner or later. Her first instinct was to whip around and call him any number of well-rehearsed names. But she didn't think that would be too polite, seeing as how she was his mother's guest.

Diana reminded, "However, just like our mistakes don't exist in a vacuum, neither do our achievements. When the WAFS proved we could be wartime pilots, that opened the door for women in flight school.

"When Sharon Danahay graduated top of her class, it opened the door for more women in the Academy. One conquest building on the back of another. That's how it has always been, that's how it always will be. We didn't get where we are today by pitching fits, and we didn't get here by quitting when progress wasn't moving fast enough for our liking. True, Anne, you may never fly combat. But, know what? I'll bet anything that your daughter will. That is, if you don't let her down by dropping your rung of the ladder."

Anne exhaled slowly, allowing the moral to sink in. She felt like she'd been diving under water and was only now coming up for air. "You must have been a hell of an instructor, Mrs. Gaasbeck."

"I had my moments."

"And you must have been one hell of a mother."

"She had her moments," Paul interjected.

Diana smiled. "Poor Paul. I'm afraid I was always practicing my classroom lectures on him. I'm surprised it didn't dissuade him from an air force career. I raised him alone, you understand, so any character flaws can only be traced back to me.''

"What character flaws?'' Paul inquired innocently.

His mother wagged her finger at him. "On the other hand, I suppose he didn't turn out too badly. What do you think, Anne?"

"Well . . ." Her eyes met Paul's.

He answered her gaze with a smile, virtually challenging Anne to articulate how she really felt. She hesitated. Whether out of politeness or something else, Anne couldn't be sure. She studied his features, noticing for the first time how his face resembled a block of marble neatly slashed on both sides below the cheekbones, leading to a stately chin and a smile that melts stone.

Anne cleared her throat. She told Diana Gaasbeck, "I think your son turned out just fine."

Neither Paul nor Anne said much during the plane ride back to the Academy. Although, right before they were about to touch down, she did ask him, "Why did you do it, Paul?"

"Why did I do what?"

"This." Anne waved her arms about the cabin, pointing out the window, across to Paul, back toward New Mexico, trying to somehow encompass their entire situation in a rather weak-for-the-occasion word. "I mean, forget that you're going to get into more trouble then there are words for. But you took me to see your mom because you knew she'd talk me out of this funk I've been in. You didn't have to do it. You could have just ignored me, and the Commander's Trophy was yours, no ifs, ands or buts about it."

"True."

"So? Why did you?"

He pretended he hadn't heard the question. Anne repeated it. Paul picked up the nav/com for a chat with Air Traffic Control.

Needing to get some sort of response out of him, Anne teased, "Maybe you just couldn't stand the thought of seeing me go."

"Right." He flicked a switch to begin lowering their landing gear. "That's exactly it."

"Come on, Paul." Anne could hear her tone sinking dangerously close to whining and pulled back. "Tell me, why did you do it?"

He turned to face her with an expression cold enough to streak frost on the windows. "Because. I don't need to win by forfeit."

Paul figured that Major Danahay was particularly furious about his stunt because he'd been so good all four years. She felt he'd lulled her into a false confidence, and played her for a fool. She said she'd expected more from him. Didn't Paul know taking Academy property for a joyride was a major offense?

Yes, ma'am, he did know that.

And did Paul realize the danger he put himself and others in, diverting off his designated flight plan?

Yes, ma'am, he knew that, too.

So, why, then? Why did Paul do it?

No reason, ma'am.

The disciplinary committee gave up. No one knew what to do with him. On the one hand, Paul had committed a serious violation. On the other, there was his exemplary record to consider. Should a promising military career be permanently derailed due to nothing more than juvenile exuberance?

The disciplinary committee decided that, no, it should not be. But then again, neither should his behavior be rewarded.

So in the end, Cadet Gaasbeck's indiscretion was not entered into his permanent record. But the Commander's Trophy, for overall excellence in flying, academics, and leadership, went to Anne.

He'd expected as much. The moment Paul broke the rules and altered his flight plan, he passed the point of no return. As he sat in his mother's house, hearing her encourage Anne to go after the Commander's Trophy, Paul knew he'd already lost the prize as surely as he knew Anne had won it. Still, knowing that he'd blown his own brains out offered small comfort in dealing with the loss.

The night their awards were announced, Paul stood off to the side, watching Anne disappear inside a throng of well-wishers and congratulatory hugs. He couldn't help thinking that if he'd been declared the winner, the celebration would have included a round of handshakes and some kind words but hardly the hoopla that erupted when the top prize went to Anne.

Two cadets lifted her onto their shoulders, bouncing Anne up and down like she'd just won the World Series. The others crowded around, swarming and shrieking from every direction. She threw her head back and laughed, hair coming loose from its carefully pinned bun and tumbling out past her shoulders. She ran a hand through her bangs, attempting to settle them into order and, lowering her arm, caught a glimpse of Paul standing off alone, silent, watching.

Oblivious to the cheers coming at her from all sides, Anne's eyes locked with his. She mouthed, "Thank you."

He nodded politely, briefly closing his eyes in recognition of her gratitude. He opened them again in time to see Anne squirm her way down the pyramid of cadets and make her way toward him.

"Hi," she said.

"Hello." Then, because he could think of nothing else to say, he offered, "Congratulations."

"Thanks." Her right hand slid self-consciously up her hair, wordlessly rubbing her neck. "I . . . we . . . a bunch of us are going into town, to celebrate. Do you think, maybe, you'd like to come?"

"No. Thank you. I'm not really in the mood."

"Yeah. I understand. But, see, I—I couldn't have won this without you. And I don't mean just because you got your mother to knock some sense into me. Although that was important."

"Yes," Paul agreed, "It certainly was."

"More important, though . . . more important was having class with you for four years. It made me push myself. It made me want to try harder. Because you were so good, you brought out the best in me. And I've never really thanked you for it."

Now Paul truly didn't know what to say. Her praise seemed to come from out of nowhere. He never dreamt she felt this way—and all he could think of to respond was a cool "You're welcome."

"Damn it, Paul." Anne flung her hands down, then raised them to the sky. "I give up. What do you want from me? What? I argue with you, I ignore you, I try to be nice . . . It makes no difference. Are you even capable of responding, one human being to another?"

"Anne, you said thank you, I said, you're welcome. That's not an adequate response? Let's consult Miss Manners."

She squeezed both fists and forced a smile. "Look. I didn't come here to fight you. Let's just start over. We're going to the amusement park, tonight. You know, the one a couple of miles out of town. Please, come. I really want you to.''

Paul was about to tell Anne that her really wanting him to in no way nullified his previous position of not feeling in the mood.

But when he opened his mouth, he heard himself say, ''Fine.''

Paul wondered why carnival people were hugging Anne. Granted, winning the Commander's Trophy was a very big deal, but he hadn't realized it mattered that much to folks who spun merry-go-rounds and hawked cotton candy for a living. However, after the ticket taker waved them all in for free, and the man at the penny-pitch hopped over his faux-crystal stack to pick Anne up off the ground and spin her madly, Paul began to suspect he was missing something.

After three hours of brooding about it, he'd embarked on this outing with a great deal of reluctance. For one thing, he thought spending an evening surrounded by cadets who knew he'd just come in second best was a less than engaging prospect. For another, he didn't even like carnivals. Frankly, he saw no point in wandering aimlessly, accumulating gum and crushed popcorn on his shoes, or in throwing money away on games of no skill that were probably rigged besides. As for the so-called thrill rides, the Ferris wheels and tilt-a-whirls, well, they weren't exactly F-15s. More like empty calories. Thrills for thrills' sake, with no legitimate objective.

He'd already half-decided to blow it off when Anne knocked on Paul's dormitory door, personally reminding him that he'd promised to come. She wore sandals and a sleeveless yellow sundress with dandelion buttons down the front. Her hair swayed loose over her bare shoulders and back, emphasizing a discernible lack of any other clothing underneath.

"Ready to go?" Anne asked.

Paul went.

And now, here he was.

He shifted uncomfortably from foot to foot, both hands in his pockets, and watched his fellow cadets scatter in every direction.

Finally, curiosity getting the best of him, Paul called Anne over and, indicating the abnormally friendly vendors periodically ambushing her with shrieked greetings, asked, "Do you know these people, or is it just one hell of a first meeting?"

She grinned. "I lived here for about a year when I was in the sixth—no, I think it was the seventh grade."

"Were your mother and father sword eaters?"

"Close. They were engineers."

"That was going to be my next guess."

Seeing Paul's confusion, she explained, "They designed roller-coasters. That's why we moved around so much when I was a kid. My mom and dad would finish one job, stick around to troubleshoot, then we'd go somewhere else. Longest we ever stayed in a spot was for eighteen months, and that was in Disneyland."

"You grew up in Disneyland?"

"Happiest place on Earth."

"Oh," Paul recalled a phrase she'd once used on him. "That explains a lot."

"I've loved roller coasters since I was a kid. Anything fast, really. Mom said I was born so quick the doctor used a catcher's mit. I was always running. I never owned a pair of jeans without holes in the knees. But it was living here in Colorado that first gave me the idea of going to the Air Force Academy."

She made his head spin. There. Finally. After four

years, Paul could finally put words to how Anne made him feel. Single-engine planes, twin-engine planes, jets fast enough to break the sound barrier, Paul climbed in and out of those without so much as a flicker of motion sickness. But, Anne, Anne made his head spin!

Great.

She said, "Looks like everyone else ran off without us."

"Yeah, well, I think Peterson mumbled something about meeting by the bumper cars."

"The bumper cars? Please. That's baby stuff. We're Academy graduates. We can do better than that." Anne grabbed Paul's hand. "Come on. I'll show you the best deal in the place. It's the one my mom and dad designed."

"Yeah? What's it called?"

"Annie's Wild Ride."

Been there, done that, Paul wanted to say.

But instead he allowed Anne to pull him toward a three-story silver-and-black zigzag at the center of the fairgrounds.

She told him, "I remember when my mom and dad started working on it. They sat every night at the kitchen table, twisting a piece of wire, making loops and shapes, trying to come up with something new. Annie's Wild Ride goes fifty miles per hour. That's not so much now, but used to be one of the fastest in the country. And my mom and dad threaded the track through these narrow passageways, so you'd feel like it's about to soar out of control. But it never really does."

"My kind of track."

"It's all an illusion. It's physics. An electric power chain pulls the car up its first hill. The rest is momentum. The next hill can't get any bigger because friction slows the car down. So what they do is make the turns at the end of the track tighter and tighter. The passengers continue to feel accelerating forces, even though their speed is actually decreasing." Anne shook her head, disgusted at ever having fallen for such chicanery. "These days, I prefer my excitement genuine, thanks."

Standing in line for the ride, she closed her eyes and spun in place. Her hair and the hem of her dress twirled in unison, like twin propellers revving to go. For the briefest of instants, Paul actually believed that Anne might take off, powered by nothing more than enthusiasm, joy, and conviction. What was worse, for that same brief instant, he, more than anything, wanted to go with her. He wanted to feel what she was feeling, he wanted to know what she was thinking, he wanted... Paul didn't know what he wanted.

And that bothered him.

That bothered him a lot.

He grabbed her roughly around the wrist, stopping Anne's whirl midrevolution. She slid to a stop, facing him. Her breath caught in her throat, her eyes quizzically lifting from his tighter-than-necessary grip on her arm to Paul's unexpected, and inexplicable, expression. Yet she made no effort to pull away. And Paul made no move to let go. He was having some trouble breathing himself.

"Next!" Annie's Wild Ride operator tapped its namesake on her shoulder, gesturing that it was their turn to climb on board.

Paul dropped her arm as if singed. Realizing his hands were shaking, he promptly thrust both behind his back, in mock at-ease.

They climbed aboard the coaster without looking at or touching each other. However, once the safety bar locked, it was impossible to ignore the close proximity. Anne's bare arm rubbed against the skin exposed by Paul's short-sleeved shirt. The sensation roared through him, every nerve in Paul's body resonating with her touch.

To make matters worse, as soon as their car lurched forward, she leaned over and whispered conspiratorially in his ear, "Every roller coaster my parents designed, they put in a special feature only we knew about. Want to see what it is?"

Paul promised himself that it would be for just this once, and allowed his curiosity to rule. "What?"

"Wait." She held up one finger, leaning back and grinning as their car dragged its way up the first, most important, hill. Paul turned his head, observing the delight in her eyes, the excitement, the anticipation, and felt a stirring in his stomach he was pretty certain had nothing to do with riding on a roller coaster.

As their car teetered along the top, ready to careen into the abyss, Anne's gaze met Paul's. And at the exact moment that they plunged downward, she tilted her head, placing her mouth atop his, lips and tongues connecting while their bodies plummeted.

The explosion of combating sensations nearly blew the lid off Paul's head. It was all he could do just to cling to the moment at hand, instead of shattering into a dozen pieces.

He cupped both hands around her face, her hair tangling in his fingers. He could taste, see, hear, feel, know nothing outside of her, his senses thoroughly hijacked. He breathed Anne in, feeling her essence pierce so deeply inside his soul, Paul doubted he could ever take another breath without sensing her presence.

On the next turn, both were flung to opposite ends of the car. They stared at each other, lips swollen, eyes glazed, cheeks red—but whether that last one resulted from the kiss or as an outcome of being flipped upside down was rather difficult to assess. Paul inhaled sharply, mind whirring ahead, looking to paste appropriate words onto what had just happened.

But, as he'd feared, Anne beat him to the punch. As Annie's Wild Ride creaked to a stop, she smiled lazily, running the tips of her fingers along Paul's mouth, wiping it clean of her lipstick.

"So, what do you think?" She brought the pink-smeared thumb to her lips, licking it leisurely like a child savoring her ice cream cone. "My folks know how to design a coaster, or what?"

Afterward, Paul hopped out first, extending his hand and pulling Anne from the car. But instead of allowing her to regain her balance, Paul continued pulling, easily crushing her against his chest and pressing his mouth against hers, this time when *she* least expected it.

Anne didn't struggle. Rather, she melted against him, parting her lips and savoring the sweep of his tongue. She rose up on her tiptoes, straining to get as close to him as possible. Now when they separated, it was Paul who got the first word in.

"What do you know?" He raised her thumb to his mouth, tongue flicking playfully along the exact same spot as hers had. "Works off the roller coaster, too."

They walked. Where, and for how long, and why—if Paul were forced to write an operational report about the next few hours, he would have felt totally stuck for details. All he knew was, they walked. And they talked.

Anne told him about her parents, their eschewing comfortable engineering jobs in favor of a gypsy life rambling from attraction to attraction, her mother's death from cancer two years before, and her father's collapse from a heart attack less than six months later.

"You're all alone?" Paul felt a wave of tenderness

overwhelm him. Her plight made him want to protect her from the world.

"Not really. I've got the Air Force, haven't I?" She asked, "How about you? What happened to your dad?"

He hesitated, uncomfortable with the topic. "Shot down. Over Vietnam. In sixty-seven." Usually, this was as far as Paul's story went. But something in the way Anne looked at him encouraged him to continue. "Dad was in the front seat. After the bird got hit, he waited to eject, because the guy in the back always goes first, you know? Otherwise the explosion from the front could crush him. So he waited. But there was something wrong with the rear eject, and by the time his copilot went, it was too late. He crashed."

Anne covered her mouth with one hand, sharing Paul's pain as deeply as if it were hers. She said, "Responsibility."

"What?"

"I was just thinking about what your mother said. How we are all responsible for everyone else. Your dad really took that maxim to heart. You must be very proud of him."

"I am. I'm very proud of him. Although, when I was a kid . . ." He smiled, mocking the entire confession, but the expression never quite reached his eyes. "When I was a kid and those two air force officers came to our door, all ashen-faced and serious, to tell us how he'd died, I got so mad. I started beating on one of them with my fists, crying, 'So, why didn't he eject first? Who cares about the stupid guy in the back? My dad should've ejected first.' I swear, I'd never seen my mother look so mortified. I think she was more devastated by what I said than by my father's death."

Anne opened her mouth, ready to make a comment, then thought better of it. Instead, she took Paul's hand in hers, rubbing her fingers along the grooves between his knuckles, and continued their stroll, mercifully changing the subject.

They passed a shooting gallery, stopping to watch a boy of no more than ten tenaciously plunk down quarter after quarter, trying to hit enough targets and earn enough points to win the top prize: a neon green, jumbo-sized water bazooka tantalizingly dangling from fishing wire strung across the roof. Legs wide, elbows propped on the booth counter, the boy stood squinting his left eye so tightly that tears formed underneath the lashes, and fired off round after round. On his ninth try, he even spit out his gum, hoping it would help concentration, but, after each tally, he still ended up a few points short of the ultimate total.

Sympathetic, Paul and Anne moved forward, offering the boy a few pointers, telling him not to lean so hard on the trigger, to release gently instead of jerking it. After two more tries, and a tip to shift his weight back on his heels, the boy finally hit the bull's-eye, racking up enough points to take home the water gun.

He jumped for joy, sneakers raising a dust tornado, and spun around, gratefully hugging first Anne, then a very surprised Paul, and promising that they could play with the water gun, too.

That's when the booth's proprietor pointed to a sign hanging above the reward stash. No one under the age of eighteen allowed to handle the air pistols. Sorry, kid, no prize for you.

"Excuse me?" Anne planted both hands on her hips. "Why the hell didn't you tell him that before he spent all his money?"

The owner shrugged, scratching a dry scab over his elbow, then twisted his arm around for a better look. "Kid can't read?"

"Listen, you—"

"Annie." Paul grabbed her hand, half-convinced she was about to leap into the booth and wrestle for the water gun. "Annie, hold on a minute."

"No, I'm not going to hold on. Do you see what he's doing?"

"Yes, I do." Paul's voice remained steady. "But your beating the crap out of him isn't going to help anyone, especially not . . ." He turned to the boy. "What's your name, son?"

The boy, eyes filled with tears, had stuffed both hands into his pockets and, head hanging down, started to walk away, kicking every pebble and crushed soda can along his path. He paused when Paul called, answering, "Walter," and swallowed hard to keep from sniffling in front of a stranger.

"Walter," Paul repeated, and beckoned the boy forward. He stepped up to the shooting gallery and flipped two quarters onto the wooden slats. Then, picking up a pair of air guns, he tossed one to Anne. Voice calm as ever, Paul pleasantly asked, "What do you say we clean the gentleman out?"

Anne smiled.

After four years of fire-arms training at the Academy, it took Paul and Anne less than a round to thoroughly master these weapons. At the end of fifty cents, each had won Walter his water-gun. But neither had any intention of stopping there. They told Walter to go and get his friends, then proceeded to win every prize under the slat roof, ranging from psychedelic plastic key chains to souvenir ash trays to a menagerie of stuffed animals.

Grinning in what Paul could only describe as lunatic delight, he and Anne spent their final hour until closing time chasing each other through the park, competing to see who could give their stash of prizes away the fastest.

They swooped down on exhausted, crying children, and startled flustered older women, offering their booty with a smile and a mock bow, like fairies gone slightly mad.

Paul watched Anne race ahead of him, her yellow dress blinking in between the trees as she darted from place to place, the golden-red sunset behind them framing her in a kaleidoscope of color. He stopped in his tracks, pretending to catch his breath, simply drunk from her image—and aware that he looked rather silly standing in the middle of the fairgrounds, a stuffed blue caterpillar under one arm and an air force of wind-up tin planes sticking out of his front shirt pockets. But to put it plainly, Paul didn't care. What was more, he didn't care that he didn't care.

And that was a new one.

Anne glanced over her shoulder, noticed Paul looking at her, and smiled. She turned around, donating the last of her trinkets to a toddler who'd fallen and skinned her knee, then slowly walked back toward Paul.

He checked his watch. It was closing time. Paul said, "Time for Cinderella to turn back into a pumpkin."

"What?" Anne's eyebrows furrowed quizzically. She stood in front of him, plucking the remaining toys out of his pockets and tossing them to the kids headed for the exit.

"It's over," he explained, then mentally kicked himself. For someone with a perfect score on the verbal S.A.T., he was doing a hell of a lousy job expressing what he really meant. Or felt.

"Over?" Anne cocked her head, then playfully slid her finger beneath the top button of Paul's shirt, hooking him forever. "Oh, no, Gaasbeck. You're not getting away from me that easily."

\*     \*     \*

"I used to hide here all the time when I was little and didn't want to go home at the end of the day," she told him.

They sat on the ground, inside a rounded thicket of bushes. Thoroughly obscured from outside view, they waited patiently for the park to close. Anne drew her knees up to her chin, resting her head on them, and peered contently up at Paul. It was as clear of an invitation as he ever remembered receiving.

He traced the moonlit outline of her bare shoulder with his eyes, then, more daring, with his fingers, and finally, with his lips. Anne purred with pleasure, tilting her head to one side and offering his mouth more room to explore. Gently, reverently, he trailed a path of kisses from the tip of her shoulder up the nape of her neck, teasing, tasting, touching, until his lips were once again atop of hers. Anne moved to unbutton Paul's shirt, her hands luxuriating in the soft, thick tangle of hair covering his chest as she whispered his name, making what he'd once considered merely a pair of syllables sound undeniably arousing.

Somewhere to the left of them, they heard the fairground gates click and lock for the night. The overhead lamps dimmed, bathing them in the bluish hue of moonlight. Without warning, Anne pulled away from Paul's embrace, springing to her feet and pulling him up along with her. Her eyes sparkled mysteriously as she pushed her way through the concealing bushes, bidding for Paul to follow. He rose, dusting the dirt off his jeans and ruefully reminding himself that he knew what he was getting into the moment he returned her kiss on the roller coaster. Annie's Wild Ride was most certainly living up to its name.

Paul followed where Anne led, verbalizing absolutely

no surprise when their journey concluded at the foot of a still dutifully whirling Ferris wheel.

Anne explained, "It's kind of old, and it takes forever to get started again in the morning. So they just let it run all night. Come on." She showed him where to jump the fence, sweeping Paul on-board one of the swaying cars before he had the chance to step back and evaluate the prudence of such an action.

They settled in, not bothering to lock the safety bar. Anne swore they wouldn't spin fast enough to need it. For one rotation, they both simply sat, watching the ground drift away, then promptly swoop closer again. Along the second upswing, Paul turned to Anne, hand lightly brushing the crook of her neck as he politely inquired, "Now, where were we, again?"

She wrinkled her brow in mock recollection. "I believe," she swept her fingers beguilingly along her throat, finally settling on the tender tip of her collarbone. "It was right about . . . here."

"Yes." He dipped his head. "That's how I remember it, too."

Paul reached to unhook the top dandelion button of her dress, but considering they sat side by side, it proved a rather awkward circumstance at best. Straining to help him, Anne pivoted, sliding her leg across his lap, her knees straddling his thighs until they were face-to-face. Her eyes met his, bidding Paul to watch as Anne slowly, deliberately, flicked loose the top button, then the next, and the next, and the next, all the way down to her waist.

Paul slipped his hands underneath the fluttering yellow satin, running both palms up her back and pressing her shoulders toward him. His tongue snaked to caress her right nipple, sucking and nuzzling till it hardened between his lips and triggered a sigh from Anne to fuel his own excitement. She dug her fingers into the wire mesh on either side of his head and arched her back as the Ferris wheel plunged downward. Paul buried his face between her breasts, covering them in kisses, the pleasures of which made her whimper with delight.

As the wheel hurled upward, Anne rose with it, and his palms slid down her back, gripping her thighs for balance. At eye level, the power of Paul's cannibalistic hunger for her unnerved at the same time as it overwhelmed him. She could sense that if he could have swallowed her whole, he would have done it. If he could have lost himself totally in her, he would have done it. No matter what the price.

Gingerly, Paul's fingers crept up the insides of her thighs, confirming, once and for all, that no, she wasn't wearing anything beneath the yellow satin. He stroked her, gently at first, then, at her urging, with more fervor. She moaned each time he touched her, responding to the rippling warmth bursting within her, and, as the wheel swept down, she thrust herself against him, crying out a bliss so primal it could only express itself in sounds, not words.

The wheel flung upward, and Anne reached for the top button of Paul's jeans, fumbling briefly as her lips reconnected with his.

"Annie?" He forced himself to pull away from the fire, his voice husky but staunch.

"What?" Her tone suggested that Anne found now a rather odd time to begin a discussion.

"Annie," her ardent kisses along his chin and up to his brows made concentrating on what Paul needed to say fairly difficult, but he persevered. "Annie, I don't understand . . . this."

"Really?" She leaned back, surveying him ironically. "Well, then, I tell you, my friend, I can't wait to see you in action when you actually do understand what you're doing.''

He smiled self-consciously, struggling to get his point across in spite of the immense . . . distractions. ''What I mean is, Anne, I—I thought we disliked each other.''

''Did we?'' She innocently tugged down the zipper of his jeans. ''I forgot.''

Paul inhaled, gritting his teeth and summoning all available self-control to keep from succumbing to her touch. He was already rock-hard and aching for a release. Her inquisitive hands weren't helping the situation any.

''But what about all our fights, our arguments, our rivalry?''

''Foreplay.''

The wheel sped downward.

Anne's mouth roamed across Paul's chest, pausing to nibble first one nipple, then the other. In between, she murmured, ''Why do you always have to analyze everything? Stop thinking, just feel. Not everything needs to be put into words, you know.''

The wheel rose.

''I like words.'' Paul rested his hands on Anne's hips, pushing her back just far enough to see her face, but not so far that he no longer felt the sweet pressure of her pelvis against his. ''Words help me keep things in order.''

The wheel fell.

''Okay, then.'' Anne lowered her arms. ''How about a word for this?'' She slipped in past Paul's jeans, feeling him pulsating and rigid in her hand, responding to her physically no matter what may have been coming out of his mouth.

He caught his breath, his hands on her hips tightening as he instinctively pulled Anne closer.

The wheel rose.

"Well?" She grazed him lightly with her fingernails, teasing and titillating until Paul was sure this was the closest he ever came, or ever would come, to losing his mind. "What's the word?"

The wheel fell.

Paul closed his eyes, perspiration dripping down his neck and chest. He wanted her. No. Worse. He needed her. And there was nothing, no amount of self-discipline or rationalization, capable of disguising that fact.

He cupped Anne's breasts between his palms, the heat from her body searing through his. She had him. Now and forever. She had him. He buried his mouth in the crook of her neck, devouring her with his lips as her hands urged him to the edge of the envelope.

"Nice," Paul finally whispered, "The word is . . . nice."

The wheel rose.

Anne rose as well, mounting and impaling herself against Paul with passion enough to deny the laws of physics. When this irresistible force met this immovable object, they not only occupied the same space at the same time, they transcended it.

Paul plunged inside her, matching his rhythm to hers, holding back until he felt Anne start to tremble. He increased his speed then, and she called out his name again, shuddering and shattering in his embrace.

Anne's candid vulnerability as she sighed and crumpled against his chest devastated the last remnants of Paul's resolve. He let himself go, relinquishing control in exchange for pleasure.

"That," he said, voice steady despite the shudder assaulting his own body, "was . . . very nice."

*     *     *

They climbed over the fence to get out of the fairgrounds. In Paul's mind, though, it was the least bizarre action he'd engaged in all night. He was still buttoning his shirt as they crossed the parking lot, heading for his car. Beside him, Anne tried to smooth down her dress so it wouldn't appear too wrinkled upon their return to the Academy, but gave up somewhere above the waistline.

She told Paul, "I had a very nice time, tonight."

He smiled at her choice of words, amazed how such bland sounds could provoke this strong a reaction in him. Paul doubted he could ever hear the expression again in quite the same way. "So did I."

"Still think we dislike each other?"

Paul opened the passenger door for her, climbing in the other side. "Actually, I think we've moved past it."

She fastened her seat belt. "So? What do you say? Same time tomorrow night?"

The thought of spending another evening with Anne filled Paul with an intense longing he'd never previously imagined possible.

His body responded as if jump-started, nerve endings snapping to attention and practically humming with desire. His mind whipped through all his obligations scheduled for the next day, then easily dismissed them one by one. This he could put off till later, this he could dump on someone else, this he could forget about entirely.

In the instant after she asked her question, nothing mattered as much to Paul as being able to say yes.

Yes.

Anything you want.

As long as you want.

Whenever you want.

Yes. Yes. Yes.

He started the engine, turning to look out his driver's-side and rear-view mirrors, despite their being the only car in the lot.

Eyes firmly on the road, Paul answered, "Sorry. Can't."

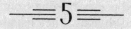

==5==

*The Present*

"Amelia?"

"Yes, Mom?"

"Come on, Ace. Stay with me here. I know you're tired. But, you've got to keep awake. If you fall asleep in this cold—"

"I know." Amelia rubbed her eyes with the back of her wrist, and shook her head, trying to clear it. "I'm trying."

Anne reached over and patted her daughter's knee reassuringly. Her own head pounded with an intensity previously reserved only for marching-band bass drums, and her arm felt like a shark was chewing it from wrist to shoulder. Her vision blurred whenever she shifted her gaze, prompting a drowning nausea that forced her to clench her teeth and count slowly up to one hundred to distract herself.

Anne sat on the floor of the shattered cockpit, Amelia tucked under her good arm. She hugged her child tightly, trying to impart as much of her own body heat as possible. The main danger facing them now was the risk of falling asleep and freezing to death. So, ignoring her own discomfort, Anne stubbornly employed any trick she could think of to keep Amelia awake.

They sang camp songs and top-40 songs and show tunes. They recited poetry ranging from William Wordsworth to childhood rhymes. They listed their fifty favorite books, movies, TV shows, and inert gasses. And every half hour, despite the torment that shot up her arm, Anne forced herself and Amelia to get up and move around, fortifying their circulation.

Still, Anne could feel Amelia slipping away. She yawned and rubbed her eyes, taking longer and longer pauses between answers, her chin drooping stealthily toward her chest.

"Amelia!" Anne prodded her daughter's legs with one foot.

"Hm?" Amelia rested against Anne's shoulder, snuggling like when she was a baby.

"Stay awake, Ace. That's an order."

"Okay, okay." Amelia grumbled, brushing hair out of her eyes. "What do we talk about now?"

"It doesn't matter. Whatever you want."

Amelia considered the possibilities. Then, eyes twinkling, "Tell me about how you and Dad fell in love and got married."

"Oh, Ace, you've heard that story a million times."

"So what? You said I could pick. Well, I want to talk about you and Dad. The first time you saw him, did you think he was like the hottest guy ever?"

Anne sighed. "I don't think this is a very good idea."

"Fine." Amelia crossed her arms, plopping backward against the wall and pursing her lips in a perfect imitation of her daddy.

On the other hand, if dissecting her checkered past with Paul was the only way Anne could keep Amelia awake and talking . . .

"All right." She buried her apprehensions, sitting up straight, braced for anything. "What do you want to know?"

An hour out of Hill Air Force Base, Paul spied his fuel-gauge needle rapping the red square labeled EMPTY. He hadn't thought to fill up the car before zooming toward Colorado Springs. Now his carelessness cost Paul precious minutes as he squinted into the distance, looking for an off ramp. Snow pricked his windshield. Paul turned the wipers on full blast. The screech of rubber on glass scraped the inside of his skull like a rake across Styrofoam.

This was all Anne's fault. Why couldn't she have just stayed put? Why did every vacation require packing and going somewhere?

Their first leave with Amelia, when the baby was barely seven months old, Paul broached the revolutionary suggestion that maybe they should think about staying home.

"Home? Home? What's the fun in that? Home's just the place where they send your mail."

They ended up backpacking across Alaska. Anne taught Amelia to swim in a lake outside Juneau, and Paul fulfilled his dream of piloting a helicopter over an active volcano. The following year, they hiked through South American ruins, where Amelia added "Inca" to her vocabulary. They went rafting in Colorado, on safari in Kenya, and, six months before their divorce, they went to Vietnam.

It was Anne's idea. She'd written the Vietnamese government, the Red Cross, village officials, and the surviving airman from Colonel Gaasbeck's last flight, and received permission for them to visit the 1967 crash site.

She thought Paul needed the closure, a chance to say a proper goodbye to his father.

He resisted at first, mostly on principle. But in the end, Paul couldn't deny the notion's appeal. It was just like Anne. To provide him with what he wanted, before he even knew he wanted it.

The three of them, Paul, Anne, and four-year-old Amelia, along with a local guide, walked half a day to reach the wreckage. They whacked aside drooping leaves the size of hubcaps and climbed over rotting trees. They took deep breaths, striving to suck in a few oxygen molecules along with watery gulps of humidity, while flies, mosquitos, and assorted other insects of unknown origin droned from each direction, hovering along the periphery, too far away to slap, too close for comfort.

Paul peeled off his shirt and sponged the sweat slithering into his eyes. He glanced over his shoulder at Amelia as she plugged along behind him, one hand tucked into Anne's, the other gripping a makeshift walking stick Paul cut for her a few miles back. She looked up, noticed him watching, and reassured, "I'm okay, Daddy."

"You're more than okay." Paul scooped Amelia off the ground and onto his back, her arms around his neck, legs around his waist. "You, Ace, are extraordinary."

Anne said, "Takes after her father."

She stood beside them, dressed in jeans, a denim shirt knotted just below her rib cage, and a khaki baseball cap. A mosquito bite throbbed on the back of her right hand like a sixth knuckle. Her cheeks glistened scarlet from the heat. Perspiration trickled down her neck, creating black patches under her arms and turning the ends of her hair limp ginger. Paul couldn't take his eyes off her.

He told Amelia, "Your mom's not too bad, either."

They reached the crash site a quarter hour past noon,

hacking through two decades of overgrown flora and fauna. Their guide, who claimed to have witnessed the crash, warned that they should tread carefully so as not to awaken ghosts still haunting the spot.

Paul took a deep breath, straightening his spine and locking it in place. Anne beckoned for Amelia to slide off his back and come stand by her. She urged Paul to go on ahead. This was his moment. She didn't want to intrude.

Thirty feet in front of them, rancid vines snaked over, under, and around the rusted remnants of an air force fighter jet. Twenty years of moss encrusted the carcass, dulling its once jagged edges, obscuring the partition between earth and machine, until the plane seemed a natural part of the landscape.

Paul didn't remember taking any steps to reach it. He felt, instead, like he'd stood still and the wreckage came to him.

His eyes grazed the splintered canopy, settling first on the fungus-capped ejector seat his father never got the opportunity to use, then on the gaping hole directly behind it, testifying to the copilot whose tardy escape cost Colonel Gaasbeck his life.

Paul listened, his face expressionless, as their guide recounted the crash, insisting that the ground shook for days afterward. He recalled putting out fires started by scalding chunks of metal, and the image of a lone parachuter shooting across the sky. Lieutenant Breen, the guide reported authoritatively, broke his ankle landing in a tree. But that didn't stop him from walking over two miles to see if his colonel had survived the crash.

The colonel, of course, was dead. No man could survive such a fiery plunge. But Lieutenant Breen came anyway, pried the body out of its half-melted cockpit, and slung it over both shoulders. He told the villagers it was his duty to bring the colonel home to his wife and son, for a proper burial.

Vietcong captured the lieutenant a half dozen miles past the crash site. He was moving slowly, because of the broken ankle and the dead weight on his shoulders. Soldiers took the lieutenant to Hanoi. They left the body to rot where they found it.

Paul's countenance didn't change. For twenty-four years, he'd believed Lieutenant Noah Breen to be the coward responsible for his father's death, the screw-up whose failure to follow orders roasted Colonel Gaasbeck alive. Now he found out that same lieutenant had risked his life in a futile rescue attempt, only to be rewarded by a sojourn at the Hanoi Hilton. And still, Paul continued standing as he was, chin up, both arms behind his back, legs planted in wide stance. He felt nothing. He understood that was wrong. He should be feeling something. Shock, guilt, indifference, even a pinch of ambivalence would have been welcome. But he felt nothing.

Paul didn't move. He didn't so much as blink. He refused to. He needed a word. If he could think of the right word to encompass his queer circumstance, then he could label it, categorize it, and set it aside for subsequent analysis. Otherwise, Paul didn't dare budge. Not until everything was properly settled.

Paul never remembered how long he stood along the edge of the wreckage. He heard the mosquitos' buzz growing louder, he felt the humidity turn into drizzle, warm as tea. The ground below his feet shifted, like sand fleeing shore on an outgoing wave. And inside his head, no matter how hard he strained to impose some discipline and order, there was only noise. A blare so thunderous, it proved deafening. A gleam so blazing, it seemed blinding.

He was drowning. Paul felt clumps of weeds beneath

his feet, air filling his lungs, the sun beating on his bare back. And yet, he couldn't shake the sense that he was drowning. Or maybe, maybe he was flying. He watched the horizon grow smaller, more distant. But instead of the exhilaration and control he usually experienced during flight, Paul merely felt . . . disconnected.

A pair of arms slipped about his waist. Anne rested her palms along his chest and her cheek against his back, not saying a word. She simply held on to him with all of her might, her heart beating steadily, soothingly, against his spinal cord.

Paul closed both eyes, blocking out all sensations except the brush of her flesh against his, immersing himself in the softness of her fingers as they grazed the hairs across his chest and in the sweet pressure of her breasts and hips along his back. With great effort, he calibrated his breathing to hers, utilizing the steady rhythm to gradually pull himself together, and find the fortitude to turn around and walk away from the site.

Later that night, back at their hotel, Anne and Paul lay side by side beneath gossamer mosquito netting, the heat so oppressive even the sheet they employed for a blanket felt excessive. Paul couldn't sleep. His mind kept returning to the afternoon's events, then darting away like a diver unable to leap off the board. He turned his head, watching Anne's drowsy profile rise and fall, and felt staggered by his ache, by his desire for her.

Yet in spite of that, or rather because of it, he forbade himself to reach out. It was bad enough she witnessed his behavior earlier. Paul refused to let her see how badly he needed her now.

Anne stirred, opening her eyes and smiling when she spied him watching her. Paul struggled to neutralize his features, lest she glimpse the conflict raging inside. He wasn't fast enough, and her smile faded, eyebrows furrowing in concern. She searched his face quizzically. Paul braced himself for an inquest.

Yet instead of grilling him, Anne rolled on her side, raised her arm, and silently caressed his cheek with the back of her hand.

Paul caught her wrist, kissing Anne's palm, her fingers, down to the crook of her elbow, then up to the sprinkle of freckles along her shoulder. She arched her back, moving to embrace him, tapping a single finger against her lips and pointing to Amelia asleep on a cot in the corner, reminding Paul they needed to be extra quiet.

He nodded, wrapping Anne in his arms and burrowing his face in her hair, inhaling deeply. "Annie . . ."

"I know." She supported his weight atop her, opening her legs, enveloping him inside her. "I know . . ."

Seven years later, screeching down a snowy highway connecting Utah to Colorado Springs, Paul reluctantly admitted that, compared to their past adventures, a skiing trip did seem the most unlikely threat to Anne and Amelia's well-being. Still, he cursed himself for not fighting harder to prevent it. If only he'd been firmer with Judge Saul . . . If only he'd taken Amelia out of state first . . . If only he'd forbidden Anne from flying in such dubious weather . . .

That last one made Paul grit his teeth and clutch the steering wheel so tightly, the leather left ridges in his hands. Since when had he ever been able to say no to Anne?

"Sorry. Can't." And the subsequent resolve that went with it lasted him only until Anne, oblivious to the labor he'd exerted issuing that first denial, shrugged and asked, "Okay. How about next Monday, then?"

She'd leaned against the passenger-side window, yellow dress rumpled, dandelion buttons dangling every which way, knees drawn up to her chest, a green smudge on her right ankle.

It was that green smudge that proved Paul's undoing.

While hiding and waiting for the park to close, Anne sat, legs tucked under her, on a patch of grass. Paul noticed the stain as soon they stood up and headed toward the Ferris wheel. It drew his attention the second time, when Anne slid her leg atop his lap and he gripped it for balance while they made love, gripped it so tightly, a portion of the stain rubbed off on his palm.

Paul glanced at his hand, wondering why a dim smudge of green should prove so adept at shattering his self-control.

Then he agreed to meet her again the following Monday.

One marriage, one child, and one divorce later now inspired Paul to classify that night, along with everything that came after, as his eight-year, ill-fated excursion on Annie's Wild Ride.

Spotting the neon of a gas station crackling through the snow, Paul pulled off the highway and up to the first pump. He hopped out of the car. The wind sliced into his uniform, reminding Paul that, in his haste to get to Colorado, he forgot his winter coat.

*Brilliant, Gaasbeck. Just brilliant.* Paul jammed the nozzle into his fuel tank. *Ten below zero outside, and you're running off to play Cavalry dressed in a cotton shirt and polyester jacket.*

Blowing on his hands and rubbing one against the other, Paul left the gas pumping and strode across the station. He tossed the cashier his credit card, then moved to the coffee machine, figuring he'd best start saturating his system with caffeine immediately, if he planned to stay awake through any more monotonous hours of empty roads and snow. He fumbled in his pockets for a pair of quarters, fed both into the slot, and made his selection.

Paul turned his head, checking on his car's progress. When he turned back toward the machine, the paper cup set to burp from its chute before filling up with coffee toppled out backward. Paul cursed and grabbed for it, attempting to position the cup upright and catch a few drops before it all spiraled down the drain. He proved too late. The machine had one fiery squirt left, and saved it not for the cup but for the back of his hand.

It seared Paul's flesh, raising an octopus-shaped blister.

He didn't make a sound.

His fingers tightened around the cup.

Without warning, Paul slammed his fist against the machine.

He cracked the plastic cover, splintering the pane into four jagged segments. His hand ripped through the paper placard touting "Coffee, uh-um, uh-um, good."

"Hey!" The cashier tore his eyes from the meter long enough to leap over the counter and sprint toward Paul. "Hey! Cut that out!"

Chipped plastic sliced Paul's knuckles and wrist. The smaller fragments burrowed underneath his fingernails. Coffee retched from the machine, spitting a murky puddle around his feet.

"Jesus Christ!" The cashier kept his distance, unsure of what sort of lunatic he was dealing with here. "Get a grip, man."

Paul's arm froze, midwhack. His fist sprung open, startled. A tremor ripped through his body. A tremor that, if Anne had been there, she would have recognized as identical to the one that shot through him fourteen years ago outside Major Danahay's office. A tremor of recognition. Of understanding.

He dropped his hand, allowing the throb of cuts and blister to reach his nervous system, welcoming the resulting discomfort as fit punishment for his actions. He squared his shoulders, inhaled, and held that breath until his chest felt set to burst from the strain.

Damn Anne.

Damn her.

Paul repeated those words as he paid his gas bill, adding in damages to the coffee machine, and he kept on repeating them as he slid back inside his car, shivering from the cold but refusing to turn on the heat lest it lull him to sleep.

He drove for a good sixty miles, thinking how he was going to let Anne have it for this. No judge in America, not even Judge Saul, could deny him custody of Amelia now. If this latest wasn't irrefutable proof of Anne's deficiency as a parent, then he didn't know what was. How much more evidence did the world need that Anne Gaasbeck was a reckless, careless, heartless human being who should not be allowed near sensitive objects like children and airplanes.

In retrospect, the fact that they'd stayed together as long as they did surprised Paul more than their final estrangement. After all, as his mother pointed out only weeks before the wedding, Paul and Anne were an "accident waiting to marry."

According to everyone they knew, the two of them were about as compatible as . . . as . . . as a snowstorm and driving.

Paul shook his head. This was ridiculous. He could barely see through the igloos on his windshield and, thanks to the slush beneath his tires, even keeping the car traveling a straight line was proving a challenge.

Up ahead, he glimpsed the red, white, and blue flicker of a police car parked perpendicular to the road. He lifted his foot off the gas pedal and coasted to a stop beside a wooden barricade. Paul rolled down his window and gestured for the lawman shivering inside his vehicle to step outside. The cop did so reluctantly, tightening his muffler and pulling on a pair of fur-lined gloves.

"Is there a problem, officer?" Paul stuck his head out the window, instantly collecting snow along his brows and lashes.

"Road's closed. You'd better turn around and head back."

"That's impossible. I need to get to Colorado Springs."

Noting Paul's uniform, the officer explained, "Sorry, Major. Nothing's getting through tonight. We're closed all the way up to the state line. Too much snow. You know how that is."

"Yes. I understand. But this is a military emergency."

"Best let the folks in Colorado take care of it, then."

Paul reached into his pocket for his military I.D., assuming his major's voice and upbraiding, "This is a federal issue. You're a city cop. You've no right to interfere with government—"

"Listen here. I don't care if you're carrying a note from the C.I.A. signed by Herbert Hoover, Ollie North, and Thomas Jefferson. I've got orders, and I intend to follow them. No one gets through to Colorado Springs tonight. Now, please turn your vehicle around and head back the way you came. The road, sir, is closed."

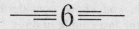

## 6

*1983*

The day before their commissions were announced, Anne and Paul jogged side by side around the Academy's track. He slowed down his pace, so Anne could match her stride to his, prompting her to run faster. Both wore the requisite phys-ed uniforms, blue shorts and a T-shirt with the Academy logo across the front. Anne pulled her hair back in a ponytail, fully aware that as soon as she received her first Air Force posting the following day, she'd be looking at twenty years of hair trimmed to regulation above the collar.

Bored with jogging at less than his maximum speed, Paul turned around, facing Anne while he ran backward, asking, "So, know what assignment you're hoping to pull tomorrow?"

"Test pilot. What else is there?"

"Test pilot, huh? First time out?" Paul grinned. "At least no one can accuse you of underestimating yourself."

"I'm a damn good flight engineer. No reason why I shouldn't be in the second seat."

"Only the second seat? Why not the front?"

"Maybe next year." Anne returned Paul's smile, and

conceded, "My second choice is a fight squadron."

"You mean combat?"

"Sure. Why not?"

"Uhm, Annie, you know, considering how . . . close . . . we've been the last couple of days, I, well, I've made a remarkable discovery. I hate to tell you this, but, you, Annie—you're a woman."

"Noooo?" She stopped in her tracks, hands pressed against her cheeks, feigning extreme shock.

"Oh, yes." Paul doubled back toward her, planting his hands on Anne's hips, pulling her to him. "I'm afraid I have mountains of evidence to support my position."

"You don't say." Anne slipped her arms around Paul's neck, playfully rubbing the base of his hairline with her fingers.

He lowered his forehead atop hers. "Definitely a woman."

"And your point is? . . ."

"Women, Annie . . ." Paul dipped his head, kissing her lightly in between each word. "Women, don't fly combat."

She cupped his face in her hands, interrupting Paul's series of kisses with one long, deep one. She slipped her tongue inside his mouth, teasing, tasting, exploring, then pulled away abruptly—"Women don't fly combat . . . *yet*"—and sprinted down the track, laughing and beckoning for Paul to follow.

"How about you?"

Anne and Paul finished their cool-down exercises, stretching in the shadow of the Academy's seventeen-spire Cadet Chapel. She asked him, "What assignment are you hoping to pull?"

Paul raised his leg to hip level, rested it on a marble

block, and reached for his foot, tugging it toward him. "Test pilot."

Anne ran her palm up his thigh. "First time out? At least no one can accuse you of underestimating yourself."

He lifted her hand off his leg, brought it to his lips, and gently kissed each finger. "Not in front of the chapel, Annie."

And never on campus. All the service academies—Air Force, Navy, and West Point—had rules against that sort of thing.

"Your self-control is remarkable, Cadet."

"Thank you." He stood up. "But let's not press the issue."

"Gosh. I thought you liked it when I pressed the issue."

Paul rolled his eyes at her but couldn't suppress a smile.

Walking toward the dormitories, Anne asked him, "What are you doing for leave?"

Academy cadets had a three-week leave in the summer between graduation and assuming their Air Force duties.

He lied, "I hadn't thought about it."

"Want to come with me?"

"Where?"

"No place in particular. I just climb on my bike and pedal whichever direction my eyes are pointing."

"How do you keep from getting lost?"

"What's to get lost? I'm not going anywhere."

Paul looked into the distance, avoiding Anne's eyes. "Give me some time think about it."

The next morning, Paul didn't even say hello to Anne before asking, "Where were you commissioned?"

He'd lain awake half the night wondering about it. As

if her appointment were somehow more significant than his own. Although, for the life of him, Paul couldn't fathom why he should feel that way. It wasn't until daybreak that he finally figured it out. His anxiety—well, you couldn't really call it anxiety, it was more of a curiosity, nothing more—over Anne's future with the Air Force stemmed from the ongoing rivalry between them. Paul was afraid she'd be assigned a better tour of duty than he. It was obvious. In retrospect, he couldn't believe it had taken him so long to properly assess the situation.

However, now that he understood the reason behind his concern, Paul felt no qualms about seeking Anne out the moment he received his own posting. He searched half the campus before locating her sitting up a tree, legs dangling from a branch thirty feet in the air, face obscured by a torrent of bright green leaves.

Ignoring the more rational part of his mind, the one wanting to know why he felt it necessary to pursue this conversation up a tree instead of at a more logical spot, like, say, the ground, Paul clambered the length of the trunk, settling beside Anne on a branch that, he hoped, would prove sturdy enough to support two people.

"Well?" He asked. "Where were you commissioned?"

She plucked loose a leaf, folding it this way and that until green juice stained all ten of her fingers. She tucked a strand of hair behind her ear, sighed and, determined to make the best of things, forced herself to smile when she told Paul, "Your mom was right. They are going to let women fly the KC-10 tanker this year. Major Danahay was right, too. I've been assigned to fly it."

A tanker? Paul let the news sink in. A tanker? A tanker was a fine assignment for some B-average cadet. But the winner of the Commander's Trophy had every right to expect something more.

Anne reassured, "It's not so bad. They're experimenting with an all-woman crew. That should be kind of interesting."

Paul's chest tightened in sympathy. He didn't know what to say. "Jesus, Annie, I'm sorry—"

"It's all right. Like your mom says, this is my responsibility. My rung of the ladder. And I'm telling you, I intend to do such a fabulous job, the next woman to graduate top of her class, they'll make her a general." Anne sighed but, resolved to stay positive, changed the subject. "What about you? What did you get?"

He blinked in surprise. Funny. A few hours ago, Paul had been racked with worry that Anne might procure a better commission. But now that the moment of truth was at hand, now that he sat at the poker table holding a royal flush to what he knew was a pair of threes, Paul felt strangely hollow. He'd expected to feel triumphant, to flash his appointment as the final stamp in their four-year, seesaw rivalry. But now he only felt . . . guilty.

No. That couldn't be right. Paul had nothing to feel guilty about. After all, it's not like he'd done anything to diminish her chances. He'd bent over backward to make it a fair fight. Hell, he'd already conceded the Commander's Trophy to her. What else did Anne want? A pound of flesh? She had no right, no right at all to make him feel this way. In a flash, Paul's guilt turned to anger. Who did Anne think she was, turning the most triumphant moment in his life into a guilt trip? Well, he'd show her!

Smugly, Paul told Anne, "Test pilot. I'm going to be a test pilot at Edwards Air Force Base."

He regretted his tone the moment he heard it. Pride was one thing, but Paul had no cause for cruelty. He hadn't the slightest idea what came over him. He'd always believed boasting testified to an appalling lack manners and, most importantly, self-control.

He opened his mouth to apologize, but was interrupted by Anne throwing her arms around him and hugging Paul so tightly, he had to grip an overhead branch to keep them both from falling out of the tree. "That's so great, I can't believe it. Test pilot your first commission out. I'm so proud of you. You must be going nuts."

"Well, not exactly—"

"I always knew you were a hell of a pilot. But, testing! And at Edwards. It doesn't get any better than that."

Okay. He was confused again. For four years, Anne had gone out of her way to prove herself Paul's superior in all feats. She battled him in class, she battled him in the air, she even battled him on the athletic field—futile as that attempt may have been. If their situations were reversed, if Anne had managed to, at the last minute, pull ahead in such a definitive fashion, Paul would have been gnashing his teeth. Gnashing his teeth, and eating his heart out. Yet here sat Anne, seemingly genuinely thrilled for him and his victory. Not only was her stance perplexing the hell out of him, but it also placed Paul in the position of feeling obligated to belittle his accomplishment for her benefit.

"You know, it's really no big deal."

"Are you kidding? It's the biggest deal. I'm so happy for you, I could burst."

He told Anne, "The posting, it should have gone to you."

"I know." There was absolutely no self-pity in her voice. No trace of despair, or surrender. "It still will. Someday."

"You're amazing." He leaned in to kiss her, thinking that if they did fall out of the tree, it would be worth it.

"Yeah," she murmured, returning his kiss. "I know that, too."

They were walking back toward the dormitories, when Anne asked Paul, "So, about my bicycle trip, want to come along?"

Last night, after a half dozen hours of tossing, turning, and other nocturnal gymnastics, he'd finally come to a conclusion about that. He couldn't go. He had too much to do before reporting to Edwards to drop everything and go bicycling across the country in no particular direction. He'd worked out exactly what he was going to say to Anne, how he would explain it so that she both understood and didn't feel hurt.

Unfortunately, all that brilliant strategy proved for naught when Paul heard himself answering, "Sure."

That night, when Paul got home, he found a letter waiting for him from the U.S. Navy. It confirmed what he'd already learned the previous day by phone. On rare occasions, the corps swapped fliers and put them through the other's test-pilot school, giving both the advantage of picking up new techniques and knowledge. An Air Force pilot with Navy training could all but write his own ticket careerwise. For a year, Paul had pulled every string he could think of, dropping both his parents' names whenever possible to get himself selected for the summer program at Patuxent River, Maryland.

Now, letter in hand, he moved to the phone, dialed, and told whoever answered that he was sorry, but he would have to decline their very generous invitation.

Something had suddenly come up.

Anne and Paul hit the road the morning following their Academy graduation. They strapped their sleeping bags onto the backs of their bikes along with a few bottles of water, some canned goods, a change of clothes, and, at Paul's insistence, a map and compass.

"Which way do we go?" Paul adjusted Anne's helmet, handing it over to her, before fitting his own.

"You pick."

Paul gave the matter some serious thought, taking a moment to peer in each direction, then finally decided, "We should head west. That way, the sun coming up in the east won't be in our eyes."

Anne smiled but didn't say a word.

For the first couple of miles, they pedaled down a mountain road, Paul a few feet ahead of her, eyes forward, back curved until his chin practically touched the handle-bars, his posture as sleek and perfect as a leader in the Tour de France.

"Paul!" Anne called from behind him. She sat upright on the bicycle seat, steering with one hand, using the other to brush hair out of her eyes, and shouted above the wind, "Look up."

He raised his head above his shoulders, turning right, then left. "What am I looking at?"

"America!" She upped her speed and coasted next to him. With her free hand, Anne reached over, wrapped her fingers over Paul's, and guided him to an upright position. She indicated the scenery flashing by. "Take a look at what you've sworn to defend."

Paul blinked, glancing quizzically first at Anne, then at the countryside. He stopped pedaling, and just glided for a stretch, drinking in the sights.

After a beat, he turned his attention back to the road. But this time, he sat up straight, his pace noticeably slower compared to a few moments earlier.

And he did not let go of Anne's hand.

For three weeks, she and Paul crisscrossed the back roads of Colorado, stopping every night either at an official campsite or one they quickly deputized for the occasion. If they happened on a lake, they strung together poles and fished. If they passed an apple orchard, they checked for property lines and picked. If they saw a waterfall, they did laundry.

In the evening, they built a fire and took advantage of the light to play chess on a miniature magnetic travel set, where, no matter how hard Anne tried, Paul beat her every time.

"It isn't fair," she pouted. "You plot out traps thirty moves in advance. How am I supposed to counter that?"

Now it was Paul's turn to smile without saying a word.

They stretched out on top of their sleeping bags, taking turns massaging each other's strained muscles. Afterward, they made love under the stars. And, on occasion, in the rain.

Paul's gentleness continued to surprise Anne. Considering how aggressively he attacked any and all duties under his jurisdiction, she'd expected him to take the same approach toward her. And yet he was so tender, so committed to pleasing and satisfying her, that the lightest brush of his skin simply took Anne's breath away.

In some ways, Paul was as meticulous in their lovemaking as he was in all other facets of his life.

He asked, "Do you like it when I do this?" as he kissed the tender spot between her collarbones, or flicked his tongue inside her navel, or slid his hand between her thighs, stroking her gently and waiting for Anne's response before continuing. She teased him about testpiloting her the same way he would an F-15.

He hovered above her in the moonlit darkness, his gaze at once dominating and delicate. He caressed her with his lips, his flesh, his fingers, bringing both of them to the edge, then pulling back, then starting over again. She raised her hips to him, wrapping her legs around his back, pressing her heels against his calves, aching to get deeper, closer, nearer, vying to break through to something nebulous and nameless and, all the same, necessary.

Her heart thundered, blood pumping two, three, four times usual speed, until it seared her veins, erupting in a flow of molten heat washing over and drowning her in the sensation.

He took her right nipple is his mouth, moistening it with his tongue, then blowing on it until her skin puckered in response and the wintergreen breeze stirred by his breath turned, unexpectedly, into an explosion of fire permeating through her, leaving Anne wet and hot and aroused to the point of agitation.

"Annie," Paul whispered her name. Just her name. It was all he ever said. But it was enough.

He responded to her need without Anne having to say a word. His kisses roamed down from her breasts and across her stomach and lower, lower, please, Paul, lower, until his mouth was at the very heart of her, flicking and tasting and licking in circles that grew narrower and narrower, crushing her body in ever expanding waves of pleasure, the tension from which made the air pressure in a soaring jet seem like a minor thrill at best.

She drew Paul upward, wrapping her arms around his shoulders, widening her legs, beckoning him to ease inside her, which he did, slowly, gradually, prolonging the enjoyment for each of them.

"Now," Anne gasped. "Please. Right now."

And Paul thrust against her, making Anne moan with delight and clutch him tighter. Her breasts burned, rubbing against the thick hair on his chest. She dug her nails along his back as he plunged into the very center of her, withdrew, then plunged again, setting up a rhythm known to just the two of them, lifting her to heights she'd never previously imagined, spinning her, rocking

her, shaking her down to the very core, until, on their
last night out before heading home, Anne couldn't stand
it anymore, and, as she arched her back and clasped his
hips between her knees, she whispered, "I love you."

She felt him stiffen. He locked his arms, as if finishing
a push-up, and straightened his back, raising his head
and glancing down on her, his face unreadable.

"It's all right," Anne rushed to reassure. "You don't
have to . . . you don't have to say it back."

For a moment, the earth stood still, heightening her
senses so that Anne grew aware of everything around
them. The murmur of the lake, the rustle of the grass,
the sweetness of the air as it blew across their naked,
sweat-drenched bodies. Yet nothing, nothing, was as
dominant as the sound of Paul's rasping breath or his
musky, masculine scent enveloping her in its redolence.
Anne wasn't sorry about what she'd said, only for the
discomfort her words seemed to cause Paul. The last
thing she'd wanted to do was upset him.

She felt obligated to apologize, but before her lips
could form the words, Paul dipped his head, brushing
his cheek against Anne's ear and softly, huskily, yet all
the same unmistakably, confessed, "I love you, too."

He was gone when Anne woke up the next morning.

She stretched languidly, yawning and taking advantage of her last day to sleep late before reporting for
duty at Sheldon Air Force Base in Northern California.

For a beat, Anne couldn't recall the reason for her
strikingly fine mood this particular morning. Then, like
a prophecy from the gods, it came back to her. *I love
you, too.*

"I love you, too." Anne repeated his words exactly
as he'd said them, inflection and all. "I love you, too,"
she informed her sleeping bag as she rolled it up and

fastened it onto her bike. "I love you, too," she told the sputtering camp-fire, covering it with dirt to prevent errant sparks from triggering a forest inferno. "I love you, too."

She went looking for Paul down by the lake. Despite being on leave, he still insisted on calisthenics and, if possible, to swim the same five miles a day he usually completed at the Academy pool. Vacation, Paul lectured, was no excuse for shirking duty. Besides, every second you weren't training, someone else was. And when you met him, he would win.

"Competitive fellow, aren't you?" Anne teased.

Paul looked at her queerly. "I thought that's what you liked about me."

She slid her arms around his waist. "It's one of the things."

Sitting on a polished rock at the edge of the lake, watching Paul freestyle his five miles, Anne silently enumerated his other positive attributes, starting with the effortless way he glided, nude, across the emerald liquid, his tanned arms and legs glinting bronze in the sun. He'd let his hair grow these past three weeks. It clung damply to the back of his neck, falling in his eyes when he raised his head to take a breath. His strokes were so regular, she could have set them to a metronome. She didn't know how he'd calculated exactly how many lake laps constituted five miles, but Anne had no doubts he would complete his requirements on the nose.

Finished, he stepped out of the water, slicking his hair back off his face with both hands. Rivulets dribbled the length of his body, bouncing off the contours of his shoulders and seeping into the concave span that was his finely muscled stomach. Seeing him like this, lit from behind by the sunrise, Anne promised herself to never again resent the number of pull-ups, sit-ups, and push-ups he insisted on fulfilling—even if that number far and away exceeded anything she could do. The results were unquestionably worth it.

Paul noticed Anne watching him. She smiled, her heart beating so loudly, she was sure he'd been able to hear it even under water.

"Better hurry up and pack." He padded by her, heading for the campsite. "We've got a long ride ahead of us."

Sometimes Anne felt she'd spent her entire life saying good-bye. Every time her parents accepted a new job, she made a round of her friends, shaking hands, hugging, and exchanging addresses. She didn't mind. Her parents always made moving to a new location such a glorious adventure, she had no time to miss the people and places she'd left behind. Until now. And the funny part was, she hadn't even said the words yet, and she was already feeling lost.

Anne watched Paul cycle back toward the Academy. Shoulders hunched, head down, legs pumping in perfect, unerring rhythm for the last fifteen miles. As if the phenomenon that began with Anne introducing Paul to America and ended with his morning swim had all taken place in the imagination—Anne's imagination.

In a couple of hours, they'd be back at school, and tomorrow both were set to report for duty—Paul in Southern California, Anne in Northern California. And after that . . . Well, frankly, she had no idea what would happen after that. Paul certainly hadn't given her any indications. In three weeks, he hadn't mentioned one word about their future, or lack thereof. Which wasn't like him. It wasn't like him at all. The man planned his accidents. Literally. Once, peeking over his shoulder, Anne spied Paul drawing up a mock-battle plan where he'd actually scheduled "problems" for 5:30 to 6:45 P.M.

She had no doubt Paul knew exactly what he intended to do once they returned to school and, in all likelihood, for the next fifty years. The question remained, what did he intend to do about Anne?

Since despite his admitted fondness for words, Paul had yet to utter one relevant to the subject, she only had his actions to go on. And what she saw, didn't exactly inspire Anne to run jumping for joy. Paul hadn't spoken to her all morning. He kept his eyes down, speeding a good thirty feed ahead of her the entire trip back to the Academy. When they pulled up to the dorms, Paul hopped off his bike, conscientiously locked it to the rack and unloaded his gear. Anne braked alongside him. She dropped both feet, balancing the bike between her thighs and, arms crossed, stood watching him.

Nothing. That's what she got from Paul. No words, no vibes, no acknowledgment. Nothing. If he noticed her watching him—and how could he not? She was planted two feet away from his face, for Pete's sake—he certainly did a fine job of hiding the fact.

"Paul!" Anne's nerves snapped right around the fifth time he managed to pass by her without making so much as eye contact.

He raised his head. "Yes?"

To be honest, she hadn't thought their conversation out this far ahead. Anne was just thrilled she'd gotten him to talk to her.

"Paul. I—I'm flying out to Sheldon tonight."

"I know. I'm going to Edwards. Would you like a ride to the airport? I still have my car."

"No. I mean, sure. A ride would be great. But. Paul."

"Yes?" No inflection.

"Would you stop saying that, please."

He shrugged, slipping his sleeping bag off his bike and onto his shoulder. "All right."

"Are we fighting?" she asked. "It feels like we're fighting."

"When I fight, Annie, you'll know it."

"Why are you being so defensive?"

"I'm an Air Force officer. When someone attacks, I defend."

"This isn't night maneuvers, Paul."

"No kidding. Night maneuvers are a lot more fun than this."

"Damn it. Don't you *want* to see me again?"

He cocked his head. "Where did that come from?"

On occasions like these, Anne wished she'd learned how to be a hysteric. The kind of girl who could burst into tears and stomp her feet and, by the end of the fit, have a man wrapped around her finger. But all Anne knew how to do was be forthright.

And so she took a deep breath, locked her stare with Paul's, and told him, "For four years, I went to bed every night thinking about you. Granted, most of the time, I was trying to think of a way to make you look bad. But, I *was* thinking about you. So, I think I deserve at least partial credit for that. I went to bed thinking about you and I woke up thinking about you and, these past three weeks, every breath I took, it felt like I was taking it for you. Now, in a couple of hours, you and I are very likely never going to see each other again. That bothers me. Frankly, Paul, it tears my heart out. You, on the other hand, are acting like, well, like—nothing. I can't even accuse you of acting indifferent, or relieved, or reluctant, because, see, that would be Something. And you—you've chosen to go with Nothing."

Paul crossed his arms along his chest, lips set in a straight line, legs planted in wide stance. He said . . . nothing.

No. That wasn't exactly true. He did grunt. Once.

Anne asked, "And how would you like me to interpret that?"

*Now,* he said nothing. Instead, Paul reached into his pocket and pulled out a creased sheet of paper. He unfolded it, flipping the document to face Anne, revealing a map of California.

"I've made a plan," he said. "The distance from Edwards Air Force Base to Sheldon A.F.B. is exactly four hundred and six miles. Factoring in typical freeway conditions, side streets, and a speed limit of seventy miles an hour—average—it is possible to drive that distance in under seven hours on one *full* tank of gas."

"Fascinating."

He continued, "Presently, our work schedules are compatible in that we both have Wednesdays and Thursdays free—"

"How did you find out my work schedule before I did?"

"I made a few calls."

"And how is it we both happened to have the same days free?"

"I made a few more calls." Seeing Anne's doubting expression, he elaborated, "And I may have called in a few blue chips."

Air Force officers who owed other officers favors called them chips. Blue chips were the biggest favors of all.

"Anyway. Seeing as how we both have Wednesdays and Thursdays free, and seeing how the drive between our respective bases is a manageable seven hours, I propose that—"

She couldn't believe it. "You had this all figured out before I even opened my mouth, didn't you?"

"Be more specific, Annie, you do open your mouth quite a bit."

Anne burst out laughing, pummeling his chest with both fists. "You son-of-a-bitch. If I hadn't made a fool of myself and brought it up, would you have just kept quiet about all your plans?"

Paul grunted. Twice.

She was making headway.

## ═══ 7 ═══

"Really?" The corners of Amelia's mouth twitched uncertainly. "You'll really tell me whatever I want to know about you and dad?"

"Well, within limits," Anne said.

Amelia giggled. It was the giggle of an eleven-year-old drunk with power. And it made Anne distinctively uneasy.

"Cool. Okay, mom. So, answer the first question, then. Did you think Dad was really hot when you first saw him?"

"Actually, the first time I saw him, I thought he was really arrogant, really condescending, really rude, and . . ."

"And . . ."

"And . . . really hot."

"What else?"

"What do you mean, what else? I may be a generation removed from the jargon, but I was under the impression that 'hot' was a pretty all-encompassing word."

"I mean, what else did you like about him? In the beginning?"

Fourteen years. Amelia was asking Anne to think back fourteen years, to a period she routinely struggled to *avoid* thinking about. Not that it had been a bad time. Quite the opposite, frankly.

"In the beginning." God, that sounded so biblical. It added weight to the pronouncement. "In the beginning, what I loved best about Paul was how..." Anne paused, rearranging her thoughts and starting a new sentence. "I wish you'd had a chance to know your grandparents, Ace. They were terrific people. Free spirits who didn't believe in schedules. All my life, I never had a curfew."

"Cool," Amelia said.

"They let me do whatever I wanted, whenever I wanted. They didn't even own watches, so they certainly didn't care if I came home in time for dinner, or, frankly, if I came home at all. They figured if I stayed out all night, well, then I must have had a damn good reason for it."

"And you went from *that* to the Air Force Academy?"

"Look up culture shock in the dictionary, and there's a photo of me my first semester."

"You must have been freaked out, Mom."

"I had my freaked-out moments. But I kind of liked it, too." Anne rubbed the crease between her eyes, remembering. "The first time I realized your dad actually *counted* on my being in class each day—that was the most bizarre feeling. He *cared* where I was, what I was doing. After a date, he either walked me to my room or, if I went alone, insisted I call him when I got there, so he'd know I made it home safe."

"And you liked that?"

"I thought it was ... different. Sweet."

"So how come when you pick me up at Dad's, and he says to call him when we get to your house, how come you get so mad at him?"

"Because." Anne spat out, certain that there was an answer. She just hadn't thought of it yet. "Because it took me a lot of years to catch on, but eventually I realized that he didn't care about *me.* He cared about controlling me. He got a thrill out of telling me what to do, then seeing me jump whenever he snapped his fingers. The few times I did something without consulting him, he went ballistic. Called me a lousy pilot, a lousy mother, a lousy wife. Any way he could envision to hurt me, he did."

Anne's voice shook with indignation, and she squeezed her left hand into a fist to hide its trembling. She couldn't understand it. Why should a six-year-old argument with a man no longer a part of her life still possess enough power to get her so upset?

"Mom?" Amelia tread carefully, hesitating a beat after each word, ready to withdraw the question at the first sign of trouble. "Mom, if you hate Dad so much, how come, then, how come you're so sure that he's going to come rescue us?"

Anne turned to Amelia, surprised by her daughter's assessment. For one thing, she never thought of herself as hating Paul. She'd felt furious with him, certainly. Exasperated, definitely. She'd felt hurt by him more times and more deeply than Anne harbored the courage to remember. But hate him? No. No matter how angry she got, no matter what Paul did, somehow, deep down inside, Anne felt convinced that no matter what she could never truly hate him.

Besides. What did her feelings matter? Paul certainly hadn't given a damn about them while they were married. Why start caring how she felt now? Anne knew Paul would rescue them for no other reason save that he was Paul. She explained as much to Amelia.

But the little girl didn't appear wholly convinced.

"It's snowing pretty hard. The rules are, no rescue operations without visibility. And Dad never ever breaks rules. You said so."

Anne shook her head, generating such dizziness, she needed to prop her chin up with her hand. Her stomach churned, trapping her breath at the base of her throat.

Still, Anne forced herself to tell Amelia, "That's the thing about your dad, though. Just when you think you know exactly what he's going to do, he goes ahead and surprises you."

Highway 24 to Manitou Springs. Up Garden of the Gods Road to Highway 25. Exit 150B to South Gate Boulevard, then onto Academy Drive. It was a trip Paul had made at least a thousand times while a cadet, and he'd been intent on doing it again that afternoon.

That is, until, "The road, sir, is closed," threw a curve into his hastily constructed plan.

Paul rolled shut his window, watching the cop rush back to his heated patrol car and climb into the front seat, brushing the snow off his hat, coat, and gloves. Once inside, the officer looked up, surprised to see Paul sitting where he'd left him and gestured for the major to "move along."

Right.

Paul shifted into reverse, blinking his headlights to signal he'd received the order and rolled back a few feet. The officer, convinced he'd done his duty for God and country, took his eyes off the road and turned his head, twisting his upper body to reach in to the backseat for a discarded newspaper.

Operating on combat instinct, Paul took advantage of his foe's vulnerability to swiftly change gears and slam his foot on the gas. He smashed through the snowy roadblock before Colorado's finest even figured out how he could turn without banging his elbow on the steering wheel. By the time the sputtering patrol car fixed to lunge forward in an attempted chase, Paul, thanks to record-breaking driving, had managed to obscure his path with a blend of blinding snowstorm and exhaust fumes. He made a mental note to send the bill for getting his bumper fixed straight to Annie.

Right after he strangled her.

Paul swerved off the highway as soon as possible, just in case his uniformed friend decided to radio ahead for reinforcements, and racked his brain, trying to dredge up fifteen-year-old memories of Colorado back roads. He could try swinging south and coming up through Bear Creek. Or heading north under Denver. But, damn it, he didn't have time to be taking the scenic route.

Paul rubbed the crease between his eyebrows with his knuckles, forcing himself to think. There had to be some way to get to the Academy without taking either a main highway or detouring through the North Pole. If Paul was in a plane, he could have followed Monument Creek, and it would bring him straight onto campus, but automobile traffic along the shoreline wasn't allowed and, and so . . . so . . . so the hell what?

Paul's hand came to a decision before he could, wrenching the steering wheel and heading for Monument Creek even as his judgment politely inquired what exactly Major Gaasbeck thought he was doing?

Eyes peeled on the nearly invisible roadway, he maneuvered his way through the storm, navigating on, God help them, instinct! and trying to formulate a coherent, cohesive plan. Short-term, Paul's goal was raw and simple: keep from plunging into the icy creek and killing himself. It was the long-term where matters grew fuzzy.

Granted, he'd had a roll of luck with improvisational tactics previously on this trip. But Paul couldn't take credit for them. It was Anne. Anne had been the one prompting all his decisions and actions. Unfortunately, it was hardly a novel occurrence.

From the moment they met, Paul doubted more than an hour had passed during which Anne hadn't been a key player in his thoughts. The worst came while they were married, when Paul was assigned to Germany for three months. As soon as his commanding officer gave the order—it didn't matter that a tour of duty in Europe would look great on his Officer Performance Report—Paul's instinct was, frankly, he didn't want to go there. Because he didn't want to leave Anne.

It was a lousy instinct, and he had no intention of giving in to it. Nevertheless, during Paul's first week in Germany, he dreamed about her every night. By the second week, he could be in the middle of a lecture, when a smell or a snatch of music or a color would flit through his mind, reminding Paul so pressingly of Anne that he lost his place and had to start a given sentence over again.

Determined to conquer the disruptive addiction, and to punish himself for even wanting to give in to it, Paul resolved to go cold turkey. If thoughts of Anne were affecting his performance, then the only reasonable course of action was to practice abstinence for the duration of his assignment. Paul ordered himself to avoid any activity which might unnecessarily remind him of Anne—including speaking to her on the phone, writing her a letter or so much as a "wish you were here" postcard.

By the time his three-month German stint was up, Paul felt so primed to come home, he spent the morning of his departure spit-polishing every button and adjusting each epaulet on his uniform to keep from arriving at the airstrip too early. At exactly thirty minutes to, Paul checked with the sergeant in charge, hooked his garment bag over the spine of a chair, and moving to the broad window facing the runway, stood at-ease—stance wide, arms behind his back—waiting to get this show on the road.

"Heading home, Captain?"

Okay. This was getting disturbing. Now he was hallucinating Anne's voice, too.

Paul turned around, dispassionately wondering whether this was what the first phase of senility felt like.

"Hi," Anne said.

If he were the sort of man who allowed his jaw to drop open in surprise, then that's exactly what would have happened. If he were the sort who could toss propriety and decorum to the wind and sweep his wife in his arms for all to see, he would have done that, too.

But he was Paul Gaasbeck. And Paul Gaasbeck could only nod his head once, bruskly, to indicate that he'd noted and processed the fresh circumstance, and then instantly progress to debriefing.

"What are you doing here, Annie?"

She looked so thoroughly pleased with herself, it was all Paul could do not to return her brilliant smile with one of his own. He wondered how she did it. How did she manage to constantly generate so much positive energy that it not only shone through her eyes and deepened the double dimples in her right cheek, but also saturated the air, like a heat mirage of good will that dared anyone in its path to just try and not experience an instant soar of mood.

"Hitchhiking." Anne pointed out the window at a swarm of enlisted men unloading the long-range four-engine C-141 Starlifter transport she'd arrived on. "Actually, I called in some chips, and got this assignment delivering medical equipment. Crew and I made a deal.

Since I worked the entire transatlantic flight on the way here, I'm relieved of duty for the trip back.'' Anne grinned. ''So. Captain. What do you say? Care to go around the world?''

She took his hand, and led Paul past the cockpit, introducing him to the crew. ''This is Lieutenant Gates, Second Lieutenant Cho, and Airman Stowe. This is my husband, the other Captain Gaasbeck.''

''Sir.''

''Sir.''

''Sir.''

Paul returned their salute, while Anne continued. ''We haven't seen each other for three months. Am I making my point clear?''

''Yes, Captain.''

''Thank you.'' Anne and Paul moved out of the cockpit and into the belly of the C-141, closing the door soundly behind them.

Because this transport was used to ferry medical equipment and supplies to Air Force base hospitals, its floor, walls, and ceiling were heavily padded, blocking the light and making every step feel like jogging on the beach. Laughing, Anne flopped on her back atop the cushioned veneer, pulling Paul down to her until they lay side by side and face-to-face inside the dimly lit cabin. She kissed him. Gently, slowly, and, after three months apart, torturously.

Her tongue flickered inside his mouth, prompting Paul to slide his hand along her body, over her waist, her breast, her neck, to cradle her cheek in his palm. ''You're killing me, here. I hope you know that.''

She smiled languidly, and playfully wrapped her leg around his hip. ''Good. You deserve it.''

He breathed in her sweet fragrance, slipping his palm beneath the crook of her knee and stroking her thigh.

This was going to be a very, very long flight home.

Anne molded her body along his, pressing her lips against his ear, and cooing, "Did you miss me, Captain?"

He couldn't say it. Not out loud.

It was one thing for Paul to respond to her physically. That was a control issue he had long ago relinquished. Besides, after three months, it was natural. It was expected. But saying the words out loud . . .

Fortunately, Paul was spared forcing an answer by the C-141's revving up its engines and drowning out all sounds. They coasted down the runway wrapped in each other's arms, laughing out loud on takeoff as, still holding each other, they rolled to the back of the plane, bouncing painlessly against the padded floor and walls. Once in the air, the cabin lights automatically shut off, plunging them into darkness until all Paul and Anne had left was their sense of taste. And touch. A strangely liberating proposition.

Even twelve years after the fact, Paul still couldn't quite put into words why the prospect of Anne being unable to see or hear him proved so emancipating. He only knew that, for the first time in his life, he felt free to follow any impulse, to let himself go.

He rolled on his back, taking Anne with him, until her thighs straddled his hips, her face pressed so near to his that they were breathing the same air. Paul squeezed his hands under her jacket, yanking it off over her head and reaching for the buttons of her blouse, snapping them one by one. The heat of her skin seared his fingers, boiling every red cell in his body until he imagined he could feel his blood gurgling though his veins. He called her name and, when Anne didn't respond and he was certain she couldn't hear him, Paul murmured, "I love you," burying his face between Anne's breasts, kissing the soft, sweet warmth before turning his head and wrapping his lips around a swollen nipple that hardened beneath his tongue and drove Anne to dig her fingernails into his shoulders.

As their uniforms melted away and his hands were free to roam across her stripped body and guide her securely on top of him, Paul whispered, "I missed you so much."

He clasped her wrists as she braced herself against his chest, fingers intertwined in kinky wisps of hair, tugging not hard enough to hurt but more than enough to excite him out of his mind. And, as he felt her start to tremble, digging her knees into his sides and riding him until neither could stand to wait a moment longer, Paul divulged the most private two words of all. "I'm sorry."

More than a decade later, especially around Amelia's birthday, whenever Paul allowed himself to recall his flight from Germany to Texas, the memory always arrived shackled to an ambivalent, queasy stir in his gut. He just wasn't quite sure what he was guilty of.

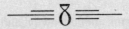

*1983*

It took them a couple of weeks, but Anne and Paul developed a routine in which they took turns trekking out to see each other. One week she drove south, one week he drove north.

At first, because Paul had a waist-high stack of manuals and computer data to pour through before taking a test jet out Friday mornings, he left Anne's at three in the afternoon and returned to Edwards by ten. That left him a couple of hours to study before falling into bed for six hours sleep and a seven A.M. pre-flight briefing. After the first month, though, he found himself leaving later and later. Three in the afternoon became six in the evening and, eventually, midnight. Instead of sleeping and studying, Paul now drove all night to reach the base in time for his flight.

And it was even worse when Anne came to see him. Even though she never left later than eight, Paul insisted she call him as soon as she arrived at Sheldon so that he'd know she made it home safe. He tried to read between hours, but more often than not his eyes strayed to the clock. He skimmed the same paragraph a dozen times without retaining a syllable, and when she finally did call, they ended up talking for hours. Or rather Anne talked and Paul listened—and missed her desperately despite the fact that they'd seen each other less than half a day earlier.

His superiors may not have picked up on the havoc his alliance with Anne was wreaking on his flying ability, but Paul felt it loud and clear. He was reminded of it whenever his response time proved just that much slower than he thought it should be, or whenever his mind wandered—even for a second—during a strategy session or briefing. And yet he felt helpless to do a damn thing about it.

Each time Paul picked up the phone to call Anne and tell her that he couldn't make it this week, he instead found himself in the car, speeding toward Sheldon A.F.B. So Paul played games with himself, in an admittedly ludicrous attempt to outsmart his own mind.

To prove that the situation wasn't as hopeless as it seemed, especially to him, Paul set his car on cruise control, refusing to drive more than seventy miles per hour no matter how free the road was or how few cops were in sight. Pulling up to Anne's quarters, he ordered himself to sit with the motor off for ten minutes rather than bounding upstairs like he longed to. If the phone rang and he knew it was her, he waited exactly six rings before answering.

Not that a single of those disciplinary exercises did him any good. The day before he was scheduled to take up a brand new F-15 *Eagle* in an attempt to test its landing capability along an extra-short runway, Paul spent the evening not reviewing data accumulated by previous pilots in identical situations, but inside a bar on the outskirts of Edwards, sitting across the table from Anne, listening to her tell him about the harassment her all-women flight crew was getting from air-traffic controllers across the country.

"Can you believe it?" She sipped a club soda, mindful of the long drive ahead of her. "One bastard actually insisted we put the *real* captain on. Like we were playing dress-up or something. When I told him we didn't have any men on board, he actually refused to bring us in. He said it would only encourage us. One of the other controllers finally had to step in and get us down."

He loved watching her when she grew this passionate, loved the way her cheeks flushed, and her eyes lit up, and her tongue darted inside her mouth, moistening her lips, until Paul could do nothing else but lean across the table and playfully suggest that they put that flicking tongue of hers to better use.

When both came up for air, Anne licked her lips regretfully, glanced at her watch, and grimaced. "Damn. Gotta head back."

Paul nodded. No matter how much he may have wanted to, he never, ever, asked Anne to stay an extra moment. It was another of those little tricks he used to outsmart himself.

She stood and grabbed her purse, heading for the ladies' room. "I'll be right back."

Paul watched her go, marvelling how Anne managed to make even an Air Force uniform that everyone else called a bus-driver getup, appear sexy. Of course, he reminded himself, the allure may have had something to do with how often he'd seen her out of it. And not just naked, either. Because of being in uniform all day, Anne favored ultra-feminine attire during her off hours. Her negligee collection alone numbered in the dozens. Satin, silk, lace, pink, yellow, peach, azure. Paul couldn't make up his mind which one he liked better. Anne said, in that case, she'd just have to keep on modeling them all, until he finally arrived at a decision.

Paul smiled, recalling the fashion show she'd entertained him with just last night, when, from somewhere to the left, he heard a slurred male voice describing, in great anatomical detail, exactly what he'd like to do to the "Army chick" who just walked into the ladies' room.

Listening, his palms tightened unconsciously into fists. His heartbeat doubled, and the heel of his neck burned.

Paul stood up slowly. He pushed back his chair, scraping it along the floor and turned around, hands on hips.

It wasn't difficult to locate the loudmouth. He was obviously the fellow with no shirt and a red bandanna tied around his head. The one who audibly gulped his beer when he noticed the muscles in Paul's arms and chest flexing against the restrictions of his uniform.

Paul crossed from his table up to the bar in three steps. He towered over the red bandanna.

"Apologize," Paul said.

Expecting to be hit, the shirtless patron did a double take, surprised that his assault came in mere words.

He smirked, downing the remnants of his beer and wiping the foam from his mouth with a bare forearm. "And what if I don't?"

"I strongly suggest you apologize," Paul repeated, proud of the way he was able to keep his voice low even while, inside, he felt more and more like a can of seriously shaken Coca-Cola.

"Right." The bandanna quivered as its owner spat, "You Army guys are pathetic. Only balls you've got are those shiny earrings dangling off your chests. Oooh. Scary. Wouldn't be surprised if that hot number of yours wasn't horny for a real man. Someone not afraid to get his pretty, little outfit dirty."

Paul said, "First off all, sir, if you're going to insult the armed forces, at least learn to differentiate which branch you're insulting." He indicated the markings on his epaulets. "This is an Air Force insignia, not Army. See the eagle?"

"Looks more like a chicken to me."

"Second of all," he raised his arm so quickly, his victim had no time to register the upswing motion before Paul's hand caught him on the way down. "Never confuse good manners with no balls."

Paul rammed his fist into the hairy belly.

The bandanna-man slumped over, hitting the floor on his knees and, seeing Paul raise his leg for a final kick, held up both arms to ward off the blow, croaking, "I thought you Army—Air Force, Air Force! guys had some officer/gentleman deal happening."

"That"—Paul pulled his last punch, only kicking hard enough to incapacitate, not induce kidney dialysis— "is the Navy."

He stood over the whimpering body, his hand throbbing lightly, his heart pumping blood.

"Problem?" Anne materialized by Paul's side, looking first up at him, then down at the gelatinous mass at his feet.

Paul shook his head, offering Anne his elbow to help her step over the body as they moved toward the door. "Solved."

In the parking lot, Paul and Anne leaned against her car. She plucked keys out of her purse and turned to kiss him good-by.

"Are you sure you're okay?" She stroked the nape of his neck.

"I'm fine."

"That bastard didn't hurt you, did he?"

"Oh, yeah. I finally had to ask him to stop slamming his gut against my fist."

She smiled, standing on tip-toe to kiss his cheek, then rubbed her lipstick off with her thumb. "See you next week, tough guy."

He waved as she pulled out of the lot, waiting until Anne was totally out of sight before moving over to his car and, bracing his arms on the hood, dropped his head and took deep breaths.

Paul could not believe what he had just allowed himself to do. He'd never done anything like it in his life. Not even when he was in grammar school and the other kids judged his reluctance to fight as proof of a definite yellow streak.

The fact was, Paul earned his first karate belt at five. It was the last thing his dad taught him before leaving for Vietnam. By twelve, he was one of the youngest black belts in the country. He knew he had the capacity to smash other kids' heads open without breaking a sweat. He also knew it was his responsibility never to unleash his skills in the heat of anger. If Paul was going to beat people up, he preferred to do so on an organized level. Football, wrestling, martial arts, he'd lettered in all three in high school. He even kept from body-checking in hockey because the practice wasn't an explicit part of the rules.

And now . . . this.

What was he thinking? No. Paul shook his head, closing his eyes. Not what. Who. Who was he thinking about?

Hell. Who'd he been thinking about, day and night, for the last four and a half years straight?

Paul drove back to base with the radio cranked up as loudly as possible to the first hard-rock station he found.

The din made it difficult to think, which was exactly the state he was going for.

At home, he planted himself in his most uncomfortable chair and, for seven hours, read his flight manual out loud. If he felt his attention wavering, he read the same sentence over and over again, committing it to memory before turning to the next page.

At two A.M., when he heard his phone ring, he let it drone six times. And then he sat by and watched the machine pick it up.

He screened his calls for the rest of the week, successfully avoiding three messages from Anne. He told himself he didn't have time to talk. He had a very important flight coming up, and Paul needed every spare minute to prepare for it.

Nevertheless, Tuesday evening, he raced through his paperwork not even bothering to stop home and shower before he hopped in his car, heading north. Paul hadn't fathomed just how much he'd missed Anne this week until he peered down and realized he hadn't lifted his foot off the gas for over two hours. His speedometer read one hundred and ten m.p.h. And, what's more, he didn't care.

He made it to Sheldon in under five hours. A record by any standards, even if Paul did have to drop his speed down to seventy once he reached the city limits.

Half a mile from Anne's apartment, Paul could only think about how badly he needed to see her again.

And that's when he ran the red light.

He hadn't even noticed he was doing it, until irate honks from all sides snatched him out of his reverie and back to reality. He slammed on the brakes, yanking his steering wheel to avoid hitting an oncoming car. With only inches to maneuver in, he skidded out of harm's way and into an empty lot.

Safe, he closed his eyes, struggling to force his heart into its assigned spot behind the lungs instead of hammering against his throat until he could neither inhale or exhale. He rubbed his hands one against the other, squeezing them to stop the trembling.

He'd almost killed someone.

Because Paul Gaasbeck—Paul Gaasbeck, of all people!—had not been looking where he was going, he'd almost killed someone.

This had to stop.

No more games, no more mind tricks, no more rationalizations. This had to stop, and this had to stop now.

He was an Air Force lieutenant. He was the number three test pilot at the number one facility in the nation. He was sworn to defend the Constitution against all enemies, foreign and domestic. Why then, was he having so much trouble with something so simple?

He wasn't.

There, Paul had decided it.

And once he decided something, he knew that it was true. He wasn't having any trouble at all. He was perfectly fine.

Pleased with his conviction, or maybe just afraid that if he didn't act promptly he would lose his resolve, Paul pulled his car out of the lot, turned around, and headed back home.

A message from Anne waited on his machine the moment he walked into his apartment. She sounded concerned, worried that something had happened to him on the way.

He stared at the blinking red light for a good minute. Then, with a shrug, he turned off the ringer, unplugged the message, and after twelve non-stop hours of driving, fell into bed for his first full night's sleep in months.

Paul intended to remain unconscious the entire weekend.

But, for some reason, he had the hardest time falling asleep.

Anne didn't know what to make of it. When Paul still wasn't at her place by daybreak Wednesday, she'd called his quarters and reached the machine. A few hours later, even it wasn't answering.

She kept calling, finally reaching Paul in person at midnight on Thursday. He sounded half-asleep, managing to stretch a drowsy hello into three reluctant syllables.

"Paul? It's Anne."

"Hey." Then, a pause. A damn long pause.

"Paul, are you all right?" He didn't sound like himself. The Paul Gaasbeck Anne knew didn't wake up slowly. Her Paul Gaasbeck snapped to attention the moment his eyes opened, barely sitting up in bed before he was on his feet, in the shower, in uniform, at the breakfast table, and out the door.

"I'm fine."

Why did she feel so disappointed when he said that? It's not like Anne had been hoping to hear he came down with bubonic plague.

She waited for Paul to elaborate. He didn't. There was only breathing on the other end of the phone. Steady, even, controlled breathing. At this point, she would have settled for a grunt.

"Well?" Anne couldn't stand the silence any longer.

"What?"

"Where were you yesterday?" Nagging wasn't her strong point. Anne wondered if she was doing it right.

"I had a report to finish."

"So why not just call and tell me that? I was expecting you."

"You were? I didn't know that."

She wavered for a moment. "Was it my week to come down? Did I lose track?"

"It was nobody's week. When you left last Thursday, I don't remember either one of us specifically saying anything about when we'd get together again."

"Well, no, not specifically, although, I could have sworn I said—oh, what difference does that make? We've been flipping weekends for almost three months now. How could you possibly not have known I was expecting you?"

"I'm sorry, Annie. But, it's not like we had a set plan or anything. I'm in deep crunch time here. I'm number three in the flight ratings now, and I've got to get to at least number two to be considered for further projects down the line. I really need to focus all my energy on the flying."

"I understand that, I do. It's just that—"

"I'll give you a call as soon as things quiet down a bit." He hung up the phone before she could wedge in another word.

For the next week, Anne walked around in a daze, wondering if she'd been dumped, and if that was so, why Paul had chosen such a roundabout way to tell her?

It took Anne another four days to get him on the phone again. Once she did, though, she didn't waste time beating around the bush. She asked Paul, "Are you mad at me about something?"

He cleared his throat and switched the receiver from one ear to the other. "Of course not. Why would you think that?"

"Well, you have been ignoring—"

"Annie, I told you. I'm swamped with work. But, know what? As soon as this project is over, I've been thinking of building my own plane from scratch. Just like I always dreamed about."

"I remember."

"Well, I'd love to get your input on it. You are, without a doubt, the best flight engineer I know."

Her spirit soared, relishing the invitation even more than the compliment. "That sounds great. When—"

"I'll call you, Annie. I've really got to take off now."

"Okay. Bye." She hesitated before adding, "I love you."

It was a risk. Anne knew it was a risk the moment she opened her mouth. But she couldn't help it. She needed to know where he stood. And despite the bizarre behavior he'd exhibited over the past few days, Anne still believed Paul was a man of his word. He wouldn't say something he didn't mean.

She waited anxiously for a response, her stomach churning in a way it didn't usually, not even during the worst turbulence.

Finally, from four hundred miles away, she heard Paul sigh and concede, "I love you too, Annie."

And then she didn't hear from him again for nearly a month.

By the last day of October, on Halloween to be precise, Anne reached the end of her rope. She still had no idea where she stood as far as Paul was concerned. In four weeks, he'd phoned a grand total of once, and that was in response to a message she left him, asking Paul to please call as soon as he got in.

It didn't matter that they'd had a wonderful talk. That he'd been sweet and reassuring and loving and funny and all those other qualities she recalled him possessing before the Big Chill set it.

He still had refused to see her for over a month.

At first, when Anne suggested she drive down the next weekend, promising not to bother him, even offering to help him study, Paul declined. He claimed he'd have no time for her, and he didn't want her getting bored. Anne took slight offense, pointing out that she was capable of keeping herself entertained for a couple of hours. Nevertheless, Paul begged off.

She kept after him, though, offering to come down just for the day, or even for an afternoon. Finally, Paul agreed. He told her he'd drive up on a Wednesday morning, spend a couple of hours up North, then head back. Thirty minutes before he was due to arrive, Anne got a call from Paul, telling her he couldn't make it.

To the average person, his actions spoke loud and clear. Paul didn't want anything to do with Anne. He just didn't have the guts to tell her so. And with any other man, Anne would have accepted the assessment. Except that this was Paul.

And Paul wasn't a liar. Or a coward.

She only *wished* he was either one of those things. Then Anne could forget about him and move on with her life. The problem was, Paul Gaasbeck was a wonderful person—when he wasn't acting in a totally incomprehensible manner.

Paul made her laugh, he touched her heart, and he turned her on like nobody's business. He was the smartest individual she ever met. The only one to whom she never had to explain anything twice, the only one who understood what she meant even when she excitedly left out a few words—or paragraphs—from her explanation. He found no problems keeping up with her, or putting her in her place when the demand arose. By laying down the gauntlet of competition, he drove Anne to strive harder, to reach further, to do—no, to be better than she previously imagined possible.

And he never, ever bored her.

She loved the way he worried about her and the way he listened to her. She thought he was an incredible pilot and an absolutely brilliant strategist, and no matter how far she peered into the future, Anne couldn't see a single day on which she wouldn't still love Paul Gaasbeck.

Which was what made her predicament all the more frustrating. If only Paul would break down and finally tell Anne to go to hell, well, then she would cry a bit—all right, she would cry a lot—but she would have her answer and she could move forward. When he insisted on keeping her dangling, acting sweet one minute, distant the next, she didn't know what to make of it.

And she was goddamn sick and tired of feeling that way.

Without waiting for an invitation, or, worse, a refusal, she hopped in her car Halloween morning, driving straight to Edwards A.F.B. without stopping for so much as a cup of coffee. Once on base, she barreled past the runways and the restricted area, with its aluminum hangars housing a stable of experimental *Eagles*, and headed for the officers' quarters.

She was waiting for Paul, in his apartment, when he walked in the door.

"Trick or treat, Lieutenant."

Another man might have expressed surprise at seeing her curled up so comfortably inside his plush chair, legs dangling over the side. Paul only slid off his garrison cap, tucking it inside the pocket of his green flight suit, and asked, "How'd you get in?"

"Let's just say you're not the only one with some blue chips to cash in."

He nodded, unzipping the suit. Perspiration trickled down his throat and into the light brown curls across his chest. "What are you doing here, Annie?"

She stood, facing him, and advanced with delicate steps, like one might approach a savage animal in danger of bolting. "I came to tell you it's time to fish, or cut bait."

"Meaning . . ."

"Meaning that I am begging. This is me, Paul, me begging you to give me a straight answer. Tell me to get lost. Please. Tell me to get out of your life, erase your phone number from my memory, head out that door and never come back. But, please, please, tell me something. Because, truth is, I'm simply not strong enough to walk away from this without some kind of prompting on your part."

He turned, walking to the bedroom. He opened his closet door and stood behind it, changing out of the flight suit.

She followed him, keeping her distance, but unable to restrain the bitter laughter bubbling out her throat. "Why the modesty? It certainly isn't anything I haven't seen before."

Paul slipped on a robe, tying the sash as he stepped out from behind the closet door. He told Anne, "If you want to end matters, I certainly have no right to stop you."

"If I? If I want to end matters? Paul, *I'm* not the one who spent the last month avoiding me."

"I wasn't avoiding you, Anne. We spoke just," he consulted a desk calendar. "Just nine days ago."

She slapped it out of his hand, grateful for the bolt of anger coursing through her veins. It was either that or tears.

"That's the problem! Nine days ago, you and I talked as if there wasn't anything wrong. So I started hoping that things were okay between us again. That's what's killing me, Paul. The hope. Just tell me to take a flying leap. Please. Otherwise, I'll keep hoping, and I'll keep coming back, and I'll keep getting hurt over and over and over again.''

"I'm sorry you feel that way. I never meant to hurt you.''

"I know. Isn't that the ultimate joke? I know. You're not the sort of person who would ever deliberately hurt anyone. That's why none of this makes any sense.''

She was crying. In spite of her best efforts, she felt tears slip past her lashes and trickle down her cheeks. Anne covered her face with both hands, embarrassed not by the show of emotion but by the discomfort her display caused Paul.

"Annie, Annie . . .'' Strapped for words, he could only wrap her in his arms, letting her sob against his chest while he soothingly rubbed her back. "Please. Don't.''

"I'm sorry.'' She pushed herself away with both palms, wiping her eyes. "This isn't what I came to do. Believe me. I wouldn't manipulate—''

"I know.'' Paul ducked his head so they could be on eye level. "Don't you think I know you by now?''

"Tell me what you want from me.'' She pulled herself together, remembering what prompted her spontaneous visit in the first place, and determined to settle things one way or the other before driving home. "I'll do whatever you say. God knows, I don't think either one of us can face any more scenes like this one.''

He clasped both of her hands between his. "I want you to marry me, Annie.''

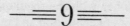

===9===

A melia wanted to know, "Did you say 'yes,' right away?"

"Actually, I said 'why?' right away."

Amelia wrinkled her nose. "That's not very romantic, Mom."

"Neither was your father's response." Anne winced and shifted her weight, trying to muffle the misery in her arm by resting it on her lap, rather than letting it dangle. She recalled every word of Paul's pragmatic answer as clearly as if he'd just delivered it.

*Because. That's what people like us do.*

In retrospect, Anne wished she'd sought clarification for his statement. What sort of people was Paul talking about? Air Force officers? Pilots? Caucasians? At the time however, she foolishly assumed Paul was talking about people who were in love.

Amelia drew her legs up to her chest, wrapping her arms around the insulated snow pants they'd dug out of their skiing luggage and yanked on over their clothes. She rested her chin on her knees, rocking to stay warm. "But Dad loved you, right? He probably just figured you already knew that. That's why he didn't say it."

"Don't!" Anne raised a warning finger, voice trembling. She was finding it increasingly harder to pinpoint

135

a spot on her body that didn't groan with pain every time she inhaled. The agony in her head had joined with the anguish in her arm to create a single wave of misery that rolled through her with the regularity of the tide. It took every ounce of concentration and military discipline Anne possessed not to whimper after each word. Hardly the prime state from which to cut her ex-husband slack. "Don't make excuses for him. That's exactly what I did. And look where it got me."

After weeks of worrying and wondering whether Paul wanted her in his life, his proposal had effectively flooded every one of her more rational senses with pure, intoxicating joy. Anne cast aside each reservation percolating in her mind—especially at three in the morning—and assured herself that everything would be fine. She told herself that Paul would be more attentive to her after they married. She told herself that the misunderstanding of the past month stemmed from their living so far apart, and how being married would certainly fix that. She told herself that she could change Paul, that she could fix some of his more bothersome habits.

She was wrong.

Anne said, "You want to know how dumb I was, Ace? Even after he spent weeks treating me like some nuisance forced into his busy schedule against his volition, I still couldn't wait to marry him."

"How come?"

"Because I loved him." Outside the icy cabin, subzero winds howled with laughter at Anne's naivete. "And because I desperately wanted to believe he loved me, too."

She gave up her post flying the KC-10 and requested a transfer—any transfer, even a desk job—to Edwards A.F.B. Anne thought Paul would be pleased. But, the day her new orders were issued, he only offered, ''Oh. Well. If that's what you want. . . .''

Anne stared at him, dumbfounded. ''Don't *you* want me to move to Edwards? I mean, call me crazy, but I read in this magazine the other day that in some cultures married couples have been known to live in the same time zone. Fancy that!''

Ignoring the sarcasm, Paul specified, ''What I want, is for you to do whatever you think is best for you and your career.''

On the surface, there was nothing in his explanation for Anne to take offense at. Yet she couldn't shake the inkling she'd been dismissed. The least he could have done was shown *some* enthusiasm at the prospect of their finally being able to live together.

Anne shivered, pulling her jacket tighter around her neck, and instinctively turned to Amelia, trying to estimate how the rapidly dropping temperatures were affecting her child. While the brutal weather was currently Anne's greatest concern, a close second was their lack of food. They hadn't eaten in twelve hours. Amelia was clearly weakening, flopping her head on Anne's shoulder, slurring her words, yawning, and constantly rubbing her eyes.

Determined to keep Amelia engrossed enough to stay awake, Anne ignored her own exhaustion and launched into yet another anecdote.

''Your father's first extended overseas assignment came after we'd been married about a year and a half. The Air Force sent him to West Germany to teach a three month test-piloting class. He got his orders. He packed his bag. He typed a single-spaced fourteen-page report for his flight squadron. He formatted a lesson plan and sent it ahead for approval by the base commander in Germany. He wrote out three months worth of checks—

car payment, house payment, cable bill—and put each in its appropriate envelope, with the day I was to send it written in the upper-right-hand corner, so I could cover it with a stamp before I mailed it.''

Amelia peeled her eyes open. ''That sounds like Dad.''

Encouraged by the lucid response, Anne pressed on. ''And yet, during all that time he was getting ready for his trip, your ultra-organized dad never once found the opportunity to mention that he might, oh, say, miss me. Or that he was looking forward to coming home. Or that he wished I could come with him.''

''Maybe he was busy. Writing checks and stuff.'' Amelia pushed herself up to sitting position.

''Very funny, Ace.''

''Just trying to help.'' She gave the matter further thought. ''Maybe he figured you already knew how he felt, so why go on about it?''

Anne raised her eyebrow. ''Now, *that* is a familiar excuse. I wonder where you heard it? You know, kiddo, if your dad wrote the Constitution, it would read, 'We find these truths to be self-evident.' Period.''

''So, what's wrong with that?''

''What's wrong is that, in Paul's case, the truth was scarcely self-evident. How would you feel, Ace, if someone you loved more than anything, someone you tried your hardest to believe loved you back, went away for three whole months and never once picked up the phone to call you and just say hello?''

Amelia squirmed. ''Dad never called you?''

''Nope. I waited. First couple of nights, I literally sat at home, looking at my watch, calculating what time it was in Germany. When he didn't call after a week, I picked up the phone—they do work both ways, you know. . . . But then I thought, no. I wanted to see how long it would take him to remember I existed."

In the end however, Anne did break down and call him. Several times. And each time Paul answered the phone, she hung up. She had her answer. He was on the base. He was free. He just didn't feel like talking to her.

The realization tortured Anne. Her own thoughts brushed Paul so many times in a given day, it would have been pointless to keep count. She couldn't solve an engineering problem, or fly over an interesting landmark, or spot a funny slogan on a passing T-shirt without instinctively wanting to tell him about it. Paul was there with every breath she took, a constant presence in her conscience, like a memorized multiplication table. She could phone him every hour on the hour and never run out of interesting things to say, or grow tired of hearing his voice.

Paul obviously suffered no such compulsion.

She told Amelia, "You think I'd get used to it. It's not like Paul did anything after we were married, that he didn't do before."

"So why'd you get so mad at him, then?"

Looking to formulate an appropriate response, Anne stalled by stealing a moment to ponder her injured hand. The flesh around her nails had lost the blue tinge that so worried her earlier. And the balls of her fingers didn't feel nearly as cold anymore. Was that a good sign or a bad one?

"I guess I just wanted . . . I guess I just needed evidence, some sign from your dad that he loved me as much as I loved him."

"What kind of sign?"

"I'm not sure." Anne bit her lower lip to keep her teeth from chattering. "I just always figured I'd know it when I saw it."

Amelia nodded, eyelids starting to shut again. "Oh."

Anne kicked Amelia's leg, coercing a hearty tone and asking, "So? Know what I did?"

"Ow!" Amelia massaged her calf. "Cut it out, Mom."

Anne shook her head ruefully, covering her eyes with her good hand, embarrassed that she'd ever taken such a track. "I decided, if I couldn't inspire passionate emotions in Paul, then I would go whole hog the other way, and make him angry."

Amelia considered the tactic. "You mean you made him mad at you on purpose?"

"I figured I'd rather brave his anger than his indifference. At least when I made him furious, I convinced myself he cared about me. People don't get angry at people they don't care for, right? And marriage isn't a fairy tale. It's hard work. Hard work your father wasn't willing to put in. I tried my best. I tried everything I could think of."

Amelia ran a mittened hand across her forehead, dabbing at the scratch under her bangs. "Mom?"

"Hm?" Anne's attention wavered between her daughter, and her latest discovery about her hand. When she pricked the balls of her fingers with her nails, she could no longer feel the puncture.

"If Dad was mean to you and stuff, why did you stay married to him for seven years? I mean, why did you have me?"

Amelia looked ready to cry, and Anne was immediately sorry for everything she'd said. Since their divorce, the one issue Anne and Paul agreed on was not to badmouth each other around Amelia. They saved those sentiments for their annual jousts before Judge Saul.

Forgetting her frozen fingers, Anne rushed to reassure, "Your dad was never mean to me, honey. Not on purpose, anyway. He never deliberately set out to hurt me."

That much Anne believed to be true. In order to want to hurt her deliberately, Paul would have had to give a damn.

She continued, "Your father loves you. And he can be very kind, very considerate. You know that. I remember one time, when we'd been married a year—we were living at Edwards then—and I got a call from a major at Reese Air Force Base in Texas asking if I'd be interested in an assignment piloting a KC-135 midair refueling tanker. Now, it wasn't exactly what I always dreamed of doing, but at least it was a chance to fly again—I was just testing computer simulations at Edwards. I was dying to request that transfer. But your dad was a test pilot, and Edwards was the best place in the world for him to be. I couldn't decide what to do. I came home that evening still trying to make up my mind about how I would tell Paul about the offer. But when I got there, he already knew. The Air Force is worse than a small town in that respect. If only our fighters could travel as fast as our gossip!"

Still talking, Anne tried squeezing a fist, growing nervous when her icy fingers refused to obey. Loathe to scare Amelia, she kept chatting on as if nothing was wrong. "Anyway, not only did Paul know, but he'd already called Reese and arranged his own transfer. They didn't have a test-pilot program, so he agreed to be assigned to a fight squadron. A fight squadron! Do you have any idea how tedious a fight squadron is after you've been a test pilot? I couldn't believe it. But he told me, 'You relocated for me. It's only fair.' Like it was no big deal."

Anne's voice grew softer and softer, virtually hypnotic. How long had it been since she'd said anything positive about Paul out loud? How long had it been since she'd even thought it? After the divorce, Anne couldn't look back at the past without bitter colors from the present splattering their streaks across each image, until she genuinely began to believe there hadn't been that many pleasant memories to start with. The conviction made signing divorce papers—not to mention enduring the past six years—much easier.

The only problem was, she'd sentenced herself to living a lie.

Briefly lost in a combination of remorse and fatigue, it took Anne a moment to yank herself back to the present and realize that her speaking voice had faded to a whisper. She turned to Amelia, noticing that her daughter's eyelids had shut again and that her breathing had slowed to a sleeping rhythm.

"Amelia!" Anne raised her voice, swallowing hard to fight the thirsty rasp in her throat. She forcefully shook her little girl's shoulder with her healthy arm. Anne's fractured one responded by firing a series of flaming arrows to burst yellow and purple hand grenades in front of her eyes. "Wake up, Amelia."

No rebuttal. Not even a groan to indicate she'd heard her.

Anne pinched Amelia's thigh, tightening her clutch through the thickly padded snow pants. "Come on, Ace, rise and shine. I'm not kidding. This isn't the first day of school, here."

Amelia didn't stir. Her head lolled off Anne's shoulder and flopped to the side, chin bobbing against her chest.

Anne grit her teeth and, for the first time in eleven years, slapped her daughter across the face. "Damn it, Amelia. Wake up. Wake up, I said! That's an order."

As Paul turned left on South Gate Blvd., steering onto Academy Drive, he knew what he planned to do, and he knew that no Air Force officer or enlisted airman in his right mind should consider going along with him. He also knew that, come hell, high water, or the Commander in Chief, Major Gaasbeck intended to get his way.

Paul drove past the USAFA Visitor Center, the Planetarium, the Cadet Field House, and the Cadet Chapel. The latter structure, with its metallic, triangular spikes jutting into the air like an armada of sailboats, was one Paul particularly avoided acknowledging. The last thing he needed now was a reminder of his wedding.

Wipers valiantly jabbing at the snowdrifts piling up on his windshield, Paul squinted through hailing golf balls at the block of houses reserved for Academy personnel. When she was still Major Danahay, the Academy's director had occupied a modest two-story home on the far-left corner of the street. Now that she'd been promoted to Brigadier General Danahay, Paul could only hope that her address remained the same.

He parked the car, opening the driver's side door, and almost immediately was slapped by a blast of wind strong enough to knock him back inside the vehicle. He thought of Anne and Amelia alone and stranded in the Rockies, facing hunger, possible injuries, and even more brutal elements, and his determination to bring them home kept Paul upright as he slipped and slid his way up the front walk to what he hoped was still Sharon Danahay's residence.

He rang the doorbell, rubbing his palms one against the other and reasoning that, on the bright side, the freezing cold did keep the blister on his hand from throbbing.

Paul winced. Jesus, things were worse than he thought. Now he wasn't just acting like Anne, he was also *thinking* like her.

The porch light came on and Paul instinctively stepped beneath the beam, willing for the general to recognize one former cadet out of a twenty-year sea of alumni. He heard the click of a lock. The door opened a crack. A man Paul had never seen in his life peeked through the slit.

"Can I help you?" He cocked his head, studying Paul's jacket. "Major, is it?"

"I'm looking for Sharon Danahay. I was a cadet here fif—"

"Paul?" The door opened and, behind the stranger, General Danahay, fifteen years older and dressed in a cardinal bathrobe over blue cotton pajamas, beckoned for him to come in, hurriedly closing the door behind him. "Paul Gaasbeck?"

"Yes, ma'am." He brushed the snow off his uniform, regretting the puddle of blizzard melting around his feet. "I'm surprised you remember me."

"Not many of my straight-A cadets throw away the Commander's Trophy by stealing a Cessna right before graduation."

"I brought it back."

"Eventually." She introduced him, "Major Gaasbeck, this is my husband, Randall Meninger."

"Hello," Paul raised his arm to waist level, unsure whether a salute or handshake, despite their being indoors, was in order. A man in a bathrobe made rank a rather tricky thing to ascertain.

"You can relax, Major, Randy's a civilian through to his toes. I found that only one pilot in the family makes life a lot easier."

Briefly, Paul contemplated how much easier the last fifteen years of his life, not to mention the past day, might have been if that fact had originally been included in his Academy curriculum.

He said, "General Danahay, do you remember my wife, Anne? We were in the same class."

"Of course. Commander's Trophy, right?"

"Yes. That's her. Anyway. She's been in an accident."

"I know. A former pupil of mine is in Air Traffic Control at Peterson A.F.B. across town. He called me this morning."

"Did he also mention that no one at Peterson is doing a damn thing to launch a search and rescue?"

"Well, in this weather, do you blame them? Besides, I thought you and Anne were divorced."

He stiffened. "Amelia is still my daughter, General."

Danahay covered her mouth with one hand. "Your daughter was on board? I didn't realize. Is there anything I can do to help?"

"Actually, there is. You could lend me an Academy helicopter so I can fly into the hills and search for them."

"Are you out of your mind, Major?"

"No, ma'am."

"Paul, the entire state of Colorado has been grounded. Do you realize what you're asking?"

"Yes, ma'am."

She sighed. "Even if I did disregard regulations and granted your request, do you really expect to secure clearance for takeoff in this storm?"

"Let that be my concern."

General Danahay crossed her arms, tapping her fingers against her elbows. "If you were in my place, what would you do?"

Paul answered without hesitation. "I would deny the major's request, and command him to obey SAR procedure. But with all due respect, ma'am, I'm not in your place. I'm in mine. And I intend to save my family. Whether the U.S. Air Force likes it or not."

# ==10==

Anne and Paul were married over six months before her request for a transfer to Edwards A.F.B. was finally approved. They moved into a one-bedroom apartment on the base, and promptly arrived at a fascinating discovery. Military life was not ideal preparation for domesticity.

On the one hand, they were both exceptionally adept at making beds tight enough to bounce quarters off. They kept the apartment so dust free it could pass white-glove inspection. Their bathroom gleamed. Their dishes were washed, dried and put away immediately after every meal.

But neither one had a clue how to cook.

Both were used to the Officer's Club at best or, at worst, the mess hall. Anne's parents never tried culinary experiments beyond sandwiches. Paul's mother was a fixture at the Academy cafeteria.

The morning she relocated to Edwards, Anne rolled over in bed and proposed, "Know what would be fun? Learning to cook together."

Paul judged it an infinitely reasonable motion. Since both of them were taking evening graduate courses to finish their Master's degrees, he offered, "I bet the university has cooking classes."

"You want to learn to cook in a *classroom*?"

"You were thinking correspondence school, maybe?" Paul dipped his head, kissing her shoulder.

"I was thinking we'd buy a couple books and experiment. It'll be fun. I've always wanted to see you smothered in molasses." She rested her chin on Paul's chest, flirtatiously blinking her lashes in comic imitation of Scarlett O'Hara.

"Sweet as that sounds—"

"No pun intended."

"You underestimate me." Paul stroked Anne's back. "Sweet as that sounds, I'm certain we'll learn more, faster and better, if we get a professional to show us the ropes."

"Wanna bet?" She kissed the tender spot beneath his rib cage, and slithered her way downward.

"Name it."

Anne's tongue flicked the inside of his navel. "You take your classes, I'll buy my books, and we'll get a third party to judge."

Paul closed his eyes as she slid to his crotch, taking him in her mouth. "Always a pleasure doing business with you."


For those who predicted that a wedding would put a lid on Anne and Paul's five-years-and-still-going-strong rivalry, the intensity with which both plunged into their culinary contest proved an eye-opener. They gave themselves a month's time limit, inviting every officer at Edwards to a dinner party during which the issue would be settled once and for all. In the meantime, Anne and Paul took turns cooking each other dinner, progressing from salads to pastas to lemon grilled chicken, eggplant parmigiana, roast veal marsala, and stuffed cod. The night of the judging, Paul and Anne prepared five dishes each, ranging from appetizers to dessert. Guests were instructed to rank them in order of preference. The chef with the lowest cumulative point total would win.

One of their guests, a colonel with twenty years experience in military rivalries, nudged his wife to observe, only half-kidding, "Patton and Montgomery were less competitive."

After results were tallied, and Paul declared the winner by a thirty-six point margin, he accepted his accolades with a smile, a nod, and raised eyebrows in Anne's direction. "Naturally."

Before their second anniversary, they'd moved to Reese A.F.B. in Texas, where Anne piloted a KC-135R Stratotanker to refuel F-15 Strike Eagles and F-16 Fighting Falcons in midair, while Paul flew those same jets as part of his fighter wing, and both waited to see if they would be promoted to captain on their first try.

In the Air Force, higher rank for officers was based on length of service, duty performance, and a vacancy in the following grade. Although it wasn't unusual for a candidate to be passed over once, twice, even three times, before attaining their next rank, it was rare for the promotion board to advance an officer below the zone.

Regardless, Anne felt convinced she and Paul were outstanding enough to warrant it their first time up. Six months before their cases were even scheduled to be evaluated, Anne strolled across the hall to scout the early promotions list, psyching herself for when it would be their turn. She skimmed the printed sheet, looking for Academy classmates who might have made the cut, when GAASBECK, ANNE jumped out at her from between FENTON, ROBERT and GRAYSON, DAVID.

She blinked, startled, then reread the list. There it still was. GAASBECK, ANNE. CAPTAIN.

She couldn't wait to tell Paul. She called out his name as she flew into their apartment, hurrying to the den. He sat at the computer, fingers poised above the keys, eyes leaving the monitor only long enough to glance at the three technical manuals spread out around him on the desk.

"Paul?"

"Hm?" He clicked a pencil against his teeth, not looking up.

"Paul, I made captain."

"I know." He reached for the manual furthest away from him. "I saw the Early Promotions list. Congratulations."

Anne blinked again, as startled now as the first time she saw her name on the wall. "That's it? Did you hear what I said?"

"I heard you." Paul pried his eyes away from the monitor long enough to offer her a quick wink, then turned back to the keyboard, typing while speaking. "That's great. I'm proud of you."

Anne let her arm drop, unsure of what sort of a reaction she'd been expecting but pretty certain this wasn't it. "Paul, this is the biggest thing that's ever happened to me. Sure, I figured you and I were a lock for promotion first time in the zone. But, early promotion? This is amazing. It's a miracle."

"It's very nice," Paul agreed.

She had no reason to be angry. He was saying all the correct things. So why then did everything feel so hollow?

Stiffly, she said, "You'll forgive me if I find your accolades a touch underwhelming."

Paul sighed, "I can't tell you what to think, Annie."

He was doing it again. God, she hated when he did this.

Biting her lip to keep from snapping something she might later regret, Anne turned to leave, telling Paul, "I'll go start dinner."

"Fine," he nodded. "I'll be down in a half hour."

Anne told herself she was acting childish. What did she want? Fire crackers? Balloons? A pony ride, maybe?

Paul had congratulated her. He said he was proud of her. He said her promotion was nice. No, strike that. He said it was *very* nice. Anne picked up a potato and, from across the kitchen, lobbed it into a pot of boiling water on the stove. Well, whoop-dee-doo.

She'd gotten the same reaction telling her CO's secretary, and that also came with a warm hug and an "I'm so happy for you." When she shared the news with Lieutenant Gates, he'd said, "Wow, making captain below the zone, you must be so psyched." And Chief Master Sergeant Thebaud patted her cheek avuncularly, saying, "I know how much this means to you."

Yet the person who mattered most to her had blown her off with a "that's nice, dear."

They had dinner in silence. Anne hoped Paul might notice that she was being less than her usual, ebullient self and mention it. He didn't.

Halfway through dessert, unable to take the silence, she lowered her fork, swallowed, and wiping her lips, asked, "Paul?"

"Yes?"

"I—I think we need to talk about this."

He stood up, carrying his plate to the sink and automatically rinsing it. "If you want."

She struggled for just the right words, reluctant to start a fight, yet certain that if she didn't get the hurt off her chest it would rise up in the night and strangle her. "I was so happy when I came home today, I was about to burst with it. And the person I most wanted to share my news with was you. But, then, your reaction—Paul, you took all the joy out of this for me.''

He loaded the dishwasher, making sure to stack each plate and cup face down, then closed the door and pushed the On button.

Anne asked, "Could I have a response to what I just said?''

As if speaking to a child, Paul repeated. "Congratulations. That's nice. You want more? I'll get the thesaurus.''

She truly didn't know what to say. Tears filled her eyes and a wet rag congealed her throat. Still, Anne managed to force out a relatively coherent, "Is that the best you can do?''

Paul turned to face her, wiping his hands on a blue-and-white dish towel. He pursed his lips, exhaling with the crisp *pop* that always indicated he was giving an issue serious consideration. For a beat, Anne dared hope that she'd gotten through to him. That he finally comprehended why his lack of excitement had cut her like a knife to the gut. Paul took a step toward her.

He said, "Yes.''

She thought her legs would give out. A swift kick to the back of the knees couldn't have toppled her more effectively than Paul's single, uninflected, favorite word. Anne spun around, disguising a need to regain her balance by hurrying toward the kitchen door and out into the hall. Blindly, she fumbled for her purse in the closet, grabbing the car keys and digging through the tangled loop until she found the one she wanted.

Paul followed, not concerned but merely curious as he asked, "Where are you going?''

Anne opened the door. "To find someone who gives a damn."

She drove around in circles for close to an hour before coming to the conclusion that this was stupid. She'd received tremendous news today and she deserved a celebration—whether her apathetic husband wanted to be a part of it or not. To that end, Anne cut short her umpteenth cruise around the landing strip and headed for the O Club. She pulled into the parking lot and walked inside.

"Hey, if it isn't Captain Gaasbeck!" A familiar voice called from the corner. Anne turned to see three lieutenants, two men and a woman, sharing a table. Lieutenant Zoe Yednok waved Anne over, offering her congratulations, which the other two enthusiastically echoed.

"Where's Paul?" Lieutenant Harvey Mirkin dipped his french fry in a pool of ketchup and popped it in his mouth.

"Still on duty," Anne lied.

"Well, snatch a chair and join us." Lieutenant Ross Lopez raised his arm to attract the waitress. "I believe it's time for a good, old-fashioned wetting-down?"

"A wetting-down?" Zoe asked.

Anne wagged her finger at Lopez, and explained. "A wetting-down is a tradition. When an officer gets promoted, she takes the difference from her last paycheck and her next paycheck and buys all her friends a round of drinks."

"Sounds good to me."

"Unfortunately," Anne punched Lopez's arm playfully with her fist. "It's a tradition in the *Marine Corps.*"

"*Semper Fi* and pass the bottle, that's my motto."

Anne pivoted in her chair, ordering a pitcher of beer from the waitress to be put on her tab.

"A toast," Zoe said. "To Captain Gaasbeck."

They clicked glasses, downed their portions, and were reaching for seconds when Zoe spoke up. "I bet Paul is really pissed, huh? I mean about your making captain before he did."

The beer suddenly burned Anne's throat, leaving a scorching trail down to her stomach. "What?"

Lieutenant Mirkin piped in. "It must be real hard, a guy like Paul, always first in everything. The day he joined our squadron, the rest of us knew we were scrambling for second place. That man's unbeatable. Bastard never makes a mistake. Tell you the truth, I'm afraid to beat him. No telling what he'll do to me."

With Mirkin's words reverberating in her ears, Anne drove home at a quarter past one A.M. It wasn't as if the thought had never occurred to her. But . . . Did she really mean so little to him? Was being first really more important to Paul than she was?

Anne turned into their driveway nursing enough dread to fill a *Friday the 13th* sequel and silently crept into their apartment, hoping Paul was already asleep. She wasn't up to facing him.

Noticing that the bedroom light had been turned off, Anne tiptoed in, sneaking into the bathroom to change, shower and brush her teeth before sliding into bed next to him. They lay back to back, Anne's eyes facing the digital clock on the bureau as she watched first minutes, then an hour, blink its way past.

No matter how hard she tried, Anne couldn't fall asleep. A single thought kept playing through her mind, over and over again like a stuck record. Winning their rivalry mattered more to Paul than her feelings—than she—did.

A tear escaped from underneath her left eyelid, dripping down Anne's cheek and teetering for a beat at the tip of her nose before splashing a gray, damp blot on her pillow. She squeezed her eyes shut, fighting to arrest the flow. But it was too late. One tear followed another with the regularity of coupled trains. They zigzagged sideways across Anne's face, strangling her breathing until she was forced to clear her throat or risk asphyxiation.

And after that, of course, the battle was lost.

One measly cough was all it took for the sobs prowling in her chest to come tumbling out. She was crying before she knew it, hugging her shoulders with both arms, knees drawn up to her chest, biting her lip to keep down the noise.

But the rigorous battle for quiet was wasted on Paul. He'd heard her come in. Hell, he'd heard her pull into the driveway. Mostly because he'd been listening for it.

He'd heard Anne sneaking into the bathroom, he'd heard her in the shower, and for the past hour, he'd lain as still as the night, regulating his breathing so that she didn't detect anything amiss, and listening to Anne's pain.

Someday he hoped to get hit with a piece of shrapnel in a non-vital, yet particularly agonizing, area so that he could confirm his suspicion that few wounds of battle could hold a candle to the misery of lying awake, listening to his wife crying, knowing that it was his fault and, also knowing, that there wasn't a damn thing he could do about it.

Or, rather, that there was something he could do. Paul just refused to do it. On principle.

He'd done nothing wrong. Nothing. And he had nothing to feel guilty about. Nothing at all.

Why, then, was he struggling with this mad urge to apologize?

Paul rolled over on his side, watching Anne's back as it shook with each muffled sob. She was doing this on purpose. She had to be. She knew the effect her tears had on him.

Well, he had no intention of falling into her trap. Reacting to her tears would be the same as admitting he was wrong. And Paul was never wrong. He had a file of successful flights to prove it.

Paul's eyes focused on Anne's shoulder blades, tracing the way they peeked out from just above the lace of her pink silk negligee. Most nights he loved to watch her getting ready for bed, loved the way Annie unfastened her hair and let it brush the very tip of her shoulders, loved the way her skin gleamed in appreciation of being set free to absorb fresh air after hours in uniform, loved the way she slipped one of her negligees over her head, and he hardened in anticipation of sliding his hands beneath all that soft satin and silk and, just as sensuously, peeling the nightgown off again.

"Annie." Paul's voice and his arm took on a life of their own as he whispered her name and cautiously reached his hand forward to lightly brush her shoulder with his fingers.

She jerked away like from a slap, curling even deeper inside herself. The tears didn't stop. If anything, her breathing grew more ragged, and her body shook so hard Paul felt it over on his side of the bed. He reached for her again, this time resting his palm on her arm and holding on even when she pulled away.

She struggled for a moment. But there was nowhere for her to go. Gradually, the strain against his grip lessened, and Anne lay back, too tired to fight. The third time he called her name, she rolled over to meet Paul, burying her face in his chest and weeping softly, unable to say a word.

He didn't know how to respond. He only knew it was

imperative he try. So Paul told Anne the only truth he could believe in.

"I'll fix it," he promised, unsure of what or how. "I'll fix this, Annie."


Paul cooked breakfast the next morning. Because it was his turn. He started to make french toast, Anne's favorite, opening the refrigerator and taking out eggs and bread before deciding, no, it was Friday. And on Fridays he always made pancakes. Always.

She came into the kitchen just as Paul was finishing setting the table, taking a sip of coffee and listlessly poking a series of holes into her top pancake with her fork. She'd put on a freshly pressed uniform and neatly pinned back her hair so that it didn't exceed regulations. On the surface, Anne appeared impeccably put together and capable of withstanding any surprise inspection. Yet there was an aura of exhaustion about her. It manifested in the slight droop of her shoulders as she sat at the table and in the absence of the smile that usually accompanied her every activity.

Anne sliced a sliver of margarine with her knife, spreading it on her pancakes, and chewed without enthusiasm before determinedly swallowing the bite and announcing, "I can't do this, Paul."

He looked up from his own stack, calmly laying down the knife and fork on either side of his plate and folding his hands neatly in front of him, fingers linked. "Okay."

"I hate fighting with you. I hate it."

"Well, then, I have a simple solution: Don't."

Anne raised an eyebrow. "It takes two to tango, Paul."

"That's quite true. It takes two to tango, two on a seesaw, and two for tea. But in this household apparently, it only takes one to start, carry on, and finish an argument.''

"You still don't think you did anything wrong, do you?'' When Paul didn't reply one way or the other, Anne pressed on. "But, then again, I never know what you're thinking. Or what you're feeling.''

"So what?'' There was no sarcasm in Paul's query, just genuine curiosity. "Why is that so important to you?''

He had her there.

"I—I don't know.'' Anne stammered. "It just . . . is.''

"Now, *there's* a good answer.''

"For God's sake, Paul, I didn't stay awake all night preparing for this like it was the S.A.T. I'm trying to have a conversation with you. This isn't a contest. No one is keeping score.''

"For the record, Annie, someone is always keeping score.''

"Wonderful. I'll write that down as my thought for the day.'' She was getting off-track. This wasn't at all how she'd wanted to approach this. Squeezing her fists, she took a moment to recenter herself, taking her time, carefully selecting each syllable before asking, "Paul, are you angry at me for making captain, first?''

"Of course not.'' The answer shot out of his mouth so quickly, it could only have been painstakingly rehearsed.

"Don't lie to me. Please.'' She kneaded her palms nervously against her knees. "I think I could handle anything but that.''

"I'm telling you the truth. I'm not mad.''

"Right.'' Anne nodded. "Right, I forgot. You don't get mad. Well, how about jealous? Do you like that word better?''

"I'm not jealous."

"Then what is it? Why are you doing this to me?" She stood up, pacing one end of the kitchen to the other, talking as much to herself as she was to Paul. "I just don't get it. I thought you'd be happy for me. Everyone on the crew, everyone I ran into on the way home, they were all happy for me. And it was nice. I was very touched. But the only thing I could think of the whole afternoon was, I've got to tell Paul. Because he's the only one who really, really understands how much this means to me. He was there when I went through my little dejection at the Academy. He was there when I got assigned to fly a tanker instead of a fighter. He knows all the crap I had to go through to be taken seriously as an Air Force pilot. And, most importantly, he loves me. That's what is going to make sharing this news with him the sweetest thing of all."

Paul drummed his fingers on the kitchen table. It started out random, then slowly mutated into "The Lone Ranger Theme." Finally, he said, "I gave you the best that I could, Annie. Why does everything with you always have to be Better! More!"

"Because the opposite of that is Worse! Less!"

"I don't know what else you want from me."

"I want the truth. I want you to tell me what you felt, what you thought when you saw my name on the Early Promotions list."

"I don't remember."

"Try."

"Jesus Christ, Annie."

"Try!" She turned on her commander's voice and, to make sure that her point was made, added, "Lieutenant," knowing exactly what effect her using *that* word for *this* conversation would have on him.

Anne didn't need to turn around to feel her attack

strike its target. The room temperature dropped until every hair on her body stood on end. She heard Paul's rage, the taut, wordless, nameless hum of anger fighting to keep itself in check. It frightened Anne at the same time as it reassured her that, if nothing else, she'd finally broken through his blasted shield of indifference.

His voice so calm it could only be a cover, Paul carefully and meticulously informed her. "All right. You want the truth? You want to know how I feel? Very well. This is how I feel. I think your promotion is a knee-jerk, politically correct attempt to prove that women in the military, especially women pilots, are receiving their fair shake. I think it doesn't mean anything. And, frankly, I don't think you deserve it." He crossed his arms. "There. Are you happy now?"

What was it the Chinese say? Be careful what you wish for. . . .

Anne wondered if it was too late to start the day—hell, the whole week—over again.

She turned around, a pickax chopping up each of her internal organs. She resolved to counter his onslaught with something sharp yet cool, reserved yet penetrating. Unfortunately, nothing of that nature was making itself available on the tip of her tongue.

The paradox left Anne with no other choice but to ask Paul the only question on her mind. "How can you say that to me?"

He shrugged. "You asked."

"You *are* jealous."

Paul opened his mouth, ready to deny and—as he once explained to her was the consequence of being an officer—defend. But he reconsidered and tossed his hands in the air, not quite conceding, more like calling a time-out. "Fine. I'm jealous."

Anne closed her eyes, simultaneously hurt and re-lieved.

He went on, "Do you blame me? I pulled the best assignment in our graduating class, I've got the best flight record. I expected to be promoted first. I *wanted* it."

Slowly, she told him the truth. "I don't blame you for wanting to be the best. That's one of the things I love about you."

"So, what the hell was this"—he waved his hand between them—"all about?"

"This," Anne copied the gesture, "was about the fact that I thought you loved me."

Paul stopped dead in his tracks. "Heads up, I've got a nonsequitur on my six."

"How can you claim to love me and, at the same time, resent me for getting your promotion?"

Paul blinked at her in surprise. "Annie, my being pissed off about missing an early promotion has nothing to do with you."

"Hello? Earth to Paul. I'm the one you resent."

"No." He shook his head emphatically. "No. Not at all. I'd be acting the same if . . . if what was his name, the pilot who finished third in our class? . . ."

"Dreger."

"I'd be acting the same if Dreger was the one to get an early promotion ahead of me. It's nothing personal."

"Well, no, not between you and Dreger. But correct me if I'm wrong, I thought there *was* something personal between you and me."

"This is a trick question, right?"

Anne struggled to make herself understood. "How can anything that happens between you and me not be considered personal?"

"To paraphrase a brilliant retort I heard only this

morning: It just . . . is. The feelings I have for Anne, my wife, are totally separate from the ones I have for Anne, my fellow officer. And if there's one thing you ought to know about me, it's that I consider every fellow officer a competitor.''

"You can so easily divide your feelings like that? Black and white, right and wrong, Anne-the-wife and Anne-the-officer?''

"Yes.'' He straightened up, practically standing at attention. "Yes, I can. All it takes is discipline.''

"Okay.'' Anne poked his shoulder with one finger. "Let's run with that. Let's make believe that you really can do what you say you can. Why then was it so hard for you to separate your envy of Anne-the-fellow-officer, from the normal, human reaction of feeling happy for the achievement of Anne, your allegedly beloved wife?''

Paul's eyes narrowed. Obviously, this was the one question he hadn't anticipated when making his game plan. Unfortunately, it was the most important one of all.

He said, "I *was* happy for you.''

"You just forgot to mention it in the middle of explaining why I didn't deserve it.''

"I was truly happy for you. I said as much, didn't I?''

"Actually, no. You said you were proud of me.''

"That's practically the same thing.''

"No, Paul. It isn't.''

Once again, they'd flown way out of the envelope where he was concerned. "I don't understand what you want from me. I said all the right things. I congratulated you. I'm not—I can't—I'm not a streamers-and-balloons kind of person, Annie.''

"I wasn't asking for streamers and balloons. I only wanted a little acknowledgment on your part. Some sense that maybe you were sharing in my excitement.

That I wasn't the only one who thought this was a big, big deal.''

''It's a big deal, okay? It's a very big deal, and it's a very big achievement, and if some woman pilot had to be the token early promotion, I'm thrilled as hell it was you.'' For all the animation in his voice, Paul might have been a teleprompter-reading presenter at the Academy Awards. ''But, right now, we are both risking being late for duty unless we get moving. I'll see you later, Annie.''

How could he not understand? The question fascinated, even as it infuriated, Anne. How could a man who never scored less than one hundred percent on any test, who eternally finished first in flight standings, who resolved, ''I never makes mistakes,'' how could a man that brilliant not understand why she was upset?

Maybe it was her fault. Maybe Anne wasn't expressing herself clearly. But, she'd tried everything she could think of. Still, the conviction remained: Paul showed no interest in her promotion because his competitiveness *with* her was stronger and more powerful than his love *for* her. And if that was in fact true, then what did it say about their marriage?

When Anne got home that evening, Paul was waiting for her. He said, ''You know Duncan from the Bombardment Squad?''

''Cowboy?'' Anne plucked bobby pins out of her hair. ''Sure.''

''His family's got a ranch an hour off base, and this weekend, they're doing a cattle drive. He asked if we wanted to come along. I figured, new experience, sleeping on the ground, two days in the saddle, risking your neck for no particular reason—that's right up your alley.'' When Anne didn't reply one way or the other, Paul clapped his hands together, repeating. ''So, what do you say? I got the directions. We could leave after dinner.''

She stuck the bobby-pins between her teeth, snapping her head forward so that her hair flipped over her face. It covered her eyes and gave Anne a chance to comb it out. ''Okay. Yeah.''

''Fine.'' She heard Paul turn away.

He walked toward the kitchen, standing with his back to her, shoulders hunched above the cutting board, neatly slicing four rows of carrots into perfectly symmetrical chunks.

Done, he hefted the board, tilting it above a simmering pot of vegetable-soup-to-be, and watched the nuggets slide their way down, landing in the boiling water with twenty satisfying plunks.

Last night he'd promised, *I'll fix it, Annie.*

She came up to stand behind him, slipping her left hand in the crook of his elbow and her right hand on his shoulder. Anne kissed the back of his neck, rubbing her cheek against it, and whispered softly in Paul's ear, ''I love you, too.''

''Head 'em out!''

Lieutenant ''Cowboy'' Duncan's father gave the command, and his paddock gates unlocked, releasing a stampede of some couple hundred cows into an open field. According to their owner, the ranch hands had nose counting and branding to finish, in addition to moving the herd from one pasture to another. The task of those on horseback was to prevent the cattle from running off in a thousand different directions during the course of their relocation.

Galloping past Paul and Anne atop their borrowed mounts, Cowboy aimed them at the rear of the herd, demonstrating how to shoo errant calves back into the pack by cutting them off midcharge. "Gotta watch them every second. They take orders about as well as some airmen I know. Miss one, and we'll have to get our ropes."

"Don't worry," Paul said. "I won't miss."

Cowboy guffawed, slapped the rump of Paul's horse, and trotted away, coming up beside Lieutenant Vandis, another visiting member of their company. He challenged, "Twenty bucks says Paul lets less of them get away than Anne does."

Lieutenant Vandis glanced over his shoulder, squinting and evaluating the possibilities, weighing Paul's resolution against Anne's zeal. "You're on. Twenty bucks on the lady."

Behind them, the two pilots Gaasbeck exchanged looks.

Anne thoughtfully wrapped her horse's reins around her wrists, observing, "Our public seems to be calling for us."

"And we are guests here," Paul mused, digging his heels into the stirrups. "It would only be polite to do as we're asked."

Anne hesitated. The wounds from their previous conference on competition were just starting to scab over. Did she really want to risk ripping them open again over something so minor?

On the other hand, she could feel the adrenaline pumping from the tips of her boots to the ends of her ponytail. It would be a lot of fun. And Paul seemed to be all for the idea. He sat poised in the saddle, the start of a strategy clicking behind his eyes.

Anne chomped at the bit, raising a Lone Ranger cloud of dust, along with her horse's hoofs. "May the best Gaasbeck win."

Paul pulled a pair of gloves from his back pocket, slipping them on. "I intend to."

Ten straight hours in the saddle later, Paul substantiated his contention. Vandis owed Cowboy twenty bucks.

Everyone stopped when it grew too dark to see, making camp and laying out sleeping bags around a campfire. Anne's body throbbed, and she nursed blisters on both hands. Still, when Paul offered, "Mr. Duncan's going to teach me to lasso. Want to come along?" What choice did she have but to say, "Sure."

Paul figured he'd have an advantage for the next day's ride if he mastered roping runaway steer, as well as chasing them. He was poised to start practicing on the herd immediately.

But the elder Mr. Duncan advised, "What say you kick off with something a speck less frisky? This tree stump, for instance."

So while the rest of the ranch hands and guests roasted hotdogs over a fire, unwrapped their sleeping bags and got some shuteye in expectation of a longer day tomorrow, Paul and Anne, under Mr. Duncan's patient tutelage, learned how to lasso a tree stump.

After about an hour, when the insistent throbbing in her hands told Anne she had no chance of breaking her personal-best record of subduing three menacing tree stumps out of five, she bade both Paul and Mr. Duncan good night and abandoned her husband to keep trying for that no-hitter.

Anne crawled into their twin sleeping bag, immediately falling asleep. Seemingly a few minutes later, she rolled over, painfully bumping her head against a rock. Anne blinked, groggily squeezing the illumination button on her watch. 1:17. She sat up. Where in the world was Paul?

Stumbling in the darkness, Anne inched toward the

clearing of trees she'd last seen him near, taking care to stay out of sight.

Paul and Duncan stood right where she'd left them, with Paul now hitting nine out of ten lasso tries.

Anne crept closer just in time to overhear Mr. Duncan asking, ". . . early promotion?"

She froze. Why, why, why did he have to bring that up? They were just starting to get over the whole fiasco, and now this?

Shadows crumpling across Paul's face made guessing what he was thinking impossible. But, then again, it wasn't like seeing Paul's face clearly ever made figuring his feelings out any easier.

He told Mr. Duncan, "Yes, sir. Only officer on the base, and the only woman on the whole list. She's incredible. Did you know she won the Commander's Trophy at the Air Force Academy? And you should see her fly. She makes maneuvering a thirty-year-old tanker with 25,000 gallons of fuel on board look as graceful as a glider."

It took another hour before Paul, after three straight sets of ten-out-of-ten, finally inched into the sleeping bag next to Anne.

He moved cautiously, trying not to disturb her. But she felt his presence and, eyes closed, snuggled drowsily against him.

"Shh." Paul stroked Anne's hair. "Go back to sleep."

She rested her head on his arm, smiling when it slipped around her waist. "This cattle drive, Paul . . ."

"Hm?"

"It was a wonderful idea."

# ═ ‖ ═

Sharon Danahay said, "I didn't think you had it in you, Paul."

"Begging the General's pardon?"

She quoted, " 'I intend to save my family, whether the U.S. Air Force likes it or not . . .' Goodness, is this the same Paul Gaasbeck who spent an hour at his disciplinary hearing espousing the merits of following all of the rules, *all* of the time?"

"That Paul Gaasbeck, ma'am, was a green cadet with an annoying habit of thinking he knew everything."

"And how have things changed in the past fourteen years?"

"Well," Paul considered her question. "I am no longer green."

General Danahay hooted with laughter, planting both her hands on her hips and shaking her head. "Yes. Yes, I can see it. Anne was certainly a wonderful influence on you."

"If you say so, ma'am."

She informed her husband, "This one was always so serious. He even intimidated me. And there aren't a lot of cadets who can lay claim to that distinction."

"General," Paul looked over his shoulder, out the window. In the few minutes they'd been talking, his car, parked outside by the curb, had managed to get shrouded in at least an inch of snowfall. The storm wasn't getting any better. Paul was running out of time. "On any other day, I would be honored to continue this discussion. But I came to borrow an Academy helicopter. And so I respectfully must repeat my request."

She sobered swiftly. "I'm afraid I already gave my answer."

"Please." The effort it took him to thrust out that word was written on Paul's face. But it in no way made his subsequent plea any easier to utter. "I'm begging you. I have served the U.S. Air Force for fourteen years. It's been my honor and my privilege and I have never, ever, asked for anything in return. Until now. If you can not loan me a helicopter to rescue a fellow officer, then, in the name of God, as one merciful human being to another, loan it to me so I can save my family."

For a beat, no one spoke. Sharon Danahay bowed her head. Her husband shifted awkwardly from foot to foot. The wind hurled free-form snowballs at the windows. And Paul remained as he was, locked at attention, waiting for the verdict not only on Anne and Amelia's lives but also on his own.

When General Danahay looked up again, she said, "I never liked you, Paul."

"With all due respect, ma'am, I don't see the relevance—"

"No, let me finish. I never liked you because the last thing I thought this world needed was yet another arrogant, macho fly-boy with a God complex."

"You're certainly entitled to your opinion, General."

"But I was wrong, wasn't I? You are an arrogant, macho fly-boy with a God complex. But congratulations, Paul, I believe you might be the first pilot I ever met who also has the potential to become a human being."

Paul felt no interest in debating, or even acknowledging, her observation. "Do I have your permission to borrow a helicopter?"

"No."

"Fine." He turned to leave. "Thank you for your time."

"Whoa. Whoa, wait a minute." Sharon Danahay's voice stopped him even as his fingers twisted the doorknob. "You do not have my permission to borrow an Academy helicopter—specifically not the just bought Apache you saw sitting on its pad on your way in, the keys for which I happen to have right here. On the other hand, if said Academy helicopter somehow, mysteriously, turns up missing for the night—as long as it's returned by morning—I have a strong feeling that I won't notice. Am I making myself clear, Major?"

He rested his head on the door frame, eyes closing, knees all but buckling in relief, and exhaled for what seemed like the first time that day. "Yes, ma'am. Thank you, ma'am."

She tucked the key in his palm. "Good luck, Paul."

He made it down the driveway without slipping and was in the process of convincing his numb fingers to insert keys in his car's locked door when Paul heard his name called: he turned to see the General's husband, winter coat thrown haphazardly over his bathrobe and pajamas, hurrying after him.

"Mr. Meninger, what are you doing?" Paul stumbled to meet him halfway. "You'll catch pneumonia."

"Don't you worry about me." Randy Meninger spit out a mouthful of snowflakes. "But it's forty below, and you're dressed for spring. I wanted to give you these." He transferred the coat over Paul's back. "There's also a pair of gloves in the left pocket."

Paul accepted the donations. "I—sir. Thank you, sir."

"Don't mention it, son." Randy squeezed Paul's shoulder. "My wife's a pilot, too."

Paul hopped in his car and loudly gunned the engine, unaware of the cautious optimism flooding his senses until he realized that he'd automatically turned on the radio. Amelia's CD twirled in the player, filling the cabin with his daughter's favorite music—what she called "oldies stuff, like the seventies."

Swerving around snowdrifts on his way to the helicopter pad, Paul sat through The Bee Gees, Gloria Gaynor and Elton-John-before-his-songs-got-deep. When Percy Sledge syruped onto the track with "When a Man Loves a Woman," he reached to bypass the selection.

Paul wondered if Percy Sledge had ever met Anne.

Certainly, Paul had never known another woman who could make him so miserable, and so happy, at the same time.

Like with that damn promotion of hers.

He'd behaved like a bastard that day. Paul knew that now. Hell, he'd even known it then. Sort of. But the truth was, the instant Paul saw Anne's name on that promotion list, he was struck with the last emotion he'd ever expected under the circumstances. He'd felt so damn proud of her, Paul thought the crown of his head would blow off like a champagne cork.

It wasn't until a moment later that the truth sunk in. Anne was the first member of their graduating class to earn captain's bars. Anne. Not Paul. Anne. And the most horrible part was *he didn't mind in the slightest.*

That's when Paul felt his blood chill. How dare he not mind? What was wrong with him? Was he going soft? If the name on that list had been anyone else's, Paul would have already been thinking of ways to crush them like an insignificant bug. But because it was Anne, he could only stand there like an idiot and marvel at how amazing she was and how lucky he was to have her in his life.

This could not possibly be the sign of a well man.

Or, at least, not the well man that Paul intended to be.

It was the Commander's Trophy all over again. Once, Paul had sacrificed an honor that was rightfully his, all in the interest of making Anne happy. And now, here he was again, allowing his love for her to dull his competitive instinct.

As he stared at the list boasting Anne's promotion, Paul vowed never to allow the worst to happen. He vowed never to let himself become this thoroughly lost to her again.

Paul's hand wavered over Percy Sledge's Off button, ready to skip ahead to another selection. Then, for the first time without Amelia trying to stop him, he let the ballad play out to its end.

The Apache that General Danahay referred to sat at the head of the Academy's six-helicopter squadron. Its twin landing skids were covered with snow, but Paul didn't foresee that causing an obstacle for takeoff. Unlike airplanes or jets, which were stored in their hangars during inclement weather, helicopters were constructed from non-rust metals that made it possible for them to remain outside.

Shivering, Paul darted out from his car and into the office of Senior Master Sergeant Henzes, who was currently in charge of the Academy's rotary wing division and had been from the day Diana Paul first became an instructor. By Paul's estimates, the man was older than God, and just as knowledgeable about all matters having to do with helicopters and all rules regarding their requisition. Who else but the most dedicated of public servants would report to his post even in the face of

Colorado's worst blizzard in sixty-one years? After all, what sort of dimwit would be reckless enough to even ask for permission to take up a chopper in this weather?

Paul introduced himself to Sergeant Henzes, receiving both a salute and a hearty cry of, "Christ, if it isn't Diana's boy? How is your mama faring these days?"

"She's fine. Living in New Mexico. Running a flight school."

"Miss her 'round here. Instructors flying now can't difference a see-three-eye from that robot in the movies, C3PO. Why'd she ever leave us, anyhow?"

"When I got my Academy appointment, she thought it would be a conflict of interest to stay." Paul didn't mean to sound rude, but he was in no mood to play This Is Your Life.

"Hell, no. We got a shit-heap of daddy's boys running round, and it's not like you didn't deserve being where you were at. Best Academy cadet ever, that's who you were. A real credit to your mama and your daddy both. A real credit."

Paul interrupted, "Thank you, that's very nice of you to say. But I am here on official business."

"Don't doubt it. What kind of dumb fuck hauls himself out in the middle of a storm just to chew the fat?"

Paul indicated the craft with a nod of his head. "That Apache you just got—"

"Isn't she a beauty?"

"I'm here to requisition it."

Henzes pointed out his window. "Right now?"

"Right now."

"Hell's bells, who signed off on that paperwork?"

Gosh, Paul wished Sergeant Henzes hadn't asked him that. "As a matter of fact, the assignment came up last minute and—"

"You haven't got your orders with you?"

"I was hoping you might make an exception—"

"You? Biggest stickler for rules and regulations we ever saw round this place, you're asking me to make an exception?"

"I wouldn't unless the situation were critical."

"This is a test, right?" Henzes leaned back, surveying Paul from a different angle. "Yeah, I got it now. They got you working on some committee testing people to see how long it takes for them to screw up and give in. Then you just slap on the cuffs and that's it, we're outta here."

"It's nothing like that, I give you my word."

"Yeah, a testing committee. I always figured you'd end up on something like it. Angling to make general, I bet."

Paul tried his best. He told Sergeant Henzes about Amelia and Anne, pulling out all the stops in an attempt to break through and convince him of the seriousness of his situation.

But Henzes only laughed, waving his beefy hand as if wiping a chalkboard. "Good one, sir. Almost had me going too, until that part about the other Major Gaasbeck crashing. No way Annie ever'll do anything that stupid."

This was pointless. Given enough time, Paul felt certain he could prepare a convincing, solid, and undeniable argument for why Sergeant Henzes should open his desk drawer, take out his keys, and unlock the eight feet high, chain-link fence standing between Paul and his Apache helicopter. But, unfortunately, time was one thing Paul didn't have to waste.

He raised both of his arms in surrender, smiling to show there were no hard feeling. "All right, Sergeant. I give up. You passed your test, and you passed it beautifully."

The older man beamed. "Damn right, I passed. I tell you, Major, I've been at this a long time."

Paul returned the salute he was given, shaking hands for good measure, and marching purposefully toward his car. He started the engine loud enough to be heard in Kansas, and made a great show of carefully pulling past the sergeant's office. He drove another few yards until wind covered the noise of tires crunching snow in the midst of a U-turn, then cut his lights and coasted to the furthest corner of the Academy's parking-lot-sized helicopter pad.

Paul peered through the fence, hoping Sergeant Henzes wouldn't get it in his head to peep across the compound and wonder what that parked, shadowy mound might be. Or else they were both in trouble.

He stepped from the car, donning his borrowed coat and gloves, while still coming to the conclusion that it was freezing outside. He contracted instinctively, drawing his arms tightly to his sides, his fingers curling into fists. Goose bumps erupted on every inch of Paul's flesh, scraping abrasively against the chilled polyester of his uniform. His pupils and cheeks burned from the icy wind.

Paul approached the fence, resting his palms on the links. He felt around, attempting to locate a comfortable grip, but the fur-lined gloves rendered his fingers too thick. He couldn't bore one in without getting the glove stuck. Wonderful.

Bracing himself, Paul yanked off the gloves, stuffing them in his pocket and, quickly, before the warmth could escape, dug his fingers into the chain-link fence. The frozen metal stuck to his skin, leaving stinging gashes each time he moved his hand, like a series of paper cuts. He clambered straight up to the top, then jumped eight feet down the other side. The soles of his shoes were hardly made for obstacle-course maneuvers in the middle of a blizzard, and he skid, landing on all fours in the snow. Paul began running even before he got up, staggering to the Apache and grabbing the door handle, using it to pull himself fully upright.

He tugged open the cabin door, vaulting into the pilot's seat. He activated the integral switches without so much as a pre-flight review. The rotary blades over his head whirled into action. No way could Paul hope for Sergeant Henzes to miss that, too.

He spotted the older man out the corner of one eye, rushing to the window, waving his arms madly to get Paul's attention.

But it was too late.

"Amelia, wake up!"

When the first slap didn't appear to do much good, Anne tried again, wincing both times. Finally, after what felt like eternity, Amelia groggily stripped back her eyelids, begging, "Come on, Mom, just a couple of minutes. I'm really, really tired."

"No." Anne rubbed her daughter's face with the tails of her scarf, trying to restore circulation. "You have to stay awake."

"But I don't want to."

"For God's sake, Ace, stop whining and act your age."

"I am acting my age."

She had a point. The problem with Amelia behaving so maturely most of the time was that, when she forgot and reverted to a normal eleven-year-old, those who'd gotten used to her elder persona felt strangely betrayed.

"Then act my age." Anne rewrapped the scarf around

Amelia's face so that her mouth and forehead were covered. The only flesh currently visible on Amelia was around her eyes and nose, and Anne intended to keep it that way. Frostbite and hypothermia inevitably assaulted exposed areas first. In fact, if Anne had her way, she'd have bundled Amelia up completely. But she was afraid covering her eyes would make her even more sleepy.

They were fighting a losing battle, and Anne knew it. If the cold didn't get them, the lack of food would. And both risks grew exponentially if either of them let down her guard and fell asleep.

She had to keep Amelia talking. But that's exactly what Anne had been doing for the last twenty hours and, to be honest, she'd run out of delightful and/or amusing anecdotes. Her parched throat rasped and crackled with each breath Anne took, and the skin of her cheeks felt deadened to the point where uttering every word was as difficult for her as for a stroke patient. She was beyond wishing for a second wind. What Anne needed was a miracle.

She thought back to all the things she'd already told Amelia about Paul, wondering if there was anything of interest she might have forgotten, when a thought popped into Anne's head.

If it worked when she provoked Paul into anger, to get him to drop his lethargy, there was no reason why a tumultuous dose of fury couldn't do an equally fine job of keeping Amelia awake.

Anne glanced down at her injured hand again, guessing that the callouslike whitish crust coating her fingers couldn't possibly be a good omen. From shoulder to wrist, Anne's arm felt like scalding needles were scraping the inside of her flesh. But from her wrist to her nails, she no longer felt anything at all.

"Hey, Ace." Anne needed to cough repeatedly before she could force the chipper words out of her mouth.

"What?" Amelia rubbed her eyes with mittened hands.

"I've got an idea. Let's play a game."

"No." It came out sounding like a whimper. "I'm tired, Mom. Can't we sit without talking for a little bit?"

"Here are the rules. For the next, let's say, couple of hours, I'm proclaiming an amnesty. Anything you say can't and will not be used against you in a court of law. Or anywhere else, actually."

Amelia dropped her hands in her lap, palms up, surveying Anne as if she were a total lunatic. "What are you talking about?"

Encouraged by the animation, even if it arose from her child's conviction that she was bonkers, Anne continued, "You, Miss Amelia Gaasbeck, are the lucky winner of a once-in-a-lifetime opportunity. Drumroll, please! Don Pardo, tell her what she's won." She tapped her knee with her left hand in a pathetic imitation of Ringo Starr. "From now until Paul shows up, you, Miss Amelia, are being handed a·chance other eleven-year-old girls only dream of. For the next few hours you get to tell your beloved mother, me, everything that you absolutely, positively, cannot stand about me."

"Huh?"

"And the best part is, like I said—amnesty. I won't hold anything that you say here against you. Scout's honor."

"You were never a scout, Mom. Dad was a scout."

"I got his honor in the divorce settlement." Anne playfully tapped Amelia's nose through her scarf. "What are you waiting for, Ace? You know how many kids would die to be in your shoes?"

"So go get a couple of them."

"This'll be fun. I promise."

"I don't want to play, okay? It's a stupid game."

"Right. That'll be number one. Your mother makes up really stupid games. What else?"

"Leave me alone."

Anne heard the beginnings of belligerence and, as far as she was concerned, it was the sweetest sound ever. "Okay. Number two. Your mother won't leave you alone. She just keeps asking the same question over and over again until she gets the answer she wants."

Amelia rolled her eyes. "Look, there's nothing about you that bugs me, okay? You're my mom. I love you."

Paul. It was like talking to Paul. Ask a heartfelt question, get a well-rehearsed banality.

"I love you too, Ace. But loving a person doesn't mean there still aren't things about them that drive you up a wall. In a way, love almost guarantees it. Because when you love somebody, everything they do, good or bad, hits you deeper, you feel it more than when it's someone you couldn't care less about."

"Really?"

There was such genuine sincerity in the question, Anne had no choice but to follow up. At this point, anything that kept Amelia interested enough to stay awake was gist for the mill.

"Really. Take your dad, for instance. I loved him. I loved him so much that—don't laugh, now—you know how, at the base of his neck, his hair kind of grows to a point, and no matter how many ways the barber tries to make it straight, there's always this little, teeny, tiny triangle right in the middle?"

"Uh-ha. Last time we went for his haircut, Dad said the first barber to get rid of it, he was going to make a general."

"Well, because I loved your father, I thought that little peak of hair was the sexiest thing I'd ever seen in my life.''

Amelia giggled. ''That's silly.''

The tension in Anne's chest melted a fraction at the sound of her daughter laughing. ''However, just because I was so head-over-heels in love with your dad that I thought his hair was sexy didn't mean he couldn't drive me out of my mind on occasion.''

''Like when he went to Germany and didn't call you?''

''He was constantly acting like that. Saying one thing, doing another. Like a spy perpetually in enemy hands. God forbid anyone should get a hint of what he really thinks or what he really feels, or who he really is. Oh, no, that's classified. I suspect he gets a kick out of keeping people off-balance. It gives him a sense of control, an I-know-something-you-don't thrill. But you tell me, Ace, who should I believe when my husband claims to love me, then does everything he possibly can to sabotage my career?''

''Dad really did that?''

''Yes. Yes, Ace, Dad really did that. When I had a chance to make history, he deliberately went to our CO and had me scratched from the mission. When I requested to be put back on active flight duty after you were born, he stuck me with a desk job. And after Iraq, your dad was ready to see me court-martialed. Now he didn't do that to any other pilot. He did it to me. Only to me. And I was supposed to believe him when he swore that our competition was most certainly not more important than I was? I'm sorry but, in those cases, actions definitely spoke louder than words.''

The hammering inside her head escalated with every sound, yet Anne couldn't stop talking. One memory unraveled another like a wool sweater caught on a nail.

"Then again, it's not like Paul was exactly consistent in that respect, either. Each time I found myself debating, "do I listen to what he says or watch what he does?" he would grab the equation and turn it on its head. He'd *do* something so considerate or sweet or loving, like when it was time for both of us to resign for another tour of duty. I wanted to ask for a written guarantee that Paul and I would always be transferred together—he talked me out of it. He sat me down and explained, logically, rationally, sensibly that when you floated a condition like that, you had to be prepared to fold cards and walk if negotiations didn't go your way. Since I had no serious intention of leaving the Air Force, I had nothing to bluff with, and in the end, I'd only lose face. It was too big of a risk for too small of a payoff."

Anne remembered, "He said that so calmly. I wanted to know, didn't he care we might be sent to separate bases? We could live apart for years. But he never answered. He acted like it didn't matter to him in the slightest. Living with me, living without me—it was the same to him. Then, a year later, I found out that he'd made no-separation a condition for his reenlistment. Do you have any idea the gamble he took? If they said no, someone with Paul's dignity would have had no option except quitting. He risked his entire career for me. But when I asked him about it, he dismissed it. 'Don't take it personally,' he said. 'I like my competitors where I can keep an eye on them.' How's that for words that speak louder than actions?"

"Maybe Daddy didn't want to talk about it. Just because you always want to talk about something right away, doesn't mean everybody does. Sometimes I don't feel like talking. Sometimes I want to think about what I should say first."

"The minute people stop talking, that's when problems start."

"Yeah, well, sounds like with you and Daddy problems started because of *too much* talking. Too much fighting. Jeez, Mom, why are you always so ready to fight?"

"Ah-ha!" Anne pounced. "So it seems we've found something else about your mom that drives you crazy. That's good, I'm glad you're getting it off your chest. But for the record, talking a problem out does not necessarily mean fighting it out. That's one nuance your father never appreciated."

"Okay, fine." Amelia turned away from Anne, making a show of surveying the cabin. "So, Dad's stupid, and I'm stupid, too. Now can we stop this?"

Anne's heart broke. Every maternal instinct she ever nurtured screamed for her to quit torturing her child this way. But the Air Force officer schooled in survival couldn't help noticing that not only was her resentment keeping Amelia awake, it was also raising her body temperature to the point where she wasn't shivering nearly as much as a few moments earlier.

"No, we can't stop. I want to hear what you think about—"

"How come you never bug Lyle like this?" Amelia rotated her head back and cut Anne off midthought, tone accusatory.

"Lyle?" It was the first time his name had come up.

"You and Lyle never fight. Not like you and dad did."

She had a point.

"W-Well," Anne stammered, "Your father was a stimulating person to talk to. He's brilliant. He knows the most amazing things. He knows the minimum NoPT transition altitude for every approach, he's fluent in

Latin, of all things. Watching his mind work is like a ring-side seat next to Leonardo da Vinci painting."

"So that's why you fought with him? Because he was smart?"

"No. Yes. Sort of." Anne offered, "Maybe I did it because making up with Paul was almost as much fun as arguing with him."

"Huh?"

Anne smiled. "I'll tell you when you're older. You want to know why Lyle and I don't argue as much as Paul and I did? It's because Lyle never tries to govern my life. He's not constantly giving me orders, telling me I should not fly this mission or that one because its too dangerous."

"Dad worried about you. He didn't want you getting hurt."

"He didn't think I was up to the job, that's what he thought."

"I worry about you sometimes. Whenever you fly far away, like Europe and stuff, I worry that something will go wrong."

"Amelia, that's silly. Don't you think I'm a good pilot?"

"You're the best."

"Well, worrying about somebody means you don't think they're smart enough to do their job. It's rather insulting, actually."

"Don't you ever worry?"

"I'll tell you about the one time I worried. Right after I moved to Edwards, your father was scheduled to take up a new F-15. He left at dawn, so I was home when I heard the Klaxon go off. It kept screaming and screaming, so I knew it wasn't a test. A plane had really gone down. I looked out the window, saw giant plumes of black smoke at the end of the runway, and, for a moment, I was sure it'd been Paul who crashed. I was being irrational, but I got this sinking feeling. Of course, every pilot knows, soon as that Klaxon goes off, it's time to call home and reassure he wasn't the one who augured. So I blew off my shift, and waited. Longest hour of my life. You can't imagine the horrors that scrambled around my mind. But, know what? It didn't do anybody any good. Say Paul had been the one who was hurt; my suffering wouldn't have helped him. And if your dad knew that I, even for a second, judged him capable of crashing, can you imagine how disappointed he'd have felt?''

"But even great pilots, stuff happens, doesn't it? Like my grandfather Gaasbeck was a terrific pilot, everybody says so, but he got shot down and he died. That could happen to you.''

"Amelia, I am not going to die. That's Paul talking.''

"It is not!'' Amelia stomped the heel of her boot against the floor. "Dad doesn't tell me what to say.''

"Granted. Paul only tells everyone what to *do*.''

"At least Dad doesn't keep asking me and asking me and asking me to tell him how I feel, then when I tell him, he doesn't say how it's wrong and I shouldn't feel that way.''

"What are you talking about, Ace?''

"You do it all the time. You told me the story yourself about how you kept asking Dad to tell you why he wasn't all jumping up and down about your making captain, then, when he finally told you the truth, you know, about how he really felt and everything, you got angry at him and said he was wrong to feel that way.''

Anne had never been hit by a lead pipe against the skull. So to be fair, she had no basis for comparison. All she knew was, the minute Amelia's words sunk in, every drop of blood in her body shot from Anne's head to her belly like a nest of snakes simultaneously leaping on a single prey. Her breath froze in her throat, chilling into a nugget that lodged just out of reach of her tongue, refusing to move up or down. Her head throbbed, cognizance proving somehow more painful than her earlier collision with the instrument panel.

"Mom?" Amelia watched all color drain from Anne's face, the dark circles under her eyes growing against a background of pallid cheeks and ashen lips. "I'm sorry. I didn't mean it. Are you mad at me about what I said?"

Anne heard her child's voice through a cavernous filter, the deadly gust outside her smashed cockpit a mere breeze compared to the shrill zephyr inside her head.

"No, Ace." She wondered how it happened that her barely awake daughter had managed to realize a truth that Anne, with her Academy diploma, her Master's in aeronautical engineering, and her supposedly gifted I.Q. had totally, thoroughly, and completely missed. "I'm not mad about what you said. I'm mad about what I *did.*"

And the recognition devastated her.

She sensed the last ounce of combat draining out of her, along with her energy. She felt hollow, bloodless, her veins deflating like stabbed balloons. Every physical pang she'd managed to ignore by distracting herself with verbal sparring, now reared up; baring its teeth, growling, sniffing for a vulnerability. Exhausted, her skin itched like poison ivy. Her fingers were too frozen for Anne to rub her eyes, and the wind had dried her corneas to such a painful extent that rapid blinking only produced a sensation akin to sandpaper scouring her pupils.

She could no longer scrounge the strength to raise her head or move her mouth. All she wanted was to curl up in a ball, close her eyes, and drift off inside a sleep so deep, the Blue Angels roaring overhead wouldn't be enough to rouse her.

After a day and night of non-stop talking, her throat finally locked, the walls sticking to each other like an airless cellophane bag. Anne could neither inhale or exhale. She couldn't even cough to try and clear it. She was simply too beat. Or maybe beaten was the more appropriate word. She was beaten.

Nevertheless, Anne fought her body's breakdown, struggling to stay conscious not for her sake but for Amelia's.

Despite the medium-to-large-sized elephant pressing his tree-trunk of a hind leg along the back of her neck, Anne grit her teeth and raised her head, holding back nausea and trying to isolate the drone in her head from another, more familiar, noise.

The whir of a helicopter, most likely an Apache, as it winged over—and away—from their crash site.

# ═══ 12 ═══

In 1986, in retaliation for a Libyan attack on a Berlin disco, President Reagan ordered the bombing of Tripoli and Benghazi. And for the first time in history, the flight crews assigned to refuel those bombers in midair would finally include women. Among those selected for deployment was Captain Anne Gaasbeck.

A year earlier, Anne, thrilled by her chance to make history, would have come running into their apartment, blurting the news to an unprepared Paul and demanding enthusiasm on the spot. But she knew better this time around. So Anne took a moment outside her front door, deflating her mood. She counted slowly to twenty, then figured that wasn't enough and started again, going up to thirty. Only when she felt properly sedate, did Anne dare step inside. She hung up her coat, cap, and purse in the hall closet, and moved into the living room, stopping with a start at the sight of their dining table covered with a sapphire cloth and set with candles, two wine glasses, and neatly aligned silverware. Paul stood in the kitchen doorway, hands behind his back as if waiting for a parade-review.

She pointed to the table, eyebrows raised questioningly. Hope swelled in Anne's subconscious like an eardrum set to burst at five thousand feet, but she didn't dare voice it.

Paul explained, "You're going to Libya."

"I know." She couldn't look at him as she inquired, "And that doesn't . . . bother you?"

Silence. Barely a second on the clock, and yet a lifetime.

"No," Paul said with conviction. "No. This is a fantastic opportunity. One for the history books. I—I'm happy for you."

Anne had been dreaming of hearing him say those words for over a year. She wanted it so badly, she'd fantasized a hundred various circumstances for the event, and tried out a dozen responses. She imagined she'd be touched, and thrilled, and maybe even a tiny bit teary-eyed. But the last sensation Anne ever rhapsodized she'd be feeling was an overwhelming urge to laugh.

He was just trying so gosh-darn hard. His body was rigid from the effort, eyes fixed on a dot exactly one inch above Anne's head, both marble cheeks taut, as if aiming a pistol at the mouth to keep it from uttering anything short of the party line. Paul might have been the dictionary definition of the word "grim." Except that Anne thought he'd never looked . . . cuter.

All that intensity, all that discipline, all that effort. And all of it for her benefit. His behavior was so sweet, it made Anne want to giggle in delight. Though she doubted he'd appreciate her gesture. So Anne did her best to stifle the impulse. She clamped shut her jaw, sucking in oxygen through her nose until it paralyzed the muscles of her face, and tried to entertain serious thoughts.

But still, the need to giggle proved overpowering. Especially when Anne, despite both their best efforts, inadvertently made eye-contact with Paul, and saw that he too realized just how carefully each one was tiptoeing around the other's sore spots.

Laughter sprayed past Anne's lips despite her hasty attempt to stop it by plastering a hand across her mouth. It hit the air like fumes from an exhaust pipe, lingering like a misshapen cloud.

And then a miracle happened. Paul threw his head back and laughed. Not a polite chortle or a distasteful snicker, but a red-blooded, all-American laugh that in the stretch of a moment, erased every tense line on Paul's face. Paul laughed!

"My God." He wiped the corner of his eye with the back of his wrist. "We're really something, aren't we? Can't either one of us do anything without taking it to the extreme? I suppose now we'll start arguing who was more gracious, me for making the overture or you for accepting it."

"You know what?"—she lifted a linen napkin from the table and waved it like a white flag of surrender, sitting down and draping it neatly across her lap—"I vote we declare this particular match a draw, and just move on."

"Excellent suggestion, Captain." Paul sat across from Anne, uncorking a bottle of wine and moving to fill her glass. "In fact, I propose a toast. To Anne Gaasbeck, the first woman to pilot non-combat aircraft in support of a military action—not counting the few who helped out during the Grenada invasion, but they were Army helicopter pilots, so it's not as if they could truly fly, anyway."

Anne laughed appreciatively at the toast and at the sentiment it expressed but covered her glass with one hand before Paul could pour. She reminded, "I've got a mission to fly tomorrow."

They ate dinner debating the Aardvark F-111 fighter

bomber versus the B-52 and the controversial art of BDA, Bomb Damage Assessment. Later Paul cleared the table while Anne packed her garment bag for the next day's departure. He came into the bedroom as she laid out her uniform, inspecting each crease, searching for wrinkles. Paul stepped up behind her and slipped his arms around Anne's shoulders. His hands dipped to pluck the buttons of her blouse.

"You can finish packing, later," Paul suggested.

Back to him, Anne leaned against Paul's chest, smiling. There was something so solid about him, something so confident and serene and masculine. Anne only had to think of him, to remember what it felt like to be in his presence, and she felt safe, no matter what the circumstances. "Just a couple more things . . ."

"Okay," Paul agreed, while calmly proceeding with the unbuttoning. He kissed the inside of her ear, his tongue easily locating every sensitive, vulnerable spot.

Anne pulled away, unconvincingly. "Dirty trick, Gaasbeck."

"If you cooperate, we can make it a lot dirtier." He moved to nibble the cleft between her shoulder and neck.

Her uniform slid through her fingers, crumpling to the floor in an unceremonial heap as Paul lifted her off the floor and carried her toward their bed. Anne pretended to fight, tapping her palms against his chest until the playful raps became caresses. Paul set Anne down, kneeling over her, one leg on the floor, weight balanced on the other knee between her thighs.

Anne, surrendering even the pretense of resistance, reached for his belt buckle, laughing, "All right, Captain, you win."

"I always do."

They made love quickly and explosively—the first time. The second time, both moved with exquisite care and stealth, prolonging every sensation until the other cried out "uncle." The third time, they simply clung to each other, trying to simultaneously exist in all past, present, and future tenses.

"Paul?"

"Hm?" He lay on his back, eyes closed, his right wrist resting along his forehead. Tiny rivulets of sweat trickled down the sides of his chest, leaving navy polka dots on the azure bedsheets.

"Paul . . ." Anne crawled on top of him, elbow balancing against his sternum, chin tickling the base of his throat. She pressed one finger to his lips. He kissed it without opening either eye. "Are you listening to me?"

"Uh-hm."

"I've got a surprise for you." Her tongue dabbed at a drop of sweat beneath his Adam's apple. Paul smiled.

"I was going to wait and tell you when I got back from Libya, but you were so great in how you reacted to everything."

"My pleasure."

"Paul, I'm pregnant."

His eyes opened slowly, like a reluctant garage. "You're . . ." His arm slid off his face. He pushed himself up to a sitting position, causing Anne to slip downward along his chest.

"West Germany," she reminded, as if that was a trip he could ever forget. "The flight home."

"But . . . You have a prescription."

"I do. I did. But I crossed ten time zones that day. I must have lost count somewhere over the Atlantic."

"How long have you known?"

"Well, I've had my suspicions for over week, but the official diagnosis came yesterday. I know how you like things official."

"You knew you were pregnant yesterday, and you still accepted the Libya assignment?"

"It's only been seven weeks, I can still fit in a cockpit."

"That's not the issue." Paul swung his legs over the side of the bed, standing up and reaching for his robe. "The issue is you accepted an assignment, an immensely important assignment, knowing you would not be in adequate physical condition to carry it out."

Her mouth dropped open. Anne sat up, allowing her blanket to slip and gather at her waist. "I'm not sick, Paul. I'm pregnant. I happen to be in fabulous condition. The doctor said so."

"Which doctor?" He crossed his arms, sliding into debriefing mode with eerie ease. "Which doctor did you go see? Major Unger, here at the base?"

"Well, no. Actually, I made an appointment in town."

"And why was that?"

Anne saw where he was leading and tried her best to sidestep the trap. "Because, I didn't want our news to be all over the base by dinner-time. I wanted to tell you first."

"Bullshit, Annie. You just didn't want Major Unger doing his duty and reporting your condition to Colonel Elbe. You knew if the truth came out, Libya would be out of the question."

"It isn't fair," Anne insisted. "I'm perfectly fine. I feel great, not even a little bit nauseous or dizzy."

"And have you given any thought to what might happen if this nausea and dizziness that you don't yet feel should suddenly makes its appearance say, in the middle of a bomber refueling somewhere over a war zone in North Africa? You'd really risk the safety of your crew, not to mention the success of our entire mission, just so that your name could go down in the history books?"

"You know I wouldn't. If I believed for one minute that my flying would endanger the baby, I'd scratch my name off the list myself. But, there's no reason to think that. It's a non-combat position. And anybody, man or woman, could, all of a sudden, feel nauseous or dizzy while flying. No one can anticipate that. This rule the military had about grounding pregnant women, it's totally arbitrary."

"Nevertheless, it is exquisitely specific. Pregnant women are not to be assigned to duties in which nausea, easy fatigue, sudden lightheadedness, or loss of consciousness would be hazardous to her or anyone else. And that includes driving, diving, operating large machinery, and, guess what, Annie?—flying."

Paul padded barefoot toward the bedroom door.

"Where are you going?" Anne asked, pleading with him. "You know how much this means to me. I've waited my whole life for this chance. And not just me. If I'm scratched from this flight because I'm pregnant— pregnant, of all things—what kind of damage will that do to women pilots in general?"

Anne reached for him, fingers outstretched, her face so open, so vulnerable, so earnest, it nearly succeeded in persuading every muscle fiber of his being to sweep her into his arms. She brushed his cheek with the back of her hand, her warm breath rustling the still damp hairs across his chest.

"Come on, Paul. Please. Just do this one thing for me." She peered up at him, smiling, coy, playful. "After all, it's not like I got into this predicament all by myself."

Paul jerked away from her caress, startling Anne into dropping her hand. Damn, but she'd almost had him. She'd almost convinced him. For a moment there, Paul'd actually felt himself weighing the possibility of forgetting the whole thing.

He took a step back, turning and marching purposefully down the hall toward the phone in the living room.

"Paul, please!" The pain in her voice stabbed him in the back like a javelin. A grenade exploded inside his chest. "I promise, I'll voluntarily ground myself right after this flight."

He kept walking, forbidding himself to stop, knowing that if he did, he'd never find enough courage to start again.

"Damn you, Paul, the least you can do is answer me. The least you can do is look at me!"

He picked up the receiver, dialing Colonel Elbe's number from memory, locking his gaze on each number pressed.

Behind him, Anne slammed shut the bedroom door.

Paul completed his call in a matter of minutes, promising to convey the Colonel's congratulations to Anne and, bracing himself, returned to their bedroom.

Still nude, Anne stood at their closet's threshold, furiously ripping her clothes out of her garment bag and tossing them back on the hangers. She heard him enter, and snapped, "No wonder you told me not to bother packing."

Paul didn't reply. Instead, he kept his distance, silently watching the graceful curve of her back as it swiveled first this way, then that. Paul's eyes leisurely stroked her body, settling curiously on the flat and toned muscle covering her abdomen. In all this drama over who could fly where and why and why not, both had forgotten the larger issue. They were going to have a baby.

Paul racked his brain for just the right word, just the right phrase to commemorate the momentous occasion. The one time he was ready and willing and downright dying to express his emotions in an unprecedented eruption of those proverbial streamers and balloons, Anne was refusing to so much as look at him.

He started to tell her that this was silly, that the personal news she'd revealed to him that evening was so much more important than any national news she may have aspired to make by piloting her tanker in Libya, when Anne turned to face him, eyes blazing so much freon, they could have submitted their room for consideration as a Winter Olympics site. She demanded, "And just who is Colonel Elbe going to get to take my place on such short notice?"

Paul cleared his throat. "Actually . . ."

"Not Maddelone, I hope. Because Maddelone can't get his plane outside without taking half a hangar with him."

"Actually," Paul repeated. "I'm going to do it."

Anne's chin dropped, stealing the lower half of her face with it. "You? But you're a fighter pilot. You don't do refueling."

"I know how."

"Of course, you know how. I never said you didn't know how." Anne turned both of her palms up. "Why would you, though?"

"You said it. We gave the Colonel extremely short notice. I felt, since we're both responsible for his predicament, the least I could do was offer to step in and help out in your place."

"The high-and-mighty Paul Gaasbeck lowering himself to flying a tanker? What did you once call them, airborne gas stations?"

"This is an emergency situation."

Anne clicked her nails against her teeth. "There's got to be more to it than that."

"Think what you want, Annie, I'm telling you—"

"You didn't get selected to do the actual bombings." Her eyes gleamed as, in Anne's mind at least, all the pieces finally clicked into place. "That's it, isn't it?"

"What's it?"

"You always tell me how frustrating it is, spending day after day practicing mock combat, knowing you might never get a chance to try out your skills in actual warfare. You would have loved going to Libya as a bomber. But they didn't send your unit. So this, my deployment, it's the next best thing, isn't it? Good God, Paul. Years out of the Academy, the Commander's Trophy long decided, both of us captains, and you're still fighting me for an imaginary lead. You couldn't stand the idea of my logging combat experience first."

"That's what you think?" Paul raised both arms in surrender, walking around the bed and pulling back the covers from his side. "Fine. You go right on thinking it, then."

"Tell me I'm wrong, Paul." In a heartbeat, her voice changed from accusatory to pleading. Anne clasped her hands together as if in prayer, rubbing her chin against her knuckles.

He punched his pillow, propping it under his head, and lay down on his back. "Okay. You're wrong."

"Damn you." She crawled in next to him, leaning forward until her face hovered mere inches above his. "Why can't you just be straight with me for once? Tell me what's really going on here."

There was so much Paul wanted to tell her, he honestly did not know where to begin. He only knew that, no matter where their talk started, it could lead to just one conclusion. If he allowed Annie to drive so much as a single chink through his armor, if he allowed himself to experience even one fraction of the sensations presently coursing through him, Paul had no doubt that, come the next day, he would be tossing aside his principles, his training, and, worst of all, his common sense, all in the name of making Anne smile again.

Just like the Commander's Trophy.

So rather than telling her how excited he was about the baby, how he could not wait to return from Libya so they could celebrate the news in style, or how his grounding of her really and truly had nothing to do with not wanting Anne to make history and everything to do with his refusal to let her control him like this, he rolled onto his side, away from Anne, and flicked off the light, yawning. "Can we talk about this later? I've got a long day tomorrow."

She woke up at the same time as Paul did the next morning, and proceeded to follow his every move with her eyes, watching him tiptoe from the bathroom to the dresser to the closet. And yet all during that period, Anne didn't say a word. Paul had to admit, he found the phenomenon more than a touch disconcerting.

He felt compelled to exaggerate his movements, almost as if he were acting in a play, performing the part of Captain Paul Gaasbeck packing, and he wanted his actions made perfectly clear even to the very back row. After a lifetime of military schools and military service, Paul was no stranger to being viewed and reviewed. Still, it was a most self-conscious way to start the day in your own home.

The sound of her steady breathing congested the room, sticking to him like leftover strips of cotton candy. Paul couldn't take a step without peeking at Anne out the corner of his eye, gauging her reaction. The problem was, she didn't seem to have any.

Not that Paul was totally blind to the irony of the situation. But, honestly, how annoying was it to sense yourself being judged, and yet have no clue of what the final verdict might be? The lady was playing hardball, and despite his annoyance, Paul had to give her credit. For Anne to sit silently for almost a half hour was a monumental achievement. Evidently, she was a great deal more upset than Paul had previously thought.

He hated to leave with matters so unsettled between them. Nevertheless, Paul only had minutes before he was scheduled to report for duty, familiarize himself with an aircraft he hadn't flown in years, and prepare to fly into enemy territory. His mind was brimming with a million details, and in all fairness, Paul knew he wouldn't be able to give Anne, or their altercation, the sort of attention both deserved. Besides, Paul hadn't had adequate time to prepare his side of the argument in a clear, concise manner. Thus, he had no intention of starting something which he had neither the time, nor the resources, presently, to finish.

So, instead of giving in to his urge to clear the air before leaving, Paul finished packing, knowing that by choosing to defray having this out until he could focus his attention solely on Annie, he had also condemned himself to an indefinite period of dwelling on it. But, that couldn't be helped. Paul had a duty to do, and duty always came before personal needs. First, last, and always, he was an Air Force officer. He was a soldier.

Dressed to go, he paused by her side of the bed, looking down at Anne. He expected her to avoid his gaze, but instead she met it head-on, eyes so filled with hurt and betrayal, it was all Paul could do to keep from turning away.

She didn't understand. She truly didn't understand why he had done this. She thought it was personal. She thought he was out to get her. She thought he was jealous. But, most of all, she didn't understand how Paul could profess his love for her with one breath and, in the next, take away her heart's desire.

Paul ached to explain, but such delicate definitions required exactly the right words, and he was too much of a perfectionist to burden her with anything less than his best attempt. Anything less than his best attempt would be an insult to his feelings for Anne.

And so he said nothing. Despite Anne's visible need to hear him say something, anything, before he left, Paul said nothing.

He bowed at the waist, tenderly smoothed Anne's hair from her face, and gently kissed her on the forehead. Paul rested his palm along her stomach, and bowing lower, kissed that, too.

Neither one of them said the word "good-bye."

In retrospect, Captain Paul Gaasbeck had only his meticulous logs and various newspaper accounts to confirm that the 1986 U.S. bombing of Libya had, in fact, been successfully executed.

Personally, he recalled very little of it since, for the bulk of the operation, his mind had been squarely on something else. If his superiors knew how little attention he was paying, they surely would have had basis for a court-martial. Hell, Paul was seriously considering turning himself in for one, at the end of the mission.

Because for weeks all Paul could think about was how to make Anne see that he had done nothing wrong on either a professional or personal level. He played out numerous conversations in his head, taking both sides of the argument, brutally ferreting out his weak points. He anticipated everything she could possibly say, plotting his rebuttal. Even as Paul flew to Washington for debriefing after the mission, one part of his mind was or-

ganizing his presentation, the another was engaged in yet
another imaginary chat with Anne.

As the only test and fighter pilot to view the bombing
from a unique, non-combat perspective, Paul was ordered to Washington for a series of discussions with Pen-
tagon officials and others involved in strategic planning.
By the time he finally got his orders to go home, over a
month and a half had passed.

He hadn't called Anne during the time he was away.
There was no point, really. She had access to information
about whether the bombing had been successful—not
that she ever worried about him, anyway; something
about how her worrying would mean she thought he was
an incompetent pilot. And, beyond that, he really had
nothing to say to her over the phone. The conversations
Paul spent weeks mapping out required the two of them
to meet face-to-face.

He got back to Texas in the middle of the day while
Anne was still at work. Paul figured he could have called
ahead to say that he was coming, but what the hell, a
few more hours of getting his thoughts together wouldn't
do any harm. Besides, there was much to be said for the
element of surprise.

He hung up his garment bag neatly in the hall closet,
then, with a few hours still left before Anne came home,
stripped off his clothes and stepped into the shower. He
set the single-blast spray to pound against his skull, tilted
his head, and let it have a shot at the tightly wound knots
in his neck and shoulders. Anne's soap was the only bar
left on the tray. He picked it up and brought it to his
face, inhaling deeply. Baby powder. Baby powder and
roses. No, baby powder, roses, and the aroma of Anne's
skin. Paul rubbed his hands together, worked up a lather,
closed his eyes and scrubbed his face until the smell
seeped into his every pore.

"Is this a private shower, or can anyone join?"

Paul's eyes sprung open.

Anne was standing right in front of him, dressed in that translucent satin robe that always made Paul yearn to rip it off her. She'd let her hair grow out, probably in retaliation for being banished to a desk job, and the warm moisture in the air had curled it ever so slightly at the edges. That same moisture also damply stuck Anne's robe to her body, stressing each curve, from the protrusions of her nipples to the newly noticeable swelling between her hip bones.

Paul blinked and, with the back of his wrist, wiped the soap from his eyes. This wasn't at all how he'd imagined their reunion. In all the debates he and Anne had convened inside his head, he was pretty sure both of them had been fully clothed.

Nevertheless, he'd been preparing for this moment for over a month, and, come what may, he was determined to say his piece.

"Annie." Paul reached up to twist the nozzle from spraying water directly into his mouth.

She smiled, loosening the sash of her robe and letting it fall open, revealing the rosy cleft between her breasts, drawing Paul's gaze downward.

He cleared his throat, inhaling more water than he expelled. "I've been thinking. About what we were discussing before I left."

"Uh-ha." Anne brushed the robe off her shoulders, kicking it aside as soon as it hit the floor.

"You see, I really think you misunderstood why I acted . . ."

She stepped over the bathtub edge, hanging onto Paul's arm for balance, and he instinctively steadied her, grasping both of Anne's elbows, touching his wife for the first time in over a month.

She rubbed her palms along his chest, twirling soapy horns out of the hairs around his nipples. "Miss me, Captain?"

"I . . . of course." He wrapped his fingers around her wrists, gently pushing back her hands. "But, Annie, listen, I really think we should talk about my reasons for . . ."

She stood on her toes, kissing the soapy dimple in his chin, running her tongue under his lower lip. "Do you want to rehash old news, or would you rather show me how much you've missed me?"

"Annie." This wasn't going at all the way he'd planned. "I thought, I . . . weren't you mad at me before I left?"

"Furious." Her mouth traveled down his neck, encircling his Adam's apple in a series of swirls that left Paul barely able to breathe, much less continue talking.

"So, don't you think we should talk? You're always the one insisting that communication—"

"Paul." She dropped her arms to her sides, standing back to look him in the eye. "A month and a half ago, I was furious, sure. But that was a month and a half ago. I'm over it now. Heck, I was over it a month and a week ago. I missed you so much while you were gone. Didn't you miss"—she traced the contours of his ribs and stomach, letting her fingers wander innocently downward—"me?"

Words failed him. An unfamiliar sensation, albeit one rather quickly usurped by a considerably more pleasurable one.

"Jesus, Annie." Paul's hands, taking on a life of their own, danced down her back and around her waist, settling on the swelling of her stomach. He did some quick math. Seven weeks pregnant when he left, six weeks out of town, seven plus six . . . it equalled three months. Anne was beginning her second trimester.

She grinned up at him. ''Bet he'll start kicking any day now.''

He stroked the taut flesh. ''That's amazing.''

''So is this.'' Her palms cradled his erection, arousing Paul into that blissful, single-minded state where everything was clear, and simple, and within his reach.

He clasped her buttocks, lifting her off the floor and leaning her against the beige tile wall. Anne wrapped her legs around his waist, nuzzling her cheek along his neck, and gasped as Paul slowly impaled himself inside her. She dug her nails into his shoulders. The muscles pulsing just beneath his skin were like iron. She felt them tighten and catch as he rocked within her, the steaming water beating rhythmically down both their bodies.

He had always been gentle with her, but now, the baby between them, there was an additional tenderness to Paul's lovemaking. He shifted his grasp, hands beneath her thighs, supporting her weight with a new reverence, the sweetness of which brought tears to her eyes. She cried out his name, not from any conscious knowledge of how much he loved to hear it but because it was the truest way to articulate her joy.

Yet just before Paul sensed her body dissolving on a wave of gratifying contractions which, in turn, triggered his own pleasure, he couldn't help wondering why, when Anne wanted to talk, Paul was expected to drop everything, while his request for discussion was something to be dismissed as a mere rehash of old news.

From the beginning, Anne felt certain their baby was going to be a girl. Paul, frankly, didn't have a preference. But Anne was so adamant in her insistence that men like him always wanted boys, he figured it was easier to agree than to argue. They moved out of their apartment and into a rental house on the base, complete with a nursery, backyard, and even an authentic white picket fence.

"Suburbia, Air Force-style," Anne called it, when the pastoral quiet was disturbed by the boom of a sonic jet screaming overhead.

They inherited a crib, changing table, teddy-bear dresser, and a diaper bag of sleepers, bonnets, and booties, from a neighbor tot whose Major father had been transferred to England and didn't feel like hauling everything with him. But while average babies settled for bleak mobiles that wobbled pathetically over their heads, Paul took a month to sketch the plans, assemble the materials, and carefully construct a fully operational air corridor to run wall-to-wall, some seven feet off the ground. Paul built it using the same principles as a model train set, except that this track was made of transparent plastic strips. And instead of tiny steam engines, it featured brightly colored planes zooming in daring loop-the-loops, disappearing not inside miniature tunnels and railroad stations but ducking through fluffy cotton-ball clouds and silver tinsel representing a storm. Anne didn't know about the baby, but she found Paul's set-up utterly enchanting. She wondered if there was anything her awesome husband couldn't figure out how to do.

Paul was as determined to be a perfect dad as he was a perfect pilot, officer, and athlete. Before buying any books, he conducted a survey on which ones were worthwhile, compiled a list, and, when two titles proved unavailable at their bookstore, ordered them from the publisher. He read each one, took notes, then typed a masterlist, complete with sub-headings, cross references, and footnotes.

Anne, at first, expected Paul to try dictating her every move. But she was pleasantly surprised to discover how respectful he was of the fact that, in the end, she was the one pregnant—not him. He went weekly to the PX and bought all the recommended food—fruit, milk, iron-rich vegetables, vitamins—but he never insisted that Anne eat them. He simply placed them in the refrigerator and let Anne decide for herself. A decade later, she would judge his actions just as manipulative and controlling as if Paul had jammed the nutritional supplements down her throat. But, at the time, she found them uncharacteristically considerate and unspeakably sweet.

He raised no objection when Anne, after consulting her doctor, continued taking her morning jog, only offering that if Anne felt tired, to call him and he would drive out and fetch her. He also didn't protest when Anne announced she'd decided on natural childbirth, no drugs of any kind.

"I want the entire experience, from beginning to end."

"Personally," Paul said, "if I were squeezing a whole, living, breathing human being out of my body, I'd want all the painkiller medical science has to offer. But, it's up to you."

One week before the baby was due, Anne was still running her standard route of seven miles every morning. Instead of going to the track like Paul, she jogged around the base, taking a different route each day in order to keep things interesting. For obvious reasons, her workout now took longer than Paul's, so he got into the habit of starting breakfast while waiting for her to come home.

On Thursday, Anne used the back door, jogging straight into the kitchen, and reaching inside their refrigerator for a container of chilled orange juice. Paul stood at the stove, scrambling eggs and slicing tomatoes to toss into the mix. He turned his head and kissed Anne as she came in, asking, "How was your run?"

"Good." She gulped down the juice and tossed the empty quart in the trash, grinning when it bounced off the rim and went in. "Oh, by the way, I had my first contraction an hour ago, then three more on the way home."

Paul's knife paused in midchop. "But you kept running?"

"Well, I'd already gone two miles one way, I had to run back."

Resolved not to take over and dominate an event that, in his mind, was about Anne's comfort, not his, Paul swallowed the impulse to give an order and, instead, inquired, "Do you think we should go to the hospital?"

"Yeah. I think maybe we should."

She had another contraction in the car, arching her back as if straining to squeeze the pain from her body like paste from a tube. Steering with his left hand, Paul offered Anne his right one, and she clenched it gratefully, leaving crimson, crescent imprints in the soft flesh just below his thumb.

"Well," Anne decreed, once the tremor had passed. "That was unpleasant."

He stroked the back of her palm. "Are you going to be okay?"

"I don't know." No fear in her voice, just statement of fact, along with sincere curiosity. "I can't wait to find out, though."

He shook his head, half in wonder, half in admiration. "This whole thing—it's all an adventure to you."

She squeezed Paul's hand. "You're going to be a great daddy."

She'd said so on numerous occasions, but somehow

hearing her reiterate that fact under these circumstances touched Paul deeper than ever before. "You really think so?"

"The best. With you for a father, our baby's going to know she's loved and thought about every minute of every day. She'll never worry that we might forget and accidently leave her behind."

Until that moment, Paul had never heard so much as a hint from Anne that growing up on a rotating series of roller coasters had been anything save the Happiest Place on Earth. He was tempted to pursue the topic. But it didn't exactly seem like the right time.

So, instead, Paul simply brought Anne's hand to his lips and kissed the knuckle beneath her wedding ring. "No. She will never have to worry about that." It was on the tip of his tongue to add, "Neither will you." But he couldn't be sure how Anne might react and, in the interest of not upsetting her, stayed silent.

At the base hospital, Anne's doctor, Major Unger, confirmed that she was indeed in labor and recommended checking in. They were assigned a private room in the north corner from which, if you peered into the distance, you could see the fighters' runways. The nurse helping Anne settle in, spotted Paul, and inquired if he'd be staying to help Anne with her breathing.

"I've been breathing by myself for twenty-five years," Anne said. "I think I've got the hang of it."

But Paul did stay. As Anne's contractions grew stronger and closer together, he stayed, letting her squeeze his hand until her nails sliced his palm, helping her to shift positions, rubbing her back, getting her cups of ice chips, holding them up against Anne's lips even as his own fingers numbed. And discounting their fights at the Academy, Paul calculated that he talked more to Anne in the hours before she gave birth than in all three preceding years of their marriage. He told her about his squadron, about Libya, about the months he'd spent teaching in Germany. He reminisced about his test-piloting days at Edwards, about the military boarding school he'd attended from grades six to twelve, about his childhood on the grounds of the Air Force Academy. Anything he thought might help keep Anne's mind from the pain.

He said, "I got tired of being the youngest wherever I went. At school, they sent me to advanced placement classes and put me on the varsity teams. Not only was I the youngest, but I was also the smallest. When I came home for breaks, the only guys to hang out with were Academy cadets, and they were older than me, too."

Eyes shut, resting in anticipation of the next onslaught, Anne murmured, "I notice you didn't say they were smarter than you."

"Now isn't the time for me to start lying to you, Annie."

Despite her weariness, Anne opened her eyes long enough to reward him with a smile.

"When I was sixteen, eighteen-year-old cadets counted the gap between them and me in dog years. They let me hang around because I was useful during a pickup basketball or touch football game. But they also made sure I knew my place. High school, my junior year, the only thing I wanted was to impress those guys."

"And I bet you made a plan."

"Several."

"And each of them was impeccably thought out and flawless."

"Quite. Unfortunately, I never got the chance to implement a one. Winter break, these cadets asked me to go rock climbing. I'd never tried it, but I figured anything they could do, I could do.''

''Better?''

''That was the general idea, yes.''

Sensing the advent of another contraction, Anne forced herself to relax, reaching for his hand and whispering, ''I knew there was a reason I loved you.''

Uncomfortably impotent in the face of her gamely engaging this new, fiercer offensive, Paul talked faster. ''Halfway up the side of the cliff, I'm hit with an idea. Damn all safety rules. I'll show these guys how tough I am. I'll scale the rock without any gear!''

Anne gasped, not in pain, as it had temporarily subsided, but in shock. ''You? You actually thought, damn all safety rules?''

Paul looked down at Anne's hand lying in his and massaged her palm, confessing, ''I slipped. This one guy lunged to grab me. He caught my arm. He also slammed his forehead against the rocks and knocked himself out for two days.''

Anne's tongue darted to dab her upper lip. ''Wait a minute. Your mother told me . . . was this the same time when you carried an unconscious guy on your back to the Academy infirmary and ripped two of your vertebrae out of alignment?''

''Same day.''

''You saved that cadet's life. If you'd waited for someone to find a phone and call an ambulance, he would have died.''

''So what? His injury was my fault to begin with. But to this day nobody knows that. Nobody knows I deliberately discarded my gear. They think it was an accident.'' Paul kissed Anne's palm. ''You're the first person I've ever told.''

She embraced the honor, suggesting, ''Maybe we

should do this more often." Another contraction hit Anne from behind, starting at the base of her spine, and she groaned, "Maybe not."

After fifteen hours of labor, despite Anne's best effort at courage, she could no longer swallow her whimpers. Perspiration slid down her forehead, cheeks, and neck, darkening her bangs from blond to brown. She inhaled sharply, clutching the bars along both sides of her bed, arching her back and nearly lifting herself off the mattress as though she could somehow press herself up and out of the pain. She'd gone so pale, Paul imagined he could trace the outline of every capillary underneath her skin. And still, despite Major Unger's regular checks, the baby hadn't dropped far enough down the birth canal for delivery.

Weakly, Anne tried to joke in between contractions, "I don't think she wants to come out."

Paul stroked her abdomen, feeling the tug-of-war beneath the strained-to-capacity skin. "I don't blame her. I rather like it in there, myself."

She lacked the strength to laugh now, managing only a faint smile before her body was ripped by another spasm. She bit down on her lip and clutched Paul's arm for support. She doubled over, curling nearly into a ball, and squeezed shut her eyes.

He helped Anne lay back down, kneading her shoulders and arms, smoothing drenched hair off her face, whispering encouragement.

But when Paul spotted a tear trickle from beneath her eyelid and slide down her cheek, mingling with the sweat along her collar, he knew he could no longer stand by and do nothing. Paul whispered in Anne's ear, "I'll be right back."

He couldn't tell if she'd heard him. Anne's entire body was shivering now, hands shaking, breath ragged like after a hysterical jag. "I'll take care of this."

It took her last ounce of effort to moan, "Yes."

Paul told the first nurse he saw that he wanted to speak to Major Unger immediately.

"The doctor is in a budget meeting."

"Where? His office?"

"Yes, but—"

"Thank you." Paul headed for the elevator.

He marched down the fifth-floor hall, knocking on the Major's door despite hearing several voices deep in discussion on the other side, and entered without waiting to be invited.

"Captain Gaasbeck?" The doctor looked up. "What is it?"

"I'd like you to take another look at my wife, sir."

Dr. Unger offered a condescending smile. "I assure you, Paul, if there was something wrong, my nurses—"

"I'd like you to take another look at my wife, sir," Paul repeated, leaving no doubt that, unless heeded, he was prepared to recite it indefinitely.

Another patronizing smile from Major Unger, then a shrug of the shoulders and a "What can you do? Nervous new fathers" for his colleagues. "Very well, Captain. I'll see what I can do."

In the elevator, Paul told him, "Please, give Annie something for the pain."

"She specifically asked for no drugs. Anne told me she wanted to experience every moment."

"Maybe she does. But, I don't. And since Anne is in no shape to be making decisions for herself right now, I'm telling you: give her something for the pain."

Dr. Unger chuckled, "I've often thought I'd be a rich man if I developed an anesthesia for expectant fathers."

But his smile faded as he walked into Anne's room

and checked the seismographic printout measuring the potency and frequency of her contractions. "I'm sorry. I didn't realize—I'd have been here sooner. I didn't realize she'd been in this much pain for so long. Most women would have begun screaming hours ago. With your permission, I'll schedule an immediate caesarean section."

"Do it."

A nurse brought Paul a mask and a scrub suit so he could be in the room for Anne's surgery. He followed her gurney down the hall, up in the elevator, and into the operating theater. He stroked her cheek, reassuring her that the pain would be over soon, while a pair of orderlies transferred her off the gurney and onto the operating table.

She tried nodding her head in response to his words but only managed to flutter her eyelashes. When a nurse—too roughly in Paul's opinion—attempted to roll Anne onto her side, Paul shoved her hands away and gently did it himself. The lieutenant nurse opened her mouth to protest his breach of etiquette, spied the expression in Paul's eyes, and thought better of it. Vigilantly, Paul watched another nurse dab alcohol along Anne's spine, followed by an anesthesiologist painstakingly inserting a needle between two of Anne's vertebrae, to numb her from the waist down. Anne nearly swallowed both of her lips from the strain of refusing to make a sound as the needle pierced her skin, drilling deep into her back.

Anne's courage overwhelmed Paul. When she opened her eyes and searched for him, Paul locked his gaze with hers, straining to suck some fraction of her misery inside himself and lessen her distress.

As the nurse bore her syringe deeper into Annie's back, Paul saw her expression change. Minutes after the fact, he would begin to rationalize and science away exactly what had happened to him—to them—in that brief instinct. All he knew was, as soon as her spinal started flowing through the needle and her eyes gripped his, Paul felt a tightening in his chest that wrenched his breath away. His heart sped into double time and his head spun. Yet Paul knew that it wasn't he who was feeling that way. It was Anne.

Even before the machines began screeching their warning, Paul grabbed the nurse's arm, stopping her from injecting further. "No. There's something wrong."

The nurse looked at Paul as if he were the moron of all time.

Then the first machine screamed. On the monitor above Anne's head, her blood pressure plummeted like mercury during a cold snap. Her face drained blue, breaths sputtering in hyperventilated gasps. Major Unger dropped the tray of instruments he'd been examining in preparation for surgery and pushed Paul out of the way to evaluate the situation. He barked out a series of orders all of which meant nothing to Paul, until he shouted for the crash cart.

Paul pressed against the operating table as if keeping Anne in his sights could somehow prevent what was happening. But Major Unger didn't even glance in his direction as he commanded the first nurse, "Escort Captain Gaasbeck to the waiting room."

"The hell I will." Paul strained for a look at Anne, but she had disappeared behind a fortified wall of blue scrubs. The nurse tugged on his arm. He refused to budge. "I am not going anywhere, until Anne is all right."

"Captain!" Major Unger turned, the green eyes above his mask devoid of the jocularity previously nested there.

"You are to take leave of this operating room immediately. That's an order."

He did not pace. Pacing would have been unproductive. So, for precisely seventy-four minutes, Paul sat on a hard-backed chair outside the operating room, eyes fixed on its swinging gateway.

Finally, Dr. Unger stepped through the doors, peeling off his scrub suit and tossing it in the trash can. He swung an arm around Paul's shoulder. "What do you say we take a walk up to my office?"

With impeccable politeness, Paul stepped aside. He did not raise his voice. He very reasonably asked, "Where's Annie?"

"We'll talk about it in my office."

Paul crossed his arms. "I want to see Anne."

"My office, Captain. Now."

They walked side by side in silence. Only after Major Unger had closed his office door behind him and pointed for Paul to take a seat, did he say, "I'm afraid we encountered some complications. It turns out that Anne is rather severely allergic to the spinal block most commonly employed during caesarean sections."

"Why didn't you know about this in advance?" Paul declined, with a shake of his head, a second invitation to sit. He stood, back against the door, trying to put as much distance as possible between him and the news and shifted his hands to his hips. "This doesn't make sense. Annie was in perfect health. Hell, she went running seven miles a day, every day, right up until she went into labor." His eyes narrowed. "You told her it was okay to run."

"Anne's running had nothing to do with her reaction."

"Whatever it was, you should have foreseen it. If

you'd taken proper care of her, you could have foreseen it and prevented it.''

"There are some things, Paul, that no amount of screening—''

"Where's Annie now?''

"She's in intensive care.'' He hesitated before breaking the next part to Paul. "When Anne's blood pressure dropped, her heart stopped. We got it started again, but the next twenty-four hours or so are critical to determine whether any permanent damage—''

"What floor is Intensive Care on?''

"The third. Come on, I'll walk you there.'' Dr. Unger stood up, shuffling toward the door. "By the way, Paul, congratulations. You have a baby girl.''

But Paul was already halfway down the hall, racing for the elevator. Over his shoulder, he said, "Later. Annie would never forgive me if I saw our baby before she did.''

$$=== 13 ===$$

He couldn't see her.

With the snow outside and condensation inside the windshield, Paul couldn't ferret out Anne's crash site from the icy terrain below him no matter how hard he strained. In the twenty-three hours since air-traffic control in Colorado lost radio contact with her, the *Amelia* could have drowned under so much snow, super-sensitive satellites would be hard-pressed to pinpoint the wreckage. And here Paul was, attempting to conduct the search visually. He scrubbed his elbow against the glass, struggling to clear even a peephole-sized window of visibility. But it was a futile task. Like a foggy bathroom mirror, as soon as he wiped one spot clean, his own breath concealed it again. If he tried rubbing a spot far enough away to avoid exhaling around it, then it also proved too far away to do him serious good. Like Paul explained to his few acquaintances who didn't fly, piloting a plane was similar to driving a car, only with an extra dimension, up and down added to the forward and backward. Unfortunately, when his fog-free spot proved too far away, he lost the down facet of the equation, which, under the circumstance, was the one he needed most.

An hour ago, even a half hour ago, Paul would have

cursed his lousy, rotten luck. But he had simply passed beyond that stage where comfort could be bought with a few choice words.

As Paul approached the twenty-four-hour mark, even the hope he'd ordered himself to feel during his drive from Utah to Colorado was fading with each tick of the minute hand. If Anne and Amelia were still alive, they wouldn't be for long. No food, no water, no shelter, plus whatever injuries they might have sustained in the crash guaranteed a grim outcome. There was no use pretending otherwise. If he was smart, Paul would start preparing himself now for the inevitable—

*No.*

Paul had no intention of preparing himself for anything short of locating his wife and his daughter.

Anne was too good of a pilot to let a little thing like a snow storm keep her from setting the *Amelia* down in anything but intact condition. So what if there'd been a deicing problem? Knowing Annie, she probably saw it as a new challenge. She probably—God help them all— thought it was interesting.

As for their safety on the ground, Paul was as sure that Anne would do anything necessary to shield Amelia as he was of his own actions under identical circumstances. Anne would probably laugh and label it one of his famous self-serving honors, but in fact that confidence was the highest compliment Paul felt he could bestow on another person.

Paul tore his gaze from the ground below him, glancing at his instruments and gnashing his teeth over the meager fuel remaining. Unfortunately, it wasn't like the Apache could be refilled at any Shell station. He'd have to return to the Academy where, for some reason, he suspected Sergeant Henzes would decline to turn his back on Major Gaasbeck a second time. But unless Paul headed back now, he risked crashing into these mountains himself, and that certainly wouldn't do Anne or Amelia any good.

Goose bumps prickled along Paul's flesh, triggered not by the frigid air sneaking in through slits in the cabin and snaking under his pants' legs like icy fingers, but by Paul's conviction—not that he had anything empirical to go on—that if he flew just a bit further—just a few yards, or just a few miles farther—he would find what he was looking for.

Of course, a few miles farther, and he wouldn't have the fuel necessary to make it back to the Academy. What advantage would it bring Anne and Amelia for Paul to locate them, if he had no means to deliver them home?

This was exactly like those hypotheticals Captain Zimmermann, their ethics instructor back at the Academy, was always throwing at them. It used to frustrate the hell—no—it used to *annoy* Paul, slightly, each time the captain judged one of Paul's answers wrong and then refused to tell him what the right one was supposed to be. Granted, Captain Zimmermann never actually came out and said Paul's solutions were wrong. But he never said they were right, either—which for Paul amounted to the same thing as an F scribbled in red across his paper. His only consolation came from the captain's never pronouncing any of Anne's characteristically asinine answers correct, either. But, then again, he also refused to declare any of them asinine. Faced with a hypothetical crisis mirroring the one they were enmeshed in now, Anne would probably say Paul should keep searching and believe that the required fuel would somehow magically be there for their flight home. It was the "wing and a prayer" approach. It was stupid.

Paul double-checked the remaining fuel, in case he had misread its low level the first time. Since he'd never made such a mistake before, the odds were slim that he'd done it now. Then again, over the last day, Paul had done so many things he'd never done before, maybe it was time for the anomaly to work to his advantage.

No such luck, though. He'd been right the first time. His fuel was drifting dangerously close to the point of no return.

Paul had no choice. He had to get back to the Academy.

Anne heard him.

Over the throbbing howls in her head and arm and the even more ominous lack of them in her fingers, Anne heard Paul's helicopter speed overhead. She knew it was Paul in the pilot's seat as surely as she knew that he hadn't spotted their crash site buried under multiple inches of snow, and as surely as Anne knew, by the drone of the blades, that he was heading away from them.

"Amelia," Anne tried to scream, but the gravel in her throat shifted with painful reluctance, scraping against her vocal cords like cracked eggshells. "Hear that, Ace? Your daddy's here."

"Uh-hm." Anne's words meant nothing to Amelia. She'd slumped forward, chin propped by the cushion-soft padding of her ski suit, shoulders rounded, hands dangling limply by her sides, eyes closed.

"Amelia, wake up." Anne moved to shake her, rolling over onto her knees for the first time in . . . she couldn't recall how many hours.

The dizziness that snatched Anne's eyesight out from under her and sent her toppling, like a crawling baby knocked over by a stiff wind, proved so oppressive it almost diverted Anne's attention from the fiery whip slashing along her arm as she grappled to remain upright, or at least on all fours. She clenched her eyes, opening them slowly and ordering both her pupils to look at the same thing at the same time.

"Ace." She tugged Amelia by the pant leg, dragging her child along as she stumbled and crawled toward the smashed cockpit door.

Eyes open a crack but with no understanding of what she was doing, and so far past the point of interest that she didn't even ask, Amelia followed her mother's lead, moving like a zombie.

Anne wanted to believe that she was utilizing her last ounce of strength to carry out what she knew would, without a doubt, be their final and most desperate attempt at rescue. But that wasn't true. She'd used up her last ounce of strength ages ago, provoking Amelia into life-saving fury when what Anne really longed to do was quietly pass out on the spot. She had no idea where her energy was coming from now, and as a result, feared its imminent, abrupt end.

As long as Anne could hear Paul's helicopter, she guessed that he was in visual range. But it was not a phenomenon fated to last much longer. His chopper was steadily but surely heading away from their wreckage. Their only chance lay in firing a signal flare to seize his attention before Paul flew too far away to notice it.

With two frozen, numb legs and only a single viable arm at her disposal, Anne clumsily crawled into the shattered remains of the *Amelia*'s cockpit, scaling shards of glass and wind-tossed piles of debris, even as a stray screw pierced its tip directly underneath her fingernail. She rummaged through the rubble, finally locating the green, metallic case that housed their emergency flares.

It had been crushed to near powder, the tools inside rendered useless, incapable of producing so much as a spark.

If Anne had more time, or any time, she would have responded to her discovery. She would have registered shock, or despair, or frustration, or even terror. But the only thing that mattered now was action, not emotion. The second she saw those crushed flares, Anne knew she only had one option left, and if she didn't exercise it immediately, she and her daughter would be dead within the hour.

Grabbing Amelia by the arm, Anne threw her weight against the cabin door, wedging an opening wide enough for them both to crawl through. The wind sliced across Anne as easily as if she'd been wearing nothing at all. It punched her chest and slammed out her back like a wind tunnel. Her breath froze in her mouth and nose, like cellophane coating her face. Snowflakes scorched her eyes, each one taking a bite of her exposed skin like a swarm of bees.

Amelia tumbled out after Anne, hitting the ground and sitting down hard. She drew her knees to her chin and dropped her head.

"No." Anne yanked the girl back to her feet, pulling her a safe thirty feet from the plane and leaning Amelia up against a tree. "Stay here. Do you hear me? Stay here until I come back."

"Mm." Amelia pressed her chin against the bark, ignoring the snow tumbling into her collar, and closed her eyes.

Anne slogged back to the plane, her every step leaving a six-inch-deep hollow in the snow. It was like jogging along the beach.

The crash had impaled the *Amelia*'s left wing deep in the earth, so that if Anne stood on the tips of her toes and raised her good arm until every muscle in her neck screamed for mercy, she could almost reach the wing's fuel cap. Anne swept her hand back and forth over frigid metal until she found it. She tightened her grip on the cap and twisted with all her might, palm first burning, then blistering from the friction. Digging into her jacket's pocket, Anne produced a cigarette lighter.

The funny part was, she didn't smoke. Never had. Neither did Paul. But he always carried a cigarette lighter with him—because you never knew when you might need one. Anne used to tease him and call him ever the Boy Scout. And yet in the six years since their divorce, she rarely left the house without one.

Anne pulled a handful of seat stuffing from out of her sleeve, tucked it under her arm, and attempted to ignite her lighter. Her fingers were so cold, it took Anne two tries before she could jerk her thumb fast enough to spark the wheel. On the third spin, she was about to touch the quivering blue flame to the stuffing, when a gust of wind snuffed it out.

Anne grit her teeth and went for it again, this time managing to catch the stuffing on fire and use her body to shield it from the wind, until she felt sure the flame wouldn't go out.

She stood on tiptoe for what she hoped would be the last time in a long, long while, and stuffed the burning insulation into the cavity of the wing, where *Amelia*'s fuel was stored.

Then Anne ran.

And in the split second during which she waited to see if her makeshift Molotov cocktail would do its job, Anne forced herself to consider the consequences of her actions.

She could no longer hear the helicopter. She had no idea if Paul would see her signal flare. And as *Amelia*'s explosion tore the air with an ear-splitting roar and sent Anne leaping to cover Amelia with her body, she faced the fact that her last-ditch effort to save them had also destroyed their only shelter.

Paul didn't hear the blast. He felt it.

Although, obviously, that couldn't be right. There must have been something, some tangible evidence Paul missed on the conscious level, that prompted him to look over his shoulder one last time.

And see the plume of smoke rising in the distance.

Paul whipped the Apache around with such speed, he practically flung himself to the other side of the cabin. He raced to the site of the fire, kicking himself for having missed it earlier. But the area was so densely covered in trees, even now he could barely make out the two snow-suited figures huddling on the ground, much less find a spot to set down his helicopter.

Realizing that even if he had the fuel to pull it off, landing was a geographical impossibility, Paul kicked open the cockpit door and lowered the Apache's ladder. He gripped the controls, vowing to keep the chopper so still that, despite the near-Arctic winds, it would seem frozen in goddamn midair.

On the ground, Anne, slowly, painstakingly, began climbing up the ladder he'd lowered. She tried getting Amelia to go up first, but her daughter was past the point of being able to follow orders. Anne guided her hands to the ladder, but as soon as she let go of her wrists, Amelia's arms slipped back to her sides. Desperate, Anne slipped her left arm around Amelia's waist, hefting their child off the ground, and wrapped Amelia's arms around her neck, legs around Anne's waist, the way she'd carried her as a baby. "Hold on, Ace."

The ladder swung beneath Anne's feet, the lower rungs, already covered with frost, slipping out from beneath her. She grabbed the upper rung with her good arm and pressed her wounded one against Amelia to prevent her falling sideways.

"Come on, Annie." Paul's heart hammered so loudly he barely heard his own screams of encouragement. "Just a little bit more." He didn't realize he was holding his breath until the trapped air almost ripped his chest open.

Anne tangled her feet in the ladder, as if climbing ropes back in gym class, and let go of the top rung just long enough to boost Amelia into the helicopter. Paul reached out his arm, grabbing and yanking her inside. He got Amelia but, for only a second, lost control of the Apache. Wind slapped its sides, spinning the nose a half-dozen degrees to the west.

And shaking Anne off the ladder.

Paul saw her head disappear below the cockpit door. He wanted to leap up, but the Apache couldn't exactly fly itself.

"Amelia." He shook his daughter by the shoulder until a sense of cognizance returned to her eyes. "Amelia, can you hear me?"

She blinked up at him. "Daddy?"

"Yes, Ace. It's Daddy. Everything's going to be fine. But, you have to listen to me carefully. You have to take the controls. Just for a minute—okay?—while I help out your mom."

"But . . . I don't know how to—"

"A helicopter is much easier than a Cessna. You can do it." Paul sat his daughter behind the controls, kissed her cheek, and whispered, "Wing and a prayer, Ace."

She had no idea what he was talking about. But his tone made her sit up straighter, gripping the controls with all her might.

Paul crawled to the door, peering out, desperately searching the landscape for Anne. But she hadn't fallen all the way down. She'd managed to grab the Apache's right skid and was now dangling several hundred feet off the ground, legs flailing.

"Annie!" Paul screamed at the top of his lungs.

She looked up. It was a difficult position for her to hold, and she was too tired to try. After a moment, Anne's head slumped down again. But not before Paul saw the bruises swelling her face and, for the first time in flight, felt sick to his stomach.

"I'm coming to get you," he shouted.

Paul lay down on his belly, reaching for her and managing to wrap his fingers around Anne's wrist. She was so heavily padded there, the ski suit plus other stuffing, that Paul didn't think she could feel him holding on to her. And because of the snow, and the angle she was dangling at, she couldn't see him. As far as Anne was concerned, the only thing keeping her from plunging to her death were her fingers wrapped around the helicopter's skid.

But Paul needed her to let go of that lifeline in order to pull her inside.

"Annie." He called her name until she painfully craned her head to meet his eyes. But she still couldn't see him holding on to her wrist. "I've got you, baby. I've got you. Now, let go of the skid. I've got you."

The wind carried Paul's voice away from his own ears, and so he couldn't be sure if Annie had heard all of what he was saying. Besides, if their situations were reversed, Paul wasn't so sure he could let go of the only thing keeping him from hitting the ground, without visual evidence that gravity wasn't the sole entity with a tight grip on his body weight.

His gaze locked with hers. "Let go of the skid, Annie."

She did.

When Paul asked Anne to put her life in his hands, she did.

Jesus.

He pulled her inside the Apache in a single, seamless motion, falling to the cabin floor with Anne on his lap, her head pressed against his chest, both of them gasping for air.

"Jesus Christ." Paul could think of nothing else to say. His head spun, leaving him to resort to the phrase that first crossed his mind when he heard about their accident. "Jesus Christ, Annie. You'll do anything to get out of honoring our custody agreement."

She twisted her neck, making sure Amelia was all right before whispering hoarsely, "Sue me."

And passed out in Paul's arms.

How they managed to make it back to the Academy, Paul would never know. Their fuel indicator read empty for at least half the distance but, somehow, the Apache remained airborne.

When they landed, Paul showed Amelia the instrument panel and told her, "That, Ace, is a wing and a prayer."

He'd radioed ahead for an ambulance, so there was one waiting for Anne and Amelia as soon as they touched down. Paul announced that he would be riding along and, after the initial time, no one tried to stop him. Anne was still unconscious when the paramedics loaded her inside, and she was still unconscious when they wheeled her stretcher through the emergency-room doors of Colorado Springs General Hospital. Paul sat with Amelia while she was examined. He signed her admission papers and promised her he'd be up to see her as soon as he straightened out the problem with Mom.

Next, he swung aside a blue curtain to peer over the

shoulder of the emergency-room resident examining
Anne. Paul was promptly asked to leave. Twice.

Paul said, "I intend to stay," in a tone of voice that
made it clear he had no interest in debating the issue.

And as the young fellow in charge had no interest in
becoming a patient of his own fine institution . . . "Uhm,
okay, sir. I guess you can stay." The resident studied
Anne's EEG and let out a long whistle. "You say she
was awake and talking an hour ago, sir?"

"She was awake and sarcastic an hour ago."

"Are you certain?"

"I assure you, doctor, despite my lack of medical de-
gree, I am capable of differentiating between conscious
and unconscious."

"It's just that, looking at the kind of blow she took,
and how bad this concussion is, Mrs. Gaasbeck—"

"Major Gaasbeck."

"Right—Major Gaasbeck, should have been knocked
unconscious as soon as she hit her head."

"She couldn't afford it. She had to take care of our
daughter."

The resident smiled, patronizing. "It's not like people
have a choice about when they're going to be knocked
unconscious."

Paul grunted.

The resident continued his examination. He moved on
to Anne's right arm, charting the severe break between
her elbow and wrist, making notes to disinfect the wound
where bone punctured skin before setting it in a cast.
When he examined Anne's fingers, the resident told
Paul, "The frostbite here is much more profound. The
break in her arm interrupted blood flow to her fingers."

"Which means?"

"Uhm, which means that, as long as we amputate the

dead tissue promptly, we can stop infection from spread—''

''What did you say?'' Paul advanced on the resident, the hands by his sides clenched into tight fists. ''Did you say you intended to *amputate* her fingers?''

''Only the three middle ones, sir. It's the best way to—''

''Are you out of your mind? This woman is a pilot.''

''Well, she'll still be able to fly. I guess.''

''Not in the United States Air Force, she won't,'' Paul said. ''I am her husband, and I refuse to give you permission to do this. I want to see your supervisor.''

''Sir, I assure you, I know what I'm do—''

''Your supervisor, young man. Now.''

A third-year resident's still-burgeoning God complex proved no match for the one Paul Gaasbeck had honed for twenty years. ''I—I'll get her for you, sir.''

Paul watched the kid leave and, while he waited for the senior doctor to arrive so he could explain that he had no intention of allowing any infection to spread up Anne's arm—ergo, slicing off her fingers would be unnecessary—continued bracing at attention by his ex-wife's bedside.

Standing vigil had brought Anne back to him before. He fully intended to make it happen again.

## $=14=$

It never occurred to him that Anne could die.

Until the day Amelia was born, and Paul saw Annie in the ICU, lying so horribly still on her back—a double discrepancy because Anne didn't sleep on her back, she slept on her side, and even in sleep, she was always in some sort of motion, eyes darting beneath her lids.

He'd considered something going wrong with the baby, the baby being sick, or even God forbid, dying. He'd prepared himself for that. Just in case. But Anne, Anne dying . . . it didn't make sense. It went against the laws of nature, the laws of physics. Anne was the strongest life force he'd ever encountered. A lightning bolt of pure energy, powerful enough to regularly knock Paul Gaasbeck's universe off its regular axis.

His mind steadfastedly refused to process the possibility of losing her. Paul's head spun, whirring on empty, struggling to summon the appropriate words to apply to their situation. But no matter how hard he strained, he drew a blank on every count. His inability to properly label and categorize what he was seeing threw Paul into paralysis. So at a loss for anything useful to do, he continued to stand as he was, arms behind his back, stance wide, eyes locked on Anne, bracing as if for review. All he needed was a rifle to grip, and he could pose for the Unknown Soldier statue.

"You know, Captain," Dr. Unger, more than a touch unnerved by the fierceness radiating from this young father's glare, tried joking to lessen the tension—"we have adequate security at the hospital. There's no need for you to stand guard."

Paul's every muscle tightened in resentment at the jocularity, but his facial expression never changed. "Understood, sir."

"It's been a long night, son. Why don't you go home, get some rest, and I'll have one of my nurses call—"

"I prefer to stay, sir."

"There's nothing you can do for her."

Paul blanched, momentarily losing his conviction and allowing his gaze to flicker from Annie to Dr. Unger. He gulped, struggling to regain his concentration, and reiterated, "I prefer to stay."

The doctor gave up.

So did the subsequent succession of nurses who, checking in to ICU in regular shifts, offered Paul a chair to sit in.

"I prefer to stand. Thank you."

The nurses exchanged nervous glances. And left him alone.

He might have been a sentry, or one of Queen Elizabeth's royal guard, the way he refused to budge from Anne's bedside, declining to move a muscle. Instead, Paul coolly shifted his gaze from Anne's face down to her feet and back again, searching for some clue, some logical, reasonable explanation as to how the hell this could have happened. He squeezed his fists by his sides, ordering his breathing to remain uniform as he contemplated Annie's inert face.

Her paleness unnerved him as much as her stillness. Anne was the sort who never needed blush, her cheeks turned pink the instant she engaged in anything physical. In other words, every moment of every day. Now her cheeks were so pale, they seemed translucent, sticking to the contours of her face like cellophane. Her throat fluttered with each breath, her chest barely rising.

Whoever brought her here had laid out her hands by her sides atop the blanket like—Paul winced at his own reflexive analogy—a corpse. Her fingers curved in the slightest bit, fluttering, as if she were trying to grasp something both large and delicate. It reminded him of the way she would curl up against him after they made love, her cupped hands playfully caressing his chest, tangling the hairs, then combing them out again with her fingers.

"Annie." It was a statement, and a question, and a plea. He willed her to open her eyes, to see him, to wake up like she always woke up—already in the middle of a conversation.

"Annie . . . please . . ."

In the end, Dr. Unger's official chart noted that it took the patient nine hours and thirty-four minutes to regain consciousness. For Paul, that period spanned a lifetime. By the time Anne finally opened her eyes, Paul Gaasbeck was a different man.

It took her a beat to focus, lids peeling open sleepily. Anne surveyed her surroundings in a daze, confused over where she was and how she'd gotten there.

"Paul?" She had to cough twice before forcing the word out.

"I'm here." He hurried to fill a plastic cup with water from the pitcher. "I'm right here."

"Did I win?"

He had no idea what she was talking about. "Excuse me?"

"The baby. Did we have a boy or a girl?"

"A girl." Paul helped her raise her head to take a sip, then lie back down again, exhausted. "We had a little girl."

"So. I won." Anne smiled, closed her eyes, and drifted back off to sleep.

Amelia Earhart Gaasbeck was ready to go home after twenty-four hours. Dr. Unger wanted to keep her mother under observation a bit longer, but after four days, Anne was hammering a contraband tennis ball against her hospital room wall to demonstrate how fit she was. Rather than risk her mutinying the other patients, Dr. Unger agreed to discharge mother and daughter on the same day.

The Air Force provided Anne with six weeks of maternity leave, and Paul had juggled his vacation time to procure the same weeks off. Since graduating from the Academy, neither one had ever gone so long without flying, or at least working. The day they brought Amelia home, Anne bet Paul, "First one caught staring longingly up at the sky owes the other a month's salary."

He didn't hesitate. "You're on."

It wasn't the money. Anne and he shared a joint bank account, so a month's salary remitted from one to the other wouldn't exactly go very far. It was the principle. It was the winning.

Unfortunately for Anne and Paul observers everywhere, Amelia quickly demonstrated how taking care of a newborn baby was harder work than perfecting computer flight simulations or leading a fight squadron. It wasn't that Anne and Paul lost their desire to stare longingly up at the sky, they simply lacked the time.

Despite Anne's victorious three-set match against the hospital wall, recovering from a complicated Caesarean pilfered much more of her energy than she had previously anticipated, leaving the bulk of child care, at his insistence, up to Paul. He was the one who got up three times a night to feed and change Amelia, ordering Anne to continue sleeping in a voice that hardly invited further argument. He gave the baby her bath in the evening and every morning took her for a walk outside, so Anne could shower and dress in peace.

A month into her leave, feeling stronger, Anne decided to join them on their outing. She slipped on a T-shirt and jeans, and set course for their front yard. Knowing that Paul couldn't see her, she paused by the door to watch him with Amelia.

He'd lifted the baby out of her stroller, hooking his thumbs under her arms, and holding her between his two palms. His fingers dwarfed her downy-fuzzed head and she kicked her tiny legs against the crooks of his elbows. The nurse who'd guided them through Baby Care 101 back at the hospital started her lecture by telling Paul, "Now, remember, Captain, she's not a yoke. We don't yank here."

Paul responded with a look so withering, it drove the nurse to thoroughly lose her train of thought and spend a minute rearranging her cornucopia of baby oils and lotions. Paul, in turn, proceeded to pick Amelia up with such tenderness, he managed to surprise not only the nurse but, subsequently, everyone who ever knew him. For some reason, the idea of a man being equally skilled at maneuvering both a million dollars worth of aircraft hardware and a seven-pound-baby girl proved rather shocking to the masses. The only soul not astonished by his deftness was Anne. For one thing, she knew how gentle he could be when the situation called for it. For another, she knew that, when he put his mind to it, Paul could do anything.

She watched him now, standing in the middle of the front yard, cradling Amelia, and Anne's heart melted. So many of the officers she knew couldn't pick their children out of a group photo. Their concern began and ended with, How Will My Kid's Behavior Affect My Performance Report? Paul's devotion to Amelia had already sparked a handful of jokes around the base. But Captain Gaasbeck couldn't care less. The fact was, anything Paul did, he expected to excel at. He was the best pilot Reese A.F.B. ever knew. He intended to be the best father, too.

Paul spied Anne eyeing him from the porch and smiled broadly, beckoning her over. "Check this out."

Paul lifted Amelia over his head, locking both elbows so that the baby floated a good seven feet off the ground. She flapped her arms excitedly, gurgling, until a spit bubble plopped past her lips and sailed like a spider web down onto Paul's cheek.

"She loves it." Paul shrugged to wipe the damp spot with his shoulder. "She's not even scared." He lowered the baby, cradling her against his chest, telling Anne, "Just like you."

Anne grinned, kissing the top of Amelia's head, then peered up to meet Paul's eyes. "Looks like you got stuck with another daredevil in the family."

"Think it's too soon to put her name down for the Academy?"

"Why, no. Not at all. She's already more than qualified. I mean, intelligence? We both know she's got that in spades."

"She's brilliant, I agree."

"And leadership? Really . . . who else do you know

that can get both Captains Gaasbeck to do their bidding?"

"And don't forget athletic ability." Paul sidestepped to the stroller, digging out a plastic toy football. He squeezed it and it squeaked, causing Amelia to laugh and reach for it. "See, she's already showing amazing aptitude."

"A regular chip off the old block," Anne agreed.

Amelia stuck the ball's pink tip in her mouth, sucking on it.

Paul and Anne exchanged looks, laughing, "Maybe not."

He wriggled the football out of Amelia's clutches, and tossed the toy, underhanded, to Anne. She caught it with both hands, and made a big show of pitching it back to him, quarterback-style.

Without needing to turn his head, Paul shifted Amelia onto his right arm and stuck out his left, wrapping five fingers around the ball in the blink of an eye. "You throw like a girl, Annie."

"I do lots of things like a girl."

"True"—he returned the football to Amelia, who, despite what any child-development books said, had tracked the flying toy with her eyes—"but them I don't mind so much."

They brought Amelia inside the house, where Anne withdrew into the bedroom to feed Amelia and Paul stepped into their den to check phone messages. She'd just gotten settled on top the bed, pulling off her T-shirt and propping Amelia up on a pillow beneath her breast, when Paul walked back in, holding a sheet of paper.

"What's this?"

Anne craned her neck for a better view, needing to read a few lines upside down before replying, "Oh, that's my request to be put back on active duty."

"You mean you want to go back to flying the 135?"

"Hell, yes. Six months of flying a desk was more than enough for me." Anne balanced Amelia's head in the crook of her elbow.

"But the work you've been doing with Design, that's much more prestigious than—"

"I joined the Air Force so I could fly, not talk about flying. You, of all people, should be able to understand that."

Paul looked down at the transfer request, carefully re-reading every word, and smiled. "Yeah. Sure. I understand." He sat down behind Anne, peering over her head at Amelia silently nursing, and kissed Anne's shoulder. "My turn next, okay?"

Colonel Elbe called the day before she was scheduled to return to duty to tell Anne that her request to commence flying again had been turned down. She stood by the phone in the kitchen, receiver clenched tightly in her right hand, too stunned to speak.

Colonel Elbe continued, "Major Sato from Design tells me that your contribution over the last half-year has been invaluable."

"But . . . I . . . my assignment there was TDY. It was temporary."

"The Air Force feels your skills would best be utilized—"

"Oh, come on." Anne regained her voice, took aim, and fired. "I'm a much better pilot than I am a flight engineer, and I've got a file full of commendations to prove it."

"Nevertheless, Paul thought that—"

"Paul?" Anne asked, "What does Paul have to do with this?"

But a part of her already knew.

*      *      *

Anne waited for Paul to come home, her anger simmering. Yet when he finally walked in the door, she almost lost her resolve. He'd been grocery shopping and came in carrying two armloads of brown paper bags. It wasn't easy to accuse a man holding milk, a pound of apples, a dozen eggs, and a package of disposable diapers.

Determined to say her piece, Anne vanquished her reluctance, and demanded, "How dare you?"

Paul turned his back on her, heading for the kitchen. He set his bags on the counter, opening the refrigerator door and holding it open with his foot, before requesting, "Could you throw another verb into that sentence, Annie?"

As always, his nonchalance drove her crazier than any attempt at a defense would have. "How dare you order Colonel Elbe not to commission me back on pilot duty?"

Paul bent his knees and squatted to open the vegetable drawer, filling it with carrots. He didn't look up. "First of all, unless the Air Force you joined is radically different from mine, I didn't realize that a captain of a fight squadron possessed the authority to order the base commander to do anything."

Figuring that two could play at this game, Anne mimicked his tone, reminding Paul, "First of all, Colonel Elbe happens to think that you walk on water. Second of all, he owes you a big chip for lowering yourself to step in and help out in Libya. And third of all, if it comes down to a choice of who Colonel Elbe would rather make happy, some woman captain, or the top-rated fight-squadron pilot in the country who just happens to be flying out of his base—well, who do you think Colonel Elbe will pick?"

Paul slammed shut the refrigerator door, standing in

front of it, hands on his hips. "Listen close to me, Annie, because I have no intention of repeating myself. I did not, *not,* order or even request Colonel Elbe to do me any favors. It was his decision to keep you behind a desk, not mine."

"A decision influenced by your telling him you didn't think I was fit to fly."

Paul hesitated. He moved to the counter, neatly folding the paper bags and stacking them underneath the sink to be recycled as garbage bags. Voice level, he said, "I simply filled Colonel Elbe in on the relevant facts."

She snatched the remaining bags out of his hands, hurling them under the sink and destroying Paul's excuse for not looking her in the eye. "You told him that I should continue to be excluded from duties that involve diving, driving, heavy machinery, and flying."

"Yes. I did tell him that."

"Jesus, Paul, that's the exact same edict you invoked when I was pregnant. Well, guess what, Paul? I'm not pregnant anymore."

"That edict specifies duties which should not be undertaken by anyone prone to sudden lightheadedness or loss of consciousness."

"Both of which are symptoms of being pregnant, which, I repeat in case you missed it the first time, I no longer am."

"Annie," Paul crossed his arms, "a little more than a month ago, you lay unconscious for almost ten hours."

"That was an allergic reaction. You can't blame me for that."

"Have you given any thought to what could happen if you suffer another allergic reaction, this time at 30,000 feet?"

She didn't know whether to laugh or cry. "Try keeping up with me here, Paul . . . I don't plan to have a C-section at 30,000 feet.''

"The risk factor is—''

"Minimal,'' Anne said. "The risk factor is minimal, and we both know it.'' She grabbed his wrists, bringing both hands to her face and kissing first one palm then the other. "Please, Paul. Tell me what's going on. Tell me why you're really doing this.''

# ═══ 15 ═══

No matter how many times and in how many ways the nurses at Colorado Springs General Hospital asked Major Gaasbeck to please leave the emergency room's examining area, Paul refused to budge. He intended to stay with Anne until she regained consciousness.

They told him, "It could take a while."

"I know," Paul said. "I've done this before."

The chief resident, a leggy blonde who looked like she'd paid her way through medical school by modeling on the runways of Paris, arrived a few minutes after Paul sent the first M.D. to fetch her. She wasted no time telling him that she agreed absolutely with her young colleague's opinion. Anne's frostbitten fingers required being amputated to prevent a spread of infection. The tissue was already dead, anyway. Even if they didn't cut them off, Anne would never regain feeling in her fingers. So his forbidding amputation only meant taking a major health risk for no earthly good reason.

Paul said, "Listen to me closely, doctors, because I have no intention of repeating myself. One: My wife *will* regain use of her hand. She has to. She's a pilot. Pilots need their hands. That is not an issue open for discussion. Two: You will do everything in your power to make sure that the above does happen, preferably as soon as possible, and three: After you've put in all the effort you humanly can, you will put in a little more. That's how we win wars, ladies and gentlemen. Have I made myself clear?''

"Major Gaasbeck. Sir,'' the chief resident informed him, "you are not being reasonable.''

"Sue me,'' Paul said. "Or better yet, take care of my wife's hand before I sue you. For negligence. And by the way, in case you're wondering how much money a career officer in the Air Force could possibly have to pursue a lawsuit of this nature, ask yourself one question: How much money does the Federal Government have? My wife is a graduate of the U.S. Air Force Academy. They've spent a lot of money to train her, and between you and me, they are not going to be too happy to lose their investment. Get the picture?''

It was the biggest crock Paul ever delivered in one place at one time. The only part of his speech with any grasp on the truth was the fact that, yes, Annie was an Academy graduate, and the tab for her education had been picked up by the government. Other than that, he was making it up as he went along.

But the word "amputation'' never came up again.

They wheeled Anne into surgery, working feverishly to set her crushed arm, restore blood flow to her hand and, possibly, somehow, save her fingers. Paul decided not to press his luck by bullying his way into the operating room.

Rather, he took advantage of the break to visit Amelia. She'd been assigned to a room in pediatrics, the incision on her forehead stitched by a plastic surgeon and every other inch of her X-rayed, looking for broken bones.

Miraculously, though, except for a touch of dehydration and hypothermia, she seemed unhurt.

Amelia lay on her side, asleep, when Paul crept into the room. In profile, she looked so much like Annie, Paul's chest contracted painfully just to look at her. The same cheeks, the same nose, the same mouth. Only Amelia's hair was longer. Much longer. Down to her waist. Paul used to needle Anne about living out her hair fantasies through Amelia. She'd never let it be cut. Although, based solely on hair, Amelia's friends always knew which parent she was staying the week with. Anne allowed her to wear it down. Paul insisted on braids, one, two, even a French one, as long as it was neat. When she'd been too little to manage on her own, he took the job on himself, tackling it as seriously as he did everything else.

He once told Annie, "It's not as easy as it looks. You've got to lay everything out just right for it to be perfectly centered."

"Sure. God forbid, anything should be even a little bit off-center."

He pulled over a chair and sat by Amelia's bed, studying the lovely, familiar face, and thanking God for the privilege of being able to see it again. Almost an hour later, she stirred, opening her eyes, and rubbing them with one fist. "Daddy?"

"I'm right here, Ace."

She propped herself up one elbow. "Where's Mom?"

"It's okay." Paul moved to reassure her, sitting on the bed, wrapping her in his arms and stroking her back. "She's fine."

"Then, where is she?"

"The doctors are fixing up her arm, that's all."

"Did she wake up?" Amelia's eyes widened at the

memory of her mother lying crumpled on the helicopter floor.

"No." Paul forced himself to sound unconcerned. "Not yet."

"Why not?"

"She—she hit her head. Hard."

"I know. It hurt her a lot. I saw her making faces when she thought I wasn't looking." Amelia asked, "When will she wake up?"

"Soon." Paul figured he'd told so many lies to so many people today, one more could hardly hurt. Besides, he liked the sound of this one himself. "Tomorrow."

"Oh." The concrete date seemed to pacify Amelia. How nice to know that, despite the mirror resemblance to Anne, she did possess a bit of her Daddy, after all.

"Are *you* all right, Ace?"

She thought about his question. "I'm okay," Amelia said. "Just kind of tired. You know, like when we go hiking. All sore like." Then, in an upside-down change of subject, she asked, "Mom was really brave, wasn't she?"

"Yes. Very brave."

"She never acted scared. Not once. The whole time, she acted like she knew we were going to be okay and you'd rescue us and—"

"What?" Paul raised his hand. "She knew what?"

"That you'd rescue us. That was the first thing she said to me. She said, now we're going to sit here and wait for your dad." Oblivious to the effect those words had on Paul, Amelia kept talking. "She was right, huh? Almost like she made everything okay, 'cause she kept saying it would be okay. You know how that is?"

Paul nodded. But it was a long time before he could force the lump from his throat to honestly tell her, "Yes, Ace, I do. I know just how that is."

\*   \*   \*

He sat with Amelia until she fell back asleep, then cautiously eased his hand out of her grip and headed back to the waiting area outside the operating room. He wondered if this was God's idea of a cosmic joke, forcing Paul, Anne, and Amelia to relive their roles from eleven years ago. Except that, eleven years ago, Paul had a wife and a family. And, these days, he had nothing.

Well, that wasn't exactly true. Paul had his rank, a display case of medals from the Gulf War, a constantly swiveling chorus of Air Force groupies who hung out at the O Club and would happily follow Paul anywhere he asked, including his apartment, and every other week, he had his daughter. But the hole that Anne left when she walked out of his life had never, ever been filled. At first, he denied that it even existed. Lately, he had moved on to resenting Anne for digging the hole in the first place. He wasn't sure that this could correctly be called progress. The notion that Anne could still get to him, nearly seven years following their divorce, was most certainly not a good thing.

Before Amelia was born, it never occurred to Paul that Anne could die. In the decade since, circumstances had obligated him to entertain the thought several times, and so he had—each time but this last one. This time, when the possibility was most real, he'd simply shut down. He tried to imagine a future without Anne in it. And he couldn't do it. He couldn't even order himself to do it.

Of course, the joke was on Paul. Even with Anne alive and well, she still wasn't available for more than a bitter cameo appearance in his future. Until the accident, Paul had resigned himself to that reality.

Now, however . . . now . . .

As soon as Anne was wheeled out of surgery, Paul followed the gurney to her room.

"Careful," he chastised the orderlies who transferred her from stretcher to bed. Both looked at Paul as if he were a nut, but he noted they did take extra care to move her smoothly.

Her right arm lay encased in a white cast from elbow to wrist, palm and fingers swathed in bandages. Paul accosted the doctor, "Is she okay? Will Anne be able to use her hand?"

"We don't know," she told him honestly. "First, we'll have to wait for the break in her arm to heal, then when the bandages come off, if she's able to move her fingers—"

"What do you mean, if?"

"Frankly, Major, at this point, if you're really looking for something to worry about, I'd suggest taking a break from the hand and stressing instead the blow she took to her head. It's not just some little bump. Considering how long it went untreated, we could be looking at serious brain damage."

"No," Paul said, "no, that's not possible. You haven't been listening to me. A couple of hours ago, she was functioning well enough to figure out how to send up a signal flare in the middle of a blizzard. She climbed a rope ladder while balancing a half-grown child. She fell out of a helicopter and managed to hang on to the skid. That is *not* the behavior of a woman with brain damage."

"Brain damage isn't always apparent right away, Major. But if you say so."

"I"—Paul's eyes narrowed—"say so."

He made the doctors explain what the fluid was inside every IV pumping into Anne's arms, and why each machine with it's persistent beeps had to be there. He refused to let a single nurse get near Anne without first explaining what she was about to do, and why.

The only time Paul left Anne's room was to visit Amelia. They had breakfast together. Amelia picked at the pancakes with sliced bananas atop her tray while Paul, sitting across from her, sipped a cup of lukewarm coffee and calculated that he had now been awake for over forty hours.

"Is Mom awake, yet?" Amelia wanted to know.

Paul swallowed the dregs at the bottom of his cup. "Not yet."

"Why not? You said she'd be awake by now. You said, Daddy."

"Hey, come on." He stabbed a slice of pancake with a plastic fork and waved it in front of her face, the way he used to when she was a toddler. "Since when has your mom ever done anything I said? Take my word for it, she's faking still being unconscious, just so she can prove me wrong."

Amelia didn't look convinced, and Paul spent the rest of their visiting hour trying to cheer her up. He read to her from a paperback off the library cart, then popped in at the gift shop, buying a portable tape player and a handful of cassettes featuring greasy rockers staring sullenly into the camera. He left Amelia to enjoy her new gadgets, and returned to Anne's room.

He picked up her chart from the foot of the bed, flipping it open and studying the doctor's notations. He had no idea what half of them meant. But he had lived his life operating on the premise that, whatever one human could do, another human, namely him, could figure out how to do.

Everyone he'd ever met had dubbed this particular doctrine of his arrogance. Except Anne. Anne was the only one who ever called it what it was. Essential. She said, "When you know the only one you can really count on is yourself, you have to believe that you can do anything. Otherwise, you'd be terrified all the time.''

They were lying in bed—Paul tried to remember the date. It was definitely a year or so after Amelia was born, because she was already walking. And if Amelia was walking, that meant they were probably living at Kessler A.F.B. in Mississippi. But they didn't have that conversation at home. They were on vacation, he was sure of it. Amelia walking . . . Kessler . . . vacation . . . Now he remembered. They were camping. It was the middle of August, and they'd gone camping in New Mexico. It wasn't a bed Paul remembered them lying in but on top of a sleeping bag. The heat had made Amelia cranky, and the only way she would sleep was if Anne kept rocking her portable crib with her foot while Paul fanned Amelia with a piece of cardboard. So at least one Gaasbeck slept that night. Paul and Anne stayed up talking in whispers. And in the darkness, with only a child's breathing and the swish of cardboard to remind them they were still on earth, Paul learned more about the woman who was his wife than he had in the eight years since they first laid eyes on each other.

She told him about her lifelong expectation that if she wasn't constantly doing something, saying something, trying something new, leading the pack, being noticed, she would be left behind. If she blended into the background, she would be lost. If she allowed a single life's moment to slip through her fingers without savoring and tasting and experiencing it fully, it would pass her by. So later, when they'd moved on to talking about him, Paul thought he heard Anne's echo as she reassured him, ''When you know the only one you can really count on is yourself, you have to believe that you can do anything. Otherwise, you'd be terrified all the time.''

Softly and, oh, so carefully, convinced that choosing any word short of the perfect one could prove shattering,

Paul dared to ask, "Do you still feel that way? Like you've got no one to count on?"

In the darkness, he couldn't see her face—only the shadowy outline of her body against the ink-black air. The silence between them sucked in every heat molecule from outside. Even Amelia felt it, rolling over on her back with a muffled meow. Paul fanned her faster. And waited for Anne's answer.

"No," she said finally, her voice an evergreen, cool breeze. "No, I don't. Because now I've got you, haven't I?"

Paul never loved Anne more than he did at that moment.

Until yesterday, when Amelia told him about Anne's belief that he would rescue them.

Paul still couldn't fully process the revelation. Despite all that they'd been through—the acrimonious divorce, the semiannual treks back into court to haggle over Amelia's custody, the brutal, spiteful insults that could never be taken back—despite all that, Anne still believed in him. She may have hated him, but she still trusted him with her life.

There had to be a logical reason for it. Paul tried to think. Obviously, Anne knew that he wasn't the sort of man to sit by while his child's life was in danger. And, naturally, Paul being a pilot familiar with the Colorado Springs area, he was the sensible choice to send on a search-and-rescue mission. So in effect, her telling Amelia that Paul would save them could have been nothing more than an intelligent woman's reasonable assessment of basic facts.

Except that it didn't explain why Anne so readily let go of the Apache's skid, the second he ordered her to.

Paul rubbed his eyes with both palms, covering his mouth to yawn, then jolting his head from side to side like a dog shaking off water. He needed coffee. Fifteen gallons seemed about right. But, he was afraid to move. As moronic and as groundless and as self-important as it sounded, a part of Paul was still convinced that only his continued presence could bring Annie back to them.

He tried to rationalize it by telling himself that it was his subconscious' way of making him feel he still had some control over this whole, horrible situation. But scientific mumbo-jumbo aside, the fact was, Paul simply believed it with all of his heart.

He watched the clock, and he watched Anne. Purple and yellow bruises dotting her cheeks and forehead had swollen one side of her face to twice its regular size. And still, despite the antiseptic-dabbed cuts, the frost-bitten redness around her eyes, the bruises, all Paul could see was the most beautiful woman he'd ever known.

He stroked her face with the back of his fingers. Then, after looking both ways to make sure no one could see, bent at the waist and delicately, gently, kissed the throbbing on her skin the same way he'd once kissed Amelia's boo-boos to make them better.

If Paul expected a Sleeping Beauty resolution to succeed his bizarre gesture, he was in for a disappointment. Kiss or no kiss, Anne didn't awaken. So much for Prince Charming.

Yet less than an hour afterward, Paul swore he detected some traces of movement beneath her lashes. The nurses told him he was seeing things, and looked at Paul exactly the same way the nurses had looked at him eleven years ago, when Paul ordered them to stop injecting the spinal block into Anne—right before she went into cardiac arrest. So rather than subscribing to the Major-Gaasbeck-is-losing-his-marbles scenario currently circulating the hospital, Paul continued keeping vigil by Anne's bed, calling her name over and over again, telling her to wake up.

When she finally opened her eyes, her pupils darted madly from side to side, settling down only when they locked on to Paul. Anne exhaled slowly, her voice barely above a whisper.

"You weren't a dream.... I was so afraid...I thought you were a dream."

He shook his head, suddenly unable to make a sound.

Anne swallowed a groan of pain, and implored, "Amelia?"

"She's fine. She's just fine."

"Her face?" Anne tried to lift her arm to indicate the cut on Amelia's forehead, but proved too weak. "Oh, God, her face."

"It's nothing. Just a superficial cut. The doctors tell me she can have the scar removed with plastic surgery, or she can just hide it behind her bangs. It's nothing to worry about."

"Good . . ."

"Annie," he hated himself for asking, when the mere formation of each word seemed to cause her such agony. But he had to know. "Annie, tell me something. Why did you let go of the skid?"

She stared at him uncomprehendingly, eyes glassy from trauma and medication.

"The skid. On the chopper. You couldn't *feel* me holding you, could you? And you couldn't *see* me holding you. So when I told you to let go, why did you do it?"

He needed to hear a logical answer. Something along the lines of how she thought about it, weighed the pros and cons, took into account what she knew about Paul and how he was likely to respond in a given situation, and . . .

"I . . . because . . ."—she struggled over the words—"it was you."

Now it was his turn to stare uncomprehendingly.

"Because it was you, Paul."

Anne fought to keep her eyes open, determined to say just one more thing before lapsing back into warm, pain-free darkness. She grabbed Paul's hand, squeezing it tightly and gazing into his face.

"Thank you," she murmured.

Paul withdrew his palm, sticking it in his pocket and politely informing Anne, "It was nothing. I'd do the same for anyone."

# ═══ 16 ═══

*1986*

Anne couldn't believe what she was hearing.

For the second time in barely a year, Paul was pulling strings to have her grounded. First Libya, and now her reassignment back on the KC-135. She was past being shocked by his actions. All she wanted now was to understand his motivation. And so she repeated, "Please, Paul. Tell me why you're really doing this."

He sighed, cupping Anne's cheeks between both his palms, and lowered his head to rest gently atop hers. "Things have changed. It's one thing to ship out at a moment's notice when you've only got yourself to look after. But you're a mother now. If you're transferred back to flying and we get orders tomorrow to take off for Libya again, are you just going to leave Amelia behind?"

Anne pulled away from his embrace. *"That's* why you're trying to ground me? Because of Amelia?" She raised a finger in the air, waving it back and forth to emphasize her point. "According to my figures, Captain, you became a father at around the same time as I became a mother. So let's try this one on for size. If you're so concerned about Amelia's being abandoned in case of

251

our deployment, why don't *you* take a desk job for a while?"

It didn't matter what the subject was anymore. Within fifteen minutes, Anne and Paul had managed to boil down a discussion about aviation safety, military protocol, and the fate of their child to the same point all their discussions boiled down to—not who was right or who was wrong, but who would win and who would lose.

Paul refused to respond to her summons, brushing past Anne as he headed out of the kitchen, up the stairs, and into the nursery. Anne followed him, determined to, once and for all, scrape to the bottom of why her husband was trying to sabotage her career.

He stood over Amelia's crib, instructing her attention to the diorama of tiny airplanes zooming above her head. Amelia stuck her fingers in her mouth and watched, enthralled.

"Paul," Anne rubbed her palm against his back, her voice low, not only so as not to upset Amelia but also to show Paul that she wasn't mad. "Please. I know you love her. But this can't be all about Amelia." She reminded, "It's not the first time you've had me grounded. Don't you think I deserve to know your real reason?"

"I'm not out to get you, if that's what you're inferring."

"Actually, Paul, I think you are."

He turned around slowly. She'd expected to see hurt in his eyes, but instead was faced with . . . nothing. His indifference stabbed Anne. And yet, she still wasn't angry with him. She just wanted Paul to understand what she was saying.

"Remember when I made Captain?"

"Yes." No inflection.

"Remember how I asked you then if you were jealous of me?"

"Yes."

"You said you weren't. That it was nothing, that you would've treated anyone else who made Captain before you the same way."

"Yes."

"You also claimed you didn't resent my success, that you were happy for me, your wife, at the same time as you were competitive with me, your fellow pilot."

"Good grief, did you have the conversation transcribed?"

"No. But, I did think about it a lot. And I tried to believe what you said, really, I did. I wanted to believe you. You will never know how badly I wanted to believe you."

"Then believe me, Annie."

"I can't. I'm not like you. I can't just command myself to feel something." She took a deep breath. "I love you, Paul. But how can I trust you when you are constantly saying one thing and then doing something else? You say that you're no more competitive with me than you are with any other pilot in the Air Force. But, Paul, darling, I don't see you going behind other pilots' backs and pulling strings to make sure they never fly again."

He didn't deny it.

Oh, God. *He didn't deny it.*

She thought she'd be pleased. She was devastated.

But she had to keep talking, she had to fill the silence.

"I mean, it's one thing for us to compete fair and square. I certainly never asked you to cut me any slack on that account, have I? And what, with your flying an F-15 and my flying a KC-135, it's not even like we're in head-to-head competition anymore like back at the Academy. That's why I don't understand. I mean, I'm

not even a threat to you. I used to think it was important
for you to be number one. And don't get me wrong, I
respect that, I do. But, lately—lately, Paul, it seems like
you care less about being number one and more just
about coming out ahead of me.''

Coolly, he said, ''Do the math, Annie. Wouldn't my
wanting to be number one automatically include coming
out ahead of you?''

She hated it when he used logic against her. Particularly in such a smug tone of voice, too. Well, if logic
was what he wanted, Anne could give as good as she
got.

She said, ''What about honor, Paul? Back at the Academy, the honor code was your own personal ten com-
mandments.''

''It still is.''

''Oh, yeah? Then, tell me something. Where in the
honor code is it acceptable to take out your competitors
by cheating? If you didn't go to Colonel Elbe in a de-
liberate attempt to undermine my career, then tell me
why you did do it. And don't you dare try hiding behind
Amelia a second time.''

Paul's eyes burned cobalt blue.

If he were the sort of man even remotely capable of
hitting a woman, Anne would have feared for her safety.
If they were in any other room save the nursery, she
wouldn't have been surprised if he put his fist through
a wall.

But because he was Paul, and because striking out at
anything would have revealed to the world that he too
possessed a semblance of human feeling, Paul did none
of those things.

Instead he simply stood straighter, hands by his sides,
chin up, and told Anne, ''Fine. If that's what you want
to hear, then—yes. I had Colonel Elbe ground you, both

now and prior to your going to Libya, because I, like everyone else in the service, know that advancement in rank most often depends on participation in a combat unit. Behind a desk, you're out of sight and out of mind—especially to the promotion board.''

Paul Gaasbeck might not have been the sort of man capable of striking a woman with his fist. But the blows he unleashed on Anne with every syllable out his mouth couldn't have hurt more if they'd left bruises on her skin.

''Let me get this straight,'' her voice shook so hard, Anne was amazed her words came out with any clarity. ''In the interest of my not getting promoted ahead of, God forbid, you! a second time, you deliberately sabotaged a huge, huge part of my life.''

''All right. Yes. Fine. That's what I did.''

She wanted to throw something at him, but found she couldn't. She wanted to scream, but found she couldn't. She didn't want to cry. But found that was all she could do.

For what felt like an eternity, but could only have been a few seconds on the clock, Paul watched the tears stream down her face.

Then he cleared his throat and, without saying another word, left the nursery.

She heard him back the car out of the garage, driving off for his first day back to work. At seven that evening, the phone rang. Anne knew exactly who it was, and what the message would be, and so she let the answering machine pick up.

Paul's voice crackled through after the third ring. ''Annie, it's Paul. Listen, I've got a lot more work to catch up with here than I thought, so, anyway, don't wait up. I'll see you later.''

The line went dead.

Anne wondered how long he intended to sulk this

time, and so didn't feel even a twinge of surprise when Paul failed to come home either that night or the following morning. She was laying bets on whether he'd deign to show up by dinnertime, when, at noon, she heard, "Annie?"

She was sitting on their bed, repeatedly stabbing her ballpoint pen along the document denying her request for a change of assignment. Despite her surprise at his unexpected appearance in the middle of the day, when Paul entered the bedroom, Anne refused to so much as glance his way. When he called her name, she growled in reply.

He coughed into his fist. "There's something I need to say to you, Annie. The thing is, though, just because there's something I *want* to say doesn't necessarily mean I know how to say it."

"You certainly had no trouble expressing yourself earlier."

He didn't argue, accepting the insult as his due. But there was clearly something else, some larger issue gnawing away at him, and he was determined to force it out before he changed his mind. "Annie, I swear to God, I'm not trying to start a fight here, but could I ask you a question?"

Her second growl hardly differed in pitch or inflection from her first, but Paul seemed to hear encouragement in it, because he took his life in his hands to ask, "Why do you think you love me?"

She raised her head slowly, meeting Paul's eyes.

"I . . ." Anne's words trailed. Her lifelong habit of starting a sentence even when she didn't know what she wanted to say, on the assumption that it would eventually come to her, failed. "Because . . ." He was obviously fishing for something specific, something he desperately needed to hear from her. Unfortunately,

Anne could not even begin to guess what that might be. Not only did she not possess Paul's deifying belief in the power of words, but, frankly, the simple word "love," had always been enough for her. She had no desire to analyze it or quantify it or dissect it. Love was something you felt, not something you thought. Otherwise, it was like repeating a sound over and over again until it lost all meaning.

Still, Paul was waiting for her to answer his question and she struggled to fulfill his request. It was so rare that he asked her for anything. She wanted to give him what he needed. "I—I love you because—because you're . . . Paul."

His face fell. "Damn it, Anne. Couldn't you at least try and work with me here. I mean, Jesus, what do I have to do? Beg?"

"I-I'm sorry," she stammered. "It's the best I can do. What's wrong? Isn't that enough?"

"No," Paul said. "No, I don't think so. See, I don't think it's a good enough reason for us to stay together."

Her eyes widened. "Are you kidding? It's the *only* reason."

"But don't you think there should be more, though? Don't you think we need a valid, logical reason for us to stay together? One that's preferably greater than all the valid, logical reasons we've got to stay apart."

Her throat went dry. "What valid, logical reasons?"

"We can't live together, Annie. We may want to. We may want to so much that it almost, almost drives us to overlook a cardinal truth: You and I hurt each other. Constantly."

"But we don't mean to," she argued. "And if we don't mean to, then it shouldn't count. We love each other, Paul."

He shook his head. "Sometimes that's not enough."

She crossed her arms. "I won't accept that."

"Annie, baby, you can accept or deny the laws of gravity, but that apple is still going to fall off the tree whether you believe in physics or not."

She rose from the bed, resting one leg on the floor, wondering how matters could have gotten so horribly out of hand without her realizing it. "What brought this on all of a sudden?"

He said, "I've been thinking about it all night. You know how you always ask me to tell you the truth? Well, when I finally did, look what happened. I hurt you. But if I'd lied, you would have been just as hurt. This relationship is irrational. We possess a million reasons for why we should part—our rivalry is just the tip of the iceberg. Meanwhile, neither of us can conjure up a solitary reason—you can't even think of *one word*—to be together."

"That's not true. You're just saying that. You're putting up this smoke screen because you know you had no right doing what you did to me, and now you can't bring yourself to apologize. Damn it, Paul, why can't you ever just admit that you were wrong?"

"I don't have to." He raised an eyebrow and reminded, "You always admit it for me."

She laughed. She couldn't help it. If she didn't laugh, she would have had to wince. Because he was absolutely right.

Paul shook his head. "You think you know me so well."

"Don't I?"

"Well, yes. But that's not the point." He matched Anne smile for smile. Then, taking a deep breath, Paul said, "You are correct about one thing, though. I had no right to go to Colonel Elbe, and I am sorry. Deeply, deeply sorry."

"I know." She linked her fingers with his, marveling at the fit. "What you did, coming to me on your own like this, it tells me more about how sorry you are than anything you could ever say."

He confessed, "I don't know what came over me. I don't know what I was thinking. I was way out of line. But you always did have that affect on me, didn't you?"

She pulled him down to sit next to her on the bed, stroking his face with the back of her hand. "Thank you for saying that."

"I'll never do it again."

She hesitated. "Paul, you do know that I still mean to fight for my right to fly, don't you? And I still intend to put my name down for every combat assignment that comes along, until I get my chance to make history. What happened before I was to go to Libya, what happened this week when I wanted to go back to flying the 135, this feeling that came over you, it could happen again."

"No, it couldn't." There was no trace of doubt in his voice. "Because, in this case—and this one case only, Annie—you were right, I was wrong. I'm giving you my word that I will never, ever block your way, again. More than that, I'm giving *me* my word. Do you understand what I'm getting at?"

Did she ever. . . . While Paul Gaasbeck might, under some valid circumstances, break a promise to another person, he would march to his grave before breaking a promise vowed to himself. By pledging an oath to his own honor, he'd found the perfect action to reassure Anne that he'd never go back on his word.

"Thank you." She wrapped her arms around him. "Thank you. I know that's a promise you'll never break."

"I'll assume you meant that as a compliment?" He

returned her embrace, hands sliding down Anne's back and resting on either side of her waist. He ducked his head, kissing the crook of her neck.

"I . . . yes. Of course, I did." She spun her chin sharply, so that they were nose to nose. "I wasn't implying—"

"Shh." Paul kissed his finger and tapped it to Anne's lips. "I know what you meant. I was teasing you. Really, Annie, you've simply got to stop taking everything so seriously."

It took her a moment to comprehend that Paul truly was pulling her leg. Once she did, however, Anne's mouth stretched into a vast grin, and she reached playfully for the top button of Paul's shirt, flicking her tongue inside the pulsating hollow beneath his throat, then peering up guilelessly to meet his eyes. "Is that a fact?"

He responded to her obviously rhetorical question in precisely the manner Anne wanted. His grasp on her hips tightened, and he pulled Anne toward him, crushing her against his chest. His hands slid up and under her T-shirt, cupping both of Anne's beasts in his hands. Her nipples, reacting instinctively to the sweet, familiar sensation, spiked to greet him, straining against the suddenly too confining lace of her bra, and Paul, acting on years of inquest and experimenting and refining, fulfilled her silent summons by raising his thumbs and sensitively running the tips of his fingers around the hotly hardened peaks. He stroked her in circles, until Anne's breathing matched the rhythm of his touch, and she arched her back, pressing her knees along either side of his hips. They slipped out of their clothes, both pleasurably proficient at removing jeans and briefs and any other articles destined to get in the way without breaking physical contact for so much as a second.

Anne leaned over him, her hair brushing his cheeks, her lips capturing his. The rest of his body was hard as stone, but Paul's tongue streaked velvet across her neck as he drew a fiery path down her chest, guiding her swollen nipple inside his mouth and pressing her shuddering body to him at the same time as he gradually raised his right knee and wedged it between her thighs.

She cried out his name, her voice hoarse, as the hot friction of flesh over flesh while he flexed and unflexed his rigid muscles propelled Anne to straddle Paul's leg, hips bucking reflexively as she rode him, one hand gripping his shoulder for balance, the other entwined in his hair.

"Yes. There, yes. Touch me there."

He obliged, lowering his leg and catching her with one hand, his fingers cupping her and triggering a tight, coiling knot in the pit of her stomach that nearly pushed Anne over the edge. But she knew enough to hold back, not to let go just yet. She trusted Paul to take her, them, even further, and so she held on with all of her might, her breath coming out ragged and uneven, her cheeks flushed a crimson red, her legs so weak she felt sure she would collapse if Paul dared remove his hand from between her thighs.

"Do you like it when I do this?"

He stroked her as deftly and delicately as a pianist coaxing the softest strains out of his instrument, his fingers moving up and down and across and oh, God, inside . . .

"Oh, yes. . . ."

"How much?" He felt her swelling and tightening against his hand. "Tell me."

"So much . . ." The moan turned into a sob as she caught her breath in response to yet another wave rising up from the depths to try and sweep her under.

Paul sat up, pulling her closer to him. "Now, Annie?"

He knew her body better than anyone, could read her every cry and sigh. She was ready to drown, ready to slip away, just another second and—"Right now. . . ."

He lifted Anne effortlessly, opening her with his fingers and guiding her on top of him. Her legs wrapped around his waist, and she strained against him, throwing her head back, falling, falling, and not even caring where she landed as long as the bliss coursing through her continued in its fervor.

Sitting up, Paul raised his knees for her to lean against and kept Anne from falling. He slipped his hands underneath her arms, holding her close.

"Like this, Annie?"

"Yes . . ." She hissed the last letter, her body contracting repeatedly until even the word she'd wept only a second ago lost all meaning. "Yes, Paul . . . yes. . . ."

He held Anne until she finished trembling, cradling her along his chest, stroking her back, her hair.

For a long while, they simply lay pasted together, wrapped in a sweet tangle of arms and legs, their hearts beating in gradually calming sync, certain that finally, finally, they had broken past and through some invisible barrier that both were aware of but neither could figure out how to bring up.

Bathed in a peace he'd previously never known, or even dreamed existed, Paul lightly kissed the top of Anne's head before asking playfully, "I don't get it. Who won?"

She rubbed her cheek against his stomach, propping her chin on his chest, and looked up at Paul, smiling.

"We did."

# ≡17≡

After two days of intoxicated drifting under the auspices of Colorado Springs General Hospital, on the first morning she felt up to peeling open her eyes without groaning a wish to slip back into unconsciousness, Anne surfaced in possession of three separate but equal musings.

*One:* Her whole body hurt. Seltzer burned the outskirts of her brain, the bubbles pressing against her skull until she thought the top of her head might burst off. Every inch of her skin felt raw, like someone had spent the forty hours she lay unconscious rubbing it with sandpaper. Her arm, besides throbbing inside its airtight plaster cast, also itched intolerably. But considering that for the last two days her aches hadn't even bothered to differentiate themselves, preferring instead to throb in a single, agonizing roar, these were all positive developments.

*Two,* and this wasn't nearly as positive of a development: She was still in love with her ex-husband. Anne wasn't precisely sure how it happened. Except that, in trying to keep Amelia awake, she lived her life over again, opening old wounds and remembering all the things about Paul that Anne simply couldn't tolerate. But, in the process, she'd also remembered all those things that she once loved—still loved—about him.

*Three:* If she confessed how she felt to Paul, and he responded with his patented indifferent stare and another, "It was nothing personal," then, quite simply, she would die.

Maybe a week ago, Anne would have felt up to accepting Paul's cold renunciation with a minimum of pain. But not now. Her nerves were stretched too tight, they were too exposed, too close to the surface. She'd spent the last of her strength huddling inside the *Amelia,* fighting to keep herself and her daughter alive. She no longer had any reserves left with which to defend herself.

So in the interest of keeping at least her emotional pain to a minimum, Anne kept her new feelings to herself and followed Paul's example whenever he came to see her, Amelia in tow. She was polite, she was cordial, and she was remote.

So what if it was dishonest? It was *safe*.

Only when Amelia left the room for a bit, rushing out to get the new tapes Dad bought her, did Anne even dare broach a subject more intimate than the weather.

She asked Paul, "When do you intend to tell me why you're so angry with me?"

He stood in the door, neck craned around the corner, looking for Amelia, one arm braced along the frame in classic Paul posture, as if he believed the building would fall down unless he personally supported it. He turned, hand sliding into his pocket. Silent.

He looked at her for a long moment.

Shook his head.

And walked away.

As soon as Anne's doctors felt satisfied that she'd suffered no brain damage, and her condition had stabilized enough for her to be discharged from the hospital, Paul bought airline tickets for the three of them to return to Utah.

Despite their taking a commercial flight, Paul wore his Air Force uniform on board. But the navy blue jacket and slacks, no matter how smartly he carried himself, certainly showed the long hours he'd spent both driving and pacing the hospital corridors. As a result, Paul, who monitored the immaculate condition of his uniform as closely as he did all other matters, looked and felt particularly uncomfortable walking into, of all places, an airport terminal. He walked briskly, gaze fixed on the trio of tickets in his hand, refusing to look up or make eye contact with anyone, Anne included. The few times she got up her nerve to ask a question, he answered curtly, staring straight ahead.

He hustled them on board with military precision, dispensing seat assignments even before the stewardess cabal loitering around the door had a chance to do their job. Still, in spite of his best efforts to get their journey over with as soon as possible, he was spotted on entry by the 747's captain, who exited the cockpit to ask, "Excuse me, Major, aren't you Paul Gaasbeck?"

Paul gestured for Amelia to climb into the window seat, then helped Anne settle comfortably between them before straightening up to answer, "I am."

"I thought you looked familiar. Captain Sam Magalnick, here. I served in Saudi Arabia with you—the 358th. I've got to tell you, sir, it's a downright honor to shake the hand of the man who got us our first kill."

For the first time that day, that week, and—considering it was January—that year, Anne saw Paul smile, even if he did look embarrassed. "Pleasure to meet you, Captain. This is my daughter, Amelia, and my—her mother, Anne."

He covered his brief verbal stumble so eloquently, the captain never noticed his slip. Only Anne, because she knew where to look, saw the muscles at the back of Paul's neck constrict, the triangle of hair at the nape arrowing his tension.

The captain saluted Paul. "Major."

Then, turning to Anne, who was dressed in civilian clothes, he nodded his head respectfully, "Ma'am," before returning to the cockpit.

It wasn't until their 747 reached its final cruising altitude that Paul managed to get the grin yanking his lips under control.

Anne peeked out of the edge of her eye, checking that Amelia sat safely under a headset before taunting Paul, "You're eating this up, aren't you?"

He leaned back in his seat, fingers linked and resting across his chest, eyes closed. "I'm not allergic to it."

"You could have told him I was a Major, too."

"True."

"But you didn't."

"Also, true. You're really racking up points, today, Annie."

"I didn't realize we were keeping score."

"Right. That would be most out of character for both of us."

She couldn't tell whether or not he was joking. It might have helped Anne's evaluation if, at any point, Paul had deigned to open his eyes and address *her* rather than the universe at large. Then again, as far as preserving Anne's sanity was concerned, obnoxious was probably the best way for Paul to act right now. The longer he continued behaving like a bastard, the longer Anne could go without remembering his other side, the one that, thanks to her recent trip down memory highway,

Anne now had to admit she'd once loved, still loved, and would, God help her, always love.

Figuring it lay in her best interests to encourage rather than diffuse Paul's antagonism toward her, Anne took the road she knew best, accusing, "Still jealous of me after all these years, Major?"

"Hardly." Paul turned his head away from her, pretending to sleep. "I gave my word eleven years ago. I never break my word."

Case closed.

Anne shook with indignation. Of all the arrogant, pompous . . . Who the hell did he think he was?

She pressed. "You're telling me all it took was one promise to yourself, and you never again felt even a smidgen of—"

"It's called self-discipline," he mumbled into his seat. "You should try it sometimes."

"You mean like a faucet? Whoosh, you just turn your feelings off, never to be bothered by them again?"

"Precisely."

Damned if she didn't believe him.

In fact, she wished she possessed the skill herself. Because then she'd be able to suppress the tickle of hope that sprung from her abdomen the instant she heard Paul proclaim his lack of rivalry toward her. After all, that competitiveness had been the root of so many of their problems that maybe, just maybe, with it out of the way, they could see clear to . . . no.

The sooner she quit thinking like that, the better.

Paul's absolute lack of rivalry toward her wasn't a sign that he still cared for her, it was exactly the opposite. At least when he'd been jealous of her accomplishments, Paul had felt *something*, negative as it may have been.

Now, without that to buffer them, Anne was finally

forced to accept that the only feelings Paul still harbored for her were, as he so eloquently asserted, "nothing personal."

She turned away from him, staring out the cabin window. She told herself, as well as reassuring an alarmed Amelia, that the tears streaming down her cheeks were simply the result of looking directly into the setting sun.

Paul escorted Anne inside her Hill A.F.B. home, turning on the light switches she couldn't reach with her broken arm and adjusting the heat. He got Anne a glass of water so she could take her pain medication, commenting that she really didn't look too great.

"Thanks," Anne said, conceding that she didn't feel too great either. The hour-long flight had exhausted her to the point where all she could think of was crawling into bed and staying there for the next millennium or so. Her head spun every time she turned it, and it took the bulk of her strength just to keep her eyes open.

"We'd better get going." Paul told Amelia, "Say good bye to your mom and pack whatever you need to stay at my house."

His daughter's eyes widened, and she took an instinctive step closer to Anne. "No, Daddy. I want to stay here."

"Your mom is in no shape to look after you, Ace."

Anne studied Paul, wondering if he was trying to goad her into a fight, waiting to beat her into submission with a host of perfect reasons for why Amelia should be living with him. She decided that he was in for a jolt of a disappointment. Anne had no inclination to have a verbal wrestling match. She just wanted him to go, to leave so that she could stop looking at him. Looking and recalling how much she loved him. And how little he cared about her.

Anne told Amelia, "Paul's right. You think you're one hundred percent recovered, but I'd feel a lot better if someone responsible was keeping an eye on you. You go home with your dad, okay? He'll look after you."

"But who'll look after you?"

Anne smiled weakly. "I'm a big girl, Ace. I can take care of myself."

Amelia crossed her arms: Paul Gaasbeck with his mind made up. "I'm not leaving you alone, Mom."

"Amelia . . ." Paul began. Then recognizing something familiar in her determined stance, threw his arms up in the air and offered, "Fine. You want to stay? Stay."

Amelia grinned, pleased not only to have gotten her way but also to have won her point. "Thank you, Daddy."

"But I'm staying with you."

"What?" Anne attributed her latest bout of dizziness to the lightning turn of her head. She needed to press her palm against the wall, steadying herself.

He shrugged. "If Ace wants to stay here and take care of you, that's her prerogative. But my job is to take care of her. If the only way I can do that is by moving in here for a few days, so be it. Those are my terms, take 'em or leave 'em, Annie."

Of course, she let him stay. But in the few seconds it took Anne to make up her mind, Paul couldn't help asking himself what it was he really wanted her to decide. Did he want her to crumble, to blink and take the bait, ordering him out of the house? Or did he want her to invite him in? As things stood, this was Paul's first step over the threshold to what had once been his own home in over six years, and he was fighting a mighty impulse to survey what Anne had changed, and what she'd allowed to remain the same.

He followed Anne upstairs to her room, meaning only tô borrow an extra pillow and blanket so that he could make himself a bed on the couch but, once in the doorway, found it impossible to leave. Everything looked different. She had a new spread over the bed, a new dresser that matched the headboard, and Amelia's school photos framed on the wall. But to Paul the bedroom was still familiar. Because it still smelled the same. It smelled like Anne.

How many nights, Paul wondered, had he gone to sleep or woken up, inhaling her sweet fragrance? Its essence drifted so engraved upon his conscience that there were mornings even now when, in that half-state between dream and wakefulness, he could swear he sensed it still, and inevitably awoke devastated by the illusion.

Seemingly oblivious to Paul, Anne crumpled on the bed, lying gingerly on her side, too tired to undress, and pulling her knees up to her chest. She looked so vulnerable. Paul realized that he couldn't, in good conscience, leave her alone.

"Annie?" He sat down beside her on the bed, brushing strands of hair from her face, frightened by how cold her skin felt.

"Go away," she whispered. "Just leave me alone. Please."

"All in good time." He kept his tone expressly light, loathe to let her hear just how much her weakened state upset him. In all the years he'd known her, Paul had never seen her in such bad form. Even during labor with Amelia, she'd had some spark. Now Paul sensed an emptiness. A surrender.

He stood, crossing over to the dresser and, on the first try, opened the drawer where Anne kept her nightgowns.

He plucked the one on top, a lavender silk, and handed it to her dispassionately. "You need to change. It'll make you feel better."

When despite a weak, affirmative nod she didn't budge, Paul moved to, at least, remove her shoes. She jerked her leg away as if he'd bitten her, gasping from the pain caused by such a sudden yank to her arm as she pulled out of his reach.

"I can do it myself, thank you."

Paul didn't know whether to feel insulted or pleased that, at least, he'd managed to somehow burst through her lethargy.

He left the room while Anne changed her clothes. When he came back, she was sitting propped against the headboard, blanket pulled up to her waist, pillow across her lap, broken arm resting on top.

"Better?" Paul asked.

She nodded, even trying a smile. "Yes. Thank you."

"Good." His nod echoed hers. "Very good."

He knew he should probably leave. Anne needed her rest, and, more importantly, she obviously didn't want him there. She'd been quite clear when she told him to go away and leave her alone. Yet for a reason Paul couldn't specify, he remained as he was, half in, half out of his former bedroom, picking at a speck of chipped paint on the door while he asked, "Is there anything you need? Anything I can get you? Are you hungry?"

"No. Thanks." She raised the pillow even higher across her chest, almost tucking it up to her neck. "Paul?"

"What?" He took a step forward, eager.

"Paul, do you ever . . . miss . . . what he had to-gether?"

Stunned by her question, he froze in place, hovering over the edge of the bed, unsure of which way to go.

Finally, he said, "I don't miss the fighting."

"Oh . . ." Anne swallowed hard. "I see."

He joked, "An accident waiting to marry, right?"

"Something like that." She studied her nails. "So why did we do it, then?"

Paul shrugged, answering by rote. "We were young . . . We were stupid . . . We were—"

"In love?" She waited for him to confirm the assertion, then, getting nothing, clarified, "At least I was."

"Why?"

Anne blinked. "Excuse me?"

"Why did you think you were in love with me?"

"Oh, God, Paul, again?"

"You never really answered it the first time I asked."

And he so desperately needed her to. He was pleading, begging Anne to give him something, anything to work with here. Something to explain and categorize the emotions that first took him hostage almost twenty years ago, and were, even as they spoke, resurfacing with a vengeance Paul never dreamed possible.

Anne squeezed the pillow with her good fist, shaking her head. "That's because I can't answer it. Not the way you need me to. I loved you with feelings, Paul, not with reasons."

He snorted, "Well, that explains it, then, doesn't it?"

"What does it explain?"

"Why our marriage was such an unmitigated disaster. We had no foundation, no basis. Face it, we were doomed to fail."

Anne flinched, her hurt scrawled as clearly on her face as if she'd scribbled it there with a marker. And, frankly, he resented it. Anne was always so candid with her feelings. Sometimes Paul suspected she used her vulnerability as a weapon. She had to know how badly it tore him up to hurt her. He wondered if, by allowing him to see that hurt, she was deliberately punishing him in return.

"Why are you so angry with me right now?" Anne asked.

"I am not angry."

"You are. I know you are. See, you're so determined to prove Paul Gaasbeck never yells or does anything that might indicate he's a human being, that the angrier you feel, the quieter your voice gets. Which, when you think about it, is no different from people whose voices get louder when they're angry—only in reverse."

*Now* she was deliberately trying to provoke him. She couldn't poke holes in Paul's claim that their marriage decomposed because it was based on feelings, not reasons, so, to win their argument, she was changing the subject, hoping to make Paul so angry that he would forget what they were really discussing. He knew he should do what he usually did under such circumstances. He should refuse to continue the conversation, refuse to give her the power to get to him like this. But, damn it, the idea of letting Anne win, the idea of even letting her *think* she'd won, especially when she was so, so wrong, stuck in his gut. He couldn't let the issue drop. He had to show her.

"You want to know why I'm so angry?" Paul raised his hands in the air, index fingers up like pistols. "I'll tell you why I'm so angry. I am angry, I am goddamn furious, because your whole life, you've been so anxious to prove that you can get away with breaking rules other people have to follow, that you've taken unnecessary risk after unnecessary risk. And, this time, you almost killed my daughter because of it."

"That's not true," she leaned forward, pupils blazing. "You have no right to accuse ..." Unexpectedly Anne's voice trailed off. She shut her mouth, falling back against the headboard and staring up at the ceiling, swallowing deep gulps of air.

"Annie, are you okay?" Paul swooped to sit down next to her, pressing a hand to her face. "What happened?"

She exhaled, shaking her head side to side. "I'm fine.

"Well, you could have fooled me. What's wrong? Your arm?"

"No, really. I'm okay. I just—I just remembered something Amelia said. About me pushing and pushing and pushing you to admit how you honestly feel, then, when you finally do, saying you've got no right to feel that way."

It was the last thing in the world Paul expected Anne to say. And so he had no idea how to react.

"She's a smart kid, isn't she?" Anne smiled, patting his hand as it rested on her cheek before returning it gently to Paul's lap. "I'm feeling tired, again. I think I'll get some sleep."

"Yes." He hopped off the bed. "Yes, you do that. I— I'll see you in the morning, Annie."

She slid under the covers, allowing him to tuck her in the way he would Amelia, and murmured drowsily, "Don't you have work in the morning? You've missed so many days already."

Paul stiffened.

And recited the lie he'd been rehearsing for days. "It's fine. I'm on compassion leave."

"Really? For how long?"

"Indefinitely."

Even asleep, Paul heard Anne scream.

He was off the couch and up the stairs and in her room before his groggy mind even registered what exactly was happening.

Anne sat upright in bed, sheets and blanket twisted around her like a whirlpool. She was shaking so violently, she made the whole frame quake with her, one hand clamped over her mouth to muffle the sobs. Still trapped in her nightmare, she cried, "I killed her."

"Annie, wake up." Paul's first impulse was to grab and shake her by both shoulders. But mindful of her injured arm, he settled for prying her hand away from her face, squeezing Anne's chin, and forcing her to look at him. "Wake up, baby."

"I killed her," she repeated, eyes unfocused and looking right through him.

"Who? Who did you kill?"

"Amelia." Her tears warmly licked the edge of Paul's fingers.

"Amelia? No, Annie, no, sweetheart, Amelia's fine."

"You said I killed her because I wouldn't follow the rules."

"I never said that." Paul shook his head frantically, hoping she could make out his gesture in the dark. "I said—oh, hell, forget what I said. You didn't kill Amelia. You saved her life."

"I never should have tried flying through that ice storm. If Amelia wasn't with me, she never would have gotten hurt."

"If Amelia wasn't with *you,* she'd have died for sure. You are the only pilot I know, Annie, who would have ever envisioned, much less risked, making the kind of emergency landing you did. And you are *definitely* the only one I know skillful enough to have pulled it off. If you'd stuck to the rules instead of improvising, both of you would be dead right now."

Overwhelmed, Anne's voice sunk to a whisper, her gaze focusing squarely on Paul. "Do you mean that?"

"I always mean what I say."

She stared up at him, wanting so badly to believe the truth of his words, but for a moment, she simply couldn't.

Then, as Paul's sincerity sank in, she squeezed his hand and impulsively kissed his palm, murmuring, "Oh, Paul. Thank you."

The brush of her lips against his skin proved Paul's downfall. All of a sudden, he was noticing how the strap of her nightgown had slipped off one shoulder. All of a sudden, he was tightening his fists to keep from peeling it the rest of the way, and wishing he'd thrown on a robe before rushing upstairs, dressed only in the cotton briefs he'd slept in.

It had, after all, been so long since he'd touched her. Since he'd held her. And they still fit together so perfectly.

"Annie . . ."

She didn't answer him. At least not in words.

Instead Anne lifted her hand, resting it on his neck, fingers caressing the velvet triangle of hair at his nape. Ever so slowly, she pulled him toward her, joining her mouth to his.

Paul could have stopped her at any time. He could have pulled away, he could have asked her to explain what it was they were doing and why. But the rudimentary truth of it was, he didn't want to.

What he wanted was to kiss her. Deeply and possessively and forever. But the instant their lips touched, Paul realized that what he'd previously identified as wanting was nothing compared to the aching hunger that possessed him now. Because now there was no more want, only need, an emotion he hinged his pride on denying.

His hands, still ostensibly on no-touch-automatic-pilot, disregarded orders and, without Paul's being aware of it, unclenched their fists, migrating to rest on Anne's shoulders. He slid his left palm down her arm, fingers dipping beneath the slipped strap of her nightgown, and tugging it downward until the lacy, lavender triangle covering Anne's breast tipped, revealing soft, warm flesh just ripe for him to cup in his hand.

He tasted her thrilled intake of breath as his tongue probed her mouth, sucking in her moan of pleasure between his lips. His thumb circled her nipple, first with the heat of skin on skin, then the chill of his nail, constantly alternating sensations until Anne was writhing beneath him, arching her back, straining.

Her left arm drifted down his back and across Paul's stomach, and, before he knew it, she'd slipped past the band of his briefs, returning the favor of cupping *him* within *her* hand and lazily rippling her nails along the length of him, stopping at the tip to rub precise, teasing circles in sync with the ones he was stroking around her equally hard nipple.

"Do you like it when I do this?" she inquired innocently.

*Yes,* Paul screamed in his head. *Yes, yes, yes to anything you say, and anything you want, and anything you want me to—*

The breadth of her power over him brought Paul to his senses much quicker than even a bucket of ice water dumped over his head. He was doing it again. Allowing her to get to him, allowing her to control not only his thoughts, but his deeds.

This was exactly what prompted all of his trials in the first place. Everything from Paul failing to win the Commander's Trophy to his rendezvous in two days time with the disciplinary committee scheduled to evaluate his actions with the Apache and judge whether Paul's temporary suspension from Air Force duty should be prolonged into a lifelong one. It all could be traced back to Anne's ability to make him lose his mind and do things he knew were wrong for him.

Like right now.

Paul knew that getting involved with his ex-wife would be suicide. And yet he wanted to. He wanted to so badly, that he was willing to ignore his common sense.

And that realization scared him most of all.

"No." He pulled away from her, mind dragging body in a feat of control unprecedented even by Paul's standards. "No, Annie. I don't like this at all."

# ═══ 18 ═══

*1991*

"I am the worst mommy in the world." The night they received order to ship out for Iraq, Anne and Paul lay side by side in their bed, his arm under her head, both staring at the ceiling. "I know how upset Amelia is going to be. But I can't wait to get there."

Paul shifted his head so that it rested on top of Anne's, and softly offered, "If that's your definition of being the worst mommy in the world, then you'd best put me down as the worst daddy. I'm dying to go. I can barely keep my mind on anything else."

Anne sighed. "We suck as parents."

He smiled, sliding his hand down Anne's arm and linking his fingers with hers. "We have been waiting for this opportunity our entire lives. Who wouldn't be roaring to go?"

Anne rolled over on her side, propping her head with her palm. "So it doesn't bother you that I'm going, too?"

Paul didn't answer at once. She felt the muscles in his arm stiffen. She was about to tell him to forget it, she didn't want to know, when he cleared his throat and asked, "Have I ever broken my promise to quit being jealous of your achievements?"

"No. Though I know it's been hard for you at times."

"Not too hard. Luckily, in the past four years, you haven't managed to outdo me. In anything."

She elbowed him in the ribs. "You bum."

"Just laying out the facts."

Anne kissed his chest, rubbing her cheek against the chestnut hairs. "Thank you, Paul."

Days into the deployment, troops in Saudi Arabia began calling the crisis "mom's war." Evidence of the 35,000 servicewomen erupted wherever anyone looked. They maintained tanks, handled petroleum, coordinated the water supply, drove trucks, handled cargo, worked as intelligence specialists, as paratroopers, shipboard navigators, flight controllers, communications experts, and ground-crew chiefs. Women pilots ferried supplies and personnel in Huey helicopters, or in Anne's case, aboard the gigantic C-141 transports.

Living quarters for U.S. Air Force personnel in Saudi Arabia consisted of khaki sheets draped between car spaces in the airport parking garage. Enlisted men lived four to a "room." Officers got their own parking spaces. Anne and Paul's quarters lay on separate levels, so the closest she got to him was on January 17, when he ran past her en route to a briefing. She called out his name, and he turned, jogging backward and slowing his pace just a fraction.

She shouted over the din, "I hear you're the first ones in."

"We're the Air Force." He indicated the whirlpool of uniforms rushing by on either side of him. "We're always first in."

"Just don't do anything stupid, okay?"

"Hey." He tapped his hands against his chest. "It's me."

She lay fast asleep when Zoe Yednock yanked the sheet around Anne's parking spot and grabbed her arm, tugging her off the bed. "Come quick, Annie. Paul's got a bandit on his tail."

Without pausing to yank on her shoes, Anne streaked after Zoe into the command center, where they maintained radar contact with all the F-16s via an AWACS craft orbiting over Saudi Arabia.

Instantly, Anne's attention was seized by the beeping green-dot representation of her husband's jet being engaged by an Iraqi MiG sitting on his six. The dots circled like a dog chasing its tail. The minute one moved, the other mirrored him.

Over the radio, Paul narrated, "Dropping down to 10,000 feet."

Zoe lay her hand reassuringly on Anne's shoulder. Anne didn't react. The whole of her being was focused on two blinking lights.

"Bandit at three o'clock." Paul's voice bypassed the fifteen other airmen in their space and addressed itself privately to Anne.

She watched the monitor. But in her mind's eye, Anne sat in the cockpit with Paul, seeing what he saw, hearing what he heard, feeling what he felt. She whispered, "Engaging," a split second prior to Paul's relaying the same information.

From AWACS came the message, "Captain Gaasbeck, be advised the bandit has received a Redcat, permission to arm weapons."

"Roger that." Paul tried rolling his F-16 forty degrees left, attempting to trap the MiG within the head-on-kill capabilities of his AIM-9L Sidewinder missiles. He stroked the missile button on his control stick with his thumb, waiting for an opening to fire.

Anne felt his calm, his detachment, the slowed-down time, the near-divine sense of invincibility. No wonder the joke around his squadron was, "You know, they say God has a Gaasbeck complex."

Anne pressed her palms together and tapped her thumbs against her lips. She was so engrossed in the monitor, the green dots reflected in her pupils.

Paul pulled down hard on the MiG, diving beneath the bandit's belly and zooming out behind him like a swimmer bobbing underneath a boat and surfacing on the other side.

"He's got an AI lock-on," Anne said.

Sympathetic, Zoe continued rubbing Anne's arm. Yet she felt obligated to point out, "Not yet."

"He's got him," Anne insisted.

Zoe and the radar operator exchanged looks.

"Ready." The Captains Gaasbeck announced in unison, prompting more than one person to turn and stare at her strangely.

"Firing." The last half of Paul's word got lost in the hiss of a Sidewinder's rocket motor igniting as the missile dropped from its wing-tipped pylon. Followed by static on the radio line.

And only one green dot remaining on the monitor.

No one moved. No one spoke. Zoe's fingers dug into Anne's shoulder, and Anne found herself patting it absently, reassuring, "It's okay. Paul's okay. He got him."

"Annie . . ."

"Captain Gaasbeck, report your status. Over."

More static.

Then, "Gaasbeck, here. Iraqis minus one bandit. Over."

\*    \*    \*

News that Captain Paul Gaasbeck had secured the first official kill of the war disseminated across their air base hours before his fighter even touched back down. Paul climbed out of his cockpit, but never made it to the ladder's bottom rung as a mass of bodies encircled him, slapping high fives, applauding, and thrusting out hands to shake. "All right!"

"Well done, Captain."

"You sure showed them."

He responded to the accolades with respectful nods and handshakes, but the whole time kept scanning the landscape, searching for something he couldn't articulate or define. Smoke filled his eyes, joining the sand that seemed perpetually stuck to the inside of his lids, and he blinked repeatedly, trying to clear them. He rubbed his eyes with the back of his sleeve, and when he lowered his hand, he saw Anne standing at the edge of the landing strip.

For a moment, neither of them moved.

He ached to reach out to her, to pull her into his arms and crush her against him with all of his strength. The feeling swept over him like a wave, narrowing Paul's vision until he could see nothing save her. So, naturally, he refused to move a muscle. He waited for her to come to him.

Which Anne did, gladly, pushing aside the throng of men, some of them nearly twice her size and weight, to jump up and throw her arms around Paul's neck. He caught her around the waist, lifting her off the ground and burrowing his face in her hair, inhaling so deeply, he felt his lungs rebelling at the smell of anything other than rubber masks, stale air, or fuel. Despite having dredged up the strength to keep from rushing over the moment he saw her, Paul knew he had no more resistance left. He'd lost the war the moment he felt her body against his. Despite the bulkiness of the flight suit, he still recognized every curve and peak. It may have been wrong to stand at the center of an airfield, in full view of his superiors, and kiss his wife so deeply that it inspired yet another round of applause from his colleagues, but Paul no longer had the strength of character to resist temptation. He promised himself he could beat himself up about it. Later.

Paul lowered Anne to the ground, and arms wrapped around each other's waists, they moved through the pack, neither of them saying a word or taking their eyes off the other.

She walked with Paul back to his room, drawing the drape shut behind them. He sat on his cot, stance wide, palms bearing down on his knees, elbows turned out, and stared straight ahead at nothing in particular. Perspiration dripped along his face, trickling down his neck and into the triangle of skin where he'd unclasped the top snap of his flight suit. "It was me or him, Annie."

"I know."

She helped Paul maneuver out of his suit, his movements torpid and perfunctory, his flesh scalding to her touch.

Anne stepped out for a moment, fetching a basin of tepid water and a sponge. When she returned, Paul still sat poised where she'd left him, naked except for cotton briefs—regulation for fliers; in a fire, synthetic fibers melted and adhered to the skin—his eyes fixed on a target only he could discern. The single sound in their room was the next-door garble of a neighbor's battery-powered AM/FM blasting Desert Storm Radio, a wartime creation broadcasting the mismatched brew of Bette Midler's peaceful "From a Distance," followed by the song bombers favored, "Another One Bites the Dust."

Paul didn't turn his head to look at Anne. He said, "I can't find the right words."

"You will." Anne set the basin down on the floor, dipped in the sponge, wrung it out, and pressed it tentatively against Paul's flushed back. His every muscle coiled so tightly in response, Anne half-expected him to ricochet away from her caress. His skin felt feverish, with purple and scarlet bruises beginning to swell along his spine. Despite the warm water, Paul shivered. He squeezed his fists to control himself, tearing the blisters he'd scoured on his palms by tightly clutching the throttle. Sweat continued to stream down his body. Anne dabbed at it gently, doing the only thing she could think of to calm him. She massaged his back, his shoulders, his neck, his chest, pretending she could wipe away his ambivalence as easily as she wiped away the lines of perspiration. She bathed his forearms and wrists, and felt his heart hammering so fiercely she feared it would rip through the fragile flesh below his palms.

She urged him to lie down, and Paul did so obediently. Anne pulled up a chair next to his cot, unsure of how much comfort her presence would bring but resolved to give him everything she had.

A week into the war, Anne's continuing requests for a transfer either persuaded, or wore down, the top brass. She received a new set of orders. A Navy pilot under attack had ejected behind enemy lines—Paul said, "Why those Navy fellows can't stick to playing with their boats, and stay out of our skies, I'll never know"—and signaled his location from the desert. The Air Force had his coordinates. Now, Anne was set to pilot the rescue helicopter and command the rescue mission. She would be flying a good fifty miles into Iraq, operating in CFM, computer flight mode, at two hundred feet, under heavy cloud cover and, God willing, below Iraqi radar. Excited by the chance to show history being made—a woman flying if not actual combat, then damn close—a CNN television crew had also talked itself on board, prepared to send back live footage.

"I know, I know," Anne told Paul, "Picking me was a knee-jerk, PC attempt to put a female-friendly face on the Air Force for TV."

"At least they picked the most qualified female in the Gulf."

She melted. "You really know how to flatter a girl, Captain."

"Just don't do anything stupid, okay?"

"Hey," she reminded, "it's me."

He was supposed to be finishing up his report on the destroyed bandit. And Paul really did try. He powered his laptop computer, he hammered the keys, he connected nouns to verbs in grammatically proper order. Yet, somehow, every time he tried to read back what he'd written, not a single thought made sense. Paul couldn't even figure out what he'd meant to say.

He could, however, have told anybody who asked precisely how many seconds had elapsed since Anne's Black Hawk took off for the Iraqi desert. And how many times he'd stopped himself from getting up, walking across the base to where CNN had set up its makeshift broadcast center, and watching Anne's progress on the satellite.

Yet no matter how hard he tried to concentrate, he couldn't. Despite the staggering piles of work stacked in order of priority across his cot, all Paul could think of was Annie. He'd promised himself he wouldn't drop by the broadcast center. He was on duty, after all. However, if Paul took a break right now, if he ran—and he meant *ran*—to CNN's broadcast center, peeked at how Annie looked on camera, satisfied his curiosity, then bolted back to his desk, he would be able to, God willing, complete his work roughly around the time it was due.

Sure he was behaving like a fool.

But at least now he was a fool with a plan.

The CNN newspeople had airlifted an armada of satellite trucks into the area. Inside, there was barely room to stand as an array of producers, directors, associate directors, switchers, audio men, graphics people, and production assistants squeezed by each other, taking turns watching the video-screen embedded walls. Everyone talked at the same time, some into headsets, others into thin air, every volume switch set at full blast. But despite the hubbub, Paul's attention lay solely on the TV monitor above the producer's head, the one showing a live feed of Anne's rescue mission.

The cameraman sat behind her in the cockpit, filming the edge of Anne's right shoulder, along with the helicopter's rotary blades whirling their shadow on the landscape. Paul saw Anne's reflection in the windshield, and felt a surge of pride. If the US Air Force wanted to put a female-friendly face on the service, they couldn't have chosen a more beautiful one.

A shotgun mike mounted on CNN's camera relayed every word Anne exchanged with her crew back into the production truck, and, as she approached the downed Navy pilot's coordinates, the producer yanked his attention away from the three other pieces he was editing and focused on the live picture.

"This is Captain Gaasbeck," Anne's voice piped in muffled but audible, as she pressed the intercom button on her cyclic control stick. "Moving into position."

Paul told himself that, despite TV's ominous depiction

of the barren landscape, Annie wasn't alone out there. She had a superb crew, and an Apache gunship overhead to cover her. The situation was under control. Everything was going to be fine.

"Three miles from target," Anne reported. "We're going in."

"Negative!" Sector AWACS crackled through her headset loud enough for everyone in the production truck to hear. "We've got a vehicle down there."

Forgetting that it was Anne doing the actual flying, not him, Paul's instinctual reaction was to lean forward, scanning the space in front of him for a nonexistent computer screen to confirm what he'd just heard. But all he saw was the back of the producer's head as he too leaned forward, pumping his intercom switch like a kid playing Space Invaders and screaming, "Show it to me!"

In a flash, his camera whipped away from Anne, zooming in on the given coordinates and revealing a tank rumbling toward their destination, moving so swiftly that, in another minute, Anne's UH-60 would swoop into its visual realm. She was flying so close to the ground, not even a blind gunner could miss shooting her down.

"Get out, Annie." Paul's breath stuck in his throat like the remnants of a particularly phlegmy cold. "Get out of there."

Yet on the monitor the Black Hawk continued on its flight plan. As did the Iraqi tank.

"What the hell?" The producer swiveled in his seat, scanning the TV-production truck for answers and, spotting Paul's uniform, figured he'd be the best one to ask. "If they can see the damn thing, why doesn't the . . . what's it called, the big chopper? . . ." He jerked his thumb toward the sky.

"The Apache?" Despite the thick wad of mucus drowning his vocal cords, when Paul answered his voice proved so modulated, he might have casually been offering a passerby the time of day.

"Yeah. That's the one. Why doesn't the Apache blow that tank away? I'd love to get a shot of it."

"It's too close. If they take out the tank, they risk killing our man on the ground." He replied by rote, watching the monitor, noting Anne listening closely to her headset and guessed, "She's being ordered to turn around."

"And just leave the pilot?"

"Better to come back for him later than have the entire rescue crew taken out by that tank."

The producer shook his head, disgusted. "Why'd this shit have to happen on *my* watch? I was promised a live rescue, goddamn it."

"She's definitely being ordered to head back." Paul nodded in agreement with the decision, feeling the lead ball pressing against both of his lungs gradually fall away.

"With all due respect,"—something in Anne's tone stopped the ball mid-dissolve. He knew that tone. Good God, did he know that tone—"I have no intention of abandoning a possibly hurt officer to the elements. What if there's a way to divert that tank long enough for the Apache to get a crack at him?"

The producer perked up. "Now we're talking, baby."

"No." Paul gripped the back of a chair. There was only one option left for her to try under these circumstance. "No, Annie. No. Don't do it."

But after eight years of marriage, she wasn't about to start listening to him now.

## ═══ 19 ═══

She'd waited almost twenty years, when, finally, Paul came to Anne on his own, wanting to talk. Unfortunately, she was no longer in the mood to listen. To her way of thinking, he'd made himself crystal clear the instant he walked out of her bedroom the night before.

It served her right, though, for getting her damned hopes up. For thinking that his telling her he didn't blame her for the crash was the sign she'd been waiting for. The symbol that would demonstrate, once and for all, that, contrary to appearances, Paul really did care about her, that he wasn't as apathetic as he acted.

What a joke. If last night demonstrated anything, it was that she couldn't even affect him physically anymore. Even at her worst times, those indigo hours at three in the morning during which she endlessly wondered why her husband's words so infrequently matched his actions, Anne had felt convinced of one thing—as long as she could still turn Paul on, he couldn't ever be totally indifferent to her presence. And now she didn't even have that to hold on to. What better evidence did Anne need of how little grasp she had on Paul than the way he'd pulled away from her kiss? So calm, so collected, so . . . nonchalant. He'd simply stood up and

turned his back on her. Not hurrying. More like . . . saun-
tering.

The following morning, when Paul felt like rehashing
the gory details, Anne wasn't nearly as motivated to re-
ciprocate. She was still in bed when he came in, trying,
with no success, to wriggle her fingers inside their bandages, and ending up with the sensation of razor blades
scraping the inside of her arm for her trouble.

Last night, despite similar discomfort, Anne had succeeded in yanking her lavender nightgown off over her
head and squeezing into a more sensible, yellow cotton
pair of pajamas. Paul, dressed for the new day in jeans
and a denim shirt he'd driven to his house to get, noticed
the change. But as expected, he didn't say a word.

Instead he told Anne, "About what happened last
night, I've been thinking . . ."

"Of course you have."

Her hostility masquerading as sarcasm went wasted
on him. The man didn't so much as blink.

"I've been thinking about how what happened—almost happened—between us, really didn't mean anything."

"Right," she snapped. "It was nothing personal. You
would have done the same for anyone. I get it."

"It wasn't real, Annie." Paul's tone was gentle, ginger even. "We were affected by our surroundings. Being
back here, together, in our bedroom, barely dressed . . .
We got carried away."

"We? As in me and you—emphasis on you?"

"Yes." He made no attempt to duck the blame. "I'll
admit it. *I* got carried away. You're a beautiful woman,
Annie. And we were once married."

"I remember." Anne nodded, wishing like hell she
could keep from smiling. But it was a losing battle.
When Paul was trying his best to act contrite, Anne's

shelf life for indignation tended to crumble under its own weight.

"As long as we both understand that the reason we almost—"

"Paul."

"Yes?"

"Congratulations. You're a grown-up."

He blinked. "I beg your pardon?"

"That was a big concession for you, admitting that you got as carried away as I did. A couple of years ago, you'd have pretended nothing happened, leaving me totally confused."

"Yes, well. That's why I wanted to make certain we were both on the same page. So that there wouldn't be any misunderstanding."

She sighed reassuringly, "It's all right. I do understand." He was being a gentleman to the end, casting aside his own discomfort about the previous night to insure she didn't get the wrong idea. He didn't want Anne thinking his almost making love to her meant that his feelings for her had strayed into the personal. He didn't want her being hurt again when she discovered that they hadn't, that their closeness had merely been a brief, physiological lapse.

"Thank you, Annie," he said, "for being so understanding."

"You're welcome."

Paul rubbed his hands together, looking not at Anne but over her head. "You're right, you know. A couple years ago I probably would have pretended nothing happened. You sure broke me of that habit." He delivered his next thought with a snicker so, if his statement elicited the wrong response, he could still pass it off as a joke. "I guess you had a good influence on me, after all."

She thought he no onger had the power to surprise her. She was wrong. Anne looked up at Paul, and rose to her knees on the bed. "Do you really mean that?"

He reminded, "I always mean what I say."

Anne rested a hand on his shoulder, admitting, "I suppose you had a good influence on my life, too."

"Well, naturally."

She snapped his cheek with her fingers, "You bum," and flopped back down on the bed.

Paul smiled, sitting down next to her. "How?"

She smacked him with a pillow. "You never quit, do you?"

"So I like concrete reasons. So shoot me."

"Don't think I haven't considered it from time to time."

"Mom!"

Amelia's voice from the hallway unexpectedly prompted Anne and Paul to spring apart, despite the fact that they hadn't been doing anything more incriminating than pillow fighting. Their daughter burst through the door without knocking, making both Anne and Paul thankful she hadn't tried it a few hours earlier.

"Mom, Lyle's on the phone."

Lyle . . .

He'd called her in Colorado, asking if Anne wanted him to fly up, and reluctantly concurring when she reassured him there was no need. She'd promised to phone him as soon as she got in.

Amelia thrust forward the portable telephone, urging Anne to take it. Anne hesitated, sneaking a peek at Paul out of the corner of her eye. He, in turn, looked away, developing a sudden, burning interest in the bedroom's decor.

If he would only look at her, if he would only give her some hint, some indication of what he was feeling.

But Paul's mask had slipped into place the minute Amelia uttered Lyle's name.

Anne looked at Amelia, the phone between them seeming to grow with every electronic pulse. Behind her Paul cleared his throat.

"Ace?" Anne made up her mind in the split second it took her to sense that she was about to lose the goodwill she and Paul had so tenuously built up over the last few minutes. "Would you do me a favor? Tell Lyle I'm still sleeping, and I'll call him later?"

Amelia's brow wrinkled in what Anne suspected was the mirror image of Paul's expression behind her back.

"Please, Ace?"

Her daughter shrugged. "Okay."

But before she could push the talk button, Paul whisked the phone out of Amelia's hand, and raised it to his ear. "Lyle? Paul Gaasbeck, here . . . Yes, it's wonderful speaking with you again, too. Listen, Lyle, Annie's kind of busy right now. She'll call when she needs you. Have a nice day. Good bye." He flicked off the switch and handed the receiver back to Amelia.

Anne cocked her head to one side. "That was certainly firm yet insulting."

Paul shrugged. "The man's a weasel." He waited for Amelia to leave the room to return the phone to its crib in the living room, before steering discussion deftly away from his atypical behavior by grilling Anne, "Why didn't you—"

"I don't want to talk about it, all right?" She sprung off the bed, rifling through her closet.

"But," his eyes twinkled, "it's important to talk everything out. I learned that from you."

She turned around, hand on her hip. "I said I didn't want to talk about it. Let's just say that's one of the things I learned from *you*, and leave it at that, okay?"

Paul fired off a salute. "Yes, ma'am."

Amelia walked back into the bedroom, and Paul slipped his arm around her shoulders, asking, "If Mom's feeling up to it, how would you girls like me to take you out for the day?"

"Yeah!" Amelia hopped up and clapped. "Can we, Mom?"

Anne wondered how she was supposed to say no to her daughter's beaming face. Then she realized that was precisely what Paul was banking on. Anne asked, "Where do you want to go?"

"Actually," he said, "I was thinking the amusement park. . . ."

She had been there at least a dozen times before with Amelia, and yet strolling the grounds with Paul, Anne saw the attraction through different eyes. She saw the paint peeling off rides promising a thrill a minute. She saw the drooping ears on the stuffed-bunny prizes. She noted that the kids sitting and bawling outnumbered the ones running around and laughing.

Anne told Paul, "No wonder you hate amusement parks."

Amelia shot her mom a strange look. "Dad and I come here all the time, don't we, Dad?"

Anne raised a questioning eyebrow. Paul shrugged. "What can I say? I've developed a taste for the place."

They wandered around for a solid half hour before Amelia gave up attempting to send her parents a hint by gazing longingly at the various roller coasters, and flat out asked, "So, can we get on?"

Paul and Anne exchanged looks. Considering the excitement of last week, both were surprised by how eager Amelia was to terrorize herself again. Reading their minds, she patiently explained, in a sort of Kid-Logic-for-Dummies, "Roller coasters aren't real scary. They're pretend scary. You always know you can get off."

Briefly, Anne wondered what it was about her ex and her child that prompted both to divide equally tangible experiences into *real* and *not real*. To Anne's mind, if something happened, then it happened. It couldn't be qualified. Her family, however, seemed to know as many ways to interpret events as the Eskimos had words for snow.

"You go if you want." Anne indicated her arm. "But I don't think I'm quite up for the roller coasters yet."

"Oh." Amelia wrinkled her nose. "That's okay, then, Mom. I don't have to."

Paul laughed. "Very convincing, Ace. Tell you what. You run and ride whatever you like, and I'll think of some way to entertain your mom for a bit." He looked at Anne. "What do you say? Think the arm's up for a spin on the Ferris wheel?"

As the attendant pressed down and locked the safety bar across their chests, Paul said, "It's been a while."

"No kidding, I think the last time I was on a Ferris wheel . . ." Anne's voice trailed off. By the look on Paul's face, she saw that he remembered perfectly well when that was. Her cheeks flushed.

"Yes," Paul remarked dryly. "That *was* a good ride."

She couldn't tell if he was being serious or sarcastic. With Paul, the two so often sounded the same.

The wheel rose.

Except for their *not real* encounter the other night, Paul and Anne hadn't sat in such close proximity for seven years. On the plane from Colorado to Utah, they'd at least had an arm-rest for a buffer. Now they sat side by side, so close that Anne felt the heat radiating from

Paul's skin caress her cheek. Their two thighs pressed one against the other, generating heat of a different sort, and prompting Anne to moderate the ongoing debate inside her brain between factions that wanted to move away, and ones that urged her to move closer. On the one hand, allowing Paul to affect her like this was just asking for trouble. The gentleman had shown her, in at least eight different ways that Anne could count, that he didn't give a damn about her except as the mother of his child. If she persisted in pursuing her dreams of the two of them somehow finding their way back to each other, then she was just setting herself up for heartache. On the other hand, Anne had thought she'd detected the teeniest, tiniest bit of jealousy when Lyle called, leaving her to hope that just maybe her ex-husband wasn't quite as indifferent to her existence as she thought.

Yet Anne refused to allow herself to leap to any conclusions. If there was one thing she'd learned about Paul over the years, it was that he couldn't, and shouldn't, be pushed.

So, rather than following what would have been her instinct in the past: hammering him with direct questions until she heard what she wanted to hear or Paul shut her out completely, Anne tried the roundabout approach, telling him, "Ferris wheels are all right. But roller coasters are more my style."

He nodded, turning his head and smiling. "Annie's Wild Ride?"

"An oldie but a goodie."

"You know," he tapped the safety bar with his thumb, "there's more than one Annie's Wild Ride in the country."

"Sure. My folks built a couple of them."

"When Amelia and I went to upstate New York last

year for that hike she wanted to do, we found a county fair that had one.''

"Right. Thornham fairgrounds. Did you ride it?''

"Well, we sort of had to, didn't we?'' Paul leaned back in the cabin. "It wasn't the best Annie's Wild Ride I've ever been on.''

Okay. Now she really couldn't tell if he was being serious or sarcastic. Nevertheless, Anne's heart beat faster.

She joked, "How many have you been on?''

"Enough.'' He sighed. "See, the problem with roller coasters is, sure, it's a thrill being at the very top of the spike, but you forget: afterward there's a long, long, long way down.''

The wheel fell.

"Then again,'' she reminded, "there's always another thrilling spike looming right around the next corner.''

"But,'' Paul raised his finger, "remember physics class. The subsequent spikes can only get progressively lower with each hill.''

Anne didn't say a word, letting him expand the metaphor.

"And, after a while, you get sick of never knowing which way a roller coaster might go. Up, down, sideways. It's fun in the beginning. But eventually you long for something calmer.''

"Like a Ferris wheel?''

"Exactly. Up-down. Up-down. It's got a set rhythm. You can predict how it's going to go. It gives you a feeling of control.''

"Sounds pretty dull.''

"Perhaps. But after a full day of roller coasters, sometimes a Ferris wheel is all you have the energy for. . . . Don't tell me that isn't the reason you hooked up with Jellison.''

The wheel rose.

Unaware that they'd switched from allegories to specifics, it took Anne a beat before she regrouped and snapped, "Of course not."

"Please." Paul rolled his eyes. "I've met the man."

"Lyle happens to be very intelligent, very caring, very—"

"If you say 'jump,' he won't even wait to ask 'how high?'"

"So what?" Anne demanded, "So he doesn't question every word I say. So he lets me win an argument once in a while."

"That must be pretty difficult, considering you never argue." To explain how he knew, Paul confessed, "Amelia told me."

"Amelia is eleven years old. You're going to let her define my relationships?"

"I repeat, I've met the man. We are talking serious snake-oil factor here. What do you do, wring him out at the end of the day?"

"Meaning?"

"Meaning, he's a slimy bastard. Have you ever noticed how he always has an answer for everything? How the hell do you trust the integrity of a man who's always got an answer for *everything*?"

"At least, when I ask him a question, he gives me an answer."

"But does he mean what he says? Or does he just say what you want to hear, so he can smooth over the circumstance and move on to something else? Jesus, Annie, was he really the best you could do? He doesn't even fly, for Pete's sake."

"Like I could ever date another pilot. Hell, all it took was one of your patented, withering looks, and I was off limits to the entire Air Force. Possibly even the whole Department of Defense.''

''Would you want to date another pilot?''

''Yes,'' Anne said, in all honesty. ''But this time I'd like for him to be worse than me.''

Paul laughed. He laughed so hard, he made their cabin shake side to side, attracting the worried glances of the attendant.

''My God, you really are something else, aren't you?''

''Why ask for problems? If I'm clearly the better pilot, we'll have nothing to argue about.''

''Oh, Annie . . .''

''Oh, Annie, what?'' When he wouldn't answer, she pressed, ''For the record, I have seen what you date. Talk about being able to do better. Air-Force groupies from the O Club? Really, Paul, where's the challenge in that? Those girls practically pick themselves up. What do you talk about? What they did in school today?''

''We,'' he cleared his throat, ''rarely talk much.''

The wheel fell.

Anne wondered whether she was a genuine masochist or merely a run-of-the-mill fool. Clearly, Paul hadn't exactly been celibate since the divorce. Not that Anne expected him to be. He was much too good-looking, especially in his uniform, and the Officer's Club was much too full of groupies for that to realistically happen. So why, then, did hearing him say what she already knew hurt so much?

Anne said, ''Lyle asked me to marry him.''

''Congratulations.''

She'd never known five syllables could be so devastating. Or that the blissful heat radiating from Paul's body could so easily chill into frost. With all of her heart, Anne wished she could say that enshrouded in those same seemingly innocent five syllables was even a dab of resentment. Or outrage. Or interest. But there was only so long that even the world's most vehement optimist could go on fooling herself.

Earlier, she'd vowed to chomp down on her tongue and keep from pushing Paul, no matter how loudly her old instincts screamed that if she'd just press the right buttons she'd manage to squeeze a few drops of response out of him—even if they only created frustration. The sole factors holding her back were Amelia's counsel and Anne's own realization that the more she pressured Paul into expressing an emotion, any emotion, the quicker he'd shut down.

Armed with such better-late-than-never awareness, she'd hoped she'd be able to keep herself from lapsing into old habits. But the reality was, without a sign from Paul that he wasn't thoroughly indifferent to her existence, Anne's uncertainty got the better of her, and she, as always, became willing to settle for any reply—even a negative one—as long as it meant he'd quit ignoring her.

To that end, Anne pulled out her big gun, knowing that once it was fired, there'd be no going back. She'd have to live with the consequences the rest of her life.

"Paul?"

"Hm?" He'd been scanning the ground, trying to locate Amelia among the carousel of brightly colored winter coats swelling from attraction to attraction.

"If you could rewind the clock and go back to the last time we rode a Ferris wheel together . . . would you?"

Paul turned his head to look at her. He smiled wistfully, or maybe Anne was just imagining things, and glanced briefly over his shoulder, running his fingers over the grid behind them, recalling a time when Anne's

holding on to similar wiring was all that kept them from
tumbling out.

He asked, "And would we then live our whole lives
over again, starting from that moment?"

"Uhm, sure, I guess so."

"Knowing what we know now, or starting at ground
zero again?"

"Jeez, Paul, I didn't plan this out like an essay question. I suppose we'd start from ground zero."

"Oh." He nodded thoughtfully, considering the suggestion from every possible angle. "Then what would
be the point?"

The wheel fell.


On their drive home—Amelia in the back chattering,
Anne in the front, silent—Paul tried to recall the last
time he'd failed a test. Especially one of his own making. Because that's what his entire day had been. The
amusement park, the Ferris wheel, Annie. He'd set himself up deliberately to prove that last night had been a
fluke, that he was quite capable of restraining himself
when Anne was around, no matter how intimate or familiar the circumstances. Like his daughter and her pen-
chant for roller coasters, Paul also spent his life pushing
the edge, doing things that frightened him to verify the
strength of his self-control. In the Gulf, Paul flew more
sorties than anyone, climbing back inside a jet even
when he was dead tired. During their divorce hearing,
Anne accused him of glory-seeking, claiming Paul guilty
of the same sin he often hurled at her—putting his own
ambition ahead of the goals of the mission. What she
didn't understand was that Paul didn't give a damn about
his place in the history books. The only one he had anything to prove to was himself. And the only subject he

cared about proving was that, no matter what, Paul Gaasbeck could remain in control.

Except where Anne was concerned.

The instant the attendant had lowered that safety bar, Paul's mind filled with images of fourteen years earlier—a summer night in Colorado Springs, and a girl in a radiant yellow dress with nothing on underneath. The sense of her then, sitting near enough to touch, near enough to taste, set the blood in Paul's veins to a slow boil, reaching overflow as soon as she asked him whether, given a chance, he would go back to that first night on the Ferris wheel.

Was the woman out of her mind?

She had to know how many nights—or worse, days—Paul had dreamed of exactly that. Of returning to specifically that night, when, even if it was only for a moment, everything seemed clear and simple, and the future shone brighter than ever before. While they were married, Anne had often referred to that night as the one when everything began. But for Paul, it was the night when everything ended. The hour before Commander's Trophy results were posted was the last one during which he felt confident of his ability to deal with any ordeal, no matter how extreme, in a calm, rational, and, most importantly, detached manner. Of course, at the time, he'd been thinking about combat, dog fights, torture by enemy soldiers. Not girls in yellow dresses.

Or lavender nightgowns.

He'd come so close this afternoon to chucking everything he'd believed in for thirty-six years and giving in to Anne's presence, that the memory of it still stung, like a bullet nicking the skin. He was furious with Anne for driving him to this point, but he was even more furious with himself for having allowed it.

Naturally, he couldn't allow Anne to glimpse the turmoil she'd sentenced him to. Although, as always, Paul suspected she already knew. She had to know. It was her weapon of choice against him, leaving Paul no other option but to fight back.

And so he matched her, silence for silence, all the way home. He barely said a word over dinner, addressing his sparse remarks to Amelia, noting that Anne did the same.

They spent the rest of the evening in front of the television, three pairs of eyes focused on a quartet of insipid sitcoms, none of which Paul found even remotely funny. He assumed he would have felt the same even if he had bothered to pay attention.

Lyle Jellison called a few minutes before the ten o'clock news started, and Anne stepped into her bedroom to take the call. When she returned, she purposely avoided Paul's eyes. He did the same.

Amelia flopped over on her stomach, chin propped against both fists, and sighed, shaking her head.

At 10:01, the lead story on the news showed the United States' renewed involvement in the Gulf. President Clinton, in response to threats from Saddam Hussein, was ordering an increase in the troops stationed in the Middle East.

Paul grit his teeth. Despite everything that had happened the first time, he was dying to get back into the action. Combat was the quickest path to promotion, and he did want his colonel's eagle very, very badly. Of course, with a possible court-martial looming in his future, Paul knew now that an eagle was a long shot.

He fought the impulse as long as he could, but finally Paul felt compelled to turn his head, to look at Anne, to somehow make her feel even a fraction of the hell she was putting him through. Except that before Paul got the chance, she bolted from her chair and ran to the bathroom, slamming the door after her and turning on the faucet.

He waited for her to come out, reluctant to waste a venomous glare on an absent target. But as the minutes ticked by, and the water continued gushing at a steady pace, Paul and Amelia exchanged worried glances. Neither could hear her moving around in there.

"Annie?" Paul stood, approaching the bathroom door, his mind instantly filling with doctors' warnings about the latent dangers of a concussion. Amelia followed, apprehensive.

"Annie?" He knocked authoritatively. "Are you all right?"

Her voice barely carried above the streaming water. "Fine." It sounded muffled, like something was covering her mouth.

"Open the door. I want to see for myself."

"Leave me alone, Paul. Please."

"Open the door, Annie." The fear on Amelia's face echoed the anxiety festering in his own gut, and the combination drove Paul to bark even harsher than he'd originally planned, "Open the goddamn door, or, so help me, I'll break it down."

"Go away, Paul. I'm begging you."

He stepped back, steering Amelia aside with his left arm and, with his right leg, carried out his promise, kicking the door with all of his might—and more than a little residual anger.

It shuddered open, doorknob lolling drunkenly. Anne sat on the border of the bathtub, facing the door, her injured arm across her lap, her left hand tightly pressed against her mouth. When she looked up, Paul realized she'd been crying.

"Oh, God." Anne whipped her face away, shielding it even more with the upraised hand. "Damn you, Paul.

I didn't want Amelia to see me like this.''

Their daughter stood in the doorway, eyes wide. She looked to Paul for an explanation, but he was having a hard time grasping it himself. "What's wrong, Mom?"

Anne shook her head, refusing to turn around. Her shoulders trembled with stifled sobs, curling forward as if she yearned to shrink and disappear from sight.

Paul stepped to the side, blocking Amelia's view of Anne and reassuring, "It's okay, Ace. Everything's okay. Your mom's just upset. You remember what the doctor told you both? About delayed shock? Well, I think maybe the last couple of days have finally caught up with her."

"Is Mom going to be all right?" Amelia strained to sneak a peek over his shoulder. Paul refused to let her. Not only for Amelia's sake, but for Anne's as well.

"She's going to be fine. Although, the best thing right now is for you to go on up to bed, okay? I'll take care of this."

"But—"

"Amelia." Paul switched on his Major's voice. "I said that I would take care of the situation."

She knew better than to argue.

Paul kissed his daughter's forehead. "That's my good girl."

"Good night, Dad."

"Good night, Ace."

She hesitated at the door. "Night, Mom."

When Anne didn't respond, Paul winked reassuringly at Amelia. "She's going to be just fine. You have my word."

Amelia disappeared around the corner.

He waited until he heard her bedroom door shut before steeling himself and turning back to face Anne.

Yet the swollen red circles around her eyes still managed to bewilder him, flooding Paul's senses with a taste of helplessness. Not his favorite emotion under any circumstances, especially where Anne was concerned. He didn't know how to proceed. This was one eventuality he'd never prepared for.

Still perched on the edge of the tub, Anne peered up at Paul, her voice hoarse. She whispered, "I didn't want *you* to see me like this, either."

In lieu of a better, or actually useful, idea, he decided to keep things light, reminding, "I've seen you cry before, Annie."

"You've never seen me give up before."

His blood chilled at her words, even as déjà vu swallowed his memory. "Actually . . ."

She shook her head. "The Academy? Major Danahay telling me I had no future in the Air Force? That was nothing. Not compared to this."

"Compared to what?"

"This!" Fresh tears drenched Anne's lashes as she thrust her injured arm forward, supporting it with her good hand. "This, damn it. I'm going to loose my fingers, Paul. As soon as the bandages come off, they're going to amputate. And then I'm finished. I am never, ever, flying again."

"You don't know that."

"Yes, I do. Finally, I do." She wiped both cheeks with her hand. "The last couple of days, I've been running around kidding myself, pretending everything was going to be okay. But seeing that deployment footage on television, it finally drove the point home. It's over for me. It's all over."

Paul's stomach churned. Fourteen years ago, her despair drove him to destroy his shot at the Commander's Trophy, all in the hope of making her smile again. But the madness that snatched him then was nothing compared to the emotions pummeling him today.

"Annie, no." Paul knelt before her, one leg up in proposal position, and cradled her hand in his, craning his neck to meet her eyes. "It's not over. Even if you can't fly anymore, there's lots of things you can still do in the Air Force. You are a wonderful engineer. Design would be thrilled to have you."

"Damn it," Anne pulled away from him. "You just don't get it, do you? Flying is all I have left."

"That's not true."

"It is. Amelia is practically grown, and I only have her half the time, anyway. I've lost you for good—I know that, now. The Air Force and flying is my whole life."

Interpreting Paul's ongoing silence as incomprehension rather than the genuine shock that it was, Anne railed at him, "But, what would you know? You've got no idea what I'm talking about. You've never sat terrified and helpless, sure that the only thing keeping you alive would be taken away from you."

His eyes darkened. Paul's grip on Anne's hand tightened until she actually winced from the tension.

"You're wrong." His voice matched his grip. "Annie, you have no idea of just how wrong you are."

$$\equiv 20 \equiv$$

*1991*

Paul's heart stopped.

In the split second it took Anne to alter her UH-60 Black Hawk helicopter's course and head straight for the Iraqi tank making its steady, rumbling trek toward the downed Navy pilot, Paul felt his heart squeeze so tight that he couldn't move. He couldn't breathe. For one frightening moment, even the vision in his eyes clouded, a gray film fogging up in front of him like factory exhaust.

She was out of her mind. Despite a direct order to abort the mission and return to base, Anne was striving to engage the Iraqi tank, hoping to lure it far enough away from the hurt pilot to give the Apache above her a clear shot at their target. A fine plan in theory, except for one thing: The only way for Anne to attract the tank's attention was by enticing it to fire at the Black Hawk.

Paul's legs gave out and he needed to grip the chair between his palms with all his might just to remain upright. Never, ever in his entire life had he previously felt like this. Certainly, he'd been scared before. More than anybody else in his squadron, Paul subscribed to the Air

Force maxim that there were bold pilots, and there were old pilots, but there were no old, bold pilots. He believed that a healthy amount of fear was mandatory to living out his thirty-year hitch, and so was used to, in fact, he counted on, the comforting, life-preserving fear that climbed into the cockpit with him for every flight. But this was a different kind of fear. This fear, instead of triggering an endorphine rush powerful enough to heighten every one of his senses and sanctifying Paul with the certain knowledge that he could do anything, pushed him over the edge of sensation and into a cavernous, numbing TILT, where he felt himself shutting down from the sheer overload of trying to put names to the turbulence of emotions raging through him. It was the same fear that had gnawed so insistently at the outskirts of his consciousness when he stood vigil over Annie the day Amelia was born. Back then, he had somehow found the strength to banish it. Now he could only sit, helpless, and watch as his wife put her life on the line.

Anne avoided the tank's first shell by engaging in a shade of stunt-flying rarely seen outside the circus, turning the Black Hawk over on its side and careening deep into the desert, taunting the Iraqis to follow. Thanks to CNN, Paul saw her eyes glowing exactly the same way they had at the crest of Annie's Wild Ride.

"All-righty! Now we've got good TV." CNN's producer cheered her acrobatics, while Paul enumerated the number of ways he knew to kill a man with his bare hands.

After Anne ducked a second shell, the producer howled for his camera to follow her every loop and, turning to Paul, demanded, "Why isn't she shooting back at the S.O.B.?"

"Because." Paul couldn't force his fingers to stop

clutching the chair. His legs felt bloodless, gutted, guaranteed to buckle if he so much as thought about taking a step. Yet when he spoke, his voice was strong, authoritative, the perfect Air Force spokesman to the end. "Women pilots are not allowed to fly combat. As a result, there is no need for them to have weaponry."

The producer pointed at the screen. "This isn't combat?"

"An SAR, search-and-rescue, is not classified as such, no."

"But she's being shot at."

Paul wondered if the gentleman thought Paul wasn't aware of the situation. Still he answered by the book. "Some non-combat positions do run the risk of attracting enemy fire."

"Uh-ha. So, let me get this straight. It's okay for women to be shot at, they just can't be allowed to shoot back?"

Paul winced. "Yes, sir."

The producer returned to his monitors. "God bless the U.S.A."

On screen, Anne lured the tank far enough away from the downed Navy pilot for the Apache to fasten a clear shot onto their target. Unfortunately, the procedure required her flying dangerously close to the tank, playing a tournament of chicken that might have seemed juvenile if not for the life-and-death stakes.

"We're hit!" Anne's declaration followed her failure to fully avoid yet another incoming discharge. The Black Hawk's engine fire-warning light flashed, as did low altitude for the radar altimeter. Anne ordered her crew, "Emergency shutdown on number one engine."

Their second engine kicked into gear but not fast enough to keep the Black Hawk from nosediving toward the tank. Addressing the Apache crew by radio, Anne informed, "If you intend to take out that tank in this century, now would be an excellent time, boys."

"No . . ." Paul shook his head. Because now it was Anne who sat too close to the line of fire. If the Apache shot now, they risked taking her out along with the tank.

"Just do it, damn it," her voice crackled across the intercom. "I'll get out of the way in time."

Not a very reassuring promise, considering her craft was still vibrating from tail rotor to cockpit after losing an engine.

"Now!" Anne barked, and the Apache obeyed.

They broke from above cloud cover to decimate the Iraqi's tank in a volcano of dust and burnt metal, while Anne, following through on her pledge to get out of their way, nosed the Black Hawk up and, fighting the charred smoke, raced toward her original destination, ordering her crew to get ready for landing.

Inside the CNN production truck, the crew clapped and whistled their approval, giving each other high fives as if they personally had been responsible for the mission's success.

"That's a wrap, folks." The producer threw off his headset, and, rather tardily remembering his manners, turned around to thank the nice Air Force captain who'd helped him during the broadcast.

But the nice Air Force captain was gone.

Paul was waiting for Anne when she came back to her quarters.

He stood by the window, still as a photo, hands locked by his sides, a quick-pulsing Adam's apple the only hint that he was even breathing. Despite being off duty, he wore his uniform.

"Paul!" Anne dumped her gear on the floor and nimbly stepped over it. "What a wonderful surprise." She moved to embrace him, but the look in Paul's eyes chilled her arms from wrapping around his neck. "What's wrong?" She reached to caress his cheek.

Paul slapped her hand aside. Grabbing Anne by both shoulders, he hurled her away from him and down on her cot.

"Paul!"

He thrust a solitary finger in her face. "You are, without a doubt, the most self-serving, dangerous, reckless pilot I have ever had the misfortune of encountering. And if your commanding officer isn't drawing up papers right now to have you court-martialed and drummed out of the service, then, believe me, I intend to make it my life's goal to do just that."

She forgot that she was fighting to get up. She forgot where she was, and why she was there, and what she was so excited about only a few minutes earlier. Paul's words slammed against Anne with such ire, they not only knocked the wind out of her, they stripped her of the ability to speak. Having managed to sit up after he'd knocked her down, she now slumped backward, catching herself with both hands behind her hips and instinctively locking her elbows to keep from collapsing all the way back into a horizontal position. She opened her mouth, but all that emerged was a questioning chirp, wordless, defenseless, and very, very confused.

Paul withdrew his finger, jamming both hands on his hips and towering over Anne, his once blue eyes turning so dark, she could no longer make out the pupils. "How dare you disregard a direct order to abort and head home? Who do you suppose you are? Do you think the rules don't apply to you? Or were you too busy imagining how heroic your little stunt would look on the evening news to care that you were risking the lives of your entire flight crew?"

Shock surged through Anne like an oil slick hungrily

gulping up every inch of clean beach along its path. Her head spun. She found that she'd forgotten how to breathe, and had to plunder her brain, trying to remember how to inhale, then how to exhale.

"Paul . . ." It was an effort to erect each word. "Why—why are you doing this?"

He turned away, too disgusted to even look in her direction, and indicated the flight gear Anne had dropped on the floor. "Is this how you treat Air Force property? Very nice, Annie. I guess that Black Hawk you flew this afternoon meant about as much to you as this crap. No wonder you're ready to sacrifice millions of U.S. dollars for your proverbial fifteen minutes of fame."

Now that he'd repeated his accusation, she was starting to get the gist of what Paul was charging her with. And her instinctive anger effectively managed to wipe away all residue of shock.

She sprung up off the bed. "You sanctimonious son-of-a-bitch."

He didn't respond. He didn't even turn to acknowledge having heard her address him. Instead, Paul bent his knees, picking her flight gear up off the floor and stacking it neatly.

She charged, "You think I disobeyed the order to abort because there was a camera stuck in my face?"

"No." The belligerence of a moment earlier was gone. "I *know* that's why you disobeyed the order."

"For your information, not that you bothered to ask, I went in because all I could think was, what if you were the one down there? What if you were the one in trouble? Wouldn't I want your SAR crew to do everything humanly possible to help you?"

"If I were the pilot in trouble, you can rest assured I'd have wanted you to obey orders. The last thing I need on my conscience is the knowledge that other lives were lost because of me."

"Well, fine. Next time I'll know. Note to myself: Next time, leave Paul to die in the desert."

He straightened up, finally turning to face her, his features arranged in a shroud of patronizing condescension it was all Anne could do to keep herself from trying to claw it off with her nails. "You should never, ever let personal feelings dictate your command decisions. You weren't thinking about your crew out there, or your duty. You were thinking about yourself. You always think only about yourself. That's why you're such a rotten commander."

Anne inhaled sharply, managing to clutch herself together long enough to inform him, "If you're telling me that as one captain to another . . . then, may I remind you, *sir,* that my time in grade happens to exceed yours. On the other hand, if you're telling me that as my husband . . ." She stepped up to Paul and, with all of her might, slapped him across the face.

He smiled. The son-of-a-bitch actually smiled. And he didn't so much as flinch. "I'm telling you that as someone who doesn't want to, one day, suffer the consequences of your glory-seeking."

"What are you talking about?"

"Five years ago, you were willing to jeopardize your country's mission in Libya, just so you could go down in the history books as the first woman to fly under combat conditions, and now today, you deliberately provoked that Iraqi tank in order prove some feminist point on national television."

"You're out of your mind." Her hand stung so severely from the blow, it was all Anne could do to keep from rubbing it against her thigh. Yet despite the swiftly reddening mark swelling up on Paul's cheek, he had yet to so much as touch it.

"You're forgetting who you're talking to, Annie. I, more than anyone, know exactly how ambitious you are, and how far you'll go to be number one."

Anne laughed, the bitterness burning her throat. "Talk about black pots throwing stones at glass pilots. Are you sure that *your* little exhibition, here and now, isn't about your jealousy over my accomplishments this afternoon?"

She'd got him. Finally, after firing a round of blanks, she'd got him. Paul flinched. "Don't be ridiculous."

"Oh, I don't know." Now that she caught a nibble, Anne wasn't about to cut the line. "I mean, you may have gotten the first kill of the war, but that was pretty anonymous. No one outside the base even knows your name. Now, me, on the other hand, I'm a hero on live television. And you know how the top brass loves to promote photogenic war heroes. How does Major Gaasbeck—no, no, how does Major *Anne* Gaasbeck, sound to you?"

If he'd so much as blinked to show that her insults affected him, Anne would have quit right there. She wasn't certain what had gotten into her. She couldn't understand where this viciousness was coming from. It had taken on a life of its own. Like all of their arguments, it had transformed into a runaway train, where the issue of the fight was no longer as important as winning it.

Yet, rather than appearing offended by her words, Paul seemed gratified by them. As if her wrath was exactly what he'd wanted.

"The only way you'll ever make major, Annie, is the same way that you made captain—as part of a quota."

She smiled sweetly. "Well, at least that's better than being grandfathered in."

He cocked his head to one side. "May I presume that you're referring to my family's illustrious history in the service?"

"It's what got you accepted into the Academy, isn't it? Your mother pulled a few strings, threw your dad's name around." Anne had no idea what she was babbling. With Paul's grades and extracurricular achievements, he could have been the bastard offspring of Adolf Hitler and Ho Chi Minn and still received an appointment.

He agreed. "The Gaasbeck name certainly didn't hurt my career, but you should know that as well as anyone. After all, it's the reason you changed your name after we were married, isn't it?"

My God, Anne thought. We've both gone insane. Neither of us has any idea what we're saying, anymore. And yet words continued spewing from their mouths, as if she and Paul were being held at gunpoint and forced to read from a script.

Barely aware of what she was doing, Anne snapped, "I changed my name when we got married because I was in love. Which, clearly, is an emotion that could never be ascribed to you."

"You don't say."

"I do say. In fact, in retrospect, I think the greatest error of my lifetime is that I didn't say it sooner. I am so tired of lying awake nights convincing myself that you love me like you say, when everything you've ever done indicates the opposite."

She wanted him to deny it. She wanted him to tell her she was wrong, and that things weren't the way they seemed. But Paul only nodded thoughtfully. "If that's how you feel, Annie . . ."

"How else can I feel? A man who truly loved me

could never, ever have attacked me the way you just did.''

He sighed. "My attack, as you call it, was not personal. I disapproved of your actions this afternoon, and I was well within my rights to tell you so.''

"Didn't you even for a second stop to think about my feelings? Even if I could, somehow, believe that there was nothing personal in your condemnation, that you were just expressing a professional opinion, still, Paul, couldn't you have at least made an effort to present it in a way that didn't rip my heart out?''

"That wasn't my intention.''

"No. It's never your intention to hurt me. I suppose that's because, to want to hurt me, you'd have to feel *something* for me.''

"Are you suggesting that I don't?''

There it was. The $25,000-dollar question, out there in black and white for everyone to see. Did Paul feel anything for her?

More important, did he love her?

He said that he did. Granted, his words usually followed her, backing him into a corner, but he would, on demand, articulate the sentiment. Still, in Anne's book, actions were the only measures that counted. And Paul's actions, culminating with his heartless accusations and insults this afternoon, were the actions of a man who cared so little, that he was willing to let anything and everything supersede her feelings. Even if she swallowed his contention that professional rivalry and personal jealousy had nothing to do with his criticism, she was still saddled with the certainty that following Air Force rules was more important to Paul than she was. That may have been love in Paul's vocabulary, but not in hers.

And so she told him, "No, I don't believe you really love me.''

It wasn't even necessary for him to out and out deny it. All it would have taken was for Paul to look the slightest bit hurt by her declaration, and Anne would have instantly taken it back. All she wanted was some sign, some little give on his part to show that he, in fact, did give a damn about her.

But Paul's expression did not flicker. He said, ''In that case, we have nothing more to say to each other.''

He nodded his head at her and, turning on his heel, stepped out of her room. And out of her life.

They'd barely been demobilized and returned to Utah, when Anne received divorce documents from Paul's lawyer—accompanied by his petition for sole custody of both Amelias.

None of it felt real. A part of Anne was still convinced that their brawl in Iraq had been nothing more than a twisted nightmare. After all, where else but in a nightmare could Anne have told Paul she didn't believe he loved her—and Paul have so readily agreed?

Yet if the divorce papers failed to drive home the reality to Anne, then Paul's behavior at the divorce hearing certainly left no doubts over how seriously he, at least, was taking the matter.

They'd barely sat down in front of Judge Saul before Paul was accusing Anne of being an unfit, neglectful, irresponsible mother. He argued that Anne's risking her life in spite of an order to turn back, proved how little she cared about orphaning her daughter. He told the court about her vagabond youth and dredged up her reckless parachute dive with Cadet Wakeman, as well as her attempt to flaunt regulations and fly to Libya while pregnant.

Years earlier, Paul had told Anne, ''I'm an Air Force officer. When someone attacks, I defend.''

Well, now, it was her turn to follow that advice.

After half a day spent sitting in shock, listening to the man she once loved tear her apart not only for the entertainment of the court, but the gossip hounds back at Hill Air Force Base, Anne told her lawyer to take off the gloves and portray Paul as a heartless, cold, emotional vacuum, incapable of accepting love or giving it. She invoked his tendency to be gone for months at a time without so much as a phone call or note. She enumerated the times Paul had been willing to destroy her in order to further his own career.

Anne knew she was being cruel. But she couldn't help herself. They'd battled so hard and for so long, neither one could stop. It was the only thing they still had left of each other.

# ═21═

"I am not wrong," Anne insisted. "You're not listening to me, Paul. You've never listened to me. It doesn't matter how many Air Force jobs I can still do, I won't be able to *fly*."

She couldn't stop shaking, muscles vibrating like plucked violin strings, flesh trembling despite the bathroom's humidity. Hysteria burned her chest and throat, attempting escape through any orifice possible—tears out her eyes, sobs out her mouth, a tingling in her ears. The feeling was awful and alien and terrifying. And she no longer possessed the strength to fight it.

She'd ruined everything, she knew that now. She sobbed, "I've been a lousy mom to Amelia. I nearly killed her because I was so determined to show you up; I decided to fly into that storm instead of around it. And for what? You don't give a damn what I do. I should've gotten the message years ago, but I kept hoping—isn't it funny? I didn't even know I was hoping, until . . ." Anne shook her head. "It doesn't matter anymore."

Paul rose from where he was kneeling in front of Anne, turning his back on her. She wondered if he'd heard a word she'd said, and whether any of it meant anything to him. Then again, why should he care whether she ever flew again? That would be almost like

321

caring about her. And they couldn't have *that*, now, could they?

Paul rolled back and forth on his heels, hands clutched behind his back, spine straight as bamboo. Finally, he intoned, "Annie."

She dabbed at her face with the corner of a towel. "What?"

"At the hospital, after I brought you in, the doctors wanted to amputate your fingers on the spot. Something about infection."

She lowered the towel slowly. "They did?"

"I refused to give them permission to operate." Paul cleared his throat. "I gave them my word that, when the bandages came off, you would be able to move your fingers."

Her mouth dropped open. "You gave ..."

"That's why these," he indicated her tears, "are un-necessary."

"Paul. I ... You only give your word when you're certain—"

"I do. I am."

"Oh."

She'd half-believed it when the doctors told her there was a small chance that she would recover. She'd half-believed it when Amelia optimistically parroted the prognosis. But hearing Paul give his word. . . . Anne started crying again, no longer sure of exactly why.

Paul, who, for a second, had allowed himself to hope that he'd finally roused up the words she needed to hear, pulled Anne off the tub's edge, cradling her against his chest. "What's wrong now?"

"I wasn't the wife you wanted, was I, Paul?"

He gripped her shoulders and forced Anne away to arm's length, studying her queerly. "Where the hell did that come from?"

"I made so many mistakes. I pushed you too hard. I asked for too much." She'd never been particularly adept at keeping what she thought to herself. Now, though, she felt like her every protective mechanism had crashed. Anne heard herself reveal things in a semi-coherent stream of consciousness that she once thought she'd take to the grave. She confessed, "Maybe I loved you too much. Do you think that's possible? To love somebody too much? I wish I could have been what you wanted. You deserved that."

"Annie, stop it." He shook her. Not hard enough to hurt, but enough to put an end to her raving. "You once told me that it took two to tango."

"But not at our house, right? At our house, it only took one person to start an argument, carry it out, and finish it. And that one person was always me."

He shifted from foot to foot. "Maybe I was wrong about that. I suppose maybe refusing to talk about something can—on certain occasions—be just as provoking as dwelling on it incessantly. I suppose it could be a reverse reaction, like lowering your voice when you're angry, instead of raising it."

Her mouth dropped open again. "You were listening to me?"

"Considering how much you talk, Annie, did I have a choice?"

The subsequent sound out of her mouth proved a cross between a laugh and a cry. Anne wondered if she was about to slide from hysterical tears into a laughing jag.

She confessed, "I don't know what's wrong with me today."

"You're scared." His tone was matter-of-fact. And a tiny bit triumphant. "No wonder, considering what you've been through."

"But I wasn't this scared on the plane. Or in the hospital when I woke up. It just sort of hit me, all of a sudden.''

"I know." He continued rubbing her back soothingly.

She leaned against him, losing herself in the sweet sensation, resting her cheek along his chest, taking deep breaths. She closed her eyes, murmuring, "You really gave the doctors your word?"

"I told them you would fly again." Realizing that her tears had wiped out the last of her strength, Paul picked Anne up in his arms and carried her down the hall to her room. He set her down gently on the bed, wiping a loose strand of hair from her forehead. "So, you see, there is nothing for you to worry about. Everything is going to be fine."

She looked up at him, moist eyes shining in the dark. "You mean that, don't you?"

"I never say what I don't mean."

She reached to caress his cheek, paralyzing Paul before he had the chance to straighten. "You care?"

He opened his mouth, as curious as her to hear what might come out. But instead of making a sound, he found himself bowing even further at the waist.

Until his lips had settled firmly on Anne's.

She gasped, surprise quickly transmuting into pleasure as Anne realized she wasn't dreaming or imagining things. She and Paul had been married for seven years, lovers almost a year before that, and yet never, ever did she remember him kissing her like this. Every sentiment he'd failed to express—anger, desire, jealousy, grief, want, need, love—she tasted in the fervor of his mouth as it conquered hers. And so she abandoned herself to it, leaping freely into the maelstrom, thinking it was the summit of madness to know she could be brutally rejected any moment and still be so quick to lay her pride on the line. But that's what she adored about Paul. He carried her to the edge. Physically, mentally, emotionally.

Anne tilted her head as Paul's kisses drifted from her mouth, down her neck. Her body responded without question, knowing better than Anne's rational mind ever had that this was how matters were supposed to be, that this was where they both belonged.

She whispered, "You've always brought out the best in me."

"Really?" He lowered Anne backward on the bed, standing over her on all fours, one knee between her thighs. "You always brought out the worst in *me.*"

She wanted to ask if that was a good thing or a bad one, but in that instant, Paul tipped his head, nibbling the edges of her mouth until Anne separated her lips and allowed him to swallow her question, along with the last simple breath destined to escape her body all night. She moved to wrap her arms about his neck, but the pain searing through her right arm the minute she even considered lifting it, put an end to that plan. She grit her teeth to keep from whimpering and ruining the mood, terrified that, just like the other night, if she somehow shattered the spell Paul seemed to be under, he would come to his senses, realize what he was doing, and once again, leave her. And she wasn't confident she'd be able to survive it a second time.

Paul sensed her tension, raising his head immediately to seek out the cause of her distress.

Realizing she'd lost the battle and had no option but to tell him the truth, Anne indicated her arm. "I'm sorry . . ."

As he glanced down at the cast, Anne saw reason return to his eyes. No longer a man overwhelmed by physical need, he became, in the second it took him to evaluate the situation, a man in control on his faculties, a man capable of making rational decisions. Her heart sank. Anne knew how Paul's mind worked. She swore she could almost hear him ticking off, one by one, the pros and cons of their continuing. What scared her most was the knowledge that, no matter how hard she tried, Anne herself couldn't come up with a solitary, logical, sensible reason for them to continue making love—except that she so very much wanted to. Yet she knew that was hardly the sort of grounds Paul would ever find acceptable.

He ran his palm along the length of her cast, pausing ever so briefly over the bandages cocooning her fingers, before swearing, "It doesn't matter. This one's on me, all right?"

She wasn't sure what he meant, until Paul further instructed, "Just lay back. Let me take care of it."

Anne did as he bid, wondering what in the world had come over them. Paul tugged the sash of her bathrobe, unwrapping Anne's body from beneath the satin. She shivered, not from cold or fear, but from the way he was looking at her, studying every contour as if it were both brand-new and hauntingly familiar. Her skin burned, but he had yet to lay a finger on her.

He inclined backwards, away from her, but Anne barely had the chance to wonder why before he was at the edge of the bed, gently cradling her right foot between his two hands, bringing it to his mouth and ever so delicately kissing the instep. Her toes curled. She gasped at the firecracker darting up her body and instinctively tried to sit up to see what he was doing. But he shook his head, smiled, and gestured for her to lie back down.

"This is my show, remember, Annie?"

She wasn't used to doing nothing. Briefly, Anne wondered if this was Paul's way of punishing her, of proving some point only he understood. But as his lips shimmered upward, kissing each toe before moving on to nibble the susceptible flesh around her ankle bone, she decided that she could live with it.

His mouth seared her calf, tongue flicking along the inside of her knee, and up her thigh. Her moans of pleasure turned to a cry of disappointment when, instead of following the inferno he started right into the core of her, he continued upward, nuzzling the taut skin around her hip bone and the tender valley below her ribs.

"Hold my place, Annie," Paul whispered between kisses. "I'll be back."

She wanted to scream, to demand why he was taunting her like this, why he was making her wait, when Paul's lips closed around the nipple of her right breast, and any words she might have formed were replaced by purrs. His tongue circled the hardened peak, and she ached to touch him, to run her hand down his back, to press him deeper against her. But she was afraid to move, afraid to disobey Paul's instructions, afraid to give him any reason to stop. And so she merely closed her eyes, reveling in the pleasures he aroused in her, not pushing, letting him set the pace.

He cupped both her breasts in his hands, lips sliding from one nipple to the other, then up her neck and back to her mouth. She tasted herself on his tongue as it plunged inside of her.

Finished, Paul pressed himself up on both arms, surveying Anne from above, eyes dancing as if deciding what to do next. Only then did she notice that, unlike her, Paul was still fully dressed.

For a beat, they simply studied each other. Then, slowly, he stood, feet hitting the floor with a thump that sliced Anne in half and prompted an unsolicited whimper.

He was leaving again. Just when she thought she was safe, he was leaving again. And there was nothing Anne could do about it.

Her body throbbed, aching to be fulfilled. But that pain was nothing compared to the one in her heart. If she had any strength left, she might have cried or called after him. But she was empty.

Paul ran both hands through his hair. "Annie?"

She raised her eyes to meet his. "Y-yes?"

"Do you want me to leave?"

Was he insane? Was he out of his mind?

If Paul had to ask, then obviously one of them was. Anne said, "No."

"So why don't you say anything?"

"Because"—she didn't realize the truth of her words until she heard herself speak them out loud—"I don't want to push you."

His hands fell by his side. Anne noticed they were shaking.

Tentatively, she asked, "What do *you* want, Paul?"

He smiled, not mocking her this time, or teasing. He smiled at her with what, to Anne's eyes, looked unexplainably like gratitude. "Thank you so much for asking, Annie."

He reached for the top button of his shirt, snapping them open one by one, and stripping in a single, fluid movement.

Watching him, dumbfounded, Anne managed to summon her power of speech back long enough to inquire, "Was this a test?"

Paul kicked off his jeans. "Something like that."

Despite the intimate predicament, she was still enough of an Air Force Academy graduate to ask, "Did I pass?"

"Flying colors." He crawled into bed next to her.

"Good." It was Anne's turn to smile mockingly. "So did you."

This time, when he kissed her, there was none of the dominance Anne sensed earlier. He wasn't trying to punish her, or tease her, or prove a point. He wanted her. Paul wanted her as badly as she wanted him. And nothing else mattered.

He suckled her tongue as ardently as he had her breasts, while propping himself on his right elbow and sliding his left hand down her belly, slipping it deftly between her thighs. The fire burning there thrilled him beyond words, as did the knowledge that all that feminine heat had been ignited just for him. Anne was already so wet and so hot, all it took was the brush of Paul's fingers for her to buck against him.

He whispered, "See? I told you I'd be back."

She'd always been so responsive, like a bow just waiting to be plucked. Paul loved to make her come merely by stroking her, loved feeling Anne's body quiver in reply to his touch. He relished her cries of pleasure, the soft sounds she made fueling his desire like nothing else, spurring him to even greater heights in his attempts to please her.

He took his time now, but that was the last thing Anne wanted. She impaled herself against his fingers, moaning Paul's name along with a plea to please, please hurry. Anne wanted him, she wanted all of him, and she didn't think she could last another second.

Her insides coiled, pleasure wrapping pleasure like ribbons on a May pole, the tension so strained she feared her tingling fingers might explode from the pressure.

Unable to wait any longer, she raised her hips to him, crying, "You're driving me out of my mind."

He cupped her buttocks between his hands, and, just

prior to diving inside her, murmured, "Now you know how I feel."

He filled her completely, effortlessly matching his rhythm to hers. She wrapped both legs around his waist, driving harder and harder against him, until she heard an odd sound forming along the back of Paul's throat, and looked up to see him biting down on his lower lip to keep her from hearing it.

How many times, in the past, had they made love? Thousands? Certainly, hundreds. And never, in all that time, had Anne heard Paul make any sort of sound.

"Oh, God, Annie," he let out the breath he'd been suppressing. "Why do you do this to me?"

She wanted to ask what he was talking about, but there was no time as he thrust inside her again and again, pushing Anne over the edge of reason and into a whirlpool of sensual, wordless elation. She felt herself lifting off the bed, levitating almost, without a trace of the pain that otherwise dogged her every move. The only thing tethering her was her left hand digging into Paul's shoulder, and her conviction that she had to hold on as long as possible, or risk losing everything.

For Paul though, the battle of his life was already lost.

He fell asleep with his chest pressed against Anne's back, arm around her waist, chin on her shoulder, legs intertwined under the blanket. For the first time in weeks, he slept soundly, and didn't dream. He didn't need to. His dreams had already come true.

Responding to a silent alarm in his head, Paul awoke at dawn. However unlike most mornings, when he was out of bed, in the shower, and out the door before his lids were fully upright, this time Paul woke up slowly, reluctantly, afraid to open his eyes and learn that what he thought was reality had actually been a wishful dream.

He buried his face in Anne's hair, swallowing deep breaths of memory. If Paul concentrated hard enough and managed to block out the right thoughts, he could almost pretend the last seven years had never happened. That it was 1991 again, and neither of them had yet blurted out anything that couldn't be taken back.

He slipped out gingerly from between the sheets, taking great pains not to disturb Anne. She stirred restlessly, and Paul held his breath, fingers freezing between the buttons on his uniform, waiting to finish the job until after he was certain she'd fallen back asleep. He considered leaving a note, but doubted anything he wanted to express would fit comfortably on a yellow Post-it.

Out of the house, Paul shifted his car into neutral, rolling silently out of her driveway. He took a deep breath and, flipping on both headlights, drove across the base. His appointment with Colonel Guzman was scheduled for nine A.M. sharp.

Paul figured the least he could do was arrive on time to find out whether he was being kicked out of the Air Force.

Colonel Guzman's staff secretary escorted Paul into the base commander's office and pointedly shut the door behind them. Paul stood at rigid attention, looking down and across the desk at his superior officer. The colonel sat by the window, leisurely leafing through Paul's most recent Officer Performance Report.

"I'd tell you, At ease, Major Gaasbeck, but I doubt that's an order you could follow under the circumstances."

"Yes, sir." Paul remained standing as he was.

Colonel Guzman sighed, and leaned forward, linking

his fingers and tapping them along the OPR. He appeared as reluctant to begin, as Paul was to get this meeting over with.

"So. Tell me. How is the other Major Gaasbeck feeling?"

"Much better, sir."

"And your daughter? Amelia, is it?"

"She's doing well also."

"I see." Colonel Guzman glanced down, for possibly the third time in ten seconds, at the file in front of him. Then, realizing that the inevitable couldn't be stalled much longer, asked, "You do know why you're here, don't you, Major?"

"Yes, sir."

"They say it's up to me to decide whether or not to put you in front of a court-martial board."

"Yes, sir."

"Frankly, I haven't the slightest idea what to do with you."

Paul didn't respond. Instead, he kept his eyes on the runway visible through Colonel Guzman's window. He counted the planes as they took off. The exercise kept his facial features neutral.

"You are, without a doubt, my best pilot, Paul. Your Officer Performance Report is spotless. Looking over your record, I'd say you're about this far from earning your eagle." The Colonel sighed again. "What in the world made you throw all that away?"

Paul said, "I had no intention of throwing anything away."

"I see. Well, what exactly did you think would happen after you stole a helicopter from the Air Force Academy? Did you think you'd get a commendation out of it?"

"No, sir."

"And I won't even mention the fact that, even if that chopper was yours to do with as you please, you again disobeyed protocol by lifting off while the entire state of Colorado was grounded."

"Yes, sir."

"Damn you, Gaasbeck." Guzman slammed shut the OPR, hoping to trigger some variety of reaction. "I don't want to see you court-martialed, but you're not making this any easier for me."

"I know what I did was wrong, Colonel. I'm ready to accept my punishment in any form the Air Force sees fit."

"So you want to be court-martialed, is that it?"

"No, sir."

Guzman stood up from his chair, walking around the desk until he stood face-to-face with Paul. He wondered how it was possible to stand eye to eye with a man and still get the feeling that he was looking right through him.

"You must have had a reason for what you did."

Paul wavered, briefly contemplating the floor before snapping his head back to attention. "With all due respect, Colonel, I do not think my reasons are relevant to this investigation. I admit that I broke the rules. Why I did so isn't important."

Not to mention, potentially humiliating.

"Seeing as how I'm the colonel and you're the major, how about if you let me decide what is and isn't important."

"Yes, sir."

"Okay. Now we're getting somewhere. Let's start again. You had a reason for what you did. What was it?"

Paul cleared his throat. He considered declining to respond. After all, what was another insubordination, more or less? His career was already in tatters, no sense tossing his pride away with it. But the fact remained, as long as he still wore the uniform, he was obligated to follow the rules that went with it.

So, truthfully, but in a staccato, emotionless bark, Paul told Colonel Guzman, "I had to rescue my family. Sir."

"You couldn't wait for SAR to do their job?"

"No, sir. They were going to wait for the storm to abate."

"Those people are professionals, Gaasbeck. You thought their judgment was less sound than yours?"

"No, sir. I'm sure they were right."

"I see. So, let me get this straight. They were right . . . and you were right?"

"No, sir. They were right. I was wrong."

"You knew that you were wrong, but you went ahead anyway?"

"Yes, sir."

Colonel Guzman circled him, looking Paul up and down, trying to make sense of the situation, and of the man. "Just one more question, Major, and then I've got to write my recommendation." He stopped his circling and deliberately blocked Paul's view of the runway. "Faced with the same circumstances as before, but knowing what you do now about its consequences, would you still respond to this crisis in exactly the same manner?"

It was a common enough question. Paul had answered it dozens of times during various debriefings over the years. Usually, he'd felt comfortable responding with a definitive yes, because he always followed the rules. Even if the result proved inadequate, his actions never were. But this time, everything flipped upside down. It wasn't his ends that people were quibbling over, but his means. And, this time, he had nothing to justify his actions.

Nevertheless, Paul obeyed the honor code. He told the truth. "Faced with the same circumstances? Yes, sir, I would do exactly the same thing."

"Even knowing it could cost you your career? Not to mention your reputation? Your honor?"

Paul swallowed hard. But there wasn't a trace of doubt in his voice. "Yes, sir."

Paul knew he should go home so he could explain to Anne where he'd vanished to. Yet, each time he tried steering in the direction of her house, he ended up driving the other way.

He was afraid to face her.

And not because Paul had lied to Colonel Guzman.

But, because he'd told him the utter truth.

If, God help them, he ever had to make another choice between Anne and . . . anything else on earth, Paul now knew, without a shadow of a doubt, that Annie would always come out the winner.

As little as a week ago, the realization of how much control she had over him would have caused Paul endless grief. He would have tried to deny his feelings, and, when that failed, he would have tried to talk and rationalize his way out of them. But not anymore. Now his acceptance of the fact only brought Paul a sense of peace. He felt like he'd just finished a brutal game of tug-of-war. He'd lost—but, oh, the relief of at last letting go.

When Colonel Guzman asked why he did what he did, Paul chose to keep silent for a pair of reasons. One: He genuinely thought that his grounds had nothing to do with the case's facts, and that his punishment ought to be based solely on the latter. And two: He doubted Colonel Guzman would've believed him, anyway.

Because, the long, short, thin, and fat of it was that everything Paul had ever done during these past nineteen years had been prompted by his fear of losing Anne for good.

Despite—or maybe because of—how close he came to losing her the day Amelia was born, Paul had taken great pains to reassure himself that such a travesty simply couldn't happen. Anne was too strong of a life force to be snuffed out. Her dying was a prospect that, before the Gulf War, Paul simply could not process. Until the minute Anne decided to play chicken with that Iraqi tank.

In the instant she got hit, during that fraction before her second engine kicked in, when it looked like Anne's Black Hawk was plummeting to the ground and right into enemy hands, Paul Gaasbeck felt himself cease to exist. It was the strangest sensation, and one he hadn't dared put into words until now. In that instant, he felt his identity fully submerge into Anne's.

If her life was over, then so was his.

The knowledge that there was no "him," anymore, only "them," effectively ripped the wings off everything Paul had ever believed in. His thoughts, his actions, his opinions, were no longer wholly his own. He felt possessed. He felt . . . controlled.

And the worst part of it was, he didn't mind.

If thoroughly surrendering his identity was the price Paul had to pay to keep Anne safe and alive and by his side, then, on that hot afternoon in the Gulf, he would have gladly given it—and a lot more—just to see that second engine start up again. It was only when the emergency had passed that Paul realized exactly how much trouble he was really in.

In the hours between Anne's rescue of the Navy pilot

and her return, Paul hated her with a raw, illogical, burning passion that he once would have gone to his grave denying he even possessed. He hated her for what she had turned him into, and for what she could make him do. Paul told himself that being with her was destroying his self-discipline, his honor. His soul. Though, naturally, he couldn't tell Anne the real reason why he was so furious with her that afternoon. Admitting how much power she had over him would have been the final nail in an already asphyxiating coffin.

Besides, Paul hadn't known the real reason himself. Not then. Not until last week, when standing vigil over Anne's hospital bed awoke every feeling he'd spent seven years burying.

Seeing Anne lying there unconscious, face scraped and bruised, he not only acknowledged what had triggered his near-breakdown that day in the Gulf, he also accepted that he was just as ready now as he was then to give up anything necessary to see her pull through this crisis—that even if it cost him his commission and his colonel's eagle, he still wasn't a bit sorry he'd chosen to break all the rules and go after Anne.

Because, without a "them," there was no "him."

Paul promised himself that when—not if—Annie woke up, he would tell her as much. And something else, as well.

He would tell her that, despite all the stupid things his love for her had made him do over the years, the stupidest thing he had ever done was let her go.

Colonel Guzman had promised to call Paul later in the day and fill him on his decision about the court-martial. But Paul wasn't even thinking about that as he leapt up the stairs to Anne's house, two at a time. He let himself in with an extra set of keys he'd borrowed off a rack in the kitchen and was already calling Anne's name as he conscientiously shut the front door behind him.

"We're in the bedroom," she shouted from upstairs, and Paul's heart spun in place.

He opened the door, scanning the room for Annie.

And found her sitting on the bed.

Next to Lyle.

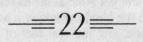

He'd dropped by right after breakfast, without calling first, a breech of etiquette that Anne, as a rule, didn't object to. Yet when she peered through the peephole and saw Lyle, it was all Anne could do to keep from pretending she wasn't home. He looked so . . . insignificant. Sandy beard trimmed to obscure chipmunk cheeks that otherwise shaved a decade off his age. Slender fingers plucking at the collar of his gray turtleneck. Charcoal slacks, though custom-made, still somehow appearing a size too big. In quantity inches, Lyle actually stood taller than Paul. But he failed to look it.

Deciding that no matter her predicament, evading confrontation wasn't Anne's style, she opened the door, flashed Amelia a be-nice-or-else stare, and agreed with Lyle that, yes, they really should talk. They ended up in the bedroom because, on the ground floor, Amelia's censoring eyes followed them from kitchen to living room. Anne perched on the bed, resting her arm on a pillow, relieved when Lyle, rather than joining her, pulled up a chair from her dressing table and straddled it, propping both elbows along the back. She tucked her legs underneath her, sliding the pillow across her lap and freezing momentarily when she realized that it, along with the sheets and even her skin, still smelled of Paul.

She hadn't showered on getting up, ostensibly because doctor's orders forbade getting her cast wet, and she figured she'd wait and get Amelia off to school before subjecting herself to the hassle of taking a bath with her arm wrapped in plastic. But the real fact of the matter was, when Anne woke up she still felt Paul's touch along every inch of her body, and she was reluctant to wash it off.

She wondered if Lyle could tell something was different. To Anne, not a single molecule in her room had passed unaffected by the events of last night. Everything looked slightly off, like a familiar television set with its color and tint readjusted. Even Lyle appeared different. Ever since Paul's characterizing him as . . . what? Slimy? Oily? She couldn't shake the image of a walking grease slick. And then there was Paul's other musing: how could she trust the integrity of a man who, now that Anne thought about it, really did perpetually offer the perfect answer to her every question?

Lyle, however, seemed oblivious both to Anne's new concept of him and the subtle, atmospheric changes of her bedroom. He asked about her health. He asked about Amelia's health. He asked—how long, exactly, did Paul plan to stay?

Actually, Anne had been wondering about that one herself. It hardly did wonders for a lady's ego to wake up in the morning and find the other half of her bed glaring empty at her.

Lyle chose his next words with what, to Anne, suddenly seemed like suspiciously surgical precision. He remarked, "Although, it's not like Paul's got anywhere to go. What, with his suspension . . ."

Anne blinked, focusing her undivided attention on Lyle for the first time since he'd crossed her threshold. "I beg your pardon?"

"We could hardly believe it back in Design when we heard. I mean, Paul's the last person you'd expect—"

"Paul?" Anne leaned forward. "Paul is suspended?"

"Well, sure. Even someone with his record couldn't expect the higher-ups to look the other way when he steals a helicopter right out from under the nose of—"

"Whoa!" Anne slashed her left hand, palm flat, from side to side as if wiping a blackboard. "Back up. Paul? My Paul? Paul *stole* a helicopter? How? Where? Good God, why?"

Lyle told her. He didn't have all the details, but as always, the base grapevine had solicited enough valid info to make piecing together a conclusion inevitable— though she did wish Lyle weren't also drawing such visible relish from relaying it.

Her voice faint, and so rich with disbelief that Anne feared speaking the words out loud would break the spell, she stammered, "Paul put his career on the line, to come after Amelia and me?"

Lyle nodded, lips crinkling to one side. "Your ex-husband is so full of himself, he probably thought he was the only one capable of doing the job right. That damn Air Force machismo sure makes me glad I get to go home a civilian at the end of the day."

Anne had no idea how to respond to that. Once she would have agreed with Lyle wholeheartedly. Well, of course she'd have agreed with him—she was the one who put the opinion in his head in the first place. It was just like Paul with his arrogance to assume no one else could conceive or pull off a rescue attempt as well as he could. If Paul Gaasbeck ever found a motive to disobey orders and break the rules, Anne could think of no better one than the wish to prove himself right, and everyone else wrong. He'd done it before. And yet she couldn't help hoping . . . what if . . . could it be? . . .

She never got the chance to finish her thought. Which was a good thing, too, because she doubted, in her present state, she'd have the guts. When Anne heard Paul downstairs, calling out to her and wondering where she was, she answered without thinking.

Paul pushed open the door, his indigo eyes registering Anne on the bed and Lyle on the chair next to her with a single, impartial glance. He stopped short. But his expression didn't change.

Anne waited. She waited for some sign, for some . . . thing from him to give her a hint about what he was thinking or feeling. She peeked from Paul to Lyle, wishing Paul might express some twinge of jealously. It didn't even have to be a twinge. At this point, she would have settled for a twitch.

What she got was Paul smiling politely at Lyle and stretching his hand out for a shake. "Hello. Nice to see you again. How was your Christmas? . . . Good to hear it. Sorry for the interruption."

He stepped outside the room again and closed the door behind him.

For the remaining half hour of Lyle's visit, Anne doubted she heard more than one out of ten words spilling from his mouth. She felt as if she needed another of her pain pills, except that her arm, along with the rest of her body, was feeling numb not pain.

She wondered why she kept doing this to herself. Was there such a syndrome as Adult-Onset-Masochism? Last night had clearly been an aberration. Paul was right. They'd been affected by the surroundings, and by the fact that, whatever else, their marital shortcomings had never been physical. They'd come together last night not from some spiritual, passionate connection, but because their bodies, quite primitively, missed each other.

And yet . . .

Last night, Paul told her she was the best pilot he ever knew. Last night, Paul held Anne in his arms and made love to her with an intensity unmatched even at the beginning of their marriage. And, this morning, she'd learned of the sacrifice he'd made in her name. Surely, taken together, his actions had to mean *something*.

Anne kissed Lyle good-bye at the door, meaning to peck only his cheek. But when she realized that Paul, sipping a mug of coffee in the kitchen while languidly thumbing through a newspaper, could see their reflection in the foyer mirror, she aimed for Lyle's lips.

Paul didn't look up when she entered the kitchen, biting into a piece of toast and swallowing as he turned the page. Anne waited for him to say something. She poured her own tepid cup of coffee, managing awkwardly with only the left hand at her disposal. She sat down next to him, reaching for the international news section he'd discarded. And she waited.

Finally, tired of breakfasting in a monastery, Anne broke the silence and asked, "Amelia get off to school okay?"

Paul nodded, neatly refolding the paper along its seams.

"How come she didn't come in to say good-bye?"

He snapped the rubber band back on, making it hard to tell the newspaper had ever been opened. "I told her you were busy."

It was the closest he'd come yet to addressing walking in on her and Lyle, and Anne figured she'd best run with the ball before her opportunity was lost.

"I wasn't. Busy, I mean."

"Is that a fact? Well. My mistake, then."

She could feel it starting, the inkling that assured Anne she could get what she needed out of Paul if only she would push him a little. Not even really push. More like nudge, in the appropriate direction. If she pressed just the right trigger, she felt certain she could pry some sort of reaction from him.

And yet—there it was again, "And yet." Even as the impulse to provoke him overwhelmed her, Amelia's censure chewed on Anne's memory like a stubborn puppy. She'd spent years provoking Paul, hoping it would bring her the words she longed to hear. And it had gotten her exactly nowhere. Maybe it was time to switch tactics.

"You certainly do get around, Annie."

She glanced up in surprise. Anne had been so busy refereeing the wrestling tournament in her head, she'd failed to notice that her uncharacteristic silence had, in fact, discombobulated Paul to the extent that he'd actually offered an unsolicited statement.

"Me in the bedroom last night, Lyle this morning. I suppose next it will be Colonel-Mustard-with-a-candlestick."

Was he making a joke? Anne couldn't be certain. Surely he couldn't be serious about the Colonel Mustard crack. Then again, how serious of an issue could he consider Lyle, if Paul was lumping him in the same sentence with a board-game character?

"Lyle and I were just talking," Anne defended.

"My dear"—Paul stood, taking his mug to the sink and rinsing it out in a single, fluid movement—"you are a grown woman. What you do, and who you do it with, is hardly a concern of mine."

It wasn't exactly what she'd wanted to hear.

"If you didn't care about finding me with Lyle, then why did you bring the subject up?"

"I didn't. You did. I was simply being polite and holding up my end of the—what was that act you claim I'm a failure at? Oh, yes—conversation."

Flip. Her heart was breaking, and Paul was acting flip.

The awareness didn't please Anne in the slightest. Why was she killing herself to suppress her faulty habits and attempt to make progress with the man, when Paul wasn't even willing to meet her halfway?

She snapped, "Well, thanks to my conversation with *Lyle* this morning, I learned a lot of fascinating things." Anne stood, one hand on her hip, blocking Paul from escaping the kitchen. "When were you going to tell me about your suspension?"

He brushed past as if she weren't even there, barely turning his head to reply, "Probably when *my* suspension affected *you*."

Anne watched him go, mouth slipping open in spite of herself, and any reservations she still harbored about not pushing him drained away with her sharp intake of breath.

She followed him upstairs, pointing out, "Considering that I am the primary reason behind your suspension—"

"Hold it right there." Paul spun around with such unexpected speed, it caused Anne to bounce off his chest, sending a crunch of pain up her arm. "Listen to me, Annie, and listen closely, because this is a fact I want to see tattooed on your tongue the next time I look at you. *I* am the primary reason behind my suspension. Me. I am the lone person responsible for my actions. No one made me do anything. I am my own man, and I alone will be held accountable."

His ex-wife wasn't the only one spending her morning snared in a conversation far different from one she'd envisioned. Paul left Colonel Guzman's determined to tell Anne everything, to confess how much he needed her, how much she meant to him, and how sorry he was for the times he'd inadvertently hurt her. But he'd planned to do it at his own pace, and in his own way.

Having her abruptly demand an answer threw Paul off count.

And walking in on her cozy tête-à-tête with Lyle hadn't exactly helped. Paul hadn't anticipated the situation, and so he'd responded the same way he responded to all unexpected situations. Rather than make a mistake with the wrong action, Paul took no action at all, biding his time, surveying the land, waiting for the perfect opportunity to implement his original plan. As sure as he knew anything, Paul knew he could never tell Anne everything he'd meant to tell her, until he knew that Lyle was no longer a factor in the equation. The last thing he intended was to make a fool of himself by confessing all, only to discover that Anne had finally accepted Lyle's marriage proposal. Their kiss at the door certainly suggested she'd come to some sort of decision. And until Paul knew what it was, he had no desire to risk making the wrong move.

Anne, though, seemed to harbor no sympathy for his predicament as she demanded, "So. Your stealing a helicopter from the Academy had nothing—nothing, right?—to do with me?"

"Don't be ridiculous. Of course, it did."

She softened. "Really?"

"Well, I didn't exactly take it out for a joyride. I took it out so that I could rescue Amelia. And you."

He was so close. So close to saying the words Anne needed, it took everything she had to keep from saying them for him. All Paul had to do was admit he did it because he loved her—no, it could even be less than that. All he had to do was admit that he did it because he cared about whether she lived or died, and Anne would instantly forgive him every past slight, every ignored phone call, every indifferent shrug.

*Say it,* she begged him silently. *Say I matter. Not just*

*as Amelia's mother, or a fellow officer, or another pilot in trouble. Say that you did it for me, for Anne. Say that you care. Say it.*

Anne repeated, "So, your taking the Apache, it did have some little thing to do with me?"

Paul's spine stiffened, even as his eyes met Anne's. Only a few hours ago, he'd been willing to let her in on everything. But Paul needed to do it on his own terms, why couldn't Anne understand that? He felt himself shutting down. He didn't will it to happen, but the second Anne began pushing him, trying to provoke a reaction out of him, Paul responded like he always did. He withdrew rather than letting Anne see how deeply, and easily, she could affect him.

Arms behind his back, shoulders squared, Paul reported, "My reasons are my own. I've already said as much to Colonel Guzman."

"But, Paul." She couldn't help forcing a few words inside his mouth, hoping the right prompt could still turn the tide. "When you disobeyed orders and stole that helicopter, you did it for me."

"I did it for me."

"I don't understand."

"I never expected you to."

His smugness pushed her over the edge. This was exactly what she deserved for daring to hope that last night had been a healing of sorts, a chance for a fresh start. They'd been so close. Now, however, the chasm between them felt wider than ever.

"Right, of course, I forgot. Everything is always about you."

He raised an eyebrow. "May I remind Major Gaasbeck that she's the one insisting *my* actions were somehow influenced by her. Talk about an ego out of control."

She had only one more card to play. "What about Amelia?"

"What about her?"

"Were your actions somehow influenced by her?"

"Of course," Paul looked at Anne as if she'd thoroughly lost her grasp on reality.

And that's when Anne knew she'd lost.

Not that she begrudged her ex his love for their daughter. In fact, it was the only feature that kept her from classifying him a thoroughly unfeeling monster. The thing that bothered Anne was the evidence that when Paul truly cared about someone, he had no qualms about expressing or admitting it. He was proud to confess that his love for Amelia drove him to forfeit his career and his principles. Just as Paul's other principle, his stubborn belief in integrity at all times, kept him from pretending that Anne ever meant any more to him than simply the extra body who'd crashed with his daughter. She supposed she should feel grateful for his honesty. Funny, she didn't feel particularly grateful.

Anne took a deep breath, slotting her emotions into their places before telling Paul, "You're a good father."

"Thank-you."

"But you are, by far, the biggest bastard I've ever known."

He wasn't unprepared for the assessment. "Yes. I can see why you'd feel that way."

She ached to ask him about last night, about how he could care so little and still make love to her with such tenderness.

"Paul." Anne cleared her throat. "I think you—"

He couldn't let her complete the directive. He had to say it first. "I'll be out of here within the hour."

\*　　\*　　\*

But he didn't go straight home. Instead, for the second time that day, Paul took a detour, ending up at Design. At the office of Mr. Lyle Jellison, to be precise.

Paul crossed his arms and blocked the door. Not that Jellison showed any inclination to run. When Paul first walked in, Lyle had opened his mouth, no doubt preparing another of his so-slick adages that usually did the trick and got him out of trouble. But before the initial syllable so much as left his lips, Paul shook his head, indicating he shouldn't even bother. So rather than speaking, the weasel continued sitting silently behind his desk.

Paul said, "When Anne and I were dating, there was a guy in a bar, who said something to her I didn't like. It wasn't very . . . what did he call it? . . . officer or gentleman of me, but I damn near took his head off. And that guy was big. Much bigger than you."

Lyle couldn't be sure if Paul was serious or not, and so only one side of his mouth raised in a smirk as the other lowered.

"If you ever"—Paul didn't need to raise his voice to make his point—"go running to my wife again with gossip that's supposed to make me look bad, I will track you down and I will very rationally, very dispassionately, and very, very slowly, render you incapable of picking up another drafting pencil. Am I making myself clear?"

"Paul, listen here, I think you misunderstood—"

"One more thing." He turned to leave, pausing briefly by the door. "If you're who Annie wants, and I find out that you've hurt her in any way—take my advice. Start running."

The phone was ringing when Paul walked through the door of his apartment, and for the briefest moment, he allowed himself to think it might be Anne. What the hell ever happened to those days when he used to kiss her good-bye, then rush home to wait for her phone call so they could spend the rest of the night talking? How in the world had two kids who thought nothing of driving hundreds of miles just to see each other for one night turned into bitter adults who couldn't pass more than twenty seconds in a room without picking a fight? And, most of all, how in the world had Paul managed to love Anne so much that he'd convinced her he didn't care at all?

"Gaasbeck." He picked up the phone, already suspecting who it really was on the other end, and feeling quite amazed by how little he cared one way or the other.

"Major Gaasbeck? Colonel Guzman, here."

"Good afternoon, Colonel." Paul shifted the receiver to his other ear and tossed his overnight bag on the sofa.

"Major, I just had a chat with General Danahay over at the Air Force Academy. Sharon tells me there's been a mistake. Seems like Sergeant Henze's got a little confused. Their Apache's right where it's supposed to be. Been there since they delivered it."

"Sir?"

"That's what the lady told me, and I've got no reason to doubt her. Way I compute it, we really don't have a situation anymore." The Colonel lowered his voice. "Brotherhood of the ring-knockers, Paul. We take care of our own. There isn't an officer here who doesn't think you did what you had to do."

"Where's Dad?" Amelia had barely hung her backpack in the hall closet before she noticed that Paul's suitcase was missing, and ran to Anne for an explanation.

Anne, back in bed, eyes closed, mind fuzzy from the extra dose of pain-killers she'd popped a half hour earlier, rubbed her lids with the back of her left hand, yawned, and told Amelia, "He left."

"Why?"

"Because he doesn't live here, Ace."

"You made him leave, didn't you?" Her daughter's voice wasn't particularly accusing, more like resigned.

"We both thought it was time."

"Did you two have another fight?"

Anne considered lying, but she didn't see the point or possess the strength. "Sort of."

"What about this time?" Amelia plopped down on the bed.

"Nothing too important. Nothing new, anyway."

Amelia crossed her arms. "Didn't he do enough, Mom? You said all you wanted was for him to do some little thing to show he cared about you. Well? Isn't him almost getting kicked out of the Air Force so he could save you, enough?"

Anne's eyes snapped open. "How did you know about that?"

"Kids at school told me."

"Wonderful." Anne rolled over on her side, burying her face in the pillow. "Everyone knew except me."

"You didn't know?"

"Not until Lyle told me."

Amelia wrinkled her nose. "He's not still here, is he?"

"No. Your father scared him away."

"Cool."

"No, it is not cool." Anne sat up, feeling the familiar sense of adrenalin drowning out pain pills. "It is not cool at all."

Deciding that was a point to be debated later, Amelia

pressed on with her original concept, demonstrating that, when she had her mind made up, she could sink her teeth into an issue as tightly as her mother. "What difference does it make who told you? You know now. You know what Dad did."

"It makes a big difference who told me. If I left it up to Paul, I'd still be stumbling around in the dark. Hell, if I left anything up to Paul, you'd only be two years old right now."

"But isn't what Dad did more important that what he didn't—"

"Ace, sweetheart." Anne sat up fully, stroking her daughter's hair. "Please, try to understand. What your dad did, he didn't do it for me. He did it for you. Because he loves you very much, and you should be very proud to have a dad who'd sacrifice not only his career and his life, but . . . you know the honor code, don't you?"

"We will not lie, cheat or steal, nor tolerate one who does."

"Exactly. Well, in order to save your life, your father lied, he cheated, and he stole. Do you know how important his honor is to him? He sacrificed it all, to rescue you."

"He did it for both of us, Mom."

"Believe me, baby, I would like nothing more in the world than to think that. But it isn't true. I know. I asked him."

"You . . . asked him?" Amelia bit her lip. "And he said no?"

"He told me, flat out and in black and white. What he did, he did for his little girl. I was just along for the ride."

Amelia's mouth opened and closed soundlessly as she tried to piece together the remnants of her theory.

Anne sighed, wishing, more than anything, that her predicament didn't also take such a toll on her daughter. "I know you'd like your dad and me to get back together. Frankly, I'd like that, too."

"Then, why—"

"Because, I can't subject myself to living with a man I adore, knowing that he doesn't feel the same way about me."

The bluntness of Anne's statement momentarily quieted Amelia. Still, like both of her parents, when she had a point to make, it would take a lot more than facts to permanently derail her. "But, the last couple of days, you and dad have been getting along a lot better. You were not fighting as much as you used to. Isn't that a good sign? Doesn't that prove he loves you now?"

Once Anne would have thought the same thing. But a lifetime with Paul had certainly chased all such romantic illusions out of her head. Frankly, she'd hoped that her daughter would be a little older before she discovered this most depressing fact of life.

"The opposite of love isn't hate, Amelia. Hate suggests that at least the other person still feels something toward you. The opposite of love is indifference. Your dad doesn't bother to fight with me anymore, because he doesn't give a damn."

## ═══23═══

Each evening on his way home from work, Paul drove past Anne's house, which was really most fascinating, considering that his own apartment was located completely in the other direction.

The problem with finally facing facts, Paul decided, was that he could no longer even amuse himself by making up excuses for why he felt this compulsion to make a nightly pilgrimage. A month ago, he might have passed many an hour pretending he was doing it out of concern for Amelia. Or because he wanted to stop at the O Club for a drink and Anne's residence was, sort of, on the way. Or because he wanted to see if the lawn needed watering.

Nowadays, though, even that pastime was lost to him. He knew, and accepted, exactly why he kept driving by Anne's house. He was worried about her. Every time he climbed in the cockpit of his F-16, and his right hand tightened around the side-stick control, he was confronted with the memory of Anne's tear-drenched face as she realized that she might never, ever fly again.

He'd felt as connected to her then as he had that day in the Gulf, felt the same submersion of his fate into Anne's, until Paul knew, without a shadow of a doubt, that her fears were his fears, her pain was his pain, and her destiny, his destiny. The primary difference was, that prospect no longer terrified him. In fact, it comforted him. At so many moments during his search for her, Paul had found himself promising to do anything, to give up anything, if only it meant Anne would be all right.

Since then, he'd amassed days wondering how God might go about collecting on that promise. Now Paul knew. And he found the barter infinitely reasonable, poetic justice at its most divine. If finally admitting the full scope of his feelings for Anne while watching her take off with another man was the tab Paul had to pay to keep her safe, then he was willing to accept the terms—he'd always believed God had one hell of a sense of humor, and he drew comfort from the conviction that, if he kept his part of their bargain, then God would do the same and heal Anne's hand as efficiently as He'd once set a bush on fire.

In the meantime, Paul wasn't certain what he thought he'd see, driving by Anne's house on a regular basis. The front porch wasn't pasted with bulletins, and the lemon tree in the front yard wasn't telling any tales. Naturally, Paul knew what he was *hoping* to see as he drove by. He was hoping to see Anne. Playing badminton with Amelia. Turning cartwheels. Even wrestling with Lyle, who, on more than one occasion, Paul had seen leaving the premises. Anything to reassure him that Anne's arm had healed and that she was once again fit for flying.

He knew it was a silly fantasy. Anne's bandages weren't even scheduled to come off for another week, and then, if—no, when she did get her fingers to move, she still faced months of therapy. Nevertheless, Paul found a strange solace in driving by the house.

As if his continuing vigil would ensure everything turning out all right in the end.

As if even God could stand a little help from Paul Gaasbeck.

The night before Anne's bandages were set to come off, Paul calculated he'd slept maybe a good seventeen minutes total. Every time he closed his eyes, he thought of Anne and how important the next day would be in the course of the rest of her life.

He didn't fool himself for a minute into thinking she'd want him there. In all honesty, she would probably want him as far away as possible. But in spite of that, Paul simply could not stay away.

He knew, even as he got up in the morning, showered, drank two cups of coffee, and buttoned his uniform that, come nine A.M., Paul would be picking up the phone, calling his squadron, and informing them he was ill. Since this was the first sick day Major Gaasbeck ever requested—and that included days when he actually was sick. The petition was instantly honored.

Paul got in his car and drove to the hospital without so much as a look back. Anne could throw him out once he got there, but at least Paul would know he'd done his best. He'd been there for her.

The only way he knew how.

She'd gotten quite adept at driving, using only her left hand. As Anne maneuvered her car into the hospital parking lot, she asked Amelia, "You think the Indy 500 would take a one-handed driver?"

"Would you stop saying stuff like that. Please, Mom." Amelia unbuckled her seat belt. "Everything's going to be okay."

"Yeah? Who says?"

"Dad."

"Oh. Well. In that case, it must be true."

Anne wasn't certain what was prompting her bizarrely buoyant mood, except the relief that, one way or another, her fate would soon be indisputably spelled out for her. No more waiting, no more hoping, no more waking up in the night shaking with dread. She'd have to accept the facts and deal—pun most certainly intended—with the hand dealt to her. One way or another, it would be over.

Either that, or she was in serious denial.

Which, considering this was the first morning she'd managed to get to sunrise without even a fleeting splash of self-pity, wasn't too bad of a state to be in, either.

The nurse at the desk took Anne's name and escorted her to an examining room, explaining that Dr. Sagara was running just a touch late but would be along shortly. Anne grit her teeth, helpless to stop the faux cheer coursing through her bloodstream from instantly transmuting into sizzling rage at the delay. She wondered what the hell was wrong with her. She'd never cared about minor things like exact promptness before. Good God, she was starting to act just like . . . just like . . . Paul.

Paul?

He stood at the far end of the examining room, dressed in full uniform as if for a parade or some other eminent occasion, staring with seeming fascination at a poster on the wall listing preferred weight in relation to height. He only turned his head halfway when Anne and Amelia entered, greeting Anne's look of surprise with one that said, "Of course, I'm here, where else could you possibly have expected me to be?"

"Dad!" Amelia's eyes lit up, and she looked eagerly from Anne to Paul, wondering if she was the first person in the room to fully comprehend the symbolism of his presence.

"Hey, Ace," Paul winked at his daughter. But the

majority of his glance never left Anne's face.

"Paul." His name was both a statement and a query.

He cleared his throat. Finding it wasn't enough, he cleared it again, and, finally, gave her a non-answer to her non-question. "I thought, after the procedure, maybe you and Amelia might need a ride home. I have my car here."

Anne shook her head and softly said, "No. It's all right. I have my car here, too. But . . . I, thank you, though."

He bowed his head respectfully.

A chair had been set up by the far wall, a tray of instruments balancing on the waist-high stand next to it, where Anne would also place her arm in preparation for the cast and bandages coming off. She found she could neither look directly at the configuration nor look away from it. It stayed no matter where she averted her eyes, blinking on the periphery like a gremlin.

Understanding the problem, Paul approached the chair, pulling it back with flourish, and gesturing for Anne to have a seat. She did so reluctantly, not realizing until she'd sat down that he had managed to position the chair so that her back faced the instrument tray. She couldn't have glimpsed it now, even if she wanted to.

Stung by his sensitivity, Anne whispered, "Thank you."

He shrugged and looked away.

Ah, yes. Now Anne remembered whom she was with.

They waited for the doctor, making two-dimensional small talk, in that Anne talked to Amelia, and Amelia talked to Anne, and Paul talked to Amelia, and Amelia talked to Paul, but never, ever, under any circumstances, did Anne and Paul actually talk to each other.

She congratulated herself on her newly developed maturity. A few weeks ago, Anne would have seized on

Paul's unexpected arrival as a sign of his feelings for her, and she would have badgered Paul into admitting it, provoking a quarrel so redundant Anne suspected both could conduct it in their sleep. Now, however, she accepted his words at face value. Paul was here because he thought she and Amelia might need a ride home. Period. End of story. It boggled her mind to think of all the heartache she could have avoided over the last nineteen years, if Anne had simply listened to what Paul actually said, instead of trying to imbue his actions with her own interpretation.

It had taken her half a decade to discover, but finally Anne understood. Her marriage to Paul didn't fail because he'd changed. Paul stayed exactly the same. Her marriage to Paul failed because *she'd* changed, because *she* kept demanding more and more, asking him for things he'd never promised to give, and, in the process, she'd obliterated whatever feelings he once might have had for her. The irony was inescapable. And very depressing.

"Amelia," Anne cut herself off middwell. "Would you do me a favor, Ace? Run down to the nurse's desk and ask when the doctor intends to get here. This waiting, it's really getting to me."

"Okay." Amelia sprung off the wall she'd been leaning on and, except for the squeak of her sneakers on the linoleum, disappeared down the hall.

Paul watched their buffer depart with an expression that, on other men, might have been curiosity.

Anne looked down at the beige floor, then up at Paul, licking her lips cautiously before revealing, "There's something I need to say to you, and I figure since I'm at the proverbial crossroad here, now's as good a time as any. Clean slate and all that."

He nodded, indicating that, if Anne felt obligated to

say her piece, he really had no license to stop her. "Go ahead."

"Thanks," she snapped from instinct, then hurried to swallow the bitterness that came with it. "I didn't mean it like that."

"I know." Paul stuffed his hands in his pockets and leaned against the wall, ready to listen, "Neither did I."

His confession gave her courage to proceed, and Anne plunged ahead with her thought, unsure of how best to articulate it but knowing the words urgently needed to be said.

"I made a mistake, Paul. I made a terrible, horrible mistake, and if you elect never to forgive me for it, I'll understand. Ever since we got back home, I've been so busy trying to coerce you and convince you and rankle you into saying that your beautiful, heroic sacrifice was done for me, that I completely disregarded the truth— that you risked your life and your rank and your self-respect, for our daughter, for Amelia. I know how agonizing it must have been for you to go against everything you've been taught to believe, and everything you stood for. You did a remarkable thing, Paul. And, in my conceit, I completely dismissed it."

Her every word seemed to be striking him precisely between the eyes. He blinked several times, and swallowed hard. But that was the only response she got. She couldn't be sure if he was agreeing with her or just meditating on the premise for the first time.

Anne went on, determined to get every word out, no matter how badly it hurt. "In the past and, well, truthfully, quite recently, whenever you didn't respond to me they way I thought you should, I accused you of having no feelings, of being cold and incapable of loving anyone. But that's not true, is it, Paul? It's not true at all, and you were just too much of a gentleman to tell me.

You are quite capable of very deep feelings, especially love. I see it when I watch you with Amelia. The problem is, you just didn't feel those things for me. It's not your fault. Looking back, I see how I forced you into everything. The damn roller coaster, the driving up and down to see each other, your proposal. I made demands, and you were too honorable of a man to hurt my feelings. I understand completely why you just decided to wash your hands of me. It must have been a lot easier than continuing to put up with my attempts to make you express emotions you didn't feel. I know how important truth is to you. I finally understand the conundrum I put you in.''

Very slowly, Paul asked, ''You think I couldn't tell you what you wanted to hear because I didn't really feel anything toward you, and I didn't want to lie?''

''Yes. Yes, exactly. I'm so glad we've finally got everything out in the open.'' Anne nodded her head maniacally, convinced that, for the first time, she and Paul were speaking the same language.

''I see.'' Inside his pockets, Paul clenched his fists.

''You're a remarkable man, Paul Gaasbeck.'' She rested her left hand in the crook of his elbow, feeling the way his muscles coiled beneath the skin. ''I just wish . . . I wish that I . . . deserved you.''

A tremor ripped through Paul's body, centering along the spot on his arm where Anne's fingers grazed his sleeve. His breathing shallowed out, lungs twisting themselves into knots.

Calmly, he removed his arm from her grip, using his free hand to adjust an out-of-line button on his uniform, and casually asked, ''Does Lyle tell you what you want to hear?''

Anne took no offense from his pulling away. It only

confirmed what she was saying. She shrugged. "I suppose he did."

"Did?" Paul's forehead wrinkled at the grammar. "You mean—"

"What?"

"Nothing. It's just that I . . . driving by our house the other day, on my way to the O Club, I saw Lyle leaving—"

"That's right." Anne turned to the door. She heard Amelia on her way back with Dr. Sagara. "You saw Lyle. Leaving. For good."

"I am so sorry I'm late, Major." Dr. Sagara swept into the room and apologized as she sat down, picking out the instruments she'd use to remove Anne's cast. "I know how anxious you must be. Let's get started."

Anne turned away from Paul, facing the dreaded tray, her heart beating so violently she imagined she felt every pulse point on her body visibly throbbing. And yet in spite of her anxiety, she also felt enormously relieved. She might lose her hand to gangrene by the end of the day, but at least another, equally gangrenous issue from her past had been resolved. If anything good was to come from this accident, her new understanding with Paul would have to be it.

Dr. Sagara easily sliced Anne's cast with what looked like an electronic pizza cutter. The skin beneath appeared wrinkled and pale, emphasizing the stitches used to sew up her skin where the bone once jutted through.

"Looks good," Dr. Sagara said.

But neither Anne nor Amelia nor Paul released the breaths they were holding. Anne's broken arm was never the problem. They knew it would heal. The real question was whether, with the bone knit, Anne would be able to move her fingers. Or whether frost bite had eaten away too many of the vital nerves.

Dr. Sagara leaned over to peel off the bandages around Anne's hand, painstakingly stripping away layer after layer. Anne's teeth began to chatter, and she bit down hard to swallow the noise. Her skin prickled, goose bumps erupting like raw sores, and her healthy arm trembled so badly that Amelia took a step forward, clutching her mother's palm between both of her own and squeezing tightly.

"It's going to be okay," Amelia murmured compulsively. "It's going to be okay. Dad said it will."

Anne nodded her head in rhythm to her words, but she knew she was only doing it to comfort Amelia. She didn't really believe her assurances. She didn't dare.

Bandages off, Anne's restored hand didn't even look like it belonged to her. The skin was darker, stiffer, and as wrinkled as if she'd been doing laundry for a century. She'd been preparing herself for this ever since pumping her doctors for details about what she was up against. Still, seeing it looking so alien was, nevertheless, a shock.

Dr. Sagara gently pressed the round end of her scissor against the ball of Anne's middle finger. "Can you feel that?"

Anne opened her mouth, words tumbling over each other. "I—I don't know."

"What do you mean you don't know?" Paul demanded, his voice coming strangely disembodied from behind her.

"I don't know if I feel it, or if I just think I feel it."

Dr. Sagara nodded. "That's very common. Phantom pain."

Anne bit her lip and, conscious that every eye in the room was boring into her, slowly, agonizingly, attempted to squeeze a fist.

She ordered her brain to send the message, willing

herself to accept that the battered hand in front of her was indeed hers, and, in the second that it took the thought to process, even amended her message. She didn't have to make a fist, not right away. She'd be willing to accept something smaller, a tiny flutter of the fingers perhaps. Just some sign that the injury was curable. She'd fight for the rest later, no matter how arduous her therapy might prove.

Perspiration broke out along Anne's skin, slithering down her back and matting her blouse beneath her breasts. She strained with all her might, vowing to never again take any movement for granted.

Behind her, she heard Paul taking a step closer, practically leaning over her shoulder, his breath wafting warmly over the top of her head. Out of the corner of her eye, she saw his hand, in sympathy, curl as if over hers, willing her fingers to move. Anne echoed his gesture instinctively, feeling, strangely, as if, in that moment, Paul's hand actually did envelop hers.

A heartbeat passed. Then, fleetingly—fleetingly, faintly, but unmistakably, Anne's fingers trembled, curling in toward her palm in a miraculous gesture of life.

Amelia laughed. She covered her mouth with both hands and laughed, rising to stand on her toes for no reason save relief.

And in spite of herself, Anne automatically pivoted to Paul, hungry for his reaction.

His expression revealed nothing. He stared down at her hand, head cocked to one side, a scientist deep in analytical thought. The furrow between his brows deepened, and he slipped his hands out of his pockets, locking them behind his back. Then, without a word, he stepped away. He didn't look at Anne. He didn't look at anyone.

Back to all of them, Paul turned and crossed two steps to the corner of the room.

He covered his face with both hands.

And wept.

# =≡24≡=

Paul was waiting for Anne and Amelia in the parking lot after her appointment. He leaned, hunched over, against the trunk of his car, hands stuffed in his pockets. He studied the asphalt beneath his feet, brows furrowed in concentration.

Anne felt afraid to approach him.

It was a most peculiar sensation. Not even in Iraq, when he'd come close to actually striking her, had Anne been afraid of him. Not the way she was now. Because for the first time since they knew each other, Anne judged Paul completely unpredictable.

Her right hand free of bandages, but still quite stiff, Anne slipped her left arm around Amelia's shoulder, using her child as a combination shield and support. They both took deep breaths and approached Paul tentatively, neither one sure of what exactly was going on here, but dying to find out.

He looked up. He saw them coming. And then he did the last thing Anne could have predicted. He smiled.

Not a phony one meant to cover what was really going on inside his head. Not a reassuring one to indicate that things were back to normal and his little lapse inside Anne's hospital room had been just that—a lapse unworthy of being mentioned ever again. But a true, genuine, downright dazzling, downright . . . happy, smile.

"Hi," Paul said.

"Hi," Anne said.

"How's your hand?" he asked.

"Hurts like hell." She didn't try hiding her joy at the proof of her muscles slow creak back to life. "Isn't that terrific?"

He nodded sincerely. "Best news I've heard in a long time."

She had no doubt he meant it. "Paul?"

"Yes?"

"Are you . . . okay?"

To anybody else, it might have sounded like the world's most benign, most banal query. But this was Paul Gaasbeck. Paul had never answered "Are you okay?" with anything short of, "Fine," in his life. He considered Anne's question with the same seriousness as he considered all questions, taking his time, mulling over every angle and implication. Finally, raising his head to meet and hold Anne's gaze, Paul told her, frankly and openly, and with no attempt at justification.

"No, Annie. I'm not okay. Isn't that terrific?"

They dropped Amelia off at school. The conversation in the car never rose above the surface level. Although, unlike plenty of other occasions, when unexpressed sentiments made it impossible for Paul to so much as look in Anne's direction, this time he had no trouble making eye contact. He even winked at Anne once when he promised Amelia she could have the scoop on what went on between her mom and him as soon as she left the car—if she would hurry up and get out of the car already, so they could get to it.

Giggling, Amelia did as she was bid, grabbing her backpack and rushing toward her school's front door.

Paul and Anne watched her go, then continued to sit quietly for another full minute, watching the door swing shut and finally settle.

Paul said, "There's something I want to show you, Annie," and, with no further explanation, drove her to the tiny airfield on the edge of town where they'd once parked the *Amelia*.

Climbing out of the car, Paul led Anne to a midsized Cessna, inviting her on board and closing the cabin door behind them before asking, "What do you think of her?"

She looked around, lost. "It's nice, I guess."

"Yeah," Paul leaned over the instrument panel, pointing out a series of key features. "She's a good little craft. Should last at least until Amelia gets her pilot's license."

"Amelia?" Anne's eyes widened.

Paul slapped the cabin wall heartily with his palm. "I bought her last week. I think it's important to get Amelia up in the air again as soon as possible. Wouldn't want her developing a phobia about flying, or anything."

"Amelia," Anne repeated, wondering when exactly it was that she'd lost her ability to make coherent conversation.

"Right." Paul spun the pilot's chair so that it faced Anne. "Meanwhile, care to take a little spin, Major?"

Anne opened her mouth. She closed it again without making a sound. It took a good beat before she could gather her energy to croak out, "Me?"

"Got to get back on that bird sometime."

She looked at her hand, the darkly scarred fingers an ominous testament to the last time she'd taken to the skies. "I don't know, Paul. I don't know if I'm ready . . ."

Paul thrust both palms on his hips. "Is this the same

Anne Gaasbeck who, a couple weeks ago, was dying to get back up here?''

"I . . . that was a couple of weeks ago."

"The one who swore her life would be over if she *couldn't* get back up here?"

"Actually, I've been giving it a lot of thought and—''

"The Anne Gaasbeck who, once, was foolish enough to think she could out-fly *me*?''

Anne cocked her head to one side, desperately trying to figure out where he was heading with this, and why he was doing it. Paul stared back at her, his expression playful and cocky and more than a little bit self-satisfied. But in no way was it malicious.

Anne slid into the pilot's seat, shaking her head and telling Paul, ''I'll never understand you, Gaasbeck.''

"Well," he took the copilot's seat next to her. "Maybe it's time to see what we can do about that.''

Anne swiveled her head, uncertain if she'd just heard what she thought she heard. Paul met her eyes and winked, indicating that indeed she had. Then he picked up their nav/com and informed the tower they were ready for takeoff.

Forgetting about Paul for a moment, Anne stared at the yoke. She'd wrapped her left hand around it easily enough, but when it came time to do the same with her right one, she could only stare at her stiff fingers, and jokingly remind Paul, ''You know, you're placing your life in my . . . hand.''

He sighed. ''What else is new?''

The tower gave them clearance for takeoff.

Anne faced the moment of truth.

Paul words ringing in her ears, she gripped the yoke with her right hand. She lifted off the runway, zooming into the air with a laugh of both recognition, and triumph. Only when they'd reached cruising altitude, could she relax enough to turn her head ever so slightly, and whisper, "Thank you, Paul."

He saluted. "Any time, Major."

The sky enveloped them, gold-kissed blue streaming in through each window. Anne sighed, tension draining out of her neck as she allowed herself to remember every thrill, mental and physical, that drove her to reach for the sky. The adrenalin rush, the euphoria, the sense of mastery over the elements.

And how she had Paul to thank for her getting it back.

"Annie . . ."

"Hmmm?"

"Annie, I . . . There's something I want to say to you. Thing is, though, just because there's something I want to say—"

"Doesn't necessarily mean you know what it is exactly?"

"Yes." He cleared his throat. "That."

Anne smiled at him warmly. "I remember."

"I *want* to tell you, really I do. It's just, the right words, if I can't find precisely the right words—"

"I can wait."

"Since when?" he asked, not unkindly.

She took no offense. "Do you know how many years I waited for you to do something to prove that you weren't indifferent to me—and then admit as much. That's why I pushed you so hard. I needed your words to match your actions. Otherwise, I didn't know what to believe about your true feelings for me. But after today, I have all I ever wanted. Now I can wait forever for the words."

Paul laughed. He laughed so hard, tears came to his eyes for the second time that morning, and he had to wipe them away with the back of his palm. "Oh, God, Annie, you and I really are some pair. Our timing is atrocious. When you want to listen, I don't want to talk, and vice versa. Do you think we'll ever get it together?''

Anne bristled, wondering briefly if she and Paul were destined to go through life perpetually misunderstanding each other. ''I did not say I didn't *want* to listen. What I said was, I didn't want to force you to talk. There is a difference.''

''I know.'' He sobered up. ''Believe me, baby, I know. And I appreciate your . . . what? restraint? I appreciate it more than you could possibly comprehend. It's just funny, isn't it? How we're always at these cross purposes.''

''Not cross purposes.'' She considered it vitally important he understand her distinction. ''We've always wanted the same thing. We both wanted out marriage to work. We just had different ways of going about it.''

''No.'' Paul looked down at his nails, flicking the one on his middle finger with his thumb, drawing blood. ''That's not true. We didn't always want the same thing.''

Anne swallowed hard, afraid of the answer, but needing to ask. ''You mean, you—you didn't want our marriage to work out?''

He leaned forward, propping his elbows on his knees, dropping his head in his hands and rubbing his face with the heels of both palms. His breathing remained steady. But the vein in his forehead throbbed like a boil.

''No,'' Paul said. ''Not all the time.''

She wanted to leap on his answer, to demand clarifications and details, and to squeeze every last ounce of blood from it until she heard what she needed. But Anne did no such thing. She knew it would only make things worse. And so she waited. She continued piloting her plane, and she waited for Paul to explain—or choose not to explain—what he meant by that.

"There were times," he flexed his fingers, "when I didn't want it to work. Because you terrified me, Annie. My love for you, *it* terrified me."

She felt nothing. Finally, after all these years, she understood what Paul meant when he claimed some ordeals were so intense, they inspired an emotional overload, and an absence of sensation.

He asked, "Can we go back to the beginning for a moment?"

She nodded her head mutely.

"From the first day," Paul cracked his knuckles. "You were a threat to everything I believed in. You were everything I detested in a pilot. In an officer. In a human being. Yet I couldn't get you out of my mind. It was like you'd cast this spell on me. The night we first made love, I had hundreds of logical, valid reasons for why we shouldn't. But I wanted to so much—you *made* me want to so much—that I blew off my instinct for self-preservation and common sense, and gave in. Just like over the Commander's Trophy."

She'd suspected as much since the day the award was announced. "You never forgave me for that, did you?"

"I never forgave *me* for it. It was the first time I realized how much control you had over me. How you could make me do things I knew were wrong, things I knew were bad for me."

"I never deliberately—"

But, he was on a roll. For almost two decades, Paul had kept his feelings locked so deep down inside, even he didn't know they existed. Now that he'd made the choice to tell Anne everything, he couldn't stop. Confessions spilled out from him, many of them as much of a revelatory surprise to Paul as they were to Anne.

He raged, "I couldn't stand it. How could Paul Gaasbeck, the self-discipline wunderkind, allow himself to be so easy controlled? Finally, I figured the easiest thing would be for me to pull away, to never see you again. But you wouldn't let me. When you came to visit me on Halloween, I truly didn't have the strength to make you leave. And that terrified me.''

She recalled that day so clearly. Not only because she'd told Amelia about it earlier, but because as far as emotional roller coasters went, that Halloween was the most turbulent she ever rode.

''So why did you ask me to marry you, then?''

''Because.'' He'd obviously given this a great deal of thought. He obviously had a logical, valid reason to explain his behavior. ''I thought marriage would neutralize the way I felt about you. I figured my infatuation was destined to wear off once we settled in to the routine of married life. Know what, though? The joke was on me. Seeing you every day made me love you more, not less. It got so bad, I almost gave up going to Germany that time, because I didn't want to leave you.''

''Wait a minute.'' Anne shook her head. ''This makes no sense. When you left for Germany, you acted like you didn't give a damn if you ever came back. And now you want me to believe it was because you actually didn't want to go?''

''I couldn't let you see how much control you had over me.''

''Why not?''

''Because then''—it was the first time Paul had taken a breath since starting to talk—''I knew I'd lose myself to you for good.''

She was trying to keep up here, really she was. But what Paul was saying seemed so fantastic to her. It was like he was speaking in a different language. ''What are you talking about?''

''Remember when you got promoted to captain?''

"Vaguely."

"You wanted to know why I wasn't enthusiastic?"

"Right. But what does that have to do with—"

"Fact is, I was thrilled for you. I was so thrilled for you, I actually didn't care that you were promoted ahead of me!"

"You certainly had an interesting way of showing it."

"I *couldn't* show it, can't you understand that? If I admitted to you that I cared more about you than I did about my own career, I'd have to admit that truth to myself, as well. And there was no way I was ready to do that thirteen years ago."

Slowly, the pieces started to click into place. "So when I asked if you were acting so strange because you were jealous—"

"I said, yes. Yes, yes, a thousand times yes, and thank you so much for giving me a sociably acceptable excuse to cover up what I knew were unacceptable feelings."

"But you *were* jealous of me. When I was going to Libya—"

"You were pregnant, I couldn't let you seduce me into breaking the rules. I couldn't let you make me ignore everything I believed in." Paul rubbed his hands together. "Though, God help us, Annie, you'll never know how close I came to breaking."

"What about after Amelia was born? You attempted to ground me then, too. What rules was I supposedly making you break then?"

Paul squeezed his fingers into a fist, pressing it against his forehead and actually wincing, as if the subsequent words from his mouth were tearing at his soul on the way out. "After Amelia was born—I mean right after, when the doctors couldn't even tell me if you were going to be okay—I stood in your hospital room, and all I could think of was . . . if Anne dies, then I die, too."

She gasped. She couldn't help it. For the first time ever in a cockpit, Anne turned her focus completely away from her instruments, so she could look him in the eye. "Paul . . ."

"Let me finish." He gestured for her to return her attention to the plane, but whether it was because he genuinely feared her losing control or simply because he felt more comfortable confessing to Anne's profile rather than to her face, she could no longer be sure. Hell, considering what she was hearing, Anne doubted she could ever feel totally sure about anything ever again.

*If Anne dies, then I die, too. . . .*

Paul said, "The prospect of my feelings, my thoughts, my life, being totally under the control of another person was unfathomable. I couldn't even entertain it long enough to dismiss it. And so I ordered myself to make it go away. I ordered myself not to think about it. Then, when you told me you wanted to go back to flying, all of a sudden, I was struck by this wordless, nameless need to stop you. I didn't know why. I was afraid to find out why. But I was a slave to it. A slave to you."

She reminded, "You told me you did it because you were jealous of me. You apologized for it. Was that a lie, too?"

"No. Absolutely not. I *thought* I was telling the truth. I genuinely thought that's where this need to ground you was coming from. But I knew it was wrong. That's why I apologized to you. That's why I promised never to do it again."

"Until Iraq."

"Iraq was different. In Iraq, I couldn't run away from the truth anymore."

"What truth?"

He sighed. "That I would sacrifice anything and anyone, even myself, to keep you safe. In Iraq, I finally had to face all those things I'd ordered myself to make go away before. I finally had to face that my self-discipline, and my honor, and my ambition, none of it meant as much to me as you did."

It took Anne's last ounce of control not to turn and look at him. But she feared doing so would spook him into silence.

Paul took a deep breath, breaking through the wall of pain and heading into his hardest lap. "Realizing that truth about myself, I'm sorry to say, also made me realize that it was not something I could live with. I had to get away from it, I had to get away from you, and I had to get away from this power you exerted over me. I had to save myself. Before I disappeared completely."

"So that's what you meant," she fought to keep any trace of censure from her voice. "About not wanting our marriage to work."

He nodded, but clarified, "That was then. This is now."

"What's changed now?"

"I have." His words were heartbreaking in their simplicity. "When I was searching for you and Amelia, after I'd lied, cheated, stolen, and spit out the honor code, I finally, at long, long last, accepted the reality I'd been struggling against for years—that I would do any thing, disobey any rule, to keep you."

She couldn't believe what she was hearing. "You mean that you still want me? After everything I've put you through?"

"Oh, Annie. When you took the blame earlier for our marriage failing, all I could think was, She's got it wrong. I was the one at fault. I kept asking why you loved me because I was desperate for you to produce a reason for us to stay together that made more sense than all my reasons for us to pull apart. You're the one who fought for us. If it wasn't for you, hell, I don't think we'd have lasted past our first Halloween.''

It all kept coming back to that. She was the one who fought for them. Translation: She was the one who pushed Paul into this relationship that caused him so much pain.

Anne blinked away her tears, resolved to be as strong as he'd been in confessing all. She asked. ''And would that have been so awful for you, our not lasting past Halloween? I mean, your life wouldn't have exactly ended if I wasn't in it.''

''Annie''—Paul's voice was so tender, it made her cry harder—''without you in it, my life would simply have never begun.''

Her eyes widened. Anne turned her head. She couldn't fight it any longer. She looked at him. The tears she'd been trying so valiantly to suppress rained down her cheeks.

Paul pointed out the windshield. ''Eyes on the road, Annie.''

''Paul, I . . .''

He gripped the yoke over on his side of the cockpit with both hands. He surveyed the instrument panel, adjusting several knobs. Then, voice conversational, he, once again, indicated the craft and asked, ''So, what do you think of this little baby?''

He was back. The old Paul, the one that she knew, and loved, and would always love, was back. For the briefest of moments, Anne had been given the only thing she ever wanted, the greatest gift Paul could offer. She'd been given a peek into his mind, into his heart. He'd ripped his soul open for her, until, at last, she knew there were no more secrets between them.

It didn't matter if he never did it again. She'd had it once. She knew the truth. It was enough.

And now, everything was back to normal. Only nothing would ever be the same again.

Anne did as Paul asked, turning her eyes back to "the road." She cleared her throat and wiped her eyes, lightheartedly offering the opinion, "It's a good machine. Handles real well."

"Yeah. I thought so, too." Paul indicated the fuel knob. "I filled her up solid before we took off. I figure we've got enough to make it to Las Vegas before it gets dark."

"Las Vegas?"

It was a question.

And an answer.

Paul knew it as well as Anne. Right now, it felt as if they didn't have to talk. They understood each other perfectly.

Paul leaned back in his seat, arms under his head. "Vegas or Reno. Or maybe Lake Tahoe if you prefer. Flight plan is cleared for all three. It doesn't matter. You can get a marriage license with no waiting anywhere in Nevada."

She matched her tone to his, marveling that the most meaningful conversation of their lives together could also be their most casual one. Frankly, Anne wouldn't have had it any other way.

"What about Amelia?" she inquired.

"Nevada's only a couple hours away. We can get there and back before she goes to bed tonight. Besides, once Ace finds out why we were gone, I don't think she'll mind too much."

Anne grinned. "You've thought of everything, haven't you?"

"I'm a very thorough man, Annie."

Her grin turned into a giggle. The giggle into a laugh.

In that moment, Anne's heart was so filled with joy, she could think of no other way to express it.

And her laughter was infectious. Paul couldn't help joining in, even if he did have to ask, "What's so funny?"

She wiped her eyes, thrilled by how quickly sad tears could turn into happy ones, and between gasps for breath, managed to tell Paul, "I was just thinking . . . you know who'll be almost as happy as Amelia about our getting back together?"

"Who?"

"Judge Saul. . . ."

Dear Reader,

If you loved the book you've just finished, then make sure you look for more terrific love stories coming next month from Avon Books. First, there's Connie Mason's TO TAME A RENEGADE. In this sassy, sexy love story a tender-hearted bad boy returns to a Wyoming town, and his life is turned upside down when he meets a falsely disreputable single mother.

There's nothing quite like a sexy hero in a kilt, so don't miss the latest in Lois Greiman's *Highland Brides* series, HIGHLAND SCOUNDREL. Pretty, pert Shonna has vowed to never marry, but her parents have other ideas. They invite all the handsome highlanders from miles around to court her. But only one—Dugald—catches her eye...

Rachelle Morgan creates western romances filled with love and laughter, and in WILD CAT CAIT you'll meet an unforgettable heroine who learns to love again when a sexy mountainman rescues her from danger.

ABSOLUTE TROUBLE, September's contemporary romance, is an exciting debut from Michelle Jerott. Stunning sensuality and taut romantic tension are hallmarks of Michelle's writing, and in this sultry love story a strong-yet-vulnerable heroine meets a dynamic man bent on revenge. Can she show him that the best choice in life...is love?

Until next month, happy reading!

Lucia Macro

*Lucia Macro*

Senior Editor

AEL 0898